68 KNOTS

A NOVEL

Michael Robert Evans

Tanglewood • Terre Haute, IN

Published by Tanglewood Press, LLC, 2007.

Cover photo by Chris Stucker
Cover and interior design by Amy Perich
Edited by Lisa Rojany Buccieri

The Publisher would like to thank Laura Maschler for her assistance with this title.

Tanglewood Press, LLC
P. O. Box 3009
Terre Haute, IN 47803

Printed in the United States of America
10 9 8 7 6 5 4 3 2 1

ISBN-13 978-1-933718-14-9
ISBN-10 1-933718-14-5

Library of Congress Cataloging-in-Publication Data

Evans, Michael Robert.
  68 knots: a novel / by Michael Robert Evans.
    p. cm.
  Summary: When a group of teenagers arrives for a summer leadership program on
board a sailing ship, the teens do not expect the counselors to bail out and the leader
of the program to commit suicide, leaving them in command without money or supplies, needing to figure out how to survive on their own.
  ISBN-13: 978-1-933718-14-9
  ISBN-10: 1-933718-14-5
  [1. Sailing—Fiction. 2. Survival—Fiction. 3. Conduct of life—Fiction.] I. Title. II.
Title: Sixty-eight knots.

PZ7.E89221Aae 2007
[Fic]—dc22
                                2007009891

7553

To my mother,
Carolyn Ruth Robinson Evans,
and to Joanna, Dylan, and Miles,
my wonderful family.
-MRE

CHAPTER ONE

Arthur stared in disbelief at the dead body sprawled across the bed. The lanky seventeen-year-old sank down into a wooden desk chair and ran his hands through his hair.

Oh shit, he thought. This could be real trouble.

He shook his head. This summer was supposed to be exciting and fun, an adventure. But it started badly and got steadily worse. And now this, he thought. Now what are we going to do?

He took in a deep breath and let it out slowly, trying to calm his nerves and clear his thoughts. I guess I'll tell the others, he said to himself. They'll freak out, but I'll try to keep them focused. Someone has to step up and lead this crew, and it might as well be me.

☠ ☠ ☠

The summer was full of promise, back when the plan involved idyllic days sailing along the coast of Maine. Arthur's father dropped him off at the docks and sped away in his black Lexus SUV. Arthur waved, but he could see that his father was already talking on his cell phone. The car cut its way into traffic and disappeared into a knot of angry drivers.

Arthur was tall for 17, with hazel eyes, straight brown hair, and an unusually deep voice. With an eager smile, he turned away from the traffic and toward the sea. He could feel the elation swell up inside him. A whole summer lay ahead of him— a summer spent on a tall ship, learning leadership and discipline and the right way to give commands so other people would follow them. He had worked for each of the last three summers in his father's law office, organizing papers and trying to absorb the intricacies of power. Now he would get a chance to sharpen his skills and show off a little on a ship off the coast of Maine.

Arthur's future seemed clear to him. Graduate from high school next year. Earn a government degree from Dartmouth. Get into law school at Harvard or Yale. Get hired by a prestigious law firm. Become a full partner by age thirty-eight. After that, who knew? With my determination and clear thinking, he said to himself, I might become a senator.

Arthur grinned. First things first, he thought. He picked up his duffel bag and looked down the dock. Rising from the bevy of white sailboats was a large, wooden, two-masted ship, with ropes in the rigging and flags flying from the top.

That must be it, he said to himself. The *Dreadnought*. My home for the summer. It looks like a pirate ship, he thought. He smiled as he shook his head. There aren't any pirates anymore. Are there? Nah, I don't think so. Besides, any adventure will be great. He started down the dock and toward the waiting ship.

But then he stopped. A couple—a young man with short dark hair and a young woman with long blonde hair—stood off to one side of the dock, wrapped in a close embrace. They stared deeply into each other's eyes. They didn't move.

Arthur was transfixed; he let his duffel fall to the dock. The couple seemed unaware of the dock, the boats, and

Arthur's stare. They didn't kiss. They just absorbed each other into a profoundly intimate gaze.

Arthur felt a pang of—of jealousy? These were strangers to him, but still he felt a wave of envy at their closeness. Arthur had never had that feeling with someone, and for an instant, he wanted it more than anything else.

Then he shook his head. "My father says emotional attachments make you vulnerable, and vulnerability is dangerous," he muttered to himself. "It's lonely at the top for a reason—and I'm going to get to the top."

He picked up his duffel and continued down the dock toward the tall ship, looking over his shoulder one last time. The couple was still there, lost to the world in each other's eyes.

At the end of the dock, Arthur was greeted by three counselors in green T-shirts; they looked at bit frazzled despite their welcoming smiles. "I'm Hoon Yin," said a thin young man with straight black hair. "That's Greg Anderson, and this is Robin Merriman. On board the ship, though, we all go by nicknames. I'm called 'Jet,' Greg is called 'Fred'—you remember Fred, the strong cool kid from the Scooby-Doo cartoons?—and Robin is called 'Grille' because she still wears braces at age twenty-two." Hoon shrugged. "It's supposed to build character. You'll get your nickname soon."

Hoon told Arthur to put his duffel on the deck near the bow and get ready to shove off. The counselors dragged the gangplank onto the ship, separating the tiny camp from the rest of the world, and a moment later the *Dreadnought* was sailing out to sea.

Arthur joined the seven other campers on a pile of vinyl mats in the middle of the boat. They introduced themselves to each other, but Arthur didn't catch many of the names. His eyes were locked onto a young woman with an incredible body and expertly styled hair. He stuck out his hand.

"Arthur Robinson," he said with a nod. The girl glanced at him and then looked away with an annoyed expression. "I'm Marietta," she said. She didn't say anything more, and she didn't shake his hand.

The other campers chatted as the ship left the bay. Arthur began to sort out a few of the names. The big guy is Jesse, he noted to himself. And his little friend is Bill. That girl with the nice smile is Dawn. But he kept returning to Marietta, who gazed with a bored scowl at the sea.

"Damn, she's hot," he whispered.

☠   ☠   ☠

Just a few hours later, on the bow of the *Dreadnought*, Joy Orejuela held onto a steel cable for dear life and prayed to God for salvation, reciting Psalms in Spanish: "*Jehova es mi pastor; nada me faltará,*" she whispered. "The Lord is my shepherd; I shall not want." The ship was leaning sharply to the right in heavy winds, ten-foot swells causing the bow to swing up and down with dizzying intensity. It was as if the bow were tied to a yo-yo string, and some unseen hand overhead was tossing it down and yanking it up for amusement. Every time the ship reached the bottom of a wave, Joy was certain that unless she prayed hard she would be splattered against the glowering wall of water ahead. Every time the ship arched over a crest, Joy was certain she would be flung toward space in a wild flailing swan dive that might never end. She kept one leg locked around the bowsprit rigging on one side, and her other leg pressed hard against the slippery wood of the bowsprit itself. She gripped the steel guy wire with both hands and squeezed her eyes closed whenever possible. The counselors had sent her to the bow to watch for boats, lobster-pot floats, and other obstacles. She chose instead to concentrate on prayer.

The *Dreadnought* had been underway for most of the day before the captain of the ship came up from below. The counselors had been showing the campers how to work the ropes and winches that adjusted the sails, but once they steered the ship into a quiet bay, they heard Captain McKinley stomp up the narrow stairs. The counselors dropped anchor and formed a green-shirted wall behind McKinley at the helm.

McKinley stared at the campers, his belly straining against the buttons of his khaki shirt. He wore a black sailor's cap and silvered sunglasses, and a pipe jutted out from the corner of his mouth. He smiled.

"I am Howard McKinley," he said in a booming voice. "Welcome to my Leadership Cruise. As you know, you're here to learn how to lead. How to take charge. How to command respect. And I'm going to teach you. You've met the counselors—Jet, Grille, and Fred. They are here to help *me*. They will explain some things, but you are not to rely on them for things you can do yourselves. They are your guides, not your nannies. Any questions so far?"

The campers stood in a loose cluster and blinked up at their so-called leader. They didn't say anything.

"Very well," McKinley continued. "There are eight of you—four boys and four girls. It's a tradition on board the *Dreadnought* that everybody goes by a nickname. You may call me 'Commodore.' Now stand in a straight line, and I'll give each of you a brand-new *Dreadnought* nickname."

The teens shuffled into a lazy line. McKinley took a clipboard from Fred and made a show of consulting it. "Which one of you is Dawn FitzWilliam?" A girl with a ponytail and a red baseball cap raised her hand. McKinley marched over to her and looked her up and down. "Baseball cap, eh? From now on, you will be called 'Shortstop.'" Dawn smiled awkwardly. She didn't seem to love the new name.

McKinley continued. "Who is Joy Orejuela?" The girl who had been praying on the bow lifted her hand. She had olive skin and dark hair. "Orejuela—that's a Spanish name, isn't it? Good. We'll call you 'Chiquita.'" Joy started to protest, but then she decided against it.

"Who is Crystal Black?" McKinley asked. A girl with very short blond hair, a tight t-shirt, and no shoes looked him straight in the eye.

"I am," she said in a defiant tone. She crossed her arms.

"Hmm," McKinley said, looking her over. "Tight, wiry, probably good at physical stuff. We'll call you 'Spider.'"

"Whatever," the girl said, not dropping her gaze.

"And the last girl," McKinley said. "Marietta Mathis. Must be you." He ogled the gorgeous girl that Arthur had noticed earlier. "Not bad. Not bad at all. We'll call you 'Bunny.'" Marietta just rolled her eyes.

He went on to hand out nicknames to the boys. Jesse, a towering boy with rippling muscles, became "Hulk." His little friend, Bill—a nervous, scrawny boy with large black glasses that kept slipping down his nose—was now "Squinty." Logan, a chubby boy with a goofy grin, became "Marshmallow." And Arthur's clean-cut good looks earned him the nickname "Boy Scout."

"Now that you all have proper *Dreadnought* nicknames," McKinley announced, "it's time to get to work. We have another few hours of daylight left, and I suggest we make good use of it. Counselors, assume your positions. I will take the helm from here."

McKinley shouted some commands, and the counselors leapt to work. They pulled on ropes and showed the campers how to tighten the sails and fill them with wind. McKinley turned the ship's wheel, and the *Dreadnought* once again nosed into the heavy waves.

As Arthur struggled with a tight rope, pulling with all his strength against the stiff wind, he noticed that sailing was different with McKinley at the helm. The counselors had tried to teach them the basics of sailing, but McKinley simply shouted orders. It was as if he expected the campers to learn everything about sailing in one afternoon. Still, Arthur thought, I didn't come here to be treated like a kid.

"Spider! Let out the jib!" McKinley hollered. Crystal, still barefoot, jumped over to a rope and began to ease it out. McKinley sighed loudly enough to be heard over the wind. "Jet, show Spider what the hell the jib is. And you there! In the stupid shirt! Uh... Marshmallow." He pointed to Logan McPhee, a pudgy sixteen-year-old who wore a tie-dyed T-shirt with the words "Bohemia Rules" across the chest. "Sheet in that main!" McKinley muttered a curse. "Do I have to spell out everything? Pull on that rope! P-U-L-L—oh, forget it. You there, Hulk, grab that rope and pull on it. Good. No, wait! Let it out! LET IT OUT!"

The "Hulk"—Jesse Kowaleweski—was the muscle-bound sixteen-year-old Arthur had met earlier. Jesse had said little since the ship left the dock, but he had tried to follow instructions whenever they were given to him. When McKinley said "pull," he hauled on the line so hard that the mainsail stiffened abruptly, and McKinley was caught heading too far downwind with a tight sail. As the Commodore cursed and pointed, the ship veered just a little bit, and the wind caught the other side of the sail from behind. The boom flew across the deck with enough force to smash a skull—and Jesse put up his hand. He caught the rocketing timber and froze it in midair. In one hand. The force would have shattered the bones of any other hand that rose in its path, but Jesse halted the boom without changing expression.

Everyone on deck stopped what they were doing and stared at Jesse. "Shit," Logan said. "I want that guy on my side."

McKinley blamed Jesse for the mishap, shouting in his face and "demoting" him from deck hand to cabin boy. "You'll sit at the foot of the table tonight!" he shouted. "And don't be so sloppy the next time!"

Jesse shrugged. Sitting farther away from McKinley didn't seem like much of a punishment.

☠   ☠   ☠

By dinnertime, Arthur was confused. He could not make sense of McKinley. The "Commodore" was charming at one moment and abusive the next, and during the late afternoon he had demoted more than half the crew to cabin boys and girls. Conversation in the dining room was taut and brief. Everyone crowded around a long rectangular table in the center of a large room near the stern of the ship. Built into the walls were a dozen bunks; most were filled with bags and boxes of gear, but three were left clear for the counselors to sleep on.

The kitchen, or "galley," was in the forward part of the ship, in a section that also contained the captain's quarters and the only bathroom. McKinley kept the door to this section locked during the day—"You kids would just love a chance to raid the pantry, wouldn't you?"—but he unlocked it at 5:30 to let two of the "deck hands" start cooking. He chose Arthur and Crystal for the task.

"Have dinner ready and on the table at exactly eighteen-hundred hours," he commanded. "That's six o'clock to you landlubbers." Then he smiled broadly and winked at them. "This is the first meal of the first-ever Howard McKinley Leadership Cruise, so do a great job. I'm counting on you!"

Arthur and Crystal squeezed themselves into the dark kitchen, which was barely larger than a small closet. It was crammed full of dented pots, bent utensils, and rusty canned goods. Crystal and Arthur looked at the tiny kerosene stove and the battered blackened pans that swung from the ceiling, and then they looked at each other.

"This is crazy," Arthur whispered, his low voice booming off the close walls. "Let's make something quick and simple and get out of here."

"We'll make some friggin' spaghetti and hope McKinley chokes on it," Crystal sneered. "Anyone who demotes me to 'deck hand' can take his pipe and—"

"Spaghetti it is, then," Arthur said with a smile.

Along one wall was a set of shelves so deep that Crystal had to stick her head into the dark spaces to reach the back. The shelves were stuffed with cans of all shapes and conditions—shining, rusty, dented, tall and thin, short and squat, pop-top and flip-top and the kind you open with a key. Most of them wore tattered labels, but many were bare. Crystal could see sardines, Spam, canned chicken chunks, gourmet mushrooms (badly dented), tomato purée, cream of broccoli soup, Vienna sausage, chipped beef, corn, pears, and random other foods. She pulled out several cans and handed them to Arthur.

Along another wall sagged a miniature sink with a hand pump, and next to it was the sheetmetal stove. Arthur read the faded instructions thumb-tacked to the wall and poured kerosene into the stove from a small oily can he found among several boxes of baking mix in an overhead cupboard. Then he opened a box of matches.

"This will either light up the stove," he said, smiling to his galley-mate, "or it will light up the ship." He touched a lit match to the pool of kerosene in the stove. The kerosene caught fire, and with some work, Arthur coaxed the stove into an impressive display of heat. No explosion.

"Oh, well," Crystal said. "Maybe the next cooks will have better luck." She smiled a tight, tough smile with thin lips and pointed teeth.

With pushing and prodding and kicking and swearing, they persuaded the water pump to cooperate, and at last, Crystal and Arthur balanced a pot of water on the burner and willed it to boil. They threw in a lot of spaghetti, and when it was tender, they drained it and dumped in the reddish-brown goo they found in several jars of ready-made sauce.

"Dinner is served," Arthur announced with a flourish as they entered the main cabin. He carried a large bowl of spaghetti, and Crystal had a box full of plates and forks.

Seated at the head of the table, beneath a banner that read "Discipline is the heart of a focused life," McKinley scowled. "You're twelve minutes late, and all you're serving us is spaghetti?" he said. "You call that a meal? Get up on deck, both of you. If that's all the effort you're going to put out, then you don't deserve to eat. Go on! Get out! We'll eat your lousy spaghetti, and tomorrow I'll lay down some cooking rules." He glowered at the crew and the counselors sitting at the table. "You people are pathetic, and it's my job to straighten you out. I intend to do exactly that."

Arthur and Crystal stood silently just inside the cabin door.

"I told you to get out!" McKinley shouted, leaping to his feet. "Get up to the deck and sit there. Jet, you go with them and keep them out of trouble. Go. Now!"

The cooks dropped the food and plates on the table and scrambled up the gangway, Crystal muttering a dark curse aimed at McKinley. Hoon Yin followed them out, shaking his head. McKinley sat back down at the head of the table.

"Now please pass me the spaghetti," he said to the others with a warm fatherly smile. "After a great day of sailing on this beautiful coastline, I'm hungry."

That evening, the air turned chilly, and the lowering sun cast a small path of gold across the waves. The *Dreadnought* was anchored on the northern side of Burnt Island at the mouth of Muscongus Bay. Lights glimmered from cottages along the rocky beaches on the mainland to the north, and Allen Island to the west blocked much of the flicker and glare from the popular vacation settlement of Boothbay Harbor. Tucked away from the noise of cities and traffic, the ship settled into a quiet evening peace.

Crystal and Arthur sat on the forward deck, watching the sun and talking quietly. Hoon Yin lingered nearby, not saying a word.

"This is bullshit," Crystal said, her hands clenched in tight fists. "This asshole doesn't have the slightest idea about what he is doing, and we're all getting fucked because of it. I feel like swimming to shore and screwing this whole project."

"I don't get it," Arthur said, leaning back against one of the storage lockers on deck. "I mean, I know we're supposed to be learning how to control our lives and make smart decisions—at least, that's what my father said when he sent me here—and maybe McKinley is acting this way on purpose for some reason. But I don't see how we're supposed to make smart decisions when we're not allowed to make any decisions at all. All we do is try to figure out the stupid orders he keeps shouting at us."

Arthur thought for a moment. "Let's try to figure *that* out," he continued. "Maybe this is some kind of test. Maybe there's something we're supposed to learn or do or something, and when we do, he'll stop treating everybody so badly."

"Bullshit," Crystal said.

"No, really," Arthur persisted. "Maybe we're supposed to organize ourselves and present McKinley with a reasonable, clear set of requests. Maybe he wants to see whether we'll react like spoiled teenagers or like rational adults. Maybe we're supposed to set the real rules for this trip—you know, so we take responsibility for making sure things get done, but we also set up rules for how to treat people. Maybe we're—"

"Maybe not." Hoon Yin quietly eased himself onto some vinyl mats. Like the other counselors, he was just a few years older than the teenagers in the crew. He wore his black hair in a casual sweep that made him look thoughtful and at ease, and he spoke in a quiet voice. "What you're saying makes sense, but it isn't right. The other counselors and I have been on board for almost three weeks, getting the boat ready for the cruise. McKinley's been like this the whole time—sometimes really nice, sometimes really obnoxious, but usually rude, arrogant, and selfish. He seems to enjoy pushing other people around. He threatened to fire me once because I wouldn't call him 'Commodore.' We all thought that he was just desperate to get everything ready to go, that he'd lighten up once the campers arrived. But here you are, and he's just as bad as ever. Today was disgusting. He insulted people, he bullied, he shouted, and he dished out those stupid demotions to nearly everyone on board. I don't know about the other counselors, but I've had just about enough of it."

Arthur looked him in the eye.

"What are you going to do about it?" he asked.

Hoon shook his head. "I don't know," he said. "But I'm going to do it soon."

☠   ☠   ☠

Sometime after sundown, when the sky turned black and sparkling and the air carried a chilling breeze, McKinley ordered the counselors to run a rope down the center of the deck. He made the campers take a vinyl mat and sit on it on the deck. He took a deep breath, grinned with his pipe clenched between his teeth, and gestured at the night sky.

"You campers will sleep out here, under the beautiful Maine stars," he said. "The four boys on the starboard side, the four girls on the port." He hitched up his belt and took a puff of his pipe. He paced as he talked, his sloppy gait showing no signs of sea legs. "The counselors will sleep below in the mess room, and I'll sleep in the captain's quarters. I do not expect to be disturbed. I will open the door to the forward compartment for just a few minutes, so you all have the chance to use the bathroom before I lock up for the night. Any questions?"

Arthur raised his hand. "Where do we get blankets and things?"

McKinley glared, his clenched pipe and sloping cap looking comical. "You will address me as 'Commodore' whenever you speak to me. Is that clear?"

Arthur shrugged and nodded.

"Counselors," McKinley snapped, his eyes suddenly dark and angry, "issue the sleeping bags."

Hoon and the other two counselors opened several large wooden boxes mounted on the deck. They pulled out a haphazard collection of old sleeping bags, all different sizes and shapes, all different colors, all different degrees of decay. Some were small and bulky, some were threadbare, some smelled strongly of mildew and rot. The counselors tossed one bag to each camper.

"Sleep in these, on top of the mats," McKinley said. "Make pillows out of your extra clothes."

"Excuse me, Commodore," said Logan—"Marshmallow"—brushing his shaggy red hair out of his eyes. "My sleeping bag's totally disgusting. I mean, I think some kinda new life-form has hatched in there, and *it* has athlete's foot. Do ya have any others I could use?"

"Do I have any others?" McKinley barked. "Do I have any others? Listen to this guy! He doesn't *like* his sleeping bag! It doesn't *suit* him. He thinks it's *disgusting*! Well, Mr. Marshmallow, that's just too damn bad. These were the best sleeping bags I could get on the lousy payment your parents paid for this trip, so you're just going to have to live with it. Understand?"

The campers were silent.

The counselors were silent.

"Good," McKinley said. "Go use the bathroom. I'll lock up in five minutes."

☠   ☠   ☠

The next day—Sunday, June 10—was no better. McKinley continued to jab his orders at people, hurling curses and insults whenever he perceived anything out of place, and then suddenly offering kind and helpful advice. When one camper let go of a line she was supposed to tie off, she was ordered to sit at the dining table for the rest of the afternoon. When another took an unscheduled break from scrubbing down the foredeck, he was told to forget about dinner that evening. But when "Bunny" Marietta failed to scramble at McKinley's command to drop the anchor, he patiently showed her how to work the winch and set the anchor properly. Later, when "Marshmallow" Logan tossed a sarcastic joke at McKinley, his sleeping bag "privilege" was revoked for the night, leaving him to face a frigid night shivering in the Maine air.

"You can sleep in your underwear, for all I care," McKinley snarled. "That should teach you some respect."

The following day was even worse. McKinley docked the counselors a day's pay "for controlling the campers so badly," and he issued half rations for everyone at dinner. Greg "Fred" Anderson, the tallest and strongest of the counselors, got into an argument with McKinley about a punishment inflicted on the campers, and it looked for a moment like he was going to swing a fist and knock McKinley over the side. Instead, Anderson turned and stormed away, and McKinley aimed his attention at some other crisis.

And so it continued, with McKinley shouting and pounding his fists, dispensing punishments at the slightest perceived infraction, and then offering warm and supportive comments at unexpected times. He also spent increasing amounts of time—hours at a stretch—locked in his quarters below. He said he was doing some planning and laying out the course, but nothing ever seemed planned, and the course seemed to change without notice. The only clue anyone could gather was the squeaky *yump-yump-yump* of the toilet flushing. The crew began to hear that sound often.

☠   ☠   ☠

It was early one morning, five days into the voyage, that things began to change. The night before, McKinley had ordered the counselors to wake the campers at sunrise "to teach them some much-needed discipline." He had given them a specific set of navigational directions heading roughly to the northeast, and so shortly after the sun's arrival, the *Dreadnought* was crashing its way through the swells. His final order was that he was not to be disturbed until o-nine-hundred hours.

At about nine o'clock, Greg Anderson, who seemed to function as the senior counselor, gave the helm to counselor Robin Merriman, who flashed a pretty, braces-filled smile. Anderson went below to wake McKinley. As the campers pulled on lines and polished the brass fittings, they could hear Anderson's knocks and calls well up from below. It was clear that he was having little success. He returned ten minutes later and resumed his place at the helm. "Door's locked," he said. "I can't wake him up."

The swells were larger than before, and Crystal, the camper assigned to bow watch, defiantly tightened her grip on the bowsprit. Every few minutes, a gush of salty water would crash against the bow and send torrents of foam slashing through the rigging and slamming against Crystal's rigid body. "Bring it on!" she shouted to the sea. "Hit me with your best damned shot. You're not knocking me off of here." She squeezed the bowsprit between her knees and clenched the rigging in her hands. A wave rose and dropped on her like a wrecking ball. Her tight T-shirt was soaked, and saltwater streamed off her short blond hair and down her neck. "Is that the best you can do?" she shouted, shaking her head like a dog to clear the sting from her eyes. "Bring it on!"

The wind had whipped into a gale by the time McKinley staggered on deck.

"What the hell's going on here?" McKinley shouted over the wind.

"Storm, sir," Anderson reported.

"I can see that!" McKinley snapped. "Why the hell didn't you steer us to a safe port? Now we're stuck out here in the middle of the ocean with—"

"With all due respect, Commodore," Anderson said sarcastically, "I had no way of knowing the storm was coming. The weather radio is locked in your quarters, and I tried several times to get you—"

"Don't give me your excuses, Mister Anderson," McKinley shouted. "You were at the helm. You were responsible. You should have—"

At that moment, a huge breaker crashed over the rails and onto the deck, unleashing a torment of foam. McKinley and Anderson clung to the wheel as the water pounded against their bodies. When the wave passed, Anderson turned the wheel and pointed the ship toward the harbor.

"You damn well better take us in!" McKinley shouted. "I'll be below, writing up my report and documenting your incompetence!"

McKinley dove down the gangway and disappeared, followed a moment later by the familiar *yump-yump-yump* of the toilet.

That night, Arthur lay on his back, his damp sleeping bag pulled tightly up to his shoulders. The *Dreadnought* had been at sea for almost a week, and everyone was exhausted. If something didn't change soon—if McKinley didn't back off and start treating people better—Arthur wasn't sure what would happen. But something had to change.

Arthur stared up at the dark sky, brilliant with stars. This trip is sure weird, he thought. When his father had brought home the brochure for "Commodore McKinley's Leadership Cruise," Arthur had been thrilled. He knew he had no choice in the matter—whenever his father handed information over like that, it was always an order and never a question—but Arthur was delighted at the chance to learn some new skills and imagined the mental and physical toughness he would gain, improving his chances of getting ahead in the world. His father had pushed him to be the very best from the start, and Arthur was grateful that the future looked so very promising. "I have the greatest father in the world," he remembered thinking when his dad gave him the check to mail off to McKinley. "With his help, I've got it made."

But this cruise didn't seem like the right sort of thing after all. Arthur was puzzled. His father was rarely wrong. He would have made phone calls, checked references, verified that this cruise was the very best place for his son to learn how to function in a tough and heartless adult world. He was a successful attorney and businessman—one of the best in Albany—and he was not in the habit of making bad investments. He would have researched this cruise thoroughly. Unless he was in one of his busy times. When Mr. Robinson got busy, Arthur knew, family life sometimes took a back seat.

But still, something was wrong here. Arthur felt like he was learning how to follow, not how to lead. And he wanted more than anything to lead. He always wanted to be in front, giving orders and making decisions and collecting the rewards. "If you fail, son, fail big," his father had told him. "And then look people in the eye and tell them why it was actually a brilliant success. People forgive big mistakes, but they never forgive weakness." How was he supposed to learn strength under McKinley? All he could do was follow orders and keep quiet and hope the "Commodore" took his rage out on someone else.

The night sky was breathtaking, and Arthur's eyes followed a faint dot of light moving slowly across the sky's arc. A satellite, he guessed, but he didn't give it much attention. He was listening instead to the few snatches of words he could make out from the argument below.

"*You listen to me . . . hired . . . address me as* COMMODORE *. . . fire you just as . . . .*" McKinley's tone was tense and angry.

"*. . . haven't paid us anything . . . rude to Greg . . . no* REASON *. . . .*" The voice belonged to Robin Merriman. Arthur smiled. She seemed to be holding her ground down there.

"*. . . orders . . . I have a job to do . . . I'll be* DAMNED *if I'll let someone . . . you can go to hell . . . .*"

After a few more exchanges, the air turned silent once again. Arthur looked across the deck. Most of the campers were asleep, but Crystal was looking back at him. She rolled her eyes.

Arthur must have fallen asleep soon after. It seemed like just a few minutes later when he woke to a scraping sound on the deck nearby. The night was still dark, but he could see three people hauling bags to the side of the ship.

The counselors. They carried their luggage to the ladder on the starboard side, climbed down, and shoved off in the *Dreadnought*'s wooden dinghy. A moment later they were gone—and Arthur guessed they weren't coming back. He pulled his sleeping bag over his shoulders and wondered how much McKinley really knew about sailing a tall ship.

☠   ☠   ☠

The next morning, McKinley was strangely pleasant. He asked two campers to cook a large breakfast for everyone—anything they wanted—and at the table, he gave a quiet speech about how leadership means getting the job done even when people you counted on let you down. It would not be easy, he said with a soft smile, but together they could make it work. The campers exchanged suspicious and worried glances. Arthur seized the opportunity to flash a reassuring smile at the stunning Marietta.

The day, June 14, was clear and bright, and a stiff wind blew steadily from the southwest. The campers hoisted the mainsail, and the *Dreadnought* inched toward shore until she was close to land. Then Jesse, responding to McKinley's polite request, jumped into the ocean and retrieved the dinghy, which was tied up at a small dock. McKinley set a course southeastward toward open ocean. He steered the ship past the last of the small islands hugging the coast, then he asked Arthur to take the wheel.

"Just keep the compass heading at roughly 140," McKinley said with a grandfatherly smile. "Two campers are on bow watch, so listen in case they see any rocks or lobster floats. Keep this heading until I ask you to change it, okay? Thanks."

He patted Arthur warmly on the shoulder, and then he squeezed down the hatch and headed below. A moment later, Arthur could hear the door to the captain's quarters lock with an audible click.

With the steady wind and easy sailing, the campers had little to do. Arthur held the course, and some of the others cleaned up the sleeping bags and mats. Mostly, though, the campers lay about the deck, talking and enjoying the morning, which seemed warmer and more pleasant without McKinley nearby.

"Boy, this is totally the life, isn't it?" asked Logan "Marshmallow" McPhee. He was pudgy and pale from long afternoons of video games and bottles of vodka smuggled into his bedroom, but the warm Maine sun was making him feel upbeat. He was talking to no one in particular. "Don't you ever wish you were rich? I mean, really rich. You know—just decide one day to go for a sail, so you call up your personal secretary, and by lunchtime she has everything arranged. The boat's been chartered, the food's been catered, the bartender's been hired, the company's been invited, and the weather's been dusted off and polished to perfection. The next thing you know, BOOM!, you're sailing the North Atlantic. You look at a map, totally choose a destination at random, and set out. If the trip takes too long for some of your guests, you just fly 'em home from the next port. When you get tired of sailing, you hop a jet back home and hire someone to sail the boat back for you. Wouldn't that be *great*?"

"It might be great at times, but I wouldn't want to be trapped in that life," said Dawn FitzWilliam.

"What do you mean?" Logan asked.

Dawn shrugged. She wore her light brown hair in a ponytail she pulled through the space in the back of a red baseball cap, and she had a pleasant smile that could turn quickly into a pensive, distant look. "These 'guests' on your boat—why are they there? Because they like you personally, or because they like the boat, and the drinks, and the money, and the travel? This secretary—does she do things for you because she believes in you, because she cares about you—or because you pay her? This destination you decided to sail to—is it exotic? Mysterious? Or just the same old country-club stuff you can get anywhere? Remember, karma works in powerful ways. The way you treat the universe is reflected in the way the universe treats you."

Logan shrugged and flicked his red hair out of his face. "Wouldn't matter to me, noooooway!" he said with a grin.

They sailed on toward the sea's horizon, passing the time with easy conversation. It was nearly three o'clock when Marietta sat on the rail next to Arthur. He was happy to have the chance to talk to her at last.

"I don't know about you," she said, "but I'm getting hungry."

"So am I," Arthur said, correcting the ship's course just a little bit to keep the compass at 140 degrees. "Why don't you see if McKinley wants us to start cooking."

Marietta looked at Arthur with a flirtatious smile. "I was hoping you would do that," she said.

"Sure," Arthur answered. "Take the wheel for a minute."

Arthur went below and knocked on the door separating the main cabin from the forward section that contained the captain's quarters. There was no sound. He knocked again, more loudly.

"Commodore?" he called. "Could I talk to you?"

There was no answer. Arthur knew that if McKinley were asleep in his cabin, he might not hear the knocking. He knocked again, waited, then tried the rusty knob. It was locked, so he jiggled and twisted it until something moved.

He would tell McKinley that the door opened "accidentally." He forced it open and entered the galley.

Rum. The galley reeked of cheap rum. The smell was stronger near the captain's quarters in the bow, and Arthur hesitated a moment. Then he knocked on the captain's door anyway.

There was no answer.

"Commodore? Are you all right?" he shouted.

Silence.

This door was locked, too, and Arthur began to feel worried. He pushed against the door and twisted the knob. No luck. No sound from inside.

"Commodore? Mr. McKinley? Hello?"

This is getting scary, Arthur thought. He raised his right foot, took a deep breath, and kicked the door with all his strength. It burst open, and Arthur leapt inside.

Three empty rum bottles lay on the table, along with two large bottles of prescription pills and several stacks of documents. The air stank of rum and vomit. McKinley lay on the bunk. He wasn't moving. Arthur slapped his face. Shouted at him. Tried to lift him up.

It was no use.

McKinley was dead.

CHAPTER TWO

"He left a note," Arthur said grimly. The campers were sitting around the dining table, a large thick slab of wood drenched in heavy layers of polyurethane. The polyurethane was yellow and cracked in places, and it was peeling off one end. The scrawny fifteen-year-old named Bill Fiona—"Squinty"—fidgeted with one of the peeling strips as Arthur read the letter out loud:

> To whoever finds me,
>
> It's all over. Everything. It's over. There's nothing left for me to do.
>
> My Leadership Cruise was the greatest idea of this century. It should have worked. It would have worked, except that people were against me from the start, like they always are. They were jealous of my success. The shipwrights. They ripped me off and damn near ended it all before it began. And the people who sold me the charts and the other stuff. They overcharged me—I have proof of it—and so I had to piece things together without the right gear.
>
> And the campers are worse than I expected. They are selfish, lazy, and stupid. Without my

guidance, they might all die—and it would serve them right. They wouldn't know leadership if it kicked them in the ass.

But the worst of all were the counselors. I chose them myself—they were supposed to be like my children. But instead loyalty, they repaid my devotion with disrespect. With rudeness. With muniny. They should all be court-martled and fed to the sharks. Damn them all! They killed me. They might well have poured the pillls down my throat

They're working now. The pills. They're working. I can feell them working. In just few minutes, Ill be gone and noone willl be able to find me and they won't be able to say bad things about me or ripme off or shit like that. All thatshit. Just don't let them get me. Bury me at sea like a sailor. I was in the Navy you kno. Not hardware store. Shit. Fuck you all.

Howard McKinley Commodore

The crew was silent for a long time. Joy was praying, reciting, "Our Father, Who art in Heaven, hallowed be Thy name," alternating between English and Spanish. Arthur was ashen and silent. Marietta twirled her blond-streaked hair and looked bored.

"If it meant so much to him," Marietta said at last, "why did he work so hard to screw it up? I mean, he yelled at everybody. He made everybody miserable. He didn't care about anybody except himself. Personally, I'm glad he's gone. Let's radio the stupid Coast Guard, go home, and have a normal summer for a change."

"I think he screwed it up because he wasn't very good at things like this," Arthur said. "I also found a bunch of files on his desk. He had them all laid out, like he was looking at them before he died."

"What were they?" Dawn asked.

"Each file was about a business that McKinley started in the past," Arthur said. "He had a desk job in the Navy for a while, but he left that and started some kind of restaurant in Savannah, Georgia."

"Oh, I'm sure that was a lovely place to dine," Marietta said sarcastically.

"Yeah," Arthur said. "It closed after a couple of years when the chef suddenly quit. Then McKinley started a magazine in Norfolk, Virginia, that published nine times and then died. Then it was a public-relations company in Connecticut, which I think closed after a year or so. And then he bought the *Dreadnought* and started this Leadership Cruise thing."

"The guy was that much of a loser, and he wanted to teach people about leadership?" Marietta said. "Give me a break."

Arthur nodded. "So when the counselors left, he must have known that this job wasn't going to work out for him, either. So he decided not to try anymore."

The teens were silent around the table. Then Bill Fiona spoke up. "I'm glad he left a note," he said, pushing his glasses up his nose. "We have to make sure no one thinks we killed him. I don't want anyone to think we killed him. 'Cause of course we didn't kill him. We didn't kill him at all. Arthur, did you touch anything in the room? I hope no one thinks we killed him."

Arthur took a slow breath. "Of course I touched things," he said. "I kicked in the door, I looked at the pill bottles, I grabbed McKinley, and I slapped him over and over again."

There was a gap of silence.

"That must've felt good," Logan said with a goofy grin. "Can I have a turn?"

Arthur smiled tightly. "Get your own Commodore," he said.

The others laughed nervously. Then another pause.

"So what do we do now?" Joy asked. Several of the teens talked at once, but Arthur tuned them out. He looked carefully around the table.

There are eight of us, he thought. Four guys, four girls. Most of us are in decent shape—he couldn't help glancing at Logan's pudgy belly—and we've done pretty well during the last few days. With some training, we could have made a good crew. It's too bad McKinley had to die before we could pull it all together. This could have been great . . .

Marietta was talking. "So we use the radio in McKinley's room, we call the police or the Coast Guard or something, and we hand him over. To hell with this burial at sea crap. I say we hand over the body. No one is going to think we killed him—what are they going to say, that we *forced* him to take a bizillion pills and drink three bottles of rum?"

Logan nodded. "We totally won't be blamed for this," he said. "The guy was obviously wacko, you know? Cooooooo-kooooo!"

This could have worked out *really* well, Arthur thought. The problem was McKinley. If it weren't for him, we would have done just fine. . . .

"It sure is creepy, though," Logan said, "sitting here talking while there's a dead guy in the next room. I hope he doesn't sit up and start yelling at us or something."

"Don't worry," Crystal said, grinning. "If he does, we'll just get Arthur to smack him again."

The eight teenagers chatted around the table, feeling serious and grown-up and aghast as they talked about their situation. They joked a little, laughed nervously, and developed a
plan. They would radio the Coast Guard, explain their situation, and follow instructions.

"After all we've been through," Joy said with a trembling
smile, "it might actually be a pleasure to go home to my parents. We just need to find God's will in all of this."

Why did we need McKinley at all? Arthur wondered. Sure,
he provided the boat. And he organized the camp. But once we
got started, what was he good for? All he did was make things
difficult. We could do a lot better without him . . . .

"This was supposed to be such a great summer," Dawn
said, her sweet smile momentarily sad, "sailing all over the
place, getting to know people, getting back in touch with the
sea and the natural air. Now I'll have to go home, and my dad
will probably make me get a job in his company for the summer. A real bummer."

"My parents are fine—I like living with them," Joy said, "and
I'd love to be closer to my boyfriend and my church. I could
help with the choir and continue with my Bible studies. But
spending the summer at home sure won't be as useful as this
was supposed to be. I was counting on this Leadership Cruise
to teach me some things about organizing a congregation."

"My folks are a real bore," Marietta said with a scowl. "I do
not want to go home."

Arthur saw his opportunity.

"Neither do I," he said. "But who says we have to?"

☠   ☠   ☠

He paused to let the others think about that for a minute. Then he continued. "Look, our parents don't expect us back until late August—three months from now. We have food, shelter, and supplies. McKinley was going to have us sail all around the Maine coast, so no one out there will know that anything has happened. We'll just sail around and have a great summer. By ourselves. Without McKinley and his stupid orders. Our parents sent us here to learn some responsibility—what better way to learn it than by taking charge of our own lives? Right now. On this boat. With no one in charge except ourselves."

Stunned silence.

"That's crazy," Marietta said.

"Isn't it illegal or something?" Joy asked.

"Parts of it might be illegal—you're right," Arthur said. It is easier to get forgiveness than it is to get permission, his father always said. "This boat doesn't belong to us, for one thing. And we'll have to do something with McKinley. But our parents paid a lot of money so we could sail this ship from June through August. As long as we're clear that we're bending certain parts of the law in favor of something more important, then that's exactly what we'll do."

More silence. Arthur enjoyed the attention, the control, the authority.

"Look at it this way," he continued. "We were promised a summer—an entire summer—on this boat. On this sea. That's what our parents paid for. That's what the brochure said we'd get. It's not our fault that McKinley turned out to be an asshole. It's not our fault that McKinley turned out to be a crook. Why should our summer be ruined just because McKinley's life was a mess? His note is wrong. People weren't trying to rip him off.

The counselors weren't traitors. And we aren't lazy or stupid. McKinley just tried to charge a lot of money for this camp and keep most of it for himself. It didn't work. That's his fault. He failed and so he killed himself. But where does that leave us? He kills himself, so we have to act like children? He can't control his own life, so we have to go home? He can't handle his own stupidity, so we have to go crawling back to our parents? Says who? Who out there is making that decision for us? I think we should make our own decisions. I think we should make our own plans. I think we should set our own course."

He paused for just a moment.

"And I intend to stay on board," he said. "This is my summer—my *life*—and I won't let McKinley mess it up for me."

There was another moment of dropped-jaw silence. Then, at last, Logan pushed his red hair out of his eyes and asked, "What'll we do if someone, like, gets hurt or sick?"

Arthur couldn't resist a small smile. He knew a "yes" when he heard one. "We'll take them to the hospital," Arthur said. "We'll use the Leadership Cruise's insurance, which is insurance that our parents paid for."

"What if we get lost or sink the boat?" asked Bill, wiping his nose on his arm. "We'd be in trouble if we got lost or sank the boat. What would we do if we got lost or sank the boat?"

"We'd radio the Coast Guard," Arthur said. "Just like McKinley would have done—I hope."

"I think this sounds stupid," Marietta said. "We'll get ourselves killed."

"I think it sounds wonderful," Dawn said. All eyes looked at her. Her eyes sparkled from beneath her baseball-cap brim. "Think of it. A whole summer of sailing and swimming and sleeping on a great old ship. Just us and Goddess Earth and the great powerful sea. At one with the ocean, at peace with the world. It's not like we're eight years old. We're perfectly capable of doing this by ourselves, and all the spirits of the sea will join together to help us. I think we can do it better than McKinley ever could."

"That's ridiculous," Marietta said.

"Like hell it is," Crystal said. "I'm with Shortstop here. There's no fucking way I'm going back to my parents for the summer. I'd rather be fighting to save my ass in some bitch of a hurricane than sitting at home watching my parents eat ice cream and listen to baseball on the radio. I vote for staying. Hell, if I had thought of this before, I would've killed the fat old geezer myself."

"Here's what I think we should do," Arthur said. "I think we should put it to a vote. We don't need everyone to stay on board—some people can go home if they want to—but we'll need at least five of us to work the ship and do the cooking and everything. And whoever goes home has to promise not to tell anyone what we're doing."

The teenagers glanced at each other as they thought about Arthur's plan. They weighed the risks of continuing against the prospect of spending the summer at home. They tried to imagine life on board, free and exciting, and they compared that image to life under the control of parents and guardians at home.

Jesse—the "Hulk"—cleared his throat. "I'm in," he said in a strong bass voice. "I won't abandon the ship."

"That makes two of us," Arthur said, looking around at the others. "Who else will join us?"

"I will," Dawn said.

"I totally will too," said Logan.

Seven of the eight agreed to stay, with Marietta the only holdout. She shook her head. "You're all crazy, and I think you're going to get in a lot of trouble," she said. "I'm going home."

"Suit yourself," Arthur said. "We have enough people to work the ship. I'm sure you'll do just fine—serving fries at McDonald's, hanging out at the mall, taking care of your little brothers and sisters, spending evenings at home helping your mom do the dishes. And don't worry about us. We'll manage somehow—sailing along the coast, holding cookouts on remote islands, going shopping in cities up and down the seaboard, singing and telling stories . . ."

"All right!" Marietta said. "All right. I still think it's stupid, but you convinced me. Count me in."

Arthur smiled. "Well, everyone, we just promoted ourselves. Thanks to McKinley, most of us were 'cabin boys' and 'cabin girls' yesterday. Well, I now declare that you are all First Mates of the schooner Dreadnought. And as our first piece of official business, I say we dump McKinley's stupid nicknames. What do you say? Bunny? Squinty? Marshmallow?"

The vote was unanimous.

☠   ☠   ☠

With awkward fumbling and clumsy lurches, they took the Dreadnought several miles out to sea, far from any other ships. Then they let her sails luff, and the entire crew, dressed in the best clothes they had on board, gathered together on the deck. Logan told some jokes about the devil and the deep blue sea. Dawn sat in a yoga position and offered a chant to the Goddess of the Maritimes. And Joy held her hands close together in deep and fervent prayer, a mixture of whispered words and spiritual communion.

McKinley's body lay on a long plank beneath an American flag. Jesse had volunteered for the unpleasant task of carrying the body up from below, placing it on the plank, and tying heavy bolts and clamps to its arms and legs. In a soft voice, Joy read some lines from the Bible she carried with her throughout the ship:

> While the people pressed upon him to hear the word of God, he was standing by the lake of Gennesaret. And he saw two boats by the lake; but the fishermen had gone out of them and were washing their nets. Getting into one of the boats, which was Simon's, he asked him to put out a little from the land. And he sat down and taught the people from the boat. And when he had ceased speaking, he said to Simon, "Put out into the deep and let down your nets for a catch." And Simon answered, "Master, we toiled all night and took nothing! But at your word I will let down the nets." And when they had done this, they enclosed a great shoal of fish; and as their nets were breaking, they beckoned to their partners in the other boat to come and help them. And they came and filled both the boats, so that they began to sink. But when Simon Peter saw it, he fell down at Jesus' knees, saying, "Depart from me, for I am a sinful man, O Lord." And Jesus said to Simon, "Do not be afraid; henceforth you will be catching people."

Joy closed the Bible. "And so we send Howard McKinley to the sea," she said, a tear sliding down her cheek. "And may the Lord have mercy on his soul."

"Amen," said Arthur. He admired the way Joy connected with people when she spoke about religion.

Jesse lifted the plank, and McKinley's body slid into the blue-green water with a fat splash. Most of the crew turned away, but Crystal watched the red and white stripes of the flag flutter softly in the water as McKinley's body spiraled downward. She knew she was supposed to feel moved, or sad, or bitter, or something, but she didn't. She just watched.

Serves him right, she thought, running a hand through her short blond hair. Pompous, mean-spirited ass. And huge! Good grief—it's a wonder the ship didn't rise up three feet when we dumped him overboard. How do people let themselves get like that? What did he do, eat nothing but doughnuts and ice cream all day? It isn't that tough, staying in shape. You run a little, you lift a little, and you eat like you have some brains. What a jerk.

She could just barely make out the swirling flag through the thick colors of the seawater. He was almost gone. She thought back to the moment—was it really just a few days ago?—when her parents had dropped her off at McKinley's dock. My folks aren't all that bad, she thought. Not in good shape. Not tough. And they argue too much. But they're all right. Her father worked as the manager of a bookstore in the mall back in Harrisburg, Pennsylvania. Her mother worked as a data-entry clerk for a chain of tire stores, typing orders and receipts into a computer all day. They weren't ambitious. They weren't go-getters. They weren't fast-lane people. But they cared about her—they *loved* her—with all their hearts, and Crystal knew that. That knowledge gave her courage. Strength. Toughness. No matter what happened in the world, she would be all right. Because she could always go home, back to that suburban split-level house with its appalling green-shag carpeting and avocado appliances, and she could regroup there, gather her strength and recharge her self-esteem, and then venture out into the world once again. It was a good feeling, knowing that the things that mattered would always be there. It let her focus her attention on the edge, where toughness and skill and icy veins counted for something. Where you could get ahead and really wield some power—or where you could be devoured by the next guy who was tougher. Crystal understood that world, and she knew that her parents didn't. But she knew that they realized the specialness of their daughter, and they supported her with every penny, every minute, and every drop of loving they could muster.

The last flicker of McKinley's flag brought Crystal back to the world before her. She shook her head.

"Hey, Boy Scout?" Crystal said, her hands on her hips.

"Yes?" Arthur winced. "Yes, *Spider?*"

"The flag is supposed to stay on board, Dumbo," she said. "McKinley's not going to need it where he's going."

Arthur sighed. "Oh, well," he said. "It's McKinley's only souvenir from his ship."

After the ceremony, Arthur and Dawn cleaned the captain's quarters. It was gruesome work, but it taught them a lot about Howard McKinley. They found personal papers, nearly $1,200 in cash, a letter he was writing to his mother, and eight different prescription medications in jars and bottles.

"He was discharged from the Navy for health reasons," Arthur told the crew, assembled once again around the dining table. "The papers don't say what the reasons were, but I'm guessing he was an alcoholic. There are six cases of rum in his cabin."

"Six cases!" Logan said. "Where do we keep the glasses?"

Arthur started to say something, but Logan lifted his pudgy body from his chair and rushed to the captain's quarters. He came back an instant later with a glass bottle of brown rum. Jesse fished eight glasses from the galley, and Marietta dug several large, dusty two-liter jugs of warm Coke from the galley shelves. The rum was dark and strong, and it mixed well with the Coke. Logan drank his rum straight. The only two who chose water instead of rum were Crystal, who said that alcohol was a cheap form of escape for people who were too weak to deal with reality, and Joy, who explained that she had vowed to meet her Maker without alcohol ever touching her lips. At first, Arthur also declined to have any rum, but when Marietta put a glass in front of him, he changed his mind. Logan stood and held his glass high.

"A toast," he said. "To the crew of the schooner *Dreadnought*! May the wind blow steady and the waves be small. Aye! Aye! And all that stuff."

They all raised their glasses.

"To us!"

"To the *Dreadnought*!"

"To small waves!" The crew clinked the glasses and drank together.

Logan made a sour face. "Like, we have *got* to get some ice," he said.

☠   ☠   ☠

Arthur considered asking the crew to elect him captain, but then he remembered something his father had told him years ago. They had been coming back from some meeting his father had attended. As usual, ten-year-old Arthur had to wait in the car during the meeting, reading books and keeping the doors locked while his father negotiated and conducted deals. Arthur had spent a lot of time waiting around since his parents' divorce. When his father returned to the car, he was in a strangely good mood. His eyes gleaming, he reached over every few minutes and patted his briefcase with genuine affection. "Arthur," he said in a gloating voice, "just remember one thing, and you'll always do well: Raise for discussion only those points you're willing to lose. Everything else—just do it."

With that advice in mind, Arthur assumed the Captain's role on board the *Dreadnought* without a word. He decided that he would let other people steer the ship, but he would be the one who chose the destinations, set the courses, and issued the commands. He moved his gear into the newly cleaned captain's quarters. No one seemed to object.

"Okay," he said to the sailors seated around the dining table as they sipped their rum, "I think there are a lot of things we need to do. It's getting close to dinnertime, so we need someone to cook."

Joy raised her hand. "*Por favor,*" she said. "Food is God's nourishment for the body, and I'm really a great cook. Lots of spices, lots of great Mexican recipes. If it's okay with you, I'll do a lot of the cooking on this trip."

She had no trouble getting the others to agree. Joy had centered her life around offering to help, serving as a support system for others who needed practical, emotional, or spiritual assistance. She hated the feeling she got when she saw a way to help someone and then chose not to do it. She wanted to increase the overall happiness in the universe, and that sometimes took a lot of work.

Leo felt the same way. Joy had met him when they were in the fifth grade, back in Austin, Texas. They became friends quickly, and they spent a lot of their time together. They would meet every evening along the banks of the river, holding hands and talking as the bats swarmed out from below the bridges. Joy had known from the beginning that they would be married, but Leo was slower to catch on. He dated some other girls in junior high and even after they started high school, but those relationships never lasted. Joy waited cheerfully each time, knowing that Leo would come back to her warmth and loyalty.

He got the picture after a painful break-up during his junior year in high school. He had been dumped, in public and with a lot of scorn, and he spent much of that evening with his "best friend" Joy. He told her all about it, he thanked her for listening so carefully, and he wondered out loud why he even bothered dating other girls when it was Joy—

That's when Leo caught on. Three weeks later, he told Joy he loved her and promised to buy her a ring as soon as he could afford one. He worked at a department store, stocking shelves and doing some checkout. He was saving his money carefully and would buy the ring once he had enough for a nice one. In the meantime, Joy worked toward her goal of founding and leading a new church back home. She planned to call it "The House of Joy," and it would be based on a particularly caring form of Christianity. Nonviolence toward all people, as children of God, would be one of the main tenets. Compassion. Helping the poor. And bringing the deep thrill of God's message to everyone through music. Lots of singing. Lots of prayerful singing. Not too many rules or requirements. Just love, laughter, and the Lord. She had signed up for the Leadership Cruise to learn how to lead the church she would create.

Joy sighed and looked around the galley table. Leo seemed very far away.

Arthur continued. "We also need to get you all decent places to sleep. It looks like there are enough bunks in this room for all of you, so we'll need someone to empty out the ones used for storage. Logan, please take care of that along with Crystal and Bill."

The three nodded.

"Great," Arthur continued. "Now, we have time to sail a little bit more today, and I'd sure like to move away from the place where we dumped McKinley's body. There are nautical maps in the—"

"Charts," Dawn said.

"What?"

"They're called 'charts.' When you're on a boat, all the ropes are called 'lines' and all the maps are called 'charts,'" she said. "Charts show landmarks, compass headings, water depths—the whole bit. I read a book about sailing after my parents signed me up for this cruise."

"Okay," Arthur said, bristling at the correction. "Dawn, would you please look at the *charts*, figure out where we are, and choose a safe place for us to anchor tonight? I'll take the helm."

"Yes, I will," she said with a freckled smile. "I'll find a safe harbor for us all."

"Great," Arthur said. "I'll need some help with the sails, so everyone else meet me on deck. We'll get under way in a few minutes."

Arthur stood, and the others followed his lead.

"And crew," Arthur said, "I'd like to take this opportunity to say that this is damn exciting! Let's have a hell of a good summer!"

They drank another toast and got to work.

☠   ☠   ☠

The sail from McKinley's resting place to Little Green Island was clumsy at best. Little Green Island was a small rock farther off the coast of Maine, and the charts made it look pleasant, inviting—and uninhabited. Arthur steered the ship with a steady hand, but he knew little about how to keep the sails full and the ship moving forward. Several times the sails, apparently without provocation, suddenly began to flutter and luff in the wind, forcing Arthur to turn off course. He gradually gained a sense of how close to the wind's source he could point the ship without losing power.

Dawn took charge of the line that controlled how far out the sail could go to the left—she explained to the others that it's called the *mainsheet*—and Jesse took the one to the right. They pulled in on the lines when they thought they should, and they released when it seemed important. At times, Jesse pulled when Dawn was pulling, straining the lines between them, but over time, they figured out which sheet was supposed to be taut, and which one loose, at any given moment.

It took a long time to go a short distance, poring over the charts and scanning the horizon for landmarks to keep from running aground, but that evening the crew anchored the ship in a sheltered bay on the east side of Little Green Island. The evening air was calm and cool, and the boat rocked gently on the waves. In the main cabin below, most of the crew sat around the dining table; Joy was banging pots in the kitchen and coaxing heat from the kerosene stove. The crew talked about the challenges that lay ahead.

"If anyone has suggestions for places to go, please bring them to me," Arthur said. "We have the whole ocean in front of us, but we shouldn't waste time debating the destinations every single day."

The dinner was Spam à la Joy, and the crew thought it was the best Spam they had ever tasted.

"To Spam!" Logan cheered. The crew toasted with glasses of warm Coke. Logan's had rum in it.

Joy also served a canned-vegetable salad, pan bread with butter, and hot cocoa for dessert. The crew ate and talked late into the night, then one at a time, they faded into the bunks—warm and comfortable in the main cabin, even though the sleeping bags were still damp—and went to sleep.

The next morning came early. The last one awake was Logan, and he looked a bit queasy.

"I shouldn't have toasted the Spam," he said on his way to the bathroom.

After breakfast, Arthur decided that they should keep moving, to get more distance between the ship and McKinley's sunken body. He asked Crystal to take the helm and steer a course for Wooden Ball Island, eighteen miles off the Maine coast and tucked just east of the larger Matinicus Island. Wooden Ball was about ten miles away, an easy day's sail, and it didn't seem to have any houses or structures on it. "Just the place to lie low for a while," Arthur said. Most of the crew worked the sails, but Dawn offered to stay below to clean the dishes. Arthur said he would join her and help out; it seemed like a good way to show the crew that he wasn't above the dirty jobs.

Once the pots and plates were clean and put away—"in a logical place, for once," as Arthur put it—the two of them began digging through the shelves and holds that squeezed storage space out of the tiny galley.

"I think this is a ham," Dawn said, lifting an oval metal tin from a damp and musty compartment. The label was missing, but the shape was right, and it had one of those little metal keys that make opening possible. Rust stained the metal in places, so Arthur suggested that they open it.

"If it's still good, we'll have it for lunch," he said. "Otherwise, it's shark food."

Dawn pried off the key with her long fingers and began to twist the metal strip around it. The stench was immediate. It was the smell of decay, of death, and of flourishing bacterial life.

"Gross!" she said. Arthur grabbed a plastic shopping bag, and Dawn dropped the offending ham inside. They proceeded to sort through the other cans, boxes, jars, and bottles in the galley, until at last, everything that was allowed to remain was relatively fresh and harmless.

Meanwhile, Joy was in the captain's quarters, tinkering with the radio. She listened carefully to one channel after another and finally settled on Channel 13, which seemed to have the most traffic on it. She heard fishermen reporting their catches to fisheries on shore. She heard ship captains reporting fog banks and floating debris. And she heard an announcement that made her dash up to the deck and gather everyone around the wheel.

"It's a whale," she said. "It's tangled in a fishing net off Ragged Island. The fisherman says he can't get the net back, so he's going back to shore. He said that the whale will probably drown by sundown, so he was warning the other boats to make sure they don't run into the body. He called it a navigation hazard."

"Don't run into the body!" Dawn said, her freckled face flashing with anger. "How sentimental. It's okay if the poor thing drowns, just don't get blood on your bow. What kind of monsters are these guys?"

"They're people who work hard to make a living from the sea," Arthur said. "And getting a whale caught in your net can threaten your whole career."

"Well, leaving it to drown doesn't seem very nice," Dawn said. "That's a living creature with a mind and a soul, just like us."

"This is the ocean, girl," Crystal said. "There's no room for 'nice' out here."

"But there is room for action," Arthur said. "The question is, what are we going to do about it?"

There was a pause.

"*Us?*" Marietta said. "You want us to go yell at that fisherman and tell him he's being mean? I don't think so."

"No," Arthur said. "I think we should go rescue the whale." He smiled. He saw the plan unfolding beautifully. The *Dreadnought* crew would set off to find the whale, and they would rescue it with skillful maneuvers and clever thinking. The crew would be elated, and his position as the leader of the group would be strengthened. He would be a hero.

Dawn nodded. "Ragged Island isn't far from here," she said. "We could get there in an hour or two."

Crystal looked around at the crew, her short blond hair reflecting the sun's light. "I think this is fucked, but I'm willing to go along with it for laughs," she said.

"This is a stupid idea," Marietta said. "I mean, the fisherman said the whale would drown soon, so what are we going to do about it? We're going to go chasing off after some stupid fish and risk our lives trying to get it out of a net? I think it's none of our business."

Crystal glared at her.

"Arthur is the captain, and he wants to go," Crystal growled. "I'm at the helm, and I want to go. So we're going."

Arthur nodded. "We'll change course and head for Ragged Island. Logan, you and Jesse raise more sails. I want to get over there as fast as we can."

☠   ☠   ☠

Ragged Island had passed on the port side, and everyone on the *Dreadnought* was looking for the whale.

"The easiest way to spot whales is by their plume," Dawn said. "When they surface, they blow air out the nose on top of their heads, and that sends spray into the air. It doesn't look like a jet of water, like in the cartoons. It looks more like a gust of spray."

Crystal looked at her. "How do you *know* all this stuff?"

Dawn smiled. "The Goddess Earth gives us a lot of gifts," she said. "Animals, weather, plants—everything. Even books. I've been reading about the Earth since I was a kid. Reading is an act of worship."

Crystal rolled her eyes and turned back to scan the sea.

No sign of the whale. Fifteen minutes passed, with all eyes searching across the waves. Sometimes the wind caught the top of a wave and sent some spray flying, causing shouts and excitement on board the ship, but again and again the plumes dissipated into false alarms. Half an hour passed, then an hour. Crystal kept the ship moving in large, slow circles, hovering around the area Joy had described. Arthur felt a bit deflated; the daring rescue he had foreseen wasn't working out.

The wind scattered another wave top, and everyone pointed and called out. Crystal turned the boat toward it, certain it would be another mirage. Then, about twenty yards off the port side of the boat, the whale surfaced and blew a misty gust into the wind.

Logan saw it first. "There it is! Wooooo-wooooo! Right here close to the side! Right over there!" he shouted.

The whale took a breath and dove, but Logan got a good look at it.

"I don't think the net's, like, stuck on the bottom or anything," he said. "I think it's just wrapped around the whale—sssssssp!—like a straightjacket. It looked like a lot of it's caught in her mouth, and the rest is totally tangled across her back and around her tail."

The crew watched closely for the whale to surface again. Five long minutes went by.

"Off to starboard!" Dawn called out. "A long way off!"

Crystal turned the boat to the right, and Logan confirmed the sighting. The whale dove again, but it surfaced just a minute later—another half of a mile out to sea.

"Come on, whale," Dawn whispered. "We can't help you if we can't catch up with you."

The *Dreadnought* made good time across the water, and the distance between the ship and the whale dwindled. The crew could see the black marks on the underside of its tail when it dove. "Look at that beautiful tail!" Dawn exclaimed. "Those marks look like an ibis beak. Come on, Ibis! Help us out!"

Ibis was swimming hard, but the net seemed to slow her down considerably. It also seemed to tire the whale; the time between surfacings was getting smaller.

Then Ibis swerved; she headed straight toward the islands off the mainland. Crystal shouted, "I'm turning the boat!" and spun the wheel hard to port. The ship veered to the left, and the sails crashed from one side to the other. Crystal heard something snap high above, and she saw the sails on the forward mast tangle in their own rigging.

"Oh, shit!" she shouted. "I'm turning it back! Damn it!"

She spun the wheel hard to starboard, and the sails swung violently across the decks again. This time, the forward boom hit Logan in the chest, knocking him far over the railing and into the sea.

"Logan fell overboard!" Marietta screamed. "Stop the boat!"

"How the fuck do you stop a sailboat?" Crystal cried out. The crew could see Logan's head above the waves, getting smaller as the *Dreadnought* whirled away.

All hell broke loose on the deck. Some of the crew pulled hard on lines, thinking they would make the boat go faster. Others let lines out, thinking the same thing. Arthur shouted instructions, but no one heard him. Crystal turned the boat dead into the wind, causing the sails to luff and flap wildly. By the time someone thought to throw a life jacket overboard for Logan, the ship was already half a mile away from him.

Then Crystal turned the ship off the wind, and the *Dreadnought* began to gain speed. It was aimed directly at Logan. The crew could see him swimming awkwardly in the frigid water, his red hair bobbing just above the waves, and nearly everyone on board shouted instructions to him in an incomprehensible babble of voices. When Logan was just a few dozen yards off the port side, thrashing and scared, Crystal turned the wheel sharply, hoping to point the bow upwind again and bring the ship to a stop. Instead, the *Dreadnought* cut a wide arc through the waves, leaving Logan behind once again.

Except this time, someone had thought clearly. While the ship was bearing down on Logan, Dawn had pulled the dinghy alongside and climbed down the ladder. Just before Crystal spun the wheel, Dawn cast off and rowed toward Logan's desperate splashing. As the dinghy drew close, Logan lunged and grabbed the side. His light-brown eyes, now bloodshot, were wide and panicked. He panted and whined as he hooked one pale leg over the edge of the boat and tried to lift his pudgy body inside. Dawn stowed the oars and grabbed his shirt. A moment later, gasping for air, Logan lay in the bottom of the dinghy. His T-shirt was torn, and his belly was scratched and bleeding from its scrape over the side of the boat. Dawn sat quietly as Logan struggled to regain his composure.

After Logan's breathing began to return to normal, Dawn asked, "Are you all right?"

"No," Logan said, his voice trembling. He rolled over awkwardly and pulled himself onto one of the dinghy's coarse plank seats. "But I'll be okay. Thanks for coming for me. I don't know how long I could have lasted."

Dawn picked up the oars and began rowing back toward the ship. Crystal had aimed the *Dreadnought* into the wind again, letting it coast to a stop, but it still took two hours for the crew to bring the ship and the dinghy together again. Logan received a warm welcome and a mug of hot soup, and Dawn was cheered for making the rescue. Only Arthur seemed angry over the whole incident. He sat off to one side, staring out to sea.

This was supposed to be a dramatic rescue, he said to himself. This was supposed to make the crew feel great. Instead, we almost got Logan killed. We sailed like idiots, and no one listened to me. Some leadership. Instead of me being a hero for saving the whale, Dawn's a hero for saving Logan. Shit. I'm the captain. I'm going to have to take charge even more.

Once the emotions of Logan's mishap had settled down, the crew turned its attention back to the missing whale.

Ibis was nowhere to be seen. The *Dreadnought* circled for the rest of the day, but the only spray they saw proved to be annoying false alarms. As sundown approached, Crystal pointed the ship toward a cove, and the crew dropped anchor.

Over dinner that night—a delicious tuna-and-pasta salad with olive oil and herbs, courtesy of Joy—the conversation centered on the day's misadventures.

"This is why we should call the Coast Guard and quit," Marietta said. "This whole idea is stupid and dangerous. We don't know what we're doing out here, and we're going to get somebody killed."

"Look, things got a little fucked out there," Crystal said. "I've never steered a big ship before, and I didn't know what to do. But I'll be damned if . . ."

"None of us is experienced at sailing," Arthur said in what he hoped was a reassuring and commanding tone, "but we had better become experienced in a hurry if we're going to stay out here. I think we should do some kind of drill every day—a sailor-overboard drill, a swamped-dinghy drill, things like that. There are books in the captain's quarters that will help us get started. We need to practice at this so we get good at it quickly. It's the only way we're going to survive out here. In the meantime, I think we should just forget about blaming each other or feeling guilty about today. Mistakes just mean we need to get better."

There was a long pause as people thought about Arthur's words.

"What about the whale?" Joy asked.

"Either she's still out there," Arthur offered, "or she got too tired to swim and she drowned. Since we don't know what happened to her, let's keep our eyes open for the next few days."

That night, in the captain's quarters, Arthur cut a rope into ten sections, each about three feet long. He tied knots into each line, and then nailed one end of each to the wooden wall alongside the bunk. The knotted lines dangled along the wall and swayed with the rocking of the boat.

Sixty-eight knots. Each knot, a day. Each day, a chance at freedom and control. Arthur had counted the days until their parents would arrive on the dock in Rockland Harbor, ready to shake McKinley's hand and take their children home. Each knot, a chance to prove himself. He hoped things would turn out all right.

With a sigh, he untied the bottom knot of the first line and crawled into bed.

CHAPTER THREE

SIXTY-SEVEN KNOTS OF FREEDOM LEFT

For the next several days, Arthur ran the crew of the *Dreadnought* through a series of drills. They lashed grimy vinyl mats together to serve as a dummy, and three or four times a day, without warning, someone would hurl it overboard.

Dawn had spent an evening reading a sailing book she found in the captain's quarters, and she taught the sailor-overboard drill to the others. Each time, the crew tried to do it the same way. The helmsman turned the *Dreadnought* until it was sideways to the wind, sailing away from the "victim," and the crew adjusted the sails. Then the helmsman turned farther, crossing the stern of the boat through the wind so the sails swung to the other side with a thud. As the crew let the sails arch farther out and fill with rescuing breezes, the helmsman held a course that brought the boat directly downwind of the dummy. With a sharp turn upwind and the sails tightened for momentum and then allowed to swing free, the *Dreadnought* eased slowly alongside the floating dummy. Some of the crew climbed down into the dinghy and pulled the dummy aboard, and with help, the "victim" was hauled to the deck for medical treatment.

After a few days of training, the crew could retrieve the dummy within a few minutes. No crashing sails, no tangled lines, no panic. Just efficiency. McKinley might even have called it discipline. Arthur was pleased. At this rate, he thought as the dripping dummy was dragged onto the deck for the sixth time, we'll become sailors yet. We just needed McKinley out of the way. I knew we could do it. I knew *I* could do it.

They also practiced the "swamped-dinghy" drill, at Arthur's insistence. Jesse, Dawn, and Joy volunteered to join Arthur in the first trial. Arthur talked Logan into participating as well; he wanted to help Logan get comfortable with the sea. After they climbed into the dinghy, they rowed a short distance away from the ship and put their feet on one side of the small boat. They put their hands on the other gunwale, with their butts in the air, and they began to rock. The heavy wooden dinghy responded grudgingly at first, dripping and complaining with waterlogged groans, but gradually they coaxed it into long swings from one side to the other. Then, with a loud whoop, they put all their weight on their feet and pulled the other side over their heads.

The icy water attacked quickly, numbing their fingers and toes, turning vision white.

"W-we have to practice this," Arthur said, his low voice booming over the waves. "These temperatures would kill us if we didn't do this well."

The five sailors, treading water and shivering with blue lips and goosebumped skin, counted off: "One! Two! Three! Four! Five!" If someone were unconscious or trapped underwater, the count would reveal the impending tragedy. Everyone was okay, so they rolled the dinghy back upright and flopped inside. It was still submerged and filled with water, like a giant wooden bathtub, its gunwales just barely touching the surface of the water from below.

"Okay, listen to me and do what I say," Arthur commanded, trying not to let his teeth chatter. "We all squat down in the boat, as far down in the water as we can. Then, when I say so, we all stand up quickly. The water level in the boat will drop, and that will give us a head start. Then we need to bail out faster than water comes in."

The others were skeptical, but they trusted Arthur. They lowered themselves in the boat until the water touched their chattering chins.

"Now!" Arthur shouted. They stood up at once, the water level dropped, the dinghy shifted unsteadily to one side—and all five teenagers lurched against each other and tipped sideways into the ocean, laughing and splashing in a tangle of arms and legs and soaked clothes. The water seemed less cold now.

They tried again. They slipped back into the dinghy, took their positions, and lowered themselves almost completely into the frigid water. Arthur gave his signal, and they all stood up—carefully, in the middle of the boat. The water level dropped, and seawater began to pour in over the sides. But the five of them bailed furiously, pitching water out with tin cans and bottomless plastic jugs, and within a minute or two, the sides of the boat were high enough to block the incoming flow. They scooped out the rest of the water and rowed the dinghy, damp but upright, back to the ship.

"It works!" Dawn announced to the crew as she wrapped a towel around her dripping brown ponytail. "It's cold, but that just helps us remember the beautiful power of the sea. Isn't it wonderful? It all makes me feel so alive, so much a part of the great web of life on earth." She smiled at Arthur, who shrugged and smiled back.

Arthur continued to put the crew through drills for the next several days as they explored the coast of Maine. They became proficient at raising, setting, and altering the sails. They developed precision in their tacks and jibes, moving the bow or the stern across the wind to fill the sails from the other side. They learned how to coax speed from the wind, how to hoist and drop the anchor with ease, and how to set a course and hold it.

With each passing day, the value of Jesse's strength became increasingly apparent. He could lift overstuffed footlockers. He could raise the largest sail by himself. And he could row the dinghy with astonishing speed, invariably causing Logan to crack a joke about him pulling the *Dreadnought* so they'd make better time.

Jesse was used to the teasing. He had been born strong, a tough and wiry baby who grew into a formidable and potent young man. He liked to wear tight T-shirts, because he enjoyed the expressions on people's faces as they watched his muscles shift and pulse beneath the fabric.

He also liked to play the harmonica. He had an odd style, holding it vertically and sliding it up and down to get the notes. But he had mastered the technique through constant practice, done out of a sense of peace and comfort more than the discipline of a musician-in-training. The harmonica was a gift from his father; it had arrived in the mail on the day Jesse turned eight. Jesse had been enduring a slow march of gray days in the shelter in the Bronx while the paperwork was being completed for his acceptance into a foster home. The harmonica came in a small white box with a note that read: "To Jesse. Happy Birthday. Dad." Jesse kept the note in his pocket for months after that, until it disintegrated into small damp wads of paper. He tucked the harmonica under his pillow, and he played lonesome tunes on it whenever he could. It was a sign that his father loved him, and it was the only such sign he had ever received. His father was living in Florida, married to—or at least living with—a woman he had met in Atlantic City. Susan was her name. Or Sharon. Something like that. Jesse's mother had died so long ago, he couldn't remember what she looked like, and his father had lived with a long line of women ever since. When he was seven, Jesse had been dropped off at the shelter after his father came back from a business trip to New Jersey. No explanation. Just "here's your new home, kid." The harmonica was the only message Al Kowaleweski ever sent. Still, he *had* mailed it. And it *had* arrived on Jesse's birthday. On the very day. Jesse didn't know why his father had left, but he took the instrument as a secret and powerful message that everything would work out all right. When the sun was setting and the air was still, he liked to sit on the bow of the *Dreadnought* and play soft sad songs about lost loves and vague yearnings.

The *Dreadnought* was sailing comfortably across the mouth of Sheepscot Bay, venturing west along the Maine coast, with Logan at the helm. The date was June 18, and the summer was still young. Gliding gracefully around the bay were several other boats, mostly sailboats with sleek bows and stout sides, their white or red or rainbow sails vivid against the blue water and green shore.

Logan spent his time at the wheel inventing silly ways to get attention. He declared, at one point, that scrawny little Bill Fiona should be called "BillFi" from then on, as though his name was BillFEE O-nah. Bill grinned and seemed to accept the nickname with pleasure. "It beats being called 'Squinty,'" he said. "Definitely beats 'Squinty.'" Logan also delighted in pushing the *Dreadnought's* bow toward the wind, causing the sails to flutter with a chaotic commotion. Then he would turn the wheel and let the sails pop full of air, just as though nothing had happened. It was just his way of passing the time and getting a rise out of the sunbathers on the deck.

Marietta was on bow watch later that afternoon. She spent more time smoothing her hair and fussing with her bikini straps than looking out at the water. The sun was beginning to set when Joy asked her to gather the crew together on the deck.

"We're getting low on food," Joy said, once everyone had gathered on the aft deck. The air was growing still and humid. Most of the sailors had traded their sweatshirts for tank tops and tees. "We have enough food to get us through another week or so, *Dios mediante*—God willing—but we're going to have to go ashore for more supplies soon. I've made up a list of things we need."

"How about a little loaves-and-fishes action, Joy?" Crystal asked with an awkward grin.

"Thou shalt not tempt the Lord thy God," Joy quoted solemnly.

"We still have the money we found in McKinley's cabin," Arthur said, his low voice carrying an air of authority. "About twelve hundred dollars. That ought to buy us a lot of food."

"But do you think we should go ashore?" Logan asked, flicking his ruddy hair out of his face. "What if somebody wonders what we're doing? What if somebody asks us about McKinley? What if somebody—"

"We need more food, Loser," Crystal said, her hands on her hips. "So quit whining. Sooner or later, we're going to have to go ashore."

"We're also low on water," Arthur said, "and our waste tank is probably getting full. We're going to have to find a marina."

Logan sighed with a wheeze. "I don't know," he said. "It seems kinda risky."

"I'll find out," Joy said. She fished a coin from her denim shorts, Saint Christopher on one side and Saint Francis on the other. With a smart flick of the wrist, she set it spinning on the polished deck. It twirled, flashing in the light, and when it stopped, Saint Christopher beamed his blessed countenance toward the heavens.

"*Muchas gracias*," she whispered toward the sky. She turned to the others. "We should go in and buy what we need. Saint Christopher is the patron saint of travelers."

Crystal shook her head with a sneer. "That's a bunch of astrological voodoo, if you ask me," she said. "But I agree with Her Holiness anyway. We have to go into town."

"Agreed," said Arthur, standing tall and speaking with a tone that he hoped would suggest that the debate was closed. "We'll find a marina tomorrow and do some shopping. In the meantime, everyone should think about things they need and let Joy know. Toothpaste, sunscreen—whatever. Let's get what we need, but we can't afford to buy anything that isn't essential. We have to make our money last all summer. Understood?"

The next day was Tuesday, and the crew spent the morning sailing up Broad Sound and the open mouth of Harraseeket River. Arthur had studied the charts in the captain's quarters and determined that the *Dreadnought* could sail in close to a small town called Freeport. It didn't look very big on the chart, but Arthur hoped it would have a store or two.

He wasn't disappointed. Freeport was a congested mass of outlet shops, upscale clothing stores, ice cream parlors, and touristy knickknack boutiques—all clustered around L. L. Bean's main complex of retail stores, a massive, sprawling network of buildings that seemed to fill the center of town. The *Dreadnought* crew rowed in on the dinghy, and Arthur gathered them together on a side street near the river.

"We don't have a whole lot of time," he said. "We shouldn't leave the ship alone for too long. So we'll divide Joy's list, split up the money, and we'll each get the things on our part of the list. Let's travel in pairs or small groups and meet back here in an hour."

"Let's make it two hours," Marietta said, smoothing her hair. "This looks like my kind of town."

The others nodded.

"Okay," Arthur said, "two hours. But no longer."

Joy tore off part of the list and handed it to BillFi and Jesse. Arthur gave them $300, and they walked off toward L. L. Bean. The others also broke off in pairs, took their $300 and their lists, and wandered into the town. Left behind were Logan, Arthur, Marietta, and Dawn.

"Where should *we* go, Arthur?" Marietta asked. "How about that woolen shop across the street? I love the sweater they have in the window. Let's take a look inside. I'm sure we'll find something on our list." Arthur started to say something, but Marietta cut him off and continued. "You won't mind if we go off together, will you?" she asked Dawn and Logan. "That way, you two can go see whatever you want to see."

Arthur smiled. "We can all go together, if you want."

"No, thanks," Dawn said, a soft smile flashing across her freckled face. "We wouldn't want to intrude. I'm sure we'll be just fine."

"Great!" Marietta said. She took Arthur's arm and walked off toward the woolen shop.

The woolen shop, not surprisingly, put forth a nautical theme, its walls painted grayish white and its trim a glossy slate blue. Wooden roughly painted seagulls sat stoically between multicolored glass lobster floats, coils of coarse rope, and replicas of ships' steering wheels. Any hope of a maritime atmosphere was shattered, however, by the heavy perfume of carpet deodorizer and the piped-in sounds of a gentle Golden Oldies station.

"Over here!" Marietta squealed, leading Arthur by the hand to a pile of cashmere sweaters stacked artfully in an upended, pristine lobster trap. The sweaters beckoned in muted shades of brown and gray, each sporting a breathtaking price tag. Marietta chose a brown sweater and scampered off to a dressing room. "Don't peek!" she called over her shoulder to Arthur as she disappeared through the swinging doors.

Arthur looked around the shop while he waited. The crew shirts were tempting with their embroidered logos on the front. The chinos looked nice with their crisp creases. The windbreakers seemed useful with their thin hoods zipped into their collars. But this store had nothing from his part of Joy's list. He dug the paper out of his jeans pocket:

—Windproof safety matches

—Kerosene

—Spatula

—Woolite

—Sponges (large)

—1 large country ham

—20 lbs. potatoes

—Small gasoline generator

—10 gals. gasoline

He could see that none of these items would be available in this store, and Arthur guessed that few of the shops in this town would offer such mundane, real-world items. After this woolen-shop visit, he would try to find a hardware store and then a basic supermarket.

"What do you think?" Marietta asked.

Arthur looked up—and fell speechless. Marietta wore the cashmere well, its flattering cut making her body all the more attractive. She smiled.

"Well?" she urged.

"It's great," Arthur said, blinking his hazel eyes. "It's really great. We should figure out some way to buy it for you someday. Because it looks good on you. I mean, it looks *really* good."

Marietta turned around slowly, like a model on a runway. "I'm glad you like it," she said softly.

Almost three hours later, the crew had gathered on the side street once again. Arthur had been waiting for nearly sixty minutes, and he was angry that the crew was failing to follow orders so completely. When at last everyone arrived, they were carrying dozens of large paper and plastic bags—most bearing designer logos on their sides.

"You didn't get the *bread?*" Arthur asked BillFi.

"Sorry," BillFi said, wiping his nose on his sleeve. "We ran out of money. Sorry. We each got a new sleeping bag, 'cause the ones we're using are really old and gross, and then—"

"And I bought some really good scotch," Logan said. "Well, I got some old guy to buy it for us—only had to give him twenty bucks. I do that all the time at home. We got *five* bottles. And six bottles of French red wine. That rum was getting pretty boring."

Arthur shook his head. "I don't believe this! How are we going to eat without bread? Joy—you were going to get pasta and some stuff for making soups. You got *that*, didn't you?"

Joy looked sheepish, her round face cast downward. "Well, we got the pasta," she said quietly. "But then we went into a shop that sells exotic herbs and things, and we got some great stuff. Maybe the best pesto sauce I have ever tasted. And some Szechwan pepper that is really hot and really good. And some—"

"Did *anyone* get what they were supposed to get?" Arthur asked in his lowest voice.

Everyone was silent. In the bags on the muddy ground around them were cotton turtlenecks ("They were sixty percent off!"), an inlaid mahogany chess set ("We have to have *something* to do at night!"), a battery-powered CD player with twelve discs ("We can't go all summer without music!"), three dozen novels, four Gore-Tex raincoats, a harmonica, two fishing rods, eight copies of the King James version of the Bible, and an impressive assembly of other odds and ends—very few of which were edible. Jesse had a paperback copy of *Moby Dick*, which he tucked into his jeans pocket. ("It's about a whale," he explained unapologetically. "I like whales.") Logan had a pewter flask and a comic book.

And the money was nearly gone.

"This is great," Arthur shouted. "This is really great! We can listen to music, play chess, dress beautifully, and starve to death!" He ran a hand through his hair and tried to think of something powerful to say. Something with authority. Something with teeth. He had to show this crew that when he gave orders, he meant them. If he let them get away with this kind of foolishness, they would just get worse as time went on.

What would my father say right now? he thought. He would know just the right words. Something like, "If you pull this kind of stunt again, I'll resign as captain—and *then* where would you be?"

No, too risky. They might just let him quit. How about, "I am your captain, and I expect you to follow my instructions. If we can't all agree to do at least that much, then we're in for a long and dangerous summer."

That might work, but someone might laugh. Like Crystal. She seemed the most likely to tell him to take a hike. Maybe he would say, "What did you think—"

"Well," Crystal asked, her hands on her hips. "Did you get the things on your list?"

Arthur scowled. "I didn't spend any of our money at all!" he said.

Marietta smiled and reached into a large bag. "A cashmere sweater," she said. "I just *had* to have something warm to wear. I didn't think Maine would be this cold in the summer."

The crew ate a late lunch on board, sailing slowly back out into Casco Bay. Most of them weren't very hungry, and Arthur guessed that some of McKinley's money had been lavished on Freeport's upscale restaurants and premium ice cream parlors. Joy boiled the pasta, added some tomato paste and a few mushrooms, and sprinkled it with Szechwan pepper. Arthur had to admit it tasted great.

Two days later, with Logan at the helm, he spotted a large powder-blue sailboat—an expensive luxury yacht—cruising nearby. A middle-aged captain was at the wheel, and several other wealthy sorts milled about the decks. For some reason, the boat began to move in closer.

"Oh, shit," Logan said, wiping his hair from his eyes. "You don't think those people, like, knew McKinley or anything, do you? Ka-BOOM! Let's put a warning shot across their bow."

Dawn was standing near the wheel. "Just stay on your course, don't change anything, and relax," she said. "These people might just like beautiful old schooners."

The blue-hulled boat took a course parallel to Logan's, matching the *Dreadnought's* speed. Only a few dozen yards of water separated the two boats, and the other captain waved respectfully to Logan.

Logan waved back. He tried to talk to Dawn without moving his lips. "What do ya think he wants?"

Dawn fixed her green eyes directly at the opposing captain. She made no effort to hide her voice. "I don't know what he wants, but right now he seems to be content just to ride along with us. Let's enjoy his company. Just two great ships sharing a brief moment in the midst of the tumultuous sea."

Logan kept his lips still. "Would you go get Arthur?" he asked.

Dawn shook her head. "We don't need him. We're doing fine," she said.

"Of course we are," Logan said. "We're doing totally fine."

A moment later, the other captain waved again. This time, he also pointed ahead, then pointed at Logan, then pointed ahead again.

"Oooo-weee, we're in trouble," Logan said. "He wants us to go with him somewhere. He wants to talk with us. He's prob-ably, like, some five-star general in the Coast Guard or something, and he knows what's going on. We're in a lot of trouble. Ka-chink! Locked in the brig forever."

"Relax," Dawn said. "I don't think the Coast Guard uses baby-blue sailboats, and I don't think they dress in designer sportswear." She stepped to the railing and raised her hands in a shrug. "We don't understand!" she shouted.

The captain signaled to a young woman on his ship, and a moment later, she brought him a bullhorn.

"Ahoy, tall ship!" he called out. "I was wondering if we could interest you in a race. Around the Black Rocks and back. The first boat to enter the bay on the south side of Damariscove Island wins. The losers provide the drinks!"

Logan and Dawn exchanged glances. They grinned.

"Attention, crew!" Logan shouted toward the bow. "All hands on deck! Hoist every sail we have! We've received a challenge, and we're accepting it! Ahoy! Avast! Scoop the scuppers! And all that stuff."

The jib sail rose, billowed, and filled with wind. The *Dreadnought* picked up speed. Logan gave a thumbs-up sign to the other captain, who turned and shouted orders to his crew.

The race was on.

☠   ☠   ☠

The blue boat was leading by a hundred yards when the *Dreadnought* rounded the Black Rocks and set course for Damariscove Island. Arthur, setting aside his anger over the shopping disaster, studied the charts and shouted navigational instructions to Logan. Joy, Dawn, Jesse, and several of the others hauled lines, adjusting the sails on Logan's command. Crystal scrambled up the rigging and dangled near the top of the main mast, scanning the water for ripples that might indicate stronger wind. Marietta sat in the dining room, reading a fashion magazine.

Halfway back across Sheepscot Bay, the *Dreadnought* had closed the gap. The two boats were nearly even, a dead heat, and the strong wind threw spray across the bows.

The other captain picked up his bullhorn. "We prefer gin martinis, on the rocks, with olives. Shaken, not stirred," he called over with a smile.

Logan smiled back. "We prefer rum and warm Coke!" he shouted. "And lots of it!" The other captain cupped his hand over his ear. He hadn't been able to hear Logan's wheezy voice across the waves.

The wind, now howling off the ocean to the southeast, was causing both boats to heel sharply to port. The tilting decks made work difficult, but the blue boat seemed to get the worst of it. Waves broke over the bow, slowing the boat and giving the *Dreadnought* the lead.

As the ships approached Damariscove Island, however, the other captain called for a sail adjustment, and the blue boat leveled and began to pick up speed. Logan called for some adjustments of his own, but they made little difference. The blue boat entered the bay twenty seconds ahead of the *Dreadnought*.

Half an hour later, the *Dreadnought* was anchored, and the blue boat was tied up alongside. Logan and the rest of the *Dreadnought* sailors stood on the blue boat's deck, introducing themselves to the well-dressed crew that had beaten them.

"It was a fine race, Captain Logan McPhee," said the other captain. "I'm Richard Turner, and this is my somewhat extended family. Welcome to the *Elkhart* of Camden, Maine."

"It is an honor to be here, Captain Richard Turner," Logan said with a formal tone and an air of mock sophistication that clashed with his pale pudgy body. "This is my crew—ta-DA!—the finest sailors on the Atlantic. Congratulations on an impressive victory. As we agreed, we have brought the drinks."

With a flourish, Jesse produced a large pitcher filled with dark, fizzing liquid. The *Elkhart* crew eyed it—and Jesse's muscular shoulders—suspiciously.

"Rum and Coke," Logan said. "It would help a *lot* if you had some ice."

The *Dreadnought* crew spent the rest of the evening lounging on board the *Elkhart*, touring the luxurious cabins, chatting with their wealthy counterparts, and drinking gin martinis on the rocks; after the first round, the *Elkhart* sailors had smiled awkwardly and declined any additional drinks from the *Dreadnought's* fizzing pitcher. The sun set in a blaze of red. Crackers and cheese, ham, salmon, and shrimp made the rounds on elegant trays. Gentle piano music drifted through the chilly air from speakers hidden throughout the yacht.

Arthur and Dawn leaned against the railing on the aft deck, talking with Turner and some of his crew. The railing gleamed of polished brass. The deck was blue fiberglass ribbed with warm teak. The conversation was charming and polite.

"So you're on a training course," Turner said. "That's fascinating. Nothing like sailing to instill a sense of discipline and order. Nothing like it at all."

Arthur smiled. "We learn more every day. And it sure hasn't been dull."

Turner took a sip of his martini, stared off at the dark sea, and sighed. "Ah, I remember learning how to sail long ago, as a boy in Portsmouth, New Hampshire. My father had given me a Laser, even though my mother protested vigorously: 'But

Bruce, he's only six! That boat's too big for such a young boy!' Father just grinned. 'Let's see who's bigger—the boy or the boat.'" Turner chuckled. He rolled his eyes. "Rumor has it— the boy was bigger."

Arthur raised his glass. "The boy is always bigger than the boat," he said. It was Dawn's turn to roll her eyes.

"So tell me," Turner asked, "who is in charge of this sailing outfit of yours? Not that you can't take care of yourselves, of course, but surely the people running this camp don't just throw a bunch of you on a tall ship and push you out to sea. Who is supervising this trip? And why isn't he over here, helping himself to our hospitality?"

Dawn didn't miss a beat. "He's down below," she said, struggling to find words that were truthful but misleading, "and he has asked not to be disturbed."

The term "down below" nearly caused Arthur to choke on a shrimp, but he managed to keep his composure.

"Ah, too bad," Turner said. "Please give him my regards. It's a pleasure to meet young people who are working to improve themselves, and I'm sure your leader must be a very interesting individual."

Marietta pried her way into the circle. She had a martini in one hand and a salmon-and-cream-cheese mini-sandwich in the other. She was wearing a low-cut blouse, and she laughed and stepped in between Arthur and Dawn. "What a beautiful boat this is, Captain," she said. "What do you do for a living? You must be very successful."

Turner cleared his throat. "Yes, well, I'm the CEO of a manufacturing firm. Paper products, mostly. Nothing terribly exciting. Probably the highlight of my dreary grind is getting out on this boat and enjoying a day off every now and then."

"Fascinating, simply fascinating," Marietta said, twirling her blond-streaked hair. "Arthur, could I show you something? I just got a tour of the boat, and there is something you have to see."

"Sure," Arthur shrugged. He didn't want to seem uninterested in Turner's pride and joy. He turned to Dawn. "I'll be back in a little while."

Marietta led Arthur across the deck and down the gangway toward the cabins below.

The captain's quarters of the *Elkhart* shimmered with polished brass, hand-rubbed mahogany, and sparkling crystal. A large bed covered with an inviting feather comforter nearly filled the room. The piano music brightened the warm air. Marietta sat down on one corner of the bed and motioned for Arthur to sit beside her.

"Wouldn't it be great to have all this?" she asked. "Wouldn't you just love to take this beautiful ship out for a sail whenever you wanted to?"

"It would be nice," Arthur said, sitting on the bed. "When I own a boat like this, it will be because I own some really cool company of my own. Something I start from scratch. Something that everyone else wishes they were doing." He smiled. Decide what you want, his father had said, and then go for it. Don't let anything stand in your way.

"And as the owner and president," Marietta said, fussing with her hair, "you'd do things to make it all worthwhile—like go golfing all over the world, and have servants cook and clean for you, and drive really fast cars. Or better yet, hire a chauffeur and make *him* drive really fast!"

Arthur smiled. "And I'll have a mansion on an island somewhere, and the only way to get to it is by boat. And I'd live out there, and I'd write fantastic novels, and I'd fly my own plane around to inspect my companies, and I'd give money to the library and the school and the Little League in town, and everyone there would think I was great. And then, when I died, I'd be buried in the little cemetery overlooking the harbor, and teachers would bring elementary-school students out to see my grave, and they would talk about me for hundreds of years, and the whole island would be preserved as a museum until one day, without warning, it disappeared into the sea and was never seen again."

Marietta stared at him. "You're kind of strange, you know that?" she said, a perplexed scowl flashing briefly across her face. "That is *really* bizarre. Fortunately, I happen to like bizarre guys. Especially when they're Captain." She pressed against his side and looked directly into his hazel eyes. She waited.

Arthur waited, too, but just for a moment. Then he kissed her, and they both leaned back across the bed. They kissed again—and at that moment, the door burst open. The *Elkhart's* meteorologist, a large and boisterous woman with a florid face and a booming voice, crashed through the door, laughing and shrieking loudly, with a man in one hand and a drink in the other.

"Whoops!" she screamed with a flushed giggle when she saw Arthur and Marietta on the bed. Arthur leapt to his feet, but Marietta stayed where she was. The meteorologist guffawed again. "Didn't know it was *occupado*! So sorry!" She laughed and shrieked again, then staggered down the hall and up the gangway, trailing the man behind her. Arthur turned to Marietta.

"We should get back on deck," he said.

It was nearly 2 A.M. when the party broke up. Arthur, concerned that late nights could weaken the discipline among his crew, stretched his tall frame and said to Turner, "I'm tired. I'm going to bed. My shipmates should, also." The two crews said goodbye, and the *Dreadnought* sailors began to climb over to their own ship.

"I have to ask you one question before I go," Arthur said to Turner as they shook hands. "About the race. You beat us by a little bit, but I noticed that your boat was heeling awfully hard out there—right up until the last minute. Did you do that on purpose, to slow yourself down and make the race more interesting?"

Turner grinned. "You'll never get me to admit it," he said.

In the dining room of the *Dreadnought*, the crew sat around the table and talked about the race and the party.

"If that's what we get for losing," Logan wheezed, "I think we should race 'em every day. Bay–BEE! Just imagine what we'd get if we *won*."

☠   ☠   ☠

Joy was at the helm in a rainstorm, two days later, when Crystal shouted from the bow. "A whale! Another whale!" She pointed off to starboard. A few seconds later, the entire crew was on deck, squinting through the glare on the turbulent waves.

A spout. Unmistakable. The large whale swam slowly, taking frequent breaths. Each time it surfaced, it blew a cloud of mist into the air. The mist cut horizontally across the choppy waves and mingled with the whitecap foam blown up by the wind.

"It's another one trapped in a net," Crystal called back. "What do you want to do?"

Joy pulled her raincoat hood tight and thought for a moment as the rain soaked the wheel and chilled her hands. On the one hand, everyone would feel better if they could rescue this whale; it might make up for losing Ibis. On the other hand, losing this whale also would make them feel even worse. And the last time they tried a rescue, Logan had nearly been killed. Still, if they could somehow get in close enough . . .

"What do you want to do?" Crystal called out.

Joy glanced nervously at the faces around her. They expected a decision, but Joy didn't want to make one. Decisions were for God to make, she thought. Our job is to follow them.

Then she pulled from her shorts pocket the coin with the saints on it. She held it above her and prayed out loud: "Our Father, Who art in Heaven, please hear our prayer. We are lost at sea without your guidance and grace, and in Christ's name we ask that you show us the way. Should we try to save this whale or not?"

She knelt on the deck, held the disk edgeways between her left forefinger and her right thumb, and gave it a spin. It twirled furiously for a moment, a silver sphere dancing on the dark wood deck, and then it slowed and wobbled to a stop. Saint Francis was on top.

"The patron saint of animals. *Muchas gracias*," Joy said, pocketing the coin. "God wants us to save that whale."

Dawn nodded. "We're going to try it!" she shouted. "Everyone gather around for instructions." She suggested a plan, gesturing and pointing with her long thin fingers. As long as the whale was swimming, she said, any attempt to untangle the net would be useless—and dangerous. "But I've been reading about the old Nantucket whalers, and I have an idea." The *Dreadnought* would sail in as close as possible, and several of the crew would row the dinghy in closer. They would take one of the large plastic floats that protected the side of the ship from damage, and when they were right next to the whale, they would clip the float line onto the net. The float would help them track the whale's movements, and the extra drag would tire the whale quickly. Once it was exhausted and resting at the surface, they could try to cut the net away. "That's what the Nantucket whalers used to do, except they used harpoons and their boats instead of clips and plastic floats," Dawn said. "And of course they killed the whale once they got close to it. This is our chance to make up for all that cruelty. Get back in the whales' good graces."

Arthur stood nearby, his arms folded across his chest. He was troubled that such an important decision was being made without his guidance, but he thought it might be a good idea to give the crew some leeway every now and then. Let them feel important and responsible. He decided to say nothing.

The crew scrambled into position, and Arthur could see that his drills were paying off. The crew handled the sails quickly and skillfully, and the ship began to gain on the whale. As the ship grew closer, Jesse, BillFi, Dawn, and Arthur pulled the dinghy alongside and prepared to climb down the ladder.

"Godspeed, sailors!" shouted Joy. "*Vayan con Dios!*" The dinghy crew leapt into the small boat and pushed away. With Jesse on one oar and Arthur on the other, they chopped through the waves. Dawn sat in the stern and directed the rowers; BillFi crouched in the bow next to a round pink float. It was about three feet in diameter and covered with a fine film of algae, and trailing from it was a stout twenty-foot rope that ended at a metal clip. BillFi's job would be to secure that clip to the net before the whale had a chance to dive and swim away.

Jesse's power made steering difficult—the dinghy veered off course several times, and Jesse had to stop rowing until Arthur could catch up—and they weren't narrowing the gap between them and the whale. It would pause, take a breath or two, then submerge again, and any gains they made during the rests would be lost in a single dive.

Then Jesse put his oar down. "Arthur, let me have both," he said.

"That'll slow us down," Arthur said. "Two of us can—"

"Trust him," BillFi called back from the bow, blinking through his thick glasses. "Give him your oar."

Arthur nodded with a frown and moved to the stern, next to Dawn. Jesse shifted to the center of the boat, picked up both oars, and began to pull.

The difference was obvious immediately. Jesse pulled against the oars with his arms, his back, and his legs. His entire body lifted off the seat as he reached forward, and then he pushed his feet against the seat in front of him as the blades dug into the water. The dinghy shot across the waves, leaving a strong wake behind it. In minutes, BillFi was just yards away from the whale.

It dove again, lifting its tail out of the water. Arthur saw the black curve, stark against the white flesh on the underside, and he shouted out loud.

"It's Ibis! It's the same whale!"

Dawn's freckled face beamed with joy, and she shouted the news back to the *Dreadnought*, which was still sailing along behind. She could see the other sailors jump and cheer on deck.

And Jesse continued to row. The dinghy moved in a straight line, and a moment later, something bumped into the portside oar from below.

"Here she comes!" Arthur called out. "BillFi, get ready!"

The shimmering black of Ibis's back broke through the waves. First came the top of her head; she blew a cloud of droplets into the air—and all over BillFi. The net was made of monofiliment fishing line, and it was nearly invisible in the water. The edges of the net were bound in heavy nylon cord, and these cords trailed back from her mouth and tangled tightly across her back. Ibis slid forward, and her blowhole dipped beneath the surface. Her black back continued to roll, and her dorsal fin cut upward, moved forward, and then began to sink again. The cords were wrapped firmly around the fin, cutting into the skin in places and exposing the white bloodless fat beneath the skin.

"Now, Bill!" Arthur said. BillFi lunged toward the whale, thrust his hands into the bitterly cold water, and tried to clip the float to the cords. The water made his fingers numb, and the moving mass of the whale made it difficult to clip the net.

"I can't do it!" he said. Ibis raised the base of her tail into the air, preparing to dive once again. "I can't make it hook on!"

Jesse threw his oars down and grabbed the clip from BillFi's stiff hands. He jammed his hands into the water, leaning far over the side of the dinghy, and he groped around in the cloud of monofiliment lines. He found a strong cable, and as he attached the clip, Ibis raised her flukes out of the water and began to dive. The strands of the net tightened around Jesse's powerful arms, and the tail slid silently beneath the waves, pulling Jesse out of the boat and far under the water.

CHAPTER FOUR

Sixty knots of freedom left

A moment passed in uncomprehending silence. Then BillFi cried out, "Hey!" and Arthur said "Oh, shit!" and Dawn said, "Oh, goddess!" The three of them lunged to the port side and searched the water for signs of their friend. They could see nothing but beams of sunlight filtering through the green murk below.

"Where is he?" Dawn asked frantically.

"He's stuck to the damn whale!" BillFi said. "He put his hands down in there, and the net got him! He's stuck to the damn whale!"

Arthur looked in all directions for signs of Ibis. He saw nothing but barren waves.

"Whales can stay under for a long time," he said. "Longer than Jesse can hold his breath."

"Jesse!" Dawn yelled. "Jesse!"

No reply. On board the *Dreadnought,* the crew had gathered anxiously at the rail. There was nothing anyone could do but watch.

"The float!" Arthur said. "The big pink float. Jesse hooked it onto the net before he went over. It's on a long line.

It'll come up before Ibis does."

They scanned the waves, the horizon, the water. Thirty seconds went by. Sixty seconds. BillFi's eyes darted from wavetop to wavetop, searching frantically for his friend. He saw nothing but seawater.

His mind flashed back to the time Jesse was knifed five years earlier. They were living in the same cinderblock shelter in the Bronx, a place for kids whose parents had decided to embrace life without them. A place where kids lived when they were between foster homes. A place where kids learned how to fight and cheat and take pride in their loss of dignity. BillFi—they called him Billy there—had arrived scared, and he spent every day and every night there scared. He was afraid for his life, he was afraid for his mind, and he was afraid for his soul. He was different from most kids—he knew that— and he had long since become accustomed to the jeers and the taunts and the harassment that the other boys dished out. But it's a long city block between accustomed and confident, and Billy had never taken that walk. He was small for his age, nearly blind without his thick tinted glasses, and nervous even when others felt at home. They laughed at him for his allergies, for his stumbling speech, for his inability to look people in the eye. They laughed at him for his intuition, for his ability to read faces and patterns and anticipate what was going to happen next. He was good at that. It was his one true gift. And it even got him beaten up more times than he let himself remember.

Jesse was always good to him, though. He could have been rough—the guy could punch his way through a wall, if he wanted to—but he saw in Billy a gentleness, a perception, a note of music that no one else in the shelter could understand. And he responded with his own kind of artistry. When Jesse was with Billy, he played songs on his harmonica that were soft and sad and sweet. And Billy listened, letting the melodies and the breathing push away all that was harsh and dirty about the world.

One day, a bunch of guys in the shelter decided that they'd had enough of Jesse's harmonica. Without warning—without even asking him to stop—they put a knife between his ribs. Jesse was sent to the hospital by cab, and he recovered quickly. When he returned to the shelter, he continued to play his harmonica. The other guys, impressed by his determination, left him alone. And Jesse devoted hours each day to running and working out, to make sure no one bothered him again.

BillFi was startled by a shout bursting from the crew of the *Dreadnought*.

"There it is!" Dawn said. "The float. It's over there."

The pink ball wobbled along the surface just fifty yards away. It was moving slowly toward deeper water. Arthur grabbed the oars and began to pull with all his strength. He made good time.

BillFi crouched in the bow and stared at the ball, knowing that his friend—his best friend—was trapped underwater below it. Then he saw the puff of mist. Ibis was surfacing for air.

Swimming with the drag of the float and Jesse's weight had clearly tired the whale. She moved slowly along the surface, taking several breaths. As BillFi watched, and as Arthur rowed, Ibis arched her back—and Jesse broke the surface.

"There he is!" BillFi shouted. Jesse's arm was still tangled in the net, but he was moving and taking large breaths. Then, as BillFi watched, Jesse reached his free hand into his pants pocket and took something out. He put it to his mouth and pulled.

"A knife!" Arthur said. "He's got a pocket knife."

Jesse reached up and began to cut the net. But he wasn't cutting the part snarled around his arm. He was cutting the cable that ran through Ibis's mouth.

"He's still trying to get her free!" Arthur said. "He's trying to cut—"

Then Ibis dove again, and all was still.

☠   ☠   ☠

More than a minute passed. Then the float crashed to the surface. This time, it didn't move. It floated in one place, bobbing low on the waves.

Arthur rowed frantically toward the pink ball. As the dinghy drew nearer, BillFi jumped up in the bow. "He's there!" he shouted. "He's holding onto the float."

Dawn and Arthur stared. They could see Jesse's head next to the float, and as they watched, Jesse raised his arm and gave them a thumbs-up sign. BillFi returned the gesture.

When Arthur had moved the dinghy within earshot, BillFi called out, "Are you all right?"

"I'm okay," Jesse called back as he grabbed the side of the dinghy. "My arm hurts a little."

"What happened?" Dawn asked.

"Who cares what happened?" Arthur yelled angrily at Jesse. "You nearly ruined everything. For everybody! You want to risk your life saving some stupid whale, that's fine. But if you get hurt or killed, this whole summer is a bust. We all go home. It's not just about you. We're all in this together."

"I just cut the net off Ibis," Jesse said, treading water calmly. "Like we were supposed to do."

"And it was wonderful," Dawn said, ignoring Arthur. Her smile beamed warmth and happiness. "Another thinking, feeling creature is alive today because of you. Because of us all. But how did you—"

She didn't finish her question. Now freed of the net and the float and Jesse, Ibis breached just twenty yards away. She shot out of the water, nose first, moving nearly straight up. Her entire thirty-ton body cleared the surface and seemed to hang in the air, dripping and outstretched. Then she arched gracefully and landed flat on her back with a loud splash that drenched Arthur, Dawn, and BillFi and nearly swamped the dinghy.

"That looks like fun," Dawn said once the waves subsided. "She's one happy whale. And I think she's trying to thank you, Jesse."

They watched for a few more minutes as Ibis waggled her tail in the air, smacked the waves with her flippers, and breached several more times. Then she leapt skyward once more—her highest breach yet—and she crashed down into the water. As the waves settled and the mist cleared from the air, nothing but silence was left.

"I'll bet she's feeding," Arthur said, his anger replaced by awe. "I don't think she could eat with that net in her mouth." They pulled Jesse into the dinghy and rowed back to the *Dreadnought*. His arm was badly bruised and cut in several places, but after some iodine, bandages, and food, he insisted that he felt just fine.

Joy patted his shoulder. "You were never in any danger," she said. "God sent you on that mission. He wouldn't abandon you."

"Well, I was damn worried," BillFi said with a smile. "Don't you *ever* do that to me again!"

☠   ☠   ☠

Two days later, Arthur had anchored the ship in a secluded bay and called the crew together around the dining table. He was pale, and he was obviously choosing his words carefully.

"Here's the situation," he said, as Logan poured himself some scotch. The others declined. "Joy says we have just a few day's worth of food left. We had twelve hundred dollars, which would have paid for a *lot* of food—and kept us out here a long time—but we spent it on 'other things' instead. We're down to just a little bit of money, so unless we can think of a way to get some money or some food, we're going to have to quit."

"So let's quit," Marietta said with a scowl. "I thought this whole thing was stupid to begin with. Let's just take the stuff we bought, go home, and find something else to do. Sailing up and down the coast is pretty boring, if you ask me."

"I don't want to quit," Logan wheezed. "Yeah, maybe buying some of this stuff was a totally dumb idea. I mean, except for the booze, of course. But I don't want to go home. Noooo way! My mom is totally murder to be around."

"I don't want to quit, either," Joy said. "I came here to learn how to lead in accordance with God's will, and I still want to do that. *Dios mediante*, God willing, I plan to start a church back home in Texas—the House of Joy—and I'll need all the leadership experience I can get!"

"Who says we have to quit?" Crystal said, her blue eyes flashing around the table. "I don't know how we're going to feed ourselves later, but for now, we have a gourmet meal at our fingertips."

The crew was silent for a moment. Then Logan downed his scotch and asked, "What do you mean?"

"Look," Crystal said, running a hand through her short blond hair, "every day, when we're sailing, someone has to be on the stupid bow. Why?"

"To watch out for lobster floats," Arthur said, annoyed that the conversation had slipped out of his control. "They could get fouled in our rudder and make it hard to steer. But the point is that—"

"Exactly, Einstein," Crystal said. "Lobster floats. Floats connected to lines that are attached to lobster traps. Lobster traps filled with—*lobsters*! Whenever we want, we can just pull up a couple of traps and help ourselves to all the lobsters we can eat!"

"I know some great recipes for lobster," Joy said. "Boiled lobster, lobster alfredo, lobster bisque. And I think I could make something decent with lobster, pasta, and Szechwan pepper. But we can't just take the lobsters. That's stealing, and stealing is wrong. It's immoral, and it's against God's will. So we can't."

"Just plain butter," BillFi said. "I like it with just plain butter and a little salt. Just butter and salt."

"Or melted cheese," Logan said, rubbing his flabby belly. "Some lobster, a lotta melted cheese, and some crusty bread. Oh, wait. We don't have any bread."

"Hold it!" Arthur said. "Think for a minute. First, Joy's right. You're talking about theft—stealing lobsters from the fishermen who put out those traps. That's illegal, and I don't—"

"It doesn't seem too bad to me," Crystal said, "compared to, you know, dumping a dead guy off the bow."

Arthur was silent for a moment. He shook his head. "Forget about it," he said. "If we get caught, we could get in a lot of trouble. We also might get shot at."

"Oh, come on!" Crystal said. "We won't get caught. We'll only do it when no other boats are around. No one can see us. I don't think—"

"No!" Arthur said. "I'm your captain, and I said no. We are not going to do something illegal and risky just because you all lacked the discipline to stick to your shopping lists."

Crystal sneered. She turned to address the rest of the crew. "Hear that?" she said. "Arthur, our fucking captain, said no. Well tell you what, Mr. Fucking Captain. Unless you have both the strength and the balls to stop me—and I doubt it on both counts—I'll go get lobsters whenever I feel like it. You got a problem with that, I won't bring one back for you."

"I see," Arthur said icily. "I'll tell *you* what. We'll put your idea to a vote, and when you lose, you'll be forbidden from diving for lobsters at any time. And if you do, we'll leave you at the next port." He looked around the table. "All in favor of violating your captain's orders and stealing lobsters, raise your hands," Arthur said.

At first, no one moved. Only Crystal's hand shot defiantly into the air. Then slowly, Logan lifted his hand, too. "Melted cheese!" he pleaded as Arthur glared at him.

"Fine," Arthur said, "that's two votes to six. Any others?"

A moment later, BillFi raised his hand, and Jesse did the same.

"I vote no," Marietta said. "I'm with Arthur."

Dawn voted yes on the grounds that the Sea Goddess would give them whatever they were supposed to have; the vote held at five in favor and three opposed. Joy just shook her head.

"Fine," Arthur said, fuming and hoping that everyone knew it. "The vote carries, and Crystal gets to lead a group to steal lobsters. Understand what we're doing, though. We just decided to break the law. Not bend it—deliberately break it. Not because McKinley tried to cheat us. Not because we were committed to a great summer on an old schooner. We're breaking the law now because we bought sweaters and sleeping bags and a boombox in Freeport."

He shook his head slowly and turned to face Crystal, who was staring at him with a smirk on her face.

"Bring back enough for everyone," he ordered.

☠   ☠   ☠

Because Jesse wasn't able to row the dinghy—his arm was still striped with purple bruises—Crystal took one oar, and Logan took the other. BillFi gave directions from the bow, and Marietta rode in the stern. Once the vote had gone against her, she jumped to side with the majority.

"Which one do you think we should take?" BillFi asked no one in particular. He pushed his glasses up his nose. "There's a red-and-white float. Should we pull up that one? The red-and-white one? Or maybe the one with the blue stripes. Should we pull that one up? The one with the stripes?"

Marietta rubbed oil over her already tan skin and scanned the lobster floats bobbing in the bay. They offered a kaleidoscope of colors, but a few patterns began to emerge. The floats were painted in eight different color patterns, and she guessed that eight different fishermen worked this area.

"I think that's right," Logan said. "I think the colors are how they, you know, tell their floats apart."

Marietta did some quick counting.

"Most of the ones out here are solid pink," she said. "I think we should try a few of those first, 'cause that fisherman is less likely to miss a few lobsters than the other ones."

"Good idea," Crystal said. "But we'll spread it around a little. If we have to check several traps to get enough lobsters, we won't do all the same color. That way, the fishermen might not notice the missing lobsters and get all pissed off. Let's go for that nearest pink one."

The dinghy glided slowly toward the float. When it was close, BillFi reached over the side and grabbed the mossy line that trailed into the shadowy water beneath it.

"Got it!" he said. "I need some help."

Crystal and Logan put their oars down and scrambled to the bow. They grabbed the line and pulled together, and slowly the wet slimy rope slithered into the dinghy.

"I see the trap!" Marietta called out. "It's almost here."

A few more pulls, and the trap broke the surface. The crew hauled it, dripping, into the dinghy.

The trap looked like a miniature Quonset hut, rectangular on the bottom and curved on the top. It was made out of small slats of wood, and netting covered the two ends. It was gray and green with algae, and water poured off it into the bottom of the boat.

One lobster lurked inside. It was dark green and about ten inches long, and it had one large, intimidating claw.

"How do you open this thing?" Marietta asked, touching it like it might explode. Then she saw a small door that was latched shut. "There it is."

"Well, go ahead," BillFi said. "Open it and get that lobster out of there. Go ahead. Go ahead and get it."

"Yeah, Marietta," Logan said with a grin. "Go ahead."

"Me? Why me? Why don't you reach *your* hand in there and get it out?" Marietta said. "I'm not sticking my hand in there."

"Oh, give me a break," Crystal said, sneering. "You people

are so afraid of everything." She turned the latch, and in motions almost too fast to see, she thrust her hand into the trap, grabbed the lobster behind its claw legs, and yanked it out. She dropped it to the bottom of the dinghy and shut the trap.

"Let's go," she said. "At this rate, this'll take us all day."

They tossed the trap back into position and rowed over to a green float. The crew pulled on that line, and the trap slowly came to the surface.

No lobsters. The trap was empty.

They rowed some more. The next trap, beneath a half-purple and half-white float, held two lobsters. Crystal plucked the lobsters out of the trap. "Only five more to go," she said. "If we each want only one, that is. We should probably get more."

Logan groaned. "I don't know how many more of these traps I can pull up," he said. "These things are like, incredibly *heavy.*"

"I know what you mean," Marietta said, rubbing more oil into her skin. "I can't do more than one or two more. This is hard work."

Crystal shook her head. "Pretty sad, ladies," she said, staring flatly at Logan. "Okay, fine. How long are these lines? How deep is the water here?"

"Not much," Logan said. "Maybe like, eight feet."

"Fine," Crystal said. "Just row us to the next trap. I'll take care of it."

Logan shrugged and rowed the creaking dinghy over to another pink float. Crystal stood up in the stern and kicked off her sneakers without rocking the boat.

"Just wait here," she said, sliding off her socks. "I'll be right back with the lobsters."

She pulled her shirt over her head and tugged her shorts down over her hips and off her legs. She stood for a moment, dressed in only a small sports bra and underwear, then took a deep breath and dove over the side.

Logan rolled his eyes. "She's totally nuts," he said. Everyone in the dinghy peered over the side, but none of them could see a thing.

Less than a minute later, Crystal swam up through the murky water, splashed through the surface, and shook the salt-water from her short blond hair. She had a lobster in each hand.

"Here," she said, tossing the lobsters at Logan. She took a few more breaths. "I'll be right back."

She dove down again and resurfaced a moment later, gripping two more lobsters behind their claw legs. She lobbed them into the dinghy, swam over to another float, and ducked her head into the water. She raised her rear end and then her legs into the air and dove downward.

Before an hour had passed, Crystal had collected a dozen lobsters in addition to the first three. Then she grabbed the gunwale, flipped herself into the dinghy, and pulled her clothes back on.

"Okay," she said. "Let's go back to the ship. I don't know about you, but I'm fucking hungry."

☠   ☠   ☠

Joy sat on the bow and tried to think and pray at the same time. She knew in her heart that stealing the lobsters was wrong—a *sin*—but she didn't think God wanted her to quit and go home. She was going to create a new church, after all, and the House of Joy was sure to do enough good to offset the theft of a few lobsters in Maine. Besides, she thought, do the lobsters belong to the fishermen just because they crawled into a trap? If we had caught them just *before* they went into the trap, that wouldn't be stealing at all. Surely God doesn't want me to quit just because we got the lobsters a minute too late, does He? But we wouldn't have gotten the lobsters at all if it weren't for the traps. So if it is stealing, then it's a direct violation of a Commandment, and surely going home was better than defying God's will. "*Dios mio*," she whispered. "Help me decide what to do."

She had started to pull her coin from her pocket when she felt a hand on her shoulder. Dawn sat down next to her and dangled her long legs over the side.

"It's no fun sometimes, is it?" Dawn asked, her green eyes staring out to sea. "We're spiritual beings trapped in a messy human existence. The answer is not always clear."

Joy nodded. "I don't know what to do," she said softly.

"I think you shouldn't do anything you can't undo," Dawn said. "If cooking and eating the lobsters are wrong, I'm sure God will forgive you. But if you leave the ship, I don't think you'll be able to come back if you change your mind."

Joy was silent.

"Just give it some time," Dawn said, pulling her red baseball cap over her light brown hair and flipping her ponytail out the space in the back. "If you don't know the answer right now, then maybe you should give it time to reveal itself."

Joy nodded again. She was silent for a while, her chubby hands holding onto supports while her mind considered her options. Then with a sudden movement, she spun her coin on the deck. Saint Christopher—the patron saint of travelers. "I'll stay," she said, putting the coin back into her pocket. "For now, anyway."

She went down into the galley and spent almost two hours banging pots and struggling with the kerosene stove. She emerged at last with lobsters in an herb-and-Szechwan-pepper butter sauce, boiled potatoes, and pesto pasta. Logan opened a bottle of dark red wine. Even Arthur enjoyed the meal.

After dinner, Arthur gathered the sailors around the table once again. He knew they didn't want to think about the reality that faced them, but as their leader he had a duty to anticipate the future.

"This is hard," he said, locking his hazel eyes on each sailor in turn. "Stealing lobsters is wrong. We can't believe it isn't. We also can't eat lobster for every single meal. But if we don't get food somehow, we're going to have to quit and go home. None of us wants to do that."

Marietta looked up and scowled. "Oh, I don't know—"

"Okay, *most* of us don't want to quit," Arthur said. "So we have to think of some way to get food. We can still take some lobsters every now and then, but we'll have to figure out something else too. Is there anything we can do—anything that's legal—to earn some money or get food somehow?"

"We could take turns, like, getting jobs and stuff," Logan said. "Nowhere fancy, just McDonald's or something. Maybe four of us at a time could get jobs for two or three weeks, you know, and earn as much money as possible, and then, like, quit."

Arthur shook his head. "I thought of that," he said. "But to save any money at all, the workers would still have to live on the *Dreadnought*. We couldn't afford to rent an apartment or hotel room or anything. And if the workers were going to work every day and come home to the ship, that would mean we couldn't sail anywhere. Suddenly, instead of cruising and exploring the coast of Maine, we'd be sitting in a harbor somewhere. The *Dreadnought* would just be a floating apartment, and this summer would be a lot like all the others. Besides, we'd get caught eventually."

The crew was silent for a while, sipping wine and soda and thinking.

Suddenly Logan smiled. "I've got it!" he said. The others leaned close around the table to hear his plan. "When I was in, like, sixth grade, my family took a trip to the Caribbean. We totally stayed at some resort on Antigua, you know, the kind with the pink cinderblock balconies along the beach. It was an absolutely great place. "Day–O!" and all that stuff. They had a rec room there, with, like, a ping-pong table, and one evening my sister and I were playing ping-pong when this guy walked in. He was maybe seventeen years old, and even though it was totally hot and humid out, he wore a black velvet vest and black velvet pants. He was from England, and he was totally cool. My sister fell for him right away. For the rest of the evening, they kept trying to get rid of me. They sent me out to check on the constellations for them, and they—"

"Is there a point to this?" interrupted Marietta.

Logan's pudgy body sagged like it had been deflated. "Well, yes," he said. "One day, while we were on the island, a couple of people came up to us on the beach and handed us a piece of paper. It was a flyer for the sailing yacht *Aurora*, a schooner—you know, a lot like this one—that these people had sailed across the Atlantic from Sweden. It was a totally great old ship, and the people on board were trying to sail it around the world. The flyer explained that they were on their way to the Panama Canal, and that to raise money for the trip—ta da!—they were offering people a chance to spend a day on board, sailing around Antigua, having a shish-kebob lunch on a secluded beach, and all that stuff. My dad jumped at the chance. He thought it sounded adventurous and romantic.

"So we all shipped out the next day and went sailing on the *Aurora*. We even got these, like, souvenir T-shirts from the trip. I don't know what it cost, but I'll bet it was pretty steep. "I think we could do the same thing with the *Dreadnought*, right here in Freeport, letting people take rides for a day, help out with the sailing and all that enchanted tourist stuff. We could charge a bundle for it, and some people would be totally happy to pay it."

"Become a tour boat?" Crystal asked with a sneer. "That's disgusting. What would we do—get cute little uniforms and sing little nautical songs on deck while we sailed around in circles?"

"No," Logan said, "nothing like that. We just take people out for a day on the water and, you know, like a nice lunch on a beach somewhere. It would mean keeping the ship pretty clean for a little while, but I think we could make some totally good money pretty quickly."

Crystal shrugged. "Your idea—your project," she said. "Personally, I'd rather steal lobsters."

The next day, Logan made his flyer:

SPEND THE DAY ON THE HIGH SEAS!
Try Your Hand at Sailing a Two-Masted Schooner!
Enjoy a scrumptious lunch on a secluded beach!

Sound good? Sound fun?
If so, stop by the main docks at 9:00 A.M.
tomorrow morning.
Bring plenty of sunscreen, a hearty appetite,
and lots of film!

Just $50.00 per person.
Children under 10 just $10.00.

He had the flyers copied, and he walked for three hours, passing them out to the shorts-and-T-shirt tourists crowding the streets of Freeport.

The next morning, Logan waited eagerly on the dock. Joy was with him, helping out as a kind of tour assistant. BillFi and Jesse were on the ship, ready to help with the sails, and Dawn and Arthur stood by at a safe distance, ready to pitch in if things got crazy but otherwise eager to stay out of the way. Marietta had gone into town to "window shop," and Crystal, once breakfast was finished, declared "I'm out of here" and jumped overboard with a paperback crime novel in her hand. She swam across the bay to a small shelf of rocks, keeping the book and her short blond hair above water the entire time. She lay out across the rocks and lost herself in the pages of the book, paying no attention to the silliness going on under Logan's leadership.

When nine o'clock arrived, the docks were full of people unloading boats, stowing gear, gawking at the yachts, and eating early-morning ice cream. None of them came over to Logan, who held a copy of his flyer hopefully high in the air.

Nothing.

By 9:05, no one had arrived.

At 9:10, someone stopped to ask Joy for directions to the public restrooms.

And at 9:12, a family lumbered down the docks toward Logan and Joy. The gaggle consisted of an enormously overweight man lugging a duffel bag, a thin and nervous woman in a dress she could have worn to church, and four running, stomping, yelling children—two boys and two girls, all under the age of 10. "I'm glad you haven't left yet!" the man said with a smile. "Sounds like fun, doesn't it?" he asked his kids, holding the flyer, sweaty and rolled up, in his beefy hand. "Sounds like fun, don't you think?" he asked Logan.

Logan wiped his hair out of his eyes and nodded with his best showman smile. "Yes, sir," he said. "I'm certain it'll be, like, totally awesome."

No one else seemed to be coming along, so Logan ushered the mother and two of the kids into the dinghy. Two trips later—one for the other two children, and one for the rotund man himself—the clan was on board and the father handed $140 in cash to Logan.

"Let's get this ship a-moving!" the man shouted, dropping the duffel bag on the deck and plopping his weight onto a crate near the gangplank.

The woman smiled tersely. "Children, you behave now, you hear?" she called out to the kids, who had already dispersed throughout the ship in a wild and noisy explosion.

☠   ☠   ☠

That evening, as the crew of the *Dreadnought* sat on deck beneath a shimmering dark sky filled with stars, Logan defended his idea.

"Okay," he said, "it was a little rough. But at least we made, like, *some* money."

"A *little* rough?" BillFi asked, wiping his nose on his arm. "Those kids nearly chewed through our hull! They were horrible. They nearly chewed through our hull."

"They did not," Logan said. "They caused a little bit of damage, that's all. They were just, you know, excited to be on board."

"They threw all our pillows overboard, Logan," Dawn said.

"And they varnished the toilet lid shut," Jesse added.

"And they poured ketchup in the cooking oil," Joy added.

"And they—"

"All right!" Logan shouted, waving his pale arms in the air. "All right. I'm sorry. We totally got the family from hell, and it was miserable. But it wasn't like I got a lot of help from you all, you know."

"Why didn't the parents control their kids?" Crystal asked, glad to have been absent during the mayhem.

"The father was too sick," Arthur explained. "We were two minutes away from the dock when he crawled down into the dining room and curled up under the table. He looked like he was going to die."

"Yeah, but we saved money on his food portion," Logan argued.

"From the looks of him," Marietta said, "we saved a *lot* of money."

"And the mother," Dawn explained, "scrambled out onto the bowsprit and rode each wave like a bucking bronco. You should have heard her up there, whooping and screaming and having a great time. While she was up there, I don't think she even remembered that she *had* children."

"Okay, it was totally shitty," Logan said quietly. "But we got some money, didn't we?" He held up the cash. "We got a hundred and forty bucks, and that'll, you know, buy us a lot of food if we're careful."

Dawn held up a clipboard. "I hate to break this to you, Logan," she said, "but we didn't exactly come out a hundred and forty dollars ahead." She looked at the clipboard. "We have to buy eight new pillows, a new ten-gallon can of cooking oil, and a new toilet seat. After we've paid for all those things, we'll have enough money left over to buy, oh . . . maybe one large tomato. The Goddess did not smile on this particular project, Logan."

Logan groaned and handed her the money. "Forget the tomato," he said. "I totally need some aspirin."

☠   ☠   ☠

"Okay, gang," Crystal said to the crew two days later. Everyone was on deck, leaning against railings or sitting on boxes. They were still trying to figure out how to get food. "This is stupid. There's only one freaking choice, and I think we had better get used to it. We can't get jobs—that's what Arthur said, and he's right. We can't buy food, because we don't have any damn money. That means that unless we can get someone to give us food or money—and I don't think that's very likely—our only choice is to take it. We're going to have to steal food."

"Not a chance!" Arthur said, straightening to his full height. "There's no way we're going to—"

"It isn't hard," Crystal continued, her hands on her hips. "I've stolen a lot of things, and it's really easy. Hell, we already stole more than a hundred dollars' worth of lobsters. It wasn't that hard. All we have to do is get good at stealing the other food and stuff we need. Every marina on the coast has expensive yachts full of things we could use. All we have to do is find a way inside and take what we need. It's either that—or we quit. And I'm *not* going to quit."

"No way," Arthur said. "I'm not—"

"Crystal's right," Logan said. "We either take what we need, or we go ashore, call our parents—'Hi, Mom and Dad. Guess what?'—and ask them to, you know, send us money for the bus ride home. And there's absolutely no way I'm doing that."

"I don't see the big problem," Marietta said, adjusting the lay of her T-shirt. "We have to be careful, we have to make sure we don't get caught, and then there's nothing to worry about. The people who own these yachts and things have more money than they know what to do with. They'll never even miss the food and stuff we'll take."

Arthur shook his head. "I think we—"

"Yeah, we know," Crystal said with a sneer. "You think stealing is wrong, and you think we should always do everything you say. Well I don't recall electing you captain. When did we put that to a vote? Just who decided you were captain anyway?"

Arthur stood up, his fists clenched at his sides. "*I'm* the one who got this whole thing going. If it weren't for me, you'd all be sitting at home right now, watching TV and listening to your parents snore. I'm the captain because I'm the one who led us when it counted. And if you don't like it"—he could hear his father's voice coming out of his mouth—"you can get the hell off this ship!"

"You led us when it counted?" Crystal tossed back. "All you did was come up with the idea. Well, I'm a part of this crew just as much as you are, and I don't feel like taking orders from you anymore. I say we raid some yachts and have a great summer— and if you don't like it, *you* can get the hell off this ship!"

The deck fell quiet; only the whisper of the breeze in the rigging and the murmur of the waves splashing the bow softened the silence. The crew sat for a long time without saying a word. Arthur sat back down on a stack of vinyl mats.

Eventually Logan spoke. "Look, Arthur," he said, "I totally like having you as our captain. I think you make good decisions. But Crystal's right. We have, like, two choices. We can steal from rich people who won't even notice, or we can give up. And Arthur—I don't want to give up. I'm totally having a great time out here."

Another long silence. No one looked at anyone else. Finally Arthur shrugged his shoulders. "You want to raid yachts, fine," he said. "I think you're out of your minds, but I won't stop you."

Crystal started to say something, but Dawn gestured for her to keep still.

"So, okay," Arthur said. "We'll steal to survive. It's wrong, but I don't see that we have much choice." He thought about pointing out that the reason they were in this bind was because the crew had violated his orders in Freeport. He thought about mentioning that if everyone had followed his instructions and bought the items on their lists—and nothing else—they would have plenty of food and gear. He thought about emphasizing that he was the obvious choice to lead this crew throughout the summer. But he decided to keep those thoughts to himself. Enter into battle only if you're sure you're going to win, his father often said. Somehow, Arthur thought, his father's advice wasn't working out too well on board the *Dreadnought*.

"We'll start tomorrow," Crystal said. "I'll take the helm and steer us to a promising harbor. We'll anchor nearby and wait for darkness. I'll assign the jobs, and I'll lead the raiding party. We should form two teams. One for water, and one for food. We'll sail into the harbor at night, row ashore, get the supplies we need, and sail out again before anyone knows we've been there. We'll have to be quick, quiet, and organized. Our parents sent us here to learn some discipline, and that's exactly what we're going to do."

Logan took a long swig from a bottle of rum and then held it aloft.

"Avast, ye maties!" he growled. "Think about it. We're sailing an old schooner. We survive by plundering other ships. Arrrrgh, ye scurvy dogs! We just totally became pirates!"

"To pirates!" they cheered, raising their glasses. Then Dawn grinned.

"I like it!" she said. "Scurvy dogs. We plunder ships. That means just one thing. We are, my friends, the Plunder Dogs!"

"To the Plunder Dogs!" Logan howled. "To doing the pirate thing!"

They drank a toast again.

To the Plunder Dogs.

Even Arthur smiled. Only Joy seemed troubled.

CHAPTER FIVE

FIFTY-THREE KNOTS OF FREEDOM LEFT

It was a perfect evening for a raid. Heavy clouds blocked the setting sun, and a steady onshore wind raised enough surf to mask the sounds of the incoming dinghy.

BillFi crouched in the stern, peering through the curve of his glasses. Jesse's injured arm kept him from coming along, so Logan took one oar, puffing with exertion as he pulled each stroke. Arthur, despite his misgivings, took the other. Make friends with the worst possible outcome, his father had said. That way, you'll never lose. Arthur yanked the oar with short angry strokes.

The dinghy splashed slowly toward the harbor at Orrs Island, a quaint and trendy collection of wood-shingled cottages and cluttered boutiques. A cluster of impressive yachts, both power and sail, bobbed at their tethers along the docks. The tide was low, and the air was thick with the smells of salt and mud. BillFi pointed through the darkness toward a shadow standing at the end of one dock. No one spoke, but the dinghy moved quietly toward it.

The shadow was Crystal. She had spent the afternoon and evening on the waterfront, sunbathing, jogging, relaxing—and taking note of which boats were occupied, how many people were staying on board, and how well-supplied each one seemed. The dinghy slid up to the dock and scraped along the splintered pilings.

Everyone knew what to do. They had discussed the plan all afternoon. BillFi climbed onto the dock, duffel bags in hand. Arthur and Logan, the Water Pirates, rowed the dinghy around the dock to find a spigot.

The Booty Pirates walked casually along the dock until Crystal, with a slight gesture of her right hand, pointed to a yacht. It was a large white cabin cruiser with the words *Sand Dollars* painted on the stern.

"Four adults," Crystal whispered. "They look fuckin' rich. They started drinking on deck about four o'clock, and they were still drinking when a limo came for them at eight. They were talking about going to a steak house and then maybe to a club. The key is above the door frame."

BillFi glanced at the glowing dial of his watch. "It's 9:15. We have plenty of time. Plenty of time. It's only 9:15." They scanned the waterfront. People were moving, but no one was close by. Crystal and BillFi stepped onto the yacht, found the key, and hurried below.

The interior was an embarrassment of polished teak: in the glare of the dock lights shining in through the small windows, warm wood gleamed from nearly every surface. Behind the gangway that led down from the deck were two small berths, each sporting a thick mattress covered with floral sheets and matching dusty-rose comforters. To the left was a long sofa, plump and paisley, that looked like it might fold out into a sleeper. Below it were compartments for storage. To the right was a thick wooden table with upholstered benches on two sides; the table had round depressions along its edge that would hold highball glasses and protect their precious contents. Beyond the table was a small stove with tidy cupboards above and below. On one side of the stove, in a tight rack, were a microwave, a coffeemaker, and a stereo CD player that operated by remote control. Standing at attention in a neat row were two dozen CDs, almost all of them reggae. Crystal scowled. These people are way too old and uptight for reggae, she thought. On the other side was a refrigerator. A doorway beyond the kitchen area led to the captain's quarters, a pointed chamber almost entirely filled by a large bed. The sheets and comforter matched the sets in the stern. To one side was a wardrobe closet and a tall narrow set of drawers. To the right was a small bathroom with a built-in showerhead. Throughout the entire boat were the details of wealth: crystal and carpeting and unrelaxed cleanliness.

"This place is cool!" BillFi said.

"This place is ripe for the picking," Crystal whispered back.

They started in the kitchen. The cupboards over the stove produced an impressive array of cans and jars, and the fridge yielded fresh meats, fruits, and vegetables.

"Get this," Crystal said, holding a jar she had found in the door of the refrigerator. "Mango chutney. What the hell do people do with mango chutney?"

They took just nine minutes. When they climbed back onto the dock, looking through the empty darkness for signs of trouble that weren't there, they hauled two stuffed duffels with them. They dragged the duffels to the end of the far dock where the dinghy had first landed, and set them down.

The next target was a bright red, tri-hulled sailboat. "One middle-aged couple," Crystal explained. "Enough lousy jewelry on her to sink the boat. They're visiting some friends in town and won't be back until late tonight."

The interior of this boat was tucked neatly into the tri-hull shape, using every possible inch for storage or comfort. The boat was less a luxury craft and more a party ship; BillFi and Crystal saw a huge sound system with speakers in nearly every room, several well-stocked bars, and a lot of beds. It seemed like the kind of boat that would be designed by people who never quite grew up. The Booty Pirates got to work, emptying the kitchen cabinets, the fridge, and the desk drawers. They were just turning their attention to the bottles behind the nearest bar when they heard footsteps on the dock. Someone was coming.

"Oh, shit!" Crystal whispered. "They're back! The owners are here!"

"Oh no," BillFi said. "Oh no. Oh no. Oh no."

They hunkered down behind the bar and listened as the steps grew closer. Then they heard a deep voice—Arthur's voice!—booming out a greeting. "Lovely evening, isn't it?" he asked. He sounded only slightly nervous.

"Spectacular!" a stranger said in a slight British accent. He seemed a bit too enthusiastic, probably drunk.

"It sure is!" agreed a woman. She seemed equally exuberant.

"So, ah . . ." Arthur was trying to think of something to say, some way to stall disaster. "Uh . . . this your boat?"

"Yessir," the man slurred clumsily. "Thass my boat. Damnfine boat, too. Damnfine. Hey, honey, we shoulda named it the *Damnfine.*"

The woman squeaked a laugh. "Robert! You're drunk!"

"Guilty!" the man answered with a chuckle.

BillFi turned to Crystal in the darkened cabin. "How are we going to get out of here?" he asked. "How are we—"

Crystal shrugged. "How the fuck should I know? I—" She was interrupted by a violent retching sound from the deck.

"Oh, my!" said the woman. "Are you all right?"

"I don't know," Arthur said weakly. "I don't feel very well. Could you both help me over to that bench?"

"Of course!" the man said. "Been there. Barfed that." He laughed loudly again.

Crystal gave BillFi a nudge. "This is it. Arthur's giving us a chance. Let's go!"

The two of them crawled toward the ship's rail, dragging their duffel bags behind them. They peered out the door and saw that Arthur and the two strangers were across a small stretch of parking lot, next to a wooden bench. Arthur was sitting on the bench with his head between his knees.

"Now!" Crystal whispered. She and BillFi scrambled out onto the dock, duffels clenched firmly in their hands. They tiptoed down the dock and into twilight.

A moment later, Arthur looked up. "I'm okay," he said to the couple. "Must have eaten some bad lobster."

The man nodded. "Ate a lot of 'bad lobster' in my day, shon. Nothing to be shamed about," he slurred.

Arthur stood up shakily, thanked his new "friends," and staggered down the dock, leaving the yacht owners by the bench. Once he joined the others in the darkness, they dashed toward the end of the dock. "We're clear," he hissed. "Let's get back to the dinghy."

A short time later, the *Dreadnought* was easing out of the harbor, flying just one small sail near the bow to avoid attracting attention. Only when the ship was well out of earshot did the Booty Pirates dare to breathe. Dawn asked Crystal how the rest of the raid had gone.

"It was close!" Crystal said.

"Too close," BillFi said. "Way too close. Far too close."

They told the story to the rest of the crew, and Joy patted Arthur on the shoulder. "That was very impressive," she said. "I don't know many people who can barf at will."

Arthur smiled. "Fingers down the throat," he said. "It's just one of my many talents."

When at last the ship was anchored in deep water off Pond Island, a small tuft of land south and a bit out to sea from Orrs Island, the crew gathered around the dining table for Show-and-Tell. The oil lamps gave the room a sense of warmth and secrecy. Marietta sat next to Arthur. Logan poured a round of scotch and root beer—extra scotch for himself, but water for Crystal and Joy. Joy eyed Logan's over-full glass with a look of concern.

Then Crystal opened the first duffel. "I present for your enjoyment," she said with a flourish, "a ham. A fucking Virginia ham, can you believe it?"

The crew cheered. Joy made a note in the ship's inventory: "One large ham. May God have mercy on our souls."

"And to go with the ham," Crystal continued, "fifteen ears of fresh corn on the cob, three large cans of New England-style clam chowder, a big jar of fucking Tang, and a jug of expensive gin."

"Gin and Tang!" Logan said. "Yeeee–haw! My favorite drink! You're so thoughtful!" He downed another large swallow of his scotch and root beer. Even he had to grimace at the foul taste.

Crystal pulled more out of the duffels. Cans of tuna, chunked chicken, peas, corned beef, Spam, kidney beans, mushrooms. Jars of spaghetti sauce, mustard, pickles, applesauce. Bottles of Coke, ginger ale, beer, liquors. Paper towels, sugar, salt, flour, corn starch. Aspirin, soap, toothpaste, shampoo. Eight hundred dollars in cash.

Show-and-Tell continued for almost an hour, and the dining table filled to overflowing with food and supplies. The crew stowed everything in the galley and then returned to the table.

"This will keep us in good shape for a while," Arthur said. "Not forever, but a while. We'll have to do one of these raids every couple of weeks or so. I still don't like it, but—"

"We'll move around a lot," Crystal said. "Never hit the same place twice. No one will even guess that the stupid raids are related."

Logan stood unsteadily and offered another toast.

"To independence!" he said.

Arthur shook his head.

"We're not independent at all," he said. "We rely on the food and supplies that other people have. This isn't independence. And it isn't right. We're committing crimes, and I don't think we should forget that. We need to realize that we're all guilty of these thefts, whether we actually went on board the yachts or not. This is something we decided to do as a group—myself included—and that makes us all guilty."

Logan drank to his toast anyway.

☠   ☠   ☠

Dawn found Joy on the bow, right where she thought she'd be. Joy was deep in thought, her dark brown eyes showing both worry and concern.

"It just gets messier, doesn't it?" Dawn asked. Joy said nothing.

Jesse was at the helm, and the *Dreadnought* cut steadily through the waves. Seagulls overhead called and squawked as they soared along with the ship. Dawn sat down next to Joy and let some quiet time go by.

Finally Joy spoke. "*No me gusta,*" she said. "I don't like it. The Commandment is perfectly clear. *No hurtarás.* Thou shalt not steal. So how can I take part in something that involves stealing? I'm supposed to help people do the right thing. I want to be a spiritual leader. Founder of the House of Joy. How can I do that if I eat stolen food and spend stolen money?" She turned to face Dawn. "I think I have to quit. I think I have to go home. I hate it—but I don't see how I can stay."

Dawn let some waves pass beneath the hull. She let the clouds sweep across the sky, and she let the *Dreadnought* sail along on its journey. After a long silence, she spoke softly, a gentle smile brightening her freckled face. "Joy," she said, "if you go, what would that say about us? Are we too evil for your company? Are we too sinful for your love? Are we too far gone for your help?"

Joy's face flashed with fear and sadness. "No!" she said. "Of course not! I just don't think I can do this with you, that's all. I can't steal things. It's against the Commandments."

Dawn nodded. "But no one's asking you to steal anything," she said.

"I can't eat stolen food or use stolen things, either," Joy said. "It's just the same thing as stealing."

"Is it?" Dawn asked. "Let me ask you this. If a church received a donation from a prostitute, would they keep the money and try to build on that relationship? Or would they throw the money back at her and say 'We can't accept money from someone like you!'?"

"They'd accept the donation," Joy said. "No church would slam the door on someone like that."

"Even though they knew how she'd gotten the money?" Dawn asked.

"It wouldn't matter," Joy said. "How she got the money isn't as important as the person herself. They'd try to help her change, of course, but they wouldn't throw her gift back in her face."

"Well, Joy," Dawn said, "we want to share food and things with you. We want you to stay on this ship and help us learn. Yes, some of the food and stuff came from raids. But how we got it surely isn't as important as we are ourselves. Is it?"

Joy thought about that for a while. Then she shook her head again. "I still can't stay. How would it look if people found out that the founder of the House of Joy once spent a summer on a pirate ship?"

"Yeah, I've been thinking about that, too," Dawn said. "Is starting a church really the best way to reach people? It seems to me that most of the people who walk through the doors are already believers. If you really want to get to people, don't you have to go to them? Shouldn't you find out where they are and spend time with them on their own turf? Shouldn't you, well, shouldn't you stay on board here and talk with us about what you believe? I see the universe differently than you do, but that doesn't mean we can't have some interesting conversations."

Joy sighed. "The House of Joy has been a dream of mine for years," she said. "It's God's will that I start my own church."

"Okay. But does a church have to have walls? Does it have to have a door? Does it have to have a sign out front that says 'House of Joy'?"

"That's the dream," Joy said. "That's what God wants me to do."

Dawn stood up and brushed off her shorts. "Yeah, about that," she said. "I mean this as a friend. I really like you a lot. But if this dream of yours is really God's will, wouldn't the sign out front say 'House of God'? I mean, isn't 'House of Joy' kind of egotistical?"

Joy's dark skin paled. She didn't speak.

"It's been a while since I've read the Bible," Dawn said, "but didn't Jesus spend his time with lepers and tax collectors and sinners, in their houses, eating their food and drinking their wine? Maybe God's will for you is to bring His love—His Joy—to people who really need it. Maybe," she said, tapping her chest, "the House of Joy is right here."

☠ ☠ ☠

That night, McKinley's sign in the dining room—the one that read "Discipline is the heart of a focused life"—had been turned around, and on the back was tacked a saying from the Bible: "For I am sure that neither death, nor life, nor angels, nor principalities, nor things present, nor things to come, nor powers, nor height, nor depth, nor any thing else in all creation, will be able to separate us from the love of God in Christ, Jesus our Lord.—Romans 8:38–39." Dawn smiled when she saw it. Joy's finding ways to share her beliefs, she thought. That sure beats quitting.

The pillow of each bunk sported a brand new leatherbound Bible, direct from the Freeport InterFaith Bookstore. In careful, sweeping calligraphy, Joy had written each person's name on the inside front cover, along with the phrase, "I accept Jesus Christ as my personal Lord and Savior.

Date:_____." Joy climbed into bed ahead of the others and opened her book reverently. She closed her eyes and lay silently for a long moment. Then she turned to the Book of Matthew and began reading aloud:

> Then Jesus called his disciples to him and said, "I have compassion on the crowd, because they have been with me now three days, and have nothing to eat; and I am unwilling to send them away hungry, lest they faint on the way."
>
> And the disciples said to him, "Where are we to get bread enough in the desert to feed so great a crowd?"
>
> And Jesus said to them, "How many loaves have you?" They said, "Seven, and a few small fish."
>
> And commanding the crowd to sit down on the ground, he took the seven loaves and the fish, and having given thanks he broke them and gave them to the disciples, and the disciples gave them to the crowds. And they all ate and were satisfied; and they took up seven baskets full of the broken pieces left over.

Marietta muttered something under her breath, and Crystal shrugged. "Whatever gets you through the night, sister," she said. "Sounds like hocus pocus to me—and we still have to raid yachts to put food on this boat."

"But we'll be fine," Joy said from her bunk. "We don't need to worry."

"Says who?" Crystal shot back. Before Joy could answer, Jesse stood up, casting a massive shadow over Crystal. Crystal glared right into his eyes, daring him to start something.

"Crystal," Jesse said in a deep and surprisingly gentle voice, "consider the ravens."

"What?"

"Consider the ravens," Jesse said. "They neither sow nor reap, they have neither storehouse nor barn, and yet God feeds them. Of how much more value are you than the birds!"

Joy, her eyes wide, whispered, "*Dios mio!* Luke, chapter twelve, verse twenty-four."

☠   ☠   ☠

The crew of the *Dreadnought* ate well the next day and throughout the following week. Joy threw enormous energy into her cooking, and she served ham and scalloped potato casserole, fresh salad with bleu cheese dressing, corn bread, red wine; western omelets with home fries and fresh biscuits slathered with mango chutney; and tuna salad sandwiches with avocado and herbed cheese, pesto pasta salad, and brownies.

On July 3, four weeks into the journey, Marietta was at the helm, the wind was strong, the sun was hot, and the crew lounged around the deck and chatted. Jesse sat by himself, shirtless, in the bow. Next to him on a vinyl cushion lay a set of permanent markers, and Jesse held the red one in his right hand. He was engrossed in drawing an intricate pattern of curves and circles and dots on the back of his left hand. The pattern was a crude version of a Maori tattoo, and Jesse added orange, black, and green lines as well. Slowly the swirls spread up his arm, past his elbow and over his bulging bicep, transforming the Bronx teenager into a New Zealand warrior and the ship into the *Pequot*.

As the others chatted, the talk eventually turned once again to harvesting lobsters.

"It was totally easy," Logan said. "Not to mention delicious."

"Easy?" Crystal said with a sneer. "I didn't see *you* diving eight feet down and sticking your hands in those fucking traps. I'll do some more diving, but no one had better think it's easy!"

"Sorry," Logan said. "I didn't mean that it wasn't—"

"Yeah, okay," Crystal interrupted. "Anyway, I'm game to do it again. Only this time, I'll wear my bathing suit."

Marietta laughed. "Good idea," she said. "Do that underwear thing again and all four guys will dive with you."

Marietta steered the ship into a long narrow bay. Logan and Jesse rowed Crystal out to a cluster of lobster floats, and in less than an hour, they were back with a dozen large lobsters.

"We can keep this up all summer," Logan said. "I wonder if you can actually get tired of eating lobster?"

"Not a chance," Marietta said, releasing the wheel to fuss with her running shorts. "It would be like getting tired of flying to Europe or driving a Porsche."

Joy boiled the lobsters for dinner that night and served them with her usual outstanding side dishes. Now that supplies were on board, the crew began to feel that theirs was a life of luxury. During the days, they sailed along the coast of Maine, exploring inlets and islands, discussing which mansions they would own if they were rich, and mastering the steering of the ship and the setting of the sails. In the evenings, once anchored, they sat on deck or around the dining table, sipping drinks and sharing their thoughts and dreams. With increasing frequency, Marietta placed herself at Arthur's side, wherever he was. She even traded bunks with Logan so she could sleep close to the captain's quarters; despite the six other people in the room, it somehow seemed more intimate. For his part, Logan began to volunteer with increasing frequency for whatever mission Crystal was on. Joy passed time by writing lengthy letters to her boyfriend back home, and BillFi and Jesse often engaged in long conversation with sparse words. Jesse continued the work on his tattoos, adding colorful swoops and swirls to his right arm and his feet and calves. BillFi drew patterns on his back.

When she wasn't on duty, Dawn spent a lot of time alone. She would take a notebook from her duffel, sit on the aft rail or the cushions on the windward side, and make sketches of the scenes she saw. Or she would lie beneath the mainsail, her head leaning against a cushion, and meditate, chanting and bringing her soul into greater harmony with the wind and the ocean and the birds and animals around her. And sometimes she would watch Arthur and Marietta for signs of disillusionment.

"Jeez," BillFi said one afternoon as he and Jesse took the bow watch shift. "It's freezing out here. It's really freezing. I mean, it's really cold. I never thought Maine would be this damn cold in July. I mean, it's really cold."

Jesse nodded. "It's cold," he said, his strong voice vibrating through the sea air. "I like the cold. Makes you strong." He searched the water ahead for lobster floats and rocks. All clear. He pulled a red marker out of his pocket and took off his pants. He began an elaborate design on his right thigh.

The sky was gray, and the water below the bow was rolling pewter. A chilly wind was blowing from the northwest. The dullness and the cold made BillFi think of the Bronx and the cinderblock pillbox he called home. About twenty kids in the foster-care system lived there in between home assignments. BillFi had moved in three months previously, when his latest foster parents were arrested for cocaine possession. He didn't mind. Even though it was scary, the shelter was more home-like than the foster home he had been sleeping in. Those fos-ter parents—George and Janet Carroll—were weird. They looked okay on the surface, but they stayed up all night long and never seemed to keep a job. They pierced each other's ears and navels, and they let people come in without knocking whenever they wanted. Billy—that's what the Carrolls called him—found himself longing for the rigid schedule and pre-dictable food of the shelter even more than he feared the aggression of the other kids.

He had been back in the shelter for a few weeks when the guy who ran the place showed him the Leadership Cruise brochure. "We have some grant money for sending kids to places like this," he said. "Wanna go? I think you'd get a lot out of it."

Billy shrugged. He was always "going." He deeply wanted to know what "staying" felt like, but he had long ago stopped fighting the Foster Machine. Besides, the other kids in the shelter made him nervous. He was never relaxed there. He didn't dare. "Sure," he said. "Sure. I'll go. Sure."

BillFi scanned the leaden waves. "Did you ever wonder," he said to Jesse, "why your guardians sent you here? Did you ever wonder? I mean, Frank at the shelter told me it would be a lot of fun. He said it would be fun. But I think he also sent me here for a reason. Some kind of reason. There has to be a reason. Something he thinks I need. He must think I need something."

Jesse nodded. "Yeah," he said. "Me, too. Don't know what, though." He drew a concentric orange maze on his knee.

BillFi looked out across the water through the tinge of his thick glasses. "I know my folks wouldn't have sent me here. They really wouldn't have. I know they wouldn't have. They didn't care if I learned nothing or not. They really didn't care.

My dad only wanted me around so he could have something to smack. That's all he wanted me for. Something to smack. And my mom didn't care if he did or didn't. She didn't care. Really. She didn't care if I was around or not. She doesn't even know where I am now. She really doesn't."

"My mom, either," Jesse said. "She's dead, remember? My dad's in Florida. He's the one that gave me to the shelter. So he could move to Florida."

BillFi smiled. "Wasn't it great the way McKinley just got himself out of the way? The way he just left, right when we wanted him to? Wasn't it great? Wouldn't it be great if our folks did that? Just left, died, right when we wanted them to? Wouldn't it be great?"

"No," Jesse said, tattooing a jagged black line on his upper thigh. "I love my dad."

☠ ☠ ☠

Three days later, Crystal was doing chin-ups on the starboard rigging, her wiry muscles rippling beneath a tight white T-shirt, when she stopped in mid-pull. "What the hell is that?" she asked.

The others were lounging around the ship, enjoying a warm and peaceful day. They straggled to their feet and looked to the east.

There, not far away, was a small raggedy sailboat. At least it seemed to be a sailboat. It was short and squat, with a stain-streaked sail that seemed far too large for its stumpy mast. In the stern was a woodstove that wheezed dark smoke into the air; the smoke trailed behind the sluggish ship like a cloud of anemic bees. The sailboat's deck was a chaotic mess of wood-en crates, large metal barrels, and tangled clumps of rope.

In place of the standard spoked wheel at the helm, this boat had two cables dangling out of a stanchion. And at the helm, tugging on the cables like a horseback rider tugging reins, stood a fat shirtless man wearing a sombrero and clenching a soggy cigar in his grinning mouth. He waved at the *Dreadnought* crew and continued toward them. The name *Chamber Pot* was painted along the boat's side.

"That thing is leaving some kind of slimy trail on the water," Logan said, pointing to the tiny boat. "Peeee-uuuu."

"It seems to be coming this way," BillFi said. "I think it's coming toward us. Right toward us. What should we do? Who is that?"

"A friend we haven't met yet," said Joy. "Let's be polite." She was at the helm, so she turned the *Dreadnought* into the wind so it would slow to a stop.

A moment later the *Chamber Pot* sagged to a stop alongside the *Dreadnought*, and the paunchy man boomed out a greeting. "Ahoy there!" he shouted, a lot louder than necessary. He had to turn his head sharply upward to look at the *Dreadnought* crew on the deck above him. "Permission to come aboard? You don't see many such fine-looking ships these days."

The stench from the *Chamber Pot* bloated its way skyward until the entire *Dreadnought* crew had suffered its gifts.

"Oh, Goddess, help us!" Dawn said in a loud whisper to the others. "What on earth is that smell?"

"For your sniffing pleasure today," Logan offered, in a whispered British accent, "I present to you the essence of rotten salmon, with potent overtones of cheap beer, kitty litter, and pickled pigs' feet, all finished nicely with a glaze of armpit sweat and underwear that has never, *ever* been washed."

"Shit!" Crystal said. "Check it out. That's not a cigar! This freak is sucking on a sausage!"

"Permission granted!" Arthur called down. The others looked at him in amazement. "Beats visiting on *his* boat," he whispered.

The man dragged his bulky mass up the *Dreadnought*'s ladder and flopped down onto a stack of vinyl mats. He took a moment to catch his breath, then he took the sausage out of his mouth. "Howdy, fellow sailors," the man puffed. "My name's Fletcher Dalyrimple. Fletcher Dalyrimple the *Third*, as a matter of fact. Please call me Smudge. My friends all call me Smudge. Don't know why—they just always have. One of those things that just sticks to a person, you know? All my friends from when I was a kid—Spinky, Bucket, Freaks, and the gang—we all had nicknames. Some good ones, too. Sometimes a nickname would just happen, you know? It would just appear and stick itself to a kid and stay there for life. That's the way it is with me. Name just jumped up and latched onto me like a tick on a horse's ass." He laughed loudly, put the sausage on the other side of his mouth, and farted. "Oooo-weeee!" he laughed again. "Seven-point-two on the Richter Scale! Hope I didn't break your boat! Snakes and scorpions! We'll need a typhoon to get rid of that one!"

The *Dreadnought* crew didn't know whether to laugh, cry, hurl over the side, or run for cover. Logan clearly liked this strange new stranger. Marietta clearly didn't. The others fell in between, mostly amused at this bizarre guest.

"So, Smudge," Arthur said. "That's quite a boat you have there."

A serious look crept across the man's face. "Ah, the *Chamber Pot*. As fine a ship as was ever built. Crafted by Neptune himself.

She can spit in the devil's eye and laugh when she tells the tale. She's tough as nails and pretty as the finest gal at the party. She's been my home and my companion for six years now, and we just follow the breezes and peddle our wares. Never hurt anybody, always have a laugh, and we'll lie to our grandmothers and blow kisses to the ladies all night long. If I ever lost the *Chamber Pot*, I'd put granite in my pockets and go for a long swim."

He was silent for a moment. "Say," he added, brightening up again and rubbing his enormous stomach. "I just mentioned how I peddle my wares. I've got some great seashells that I found all up and down the coast, and I carve animals out of driftwood. I even glue rocks together to make interesting conversation pieces. Care to see 'em? They don't cost much, and they add joy to every living day."

"No, thanks," Marietta said sharply.

"Ah, well. Can't fault a fellow for asking. Learned that from a cat I had a while back. She'd ask for her dinner, and then she'd ask for half of yours, and you couldn't help lovin' her all the same," Smudge said with a belch. "Well, if you're not interested in some fine New England folk art, maybe I can interest you in a story. I know some of the best stories ever told around the sea, and I'd be happy to tell you one or two of them now. Of course, I don't accept money for telling my stories—wouldn't be right, you know—but I might let you talk me into trading one for a sip or two of rum. You *do* have some rum, don't you?"

Before Arthur could respond with a prudent lie, Logan jumped to his feet. "I'll fetch you some, Captain Smudge," he said. "Be right back."

With a very full mug of rum in his hand and an audience of amused teenagers sitting around the deck, Smudge took a drink and a deep labored breath—and began.

"This takes place down in the Chesapeake Bay, down in Maryland, you see," Smudge said, wiping sweat from his neck. "If you've ever been down to the Chesapeake, you know what I'm talking about. Along the western shore there, the road goes gradually up a long gentle hill. The farther up that hill you go, the houses keep getting bigger and bigger, with more and more columns and verandas and flower boxes on the front. And the yards keep getting bigger and bigger, turning into pastures and stables and polo grounds. And the cars get more expensive the higher up that hill you go. And the people get better dressed, with nicer and nicer hairdos and worse and worse manners.

"But before you start up that long hill, just near the base of it, you'll see a little spit of land that sticks out into the bay. The road along it isn't much more than a couple of tire ruts through the beach grass, and if you push your way to the very end of that little peninsula, you'll come to Annie's.

"Now Annie's is a pub. A nice pub it is, with big wood tables and music playing that'll either eat your heart out or make you laugh till you puke up last week's breakfast. It's where all the sailors hang out. Not the sailors who live on the top of the hill, with their silk blazers with little gold crests embroidered on them. No, sir. I'm talking about the sailors who work the tankers and the freighters that come and go on the shipping lanes, right up the middle of the Chesapeake. These are big, nasty, funny guys with short fuses and iron jaws. The kind of guy you want next to you when the storm hits, or when your girlfriend's husband comes home early, if you know what I mean.

"And behind the counter was Annie. She was this scrappy old woman, thin as a soda straw and tough as jerky. She grew up in that house, just her and her mom and dad. When she was a little girl, her dad bought her this little sailboat. Oh, she loved that boat. She sailed it up and down the bay, exploring all the little inlets and islands that color up the shoreline. She learned independence on that boat, she did. She learned how to take care of herself, and to fear nothing. When she was a teenager, she'd sail that boat clear across the bay—right through the shipping lanes—and explore the eastern shore. She'd be gone for days at a time, eating biscuits and drinking water she had packed on board, and sleeping out in the open on the deck of the little boat. She was almost as tall as the boat was long, but she didn't mind discomfort, and she loved the freedom she felt on the water.

"Then, when she was just sixteen years old, her daddy died. He was a deck hand on a tanker that sailed between Baltimore and some ports in South America, and the ship went down one day in the bowels of a hellish storm. All hands were lost in one quick moment.

"When her dad died, Annie stopped sailing. She sold the little boat and set up the pub in the downstairs part of the house. She and her mom lived upstairs, and Annie worked the pub seven days a week. She cooked the food and hauled the kegs and served the drinks, and she kept all the sailors happy with her grog and her spunk. She could stare down the meanest sailor on the bay, and the guys all loved her for it. She grew old and stooped, bent nearly double from lifting all those cases of booze, and she wore thick glasses that still couldn't hide the spark of fire in her eyes."

Smudge paused for effect, scanning the eyes of the attentive listeners around him. "I don't suppose you have any more rum," he said, lifting his empty glass. "And a bite of something sure would hit the spot."

In no time, Smudge had another tall glass of rum and a ham sandwich in his hands. He took a huge bite of the sandwich, washed it down without chewing with a big swallow of rum, belched loudly, grinned, and continued.

"This one Saturday night, all the old sailors were there. They were drinking and laughing and varnishing up a bunch of old lies. Oh, it was a great night to be at Annie's. Guys were throwing darts and arm wrestling and bragging about their women, when—when this man showed up in the doorway.

"He was tall and thin, and he was dressed all in white. White shirt, white sportcoat, white pants, white shoes. Black tie. He was pale, with black hair and a black goatee. And as he stood there"—Smudge leaned forward, his eyes wide—"as he stood there, the whole room fell quiet." Smudge paused again. "Every single man in that room was thinking back to the last time he had seen this man in the white suit.

"One old guy, a grizzly stocky fellow with forearms like barrels, remembered back to a time years before when he had shipped out on the *Ethel M. Conrad*, a freighter that was crossing the Atlantic heading for South Africa. The ship was caught in a terrible storm, and all the rookie sailors on board were scared for their lives, but this old sailor wasn't worried. He had shipped out on the *Conrad* before, and he knew that the old boat would hold up just fine. She was a tough old boat, and she had been through worse before without a scratch.

"Well, on the second day of the storm, the waves were breaking over the bow and the wind was howling like the dogs of hell. The rookies were sick and terrified, but this old guy just went about his job. The *Conrad* was a loyal friend, and she wouldn't let them down.

"It was on the third day of the storm, when the wind and the waves were fiercer yet, that the old sailor heard something he had never heard before. It was a groaning shrieking sound, and it came from deep within the guts of the ship. The *Conrad* was buckling, twisting beneath the force of the waves, and she was starting to break apart from below.

"The sailors all screamed and scrambled up the gangways, but water gushed in like a linebacker and knocked them to the floor. The lights went out and the sea was pouring in with a vengeance. The sailors were doomed and they knew it, and they were crying and screaming and struggling against the water and each other, scrambling for a last gulp of air—and it was then that this old sailor *said something he shouldn't have said.* An instant later, the lights came back on. The waves eased. The storm slackened. And the *Conrad* righted herself, strong enough to get to the nearest port. It was then that this sailor saw the man in the white suit, and the man in the white suit just nodded and said, 'I'll be back for you later.'

"And then he was gone."

Logan whistled low. "I hate it when that happens," he whispered. Crystal elbowed him in the ribs.

Smudge swallowed more rum and continued. "Another of the sailors there at Annie's that night, he was a scrawny young guy with short hair and mean eyes. He remembered the time he had seen this man in the white suit before. It was just a year earlier, and this young fellow had shipped out on a tanker that had stopped in some dark little port in Southeast Asia. This fellow was in a foul mood, it seems, and he found himself in a shitty little bar drinking more than was smart under the circumstances. He was spoiling for a fight, and so he turned to the guy next to him and knocked him to the floor. The guy stood up and moved away, so this young fellow smacked the guy on his other side. An instant later, four men had pinned this young fellow to the floor, and the guy he hit was coming toward his face with a broken bottle. It was at that moment that this young fellow *said something he shouldn't have said.* The next instant, this man in the white suit was there, pulling the guys off him and dragging him out the door to safety. When they were outside and away from danger, the man in the white suit just turned to the young fellow and said, 'I'll be back for you later.' And then he was gone.

"And every sailor there at Annie's that night remembered back to the time he had seen this man in the white suit before. And the man in the white suit just stood in the doorway, looking out at all those sailors, and he smiled. The sailors all stared back at him, or they looked away, or they kept their eyes pointed down at their shoes. And every single one of them knew how this evening would end."

Smudge paused, then whispered, "'*Cause when you sell your soul to the devil, you have to go with him when he calls.*"

Joy stiffened and grabbed the cross she wore around her neck. Her eyes never left Smudge's face, but she whispered a prayer to herself: "*Padre neustro que estas en los cielos . . . .*"

Smudge leaned forward and continued. "The devil grinned as he looked at all those sailors. 'My, my, my, my my!' he said. 'Just look at all of those souls—and all of them mine!'

"He started walking up and down among the tables, calling each sailor by name just to prove that he remembered. 'Reynolds, good to see you again. Mr. Green, how are the children these days? Gonzalez, you've *almost* saved up enough for law school, haven't you?' And he just walked among them, calling them by name, his eyes glittering black and evil.

"And when he got to the counter, he saw Annie. He saw the fire in her eyes and the grit in her heart, and he said, 'My, my, my, my my—now *there's* a soul I'd like to have for my own.'

"He thought for a moment, and then he spun on his heel.

"'Tell you what, boys,' he said to the sailors in the room, 'I'll make you a little wager. I'll challenge any one of you to the contest of your choosing, but the stakes will be high. If you win, you all get your souls back for free. But if I win, I keep all your souls—and I get hers, too. What do you say?'

"He began walking among the tables again, challenging each sailor by name. 'Reynolds, you're a strong man. How about a little arm wrestling? Hmm? Green, you've got good aim. Care for a round of darts? Mr. Gonzalez, you're pretty smart. How about a game of chess?'

"But as he walked among the tables, challenging each sailor by name, they all kept their eyes down and their mouths shut. As much as they all desperately wanted to win their souls back, they all loved Annie too much to risk her soul in the bargain.

"When the devil got no takers, he spun on his heel and stormed toward the door. 'In that case, gentlemen,' he hissed, 'it's time to go.'

"It was at that moment that Annie spoke up. She was still behind the counter, with a dishtowel in her hands. She peered out at the devil from behind her thick glasses, and she called out in a strong voice, 'You didn't ask me, Devil,' she said. 'You didn't ask me.'

"The devil bounded over to the counter and looked down at Annie. 'My dear little Annie,' he crooned, 'what sort of contest could you possibly propose? Knitting, perhaps? Crochet?'

"'Sailboats,' Annie said. 'I'll race you across the bay.'

"The devil laughed out loud. 'My dear little Annie, not even *I* could accept such an offer. Look at you! You're old. You're frail. You can't see. You—'

"'It's all right, Devil,' Annie interrupted, patting the devil reassuringly on the arm. 'It's all right. I know what it's like to be *afraid*.'

"The devil's eyes blazed in anger. 'Very well, Annie,' he hissed. 'You've got yourself a race.'

"'That's fine, Devil,' Annie said. 'But there are two conditions. The first is, you'll have to provide the boats. It's been a long time since I've had a boat of my own.'

"'Very well,' the devil replied.

"'And secondly, Devil,' Annie said, 'I don't trust you. I never have, and I never will. I think if we race head-to-head, we'll get out there in the middle of the bay, and you'll do something to me. Or you'll do something to my boat. So we won't race head-to-head. One of us will start at six o'clock tomorrow morning, and the other will start at eight. Whoever gets across the bay in the shortest amount of time, that's the winner. And if it's all the same to you, Devil, I'll start at eight.'

"The devil, sensing a trap, reeled back and thought about that for a moment. He knew that the breezes around the Chesapeake blow offshore—from land to sea—at night, and they blow onshore during the day. Around sunrise, the breezes cancel each other out, and the air is nearly still. But by eight o'clock, with the sun higher in the sky, the onshore breeze is strong. So whoever started at eight o'clock would have the advantage.

"'Fine,' said the devil, 'but *I'll* start at eight, and *you'll* start at six.'

"Annie nodded grimly. 'I'll beat you anyway, Devil,' she said. 'Just wait and see.'

"Just before six o'clock the next morning, all the sailors were gathered on the beach outside of Annie's. Annie was there, too, and so was the devil. True to his word, he had provided two boats.

"On the stern of one, it read *Annie*.

"On the stern of the other, it read *Me*.

"And the boats were *technically* identical, but there were a lot of subtle differences between them. Annie's boat sat low and fat in the water, and the sail didn't seem to fit quite right. But the devil's boat danced on the waves, as if it were eager to get the race under way. There was nothing Annie could do about it, though. She marched up to the devil and looked him in the eye. 'Just remember, Devil,' she said, yanking him on the sleeve three times. 'When you feel a little tug, look behind you.'

"The devil laughed, and the sailors helped Annie climb into her boat. At six o'clock sharp, they pushed her boat into deeper water, running behind it as far as they could. Annie set her sail, and the faint breeze pushed the boat ever so slowly away from the beach.

"By eight o'clock, the breeze was strong and fresh. The devil jumped into his boat and filled his sail with a pop. He cut away from the beach, leaving a steady wake behind him."

Smudge paused and looked around intently at his silent audience. Logan slipped below and returned with a bottle of rum, which he poured into Smudge's empty glass and one he brought for himself. Smudge took a long drink, wiped his mouth on the back of his hairy forearm, and continued.

"The devil had sailed for just over an hour, and he was in a pretty good mood. He could see Annie's boat up ahead, growing larger and larger. At the rate he was gaining on her, he would not only beat her overall time, he would actually pass her in the bay!

"Now, he noticed a tanker far off on the horizon to his right. He paid it no mind, because it was so far away that it couldn't possibly do him any harm. *But what the devil didn't know* was that tankers and freighters on the Chesapeake move so fast that if you see one on the horizon, you could be on a collision course.

"Well, the devil kept sailing on, watching that tanker growing larger and larger. But he held his course, confident that he would pass well in front of the big ship. The tanker steamed closer. The devil could see the waves pushed by its bow. But he held his course still, like the stubborn devil that he is.

"Then at the last minute, when it was clear that the sailboat would be crushed by the tanker if the devil didn't do something, he let fly the mainsheet and sat there motionless in the water, the mainsail luffing loudly and Annie sailing farther and farther away. The devil cursed at Annie and he cursed at the tanker, 'cause he was sure that he had been set up somehow and that this was some kind of trap.

"It took the ship and its wake three minutes to churn by, and then the devil tightened his mainsheet and started sailing again. He could still see Annie's boat far off in the distance, and he was determined to make up the lost time.

"He sailed on for another hour, gaining steadily on Annie in her wallowing little boat. He began to smile again, confident of a clear victory.

"That's when he saw the tugboat far off to his left. It was coming his way, but the devil had learned his lesson this time. Instead of sailing on at full speed, and then waiting dead in the water while the tugboat went past, the devil slowed up just a bit. That way, the tugboat would pass in front of his sailboat without forcing him to come to a complete stop.

"And sure enough, the tugboat grew larger and larger, and it slid past the devil's bow with only fifty yards of clearance. The devil smiled, pleased with his timing, and he tightened his mainsheet and picked up full speed once again.

"Then BAM! The sailboat smashed to a stop, and the devil lurched forward, gashing his cheek on the gunwale. He scrambled to his feet and glared down into the water, trying to find out what he had hit. And there, just below the surface, was a big thick cable, moving from left to right. See, *what the devil didn't know* was that barges on the Chesapeake are sometimes so big that tugboats let out a mile or more of cable to keep the barge from crashing into the tugboat's stern when it stops. The devil looked far off to his left. Sure enough, there was a barge way off, clipping toward him, pulled by the tug. The devil howled at the delay and cursed the tug.

"*The tug.* Annie's words came back to him. 'When you feel a little tug,' she had said, 'look behind you.' Well, the devil felt that tug all right—he had sailed smack into the cable it was pulling—and so slowly, ever so slowly, the devil looked over his shoulder.

"There was nothing there. The devil relaxed. Crazy old woman, he thought. But then, as he stared past his stern, his eyes picked out the tiny distant shape—of another tugboat.

"See, *what the devil didn't know* was that some barges on the Chesapeake get so big that it takes two tugboats to pull them. One tug hooks onto the bow of the barge and swings far out to port. The other hooks on and swings far out to starboard. And when the devil realized that he was caught between those two cables, he brought his sailboat about and whizzed back—too late. He hit the second cable. He came about again and shot back, but he hit the first cable once again. He kept on trying, zigging and zagging back and forth and back and forth and backandforthandbackandforth—until finally, *the barge was there. And the devil?"* Smudge grinned and leaned back. "Well, the devil lost that race."

"Back at Annie's that night, the whole crowd of sailors was there, laughing and joking and thanking Annie and their lucky stars. And Annie explained how she had tricked the devil into starting at eight o'clock. She knew the shipping schedule better than anyone alive, and she knew that the devil would sail right in between those two tugs.

"And sailors, they're a superstitious lot. They like to give names to things that scare them, just to make them seem less threatening. And that night, there at Annie's, they gave names to those two cables that stretch out from a barge when two tugboats clip on. The cable to port—the first one the devil hit—well, they named it after the devil himself. And the cable to starboard—the one that made the devil realize that he was going for a long swim—well, they named that cable after the deep blue sea.

"And so, if you're ever caught between the devil and the deep blue sea—well, you know you're in a trap that the devil himself could not escape."

And with those words, Smudge drained the rest of his rum, belched three times in rapid fire, and fell sound asleep on the vinyl mat. He stayed there for nearly twenty-four hours, until he finally got up, relieved himself over the rail of the *Dreadnought*, and with a smile and a wave, climbed back down into the *Chamber Pot* and sailed off.

CHAPTER SIX

FORTY-THREE KNOTS OF FREEDOM LEFT

July 10th was hot, and little wind blew at all. Logan was at the helm, squinting through his shaggy red hair, but there wasn't much for him to do. The *Dreadnought* drifted slowly along Isle au Haut bay. Rockland, where the *Dreadnought* had first launched several weeks before, was off to the west, but the upscale island of Vinylhaven loomed between the town and the ship. Somehow, even though no one in Rockland knew or cared where the *Dreadnought* teens were, it seemed safer not to venture too close. The crew donned hats, passed around a bottle of sunscreen, took off nearly all their clothes, and lay on the vinyl mats on deck, absorbing the sun and floating off into daydreams.

The ship creaked mournfully in the gentle swells; the sails filled, then fluttered, then popped full again.

The day was taking a long time to pass.

Dawn was lost in her favorite daydream, featuring a hammered dulcimer. Her favorite instrument, the dulcimer is a large wooden box strung with wires. Handheld hammers striking the wires make a beautiful sound, like the hammers striking wires in the back of a grand piano. The daydream involves a large and quiet crowd and some lyrics Dawn has written herself. With flowers in her hair, she stands poised on stage, smiles a soft freckled smile to the throngs that begin at her feet and rise slowly toward the back of the hall, and then strikes the first chord with her leather-faced hammers.

> *It was an early-morning highway,*
> *And the cars just kicked up dust.*
> *No one slowed down, a soul could drown,*
> *There's no one I can trust.*
>
> *A limo stopped, a man peered out,*
> *He offered me a ride.*
> *"Just climb on in, and show some skin,*
> *There's lots of room inside."*
>
> *Another guy pulled over fast.*
> *He said, "Babe, you're in luck.*
> *I am the best, forget the rest,*
> *Just climb up in my truck."*
>
> *But I told them all to drive away,*
> *I don't want trucks and cars.*
> *The soul I seek is strong and meek*
> *And dreams about the stars.*
>
> *If you want to walk with me,*
> *You'll have to ditch those wheels,*
> *And find out what the earth is like*
> *And how the Spirit feels.*

The crowd listens, hushed, as Dawn sings about energy, about life, and about the things that matter. She sings about the inhuman distractions that are injected into our lives by television and gadgets and material success. She sings about the importance of love, and sensitivity to the pulses of the Earth, and the power of the Goddesses that rule our—

"*El almuerzo!* Lunchtime!" Joy called out. She emerged from below with a tray piled high with ham and baby Swiss sandwiches. Dawn shook her head to clear her thoughts and return to the tragically mundane world.

Logan grunted. "Oh, boy," he said. "Mmmmmm–mmmm! Ham again. More preserved meat. Joy, you make wonderful meals outta totally ordinary food, but I'm getting so tired of food out of cans, or stuff that has been, like, salted, cured, and embalmed." He took a bite of his sandwich as Joy watched with a sweet and hopeful look. "This is good, Joy. It's really good. But I totally want steak. I demand steaks for everyone! Grilled on a charcoal fire, with, like, baked potatoes, gravy, and sourdough biscuits. But mostly, I'm talking steaks. Big enormous steaks, steaks that spill over all sides of your plate, bright red, medium-rare, hot and juicy and—"

"Enough!" Dawn laughed. "We still have some money from our raid. We can go ashore, buy some steaks and some charcoal, and maybe a little disposable grill, and cook up the best food you ever tasted."

"I have this trick I do with juniper branches that gives the steaks a taste you'll never forget," Joy added.

The crew, drowsy but paying attention, murmured assent. They would go ashore for steaks.

"Lobster float, dead ahead!" Arthur boomed out from the bow. "Turn to port!"

Logan spun the wheel gently counterclockwise. "Aye! Aye! Turning to port!" he chanted back in his best *Mutiny on the Bounty* accent. The ship creaked and changed direction lazily.

"Okay!" Arthur shouted. "All clear!"

Logan brushed the ruddy hair out of his eyes and nodded. He held the wheel steady.

"Wait!" Arthur called again. "There's another float. Turn to starboard."

Logan turned the wheel in the other direction. The ship responded with a yawn.

"Okay!" Arthur said. "All clear."

The ship drifted farther into the bay, visions of juicy grilled steaks dancing in the heads of the crew.

"Jesse," Logan said, "how's your arm feeling? You feel up to rowing ashore with Joy and me to do some shopping?"

Jesse nodded from beneath a cap pulled down across his face. "I'm okay. I'll do anything people want."

"Great," Logan said. "We'll totally go ashore as soon as we find a town."

"That would be Stonington," Dawn called out. She was sitting in a yoga position on an orange mat, her white skin shining in the sun. "I looked at the charts last night. It's just up ahead."

"Hold it!" Arthur called from the bow. "Lobster float, dead ahead again. Damn it! I thought we were clear. It's like these things are moving or something. Turn to port again."

Logan moved the wheel counterclockwise once again, and the ship began to turn.

"Wait a minute!" Arthur gestured for Logan to stop the boat. Logan chuckled. "It's gone!" Arthur yelled. "The float is gone! It was here right in front of us, just a minute ago, and now it's—"

Arthur was silent.

"It's what?" Logan called forward.

"It's back!" Arthur said. "It was gone, and now it's back."

The crew rushed to the bow, leaving only Logan to steer the ship.

"Seals," Dawn said. "They're watching us."

In the bay, ahead of the *Dreadnought*, the glistening dark-brown heads of almost three dozen seals bobbed just above the gentle waves. One would disappear, without a sound, and then a few minutes later, another one—or the same one— would surface somewhere else.

Arthur looked to the starboard. He saw more than fifteen clusters of low, flat rocks, barely dry above the ocean's surface. On them were dozens of large beige and brown masses.

"Look at them all!" he said. "This place is thick with seals!"

As the *Dreadnought* slid slowly up the bay, the crew watched seals in the water and on the rocks.

"Those are the Scraggy Ledges," Dawn said. "The charts show good water depth in most of this area. And over there is Brown Cow Island. Obviously, the seals like it here."

On one of the ledges, a large dark seal lifted its head above the others sleeping in the sun. It flopped awkwardly to one side, then flipped into the water with a nose-down-then-nose-up movement that left it ten feet away from the rock, treading water and peering at the boat.

Another seal that had been watching the ship from dead ahead sank slowly beneath the green waves, then resurfaced in exactly the same spot, staring once again as though nothing had changed. As the *Dreadnought* drew near, the crew could make out details: the patches of dark and light fur; the large, round, brown eyes; the whiskers. From time to time, one of the seals would bark—usually sending several others scurrying for the safety of the water—but mostly the seals were silent. They simply watched.

Near the bow, Joy gazed down at the seals with an expression of deep affection. "*Muy bonito.* Very beautiful," she said to Jesse. "They look like cute, patient little friends."

Jesse nodded, his homemade tattoos rippling in the sweaty sunlight. "They stick together. Like family."

"What do you think their view of the world is?" Joy asked.

"Peaceful," Jesse said. "Peaceful and relaxed and trusting. Not bad. Lie around in the sun. Spend time with each other. Dive into the water and eat all the food you want. Always trusting your friends to keep you safe. Friends and family."

Joy shook her head slowly. "They're so lucky," she said.

In the stern, at the wheel, Logan suddenly grinned. "Hey!" he called out, spotting a chance to be a hero for once. "Is anyone else, like, thinking what I'm thinking?"

Marietta scowled. "I doubt it," she said.

"Steaks," Logan said.

Marietta eased herself back down on her mat, rolled her T-shirt up into a tight tuck across her chest, and sighed. "We've been over that," she said. "With juniper."

"Not *those* steaks," Logan said. He gestured toward the seals. "*These* steaks. We've caught lobsters to feed ourselves. So like, why not catch a seal?"

"What are you talking about?" Marietta said drowsily.

"For dinner," Logan said. "We'll row over to those rocks in the dinghy, and we'll go on, like, a seal hunt! Ready—aim—fire! We'll bring back fresh seal steaks for everyone!"

It didn't take long for word of Logan's idea to spread throughout the ship. The crew gathered around the wheel.

"Count me out," Arthur said. "For all we know, seal meat tastes like shit. I mean that literally. Besides, I'm not going to kill some seal just because we're tired of eating ham."

"Neither am I," Dawn said, her green eyes angry. "These creatures have done us no harm, and it would be cruel to shatter their lives with our greed."

"Actually, I don't see the difference," Joy said. The others stared at her in surprise. "Look, I take live lobsters, drop them into boiling water, and clamp a lid on so they can't get out. To eat, we have to kill. God gave us these animals so we could live. If you get your food from a supermarket, that just means you have someone else do the killing for you."

The argument continued until Logan raised his hand. "Excuse me, everyone!" he said. "I'm totally going on a seal hunt, and whoever wants to come along can go. If you don't like it, don't go—and don't eat the steaks. Now who's going with me?"

Joy agreed to go, which surprised everyone again. "Hey," she said, "I'd rather hunt for food than steal it." BillFi joined also. Crystal looked over at the seals, then she shook her head.

"Not me," she said. "My money is on the seals."

"That makes three of us," Logan said. "That's perfect. Now—we'll need something to use as clubs."

Crystal nodded. "Belaying pins," she said.

"What pins?" Logan asked.

"Belaying pins, nimrod," Crystal said, putting her hands on her hips. "Long wooden pins with handles on the ends. Perfect for cracking a skull."

"Where are they?" Logan asked.

"Right over there." Crystal pointed to the rigging on the starboard side. "Help yourself."

"Then we're all set," Logan said. "Let's drop anchor and get started."

A short while later, the seal hunters hunkered down in the dinghy, trying not to scare their prey. Their bare feet chilled in the puddle of seawater that always seemed to slosh on the dinghy floor. Logan rowed the boat slowly across the water toward a small cluster of glistening seal-covered rocks. BillFi, crouched in the bow, whispered back that eight seals were basking just up ahead. Joy, next to him, shrugged. She could see nothing but an undulating mass of beige fur.

"Here's the plan," Logan wheezed. He felt excited at the prospect of leading an adventure. He grinned as the others looked to him for guidance. When I bring back a big seal and we all have seal steaks tonight, he thought, Crystal will pay attention to me then. She'll have to. I'll be a hero.

He paused at the oars and peered ahead through sunglasses and the low brim of a baseball cap. "We'll, like, glide up to the rocks very quietly, tie up on a rock, and get out. Then we'll creep up to a seal, and when I nod, we'll swing our clubs and totally hit it in the head. Badda-bam! We'll have to be quick so we don't scare it away."

The others nodded. Joy moved her arm slowly and pointed ahead.

"We're almost there," she whispered. "We should get out right there between those two rocks."

"Okay," Logan said. "We'll wait till the water is, like, shallow, then we'll go. Jump out at my command."

He guided the dinghy between the rocks, and Joy got ready to jump. The boat was just five feet away from dry granite. Logan raised his hand.

"No!" BillFi said to Logan. "Too soon! We're not—"

"NOW!" Logan whispered. Joy swung her legs over the rail, pushed off, and vanished deep under the water.

On board the *Dreadnought,* Arthur was watching the action through binoculars. It was all he could do to keep from laughing out loud.

Joy lunged up through the surface, sputtering, and grabbed onto the dinghy's rail.

"I thought you said to—" she said.

BillFi laughed. "I tried to tell you," he said. "I tried to tell you. It gets deep really fast here. Really deep. You have to get out on the dry rock, or you could be in twenty feet of water. It gets deep really fast here."

"Great," Joy said. "*Muchas gracias.* Thanks for telling me."

BillFi looked crestfallen. "I'm sorry," he said. "I tried. I'm sorry."

With Joy holding onto the rail, Logan rowed the boat closer to the rocks. Joy tossed her belaying pins onto the granite and scrambled up out of the water.

The seals were gone.

"Oh, shit," BillFi said, pushing his glasses higher up his nose. "They're not here. They're gone. Not here anymore. Let's go find another rock."

Logan rowed the hunters a few hundred feet farther into the bay, and they started the drill over again. They kept their heads down, they waited without a sound, and—when the boat was bumping against hard rock—they clambered over the rail.

"Get down!" Logan whispered. They dropped to their bellies. The ashen granite was cool and rough, and it smelled of moss and seagull droppings. The hunters lay low and motionless.

"Okay," Logan said. "Follow me." He raised his head slowly. Twenty yards in front of him were a dozen seals, slowly raising their heads. "This way." He squirmed forward on his stomach, clutching a belaying pin in his right hand. After about ten yards, he stopped. "Lie still," he wheezed. "Let them, like, calm down. Get used to us."

The three hunters pressed their cheeks against the ragged rock. They didn't move. Three minutes went by, then Logan looked up.

Twenty yards in front of him were a dozen seals, watching him closely.

"Shit! They keep moving away," he said. "Let's try it again, but stay low this time! Lll–oooooo–www!"

They crawled forward another ten yards. Logan looked up. The seals looked back at him. They were twenty yards away.

"Damn it!" Logan whispered. "Somebody isn't staying low enough. They totally keep seeing us."

"Logan," Joy said. "I have a feeling it doesn't matter how low we go. Watch this."

She stood up.

The seals didn't move.

"Hello, seals," Joy called out in a loud voice. "*Buenas dias.* Lovely day, isn't it? God does good work, wouldn't you say?"

They didn't move.

"You can get up now," Joy said to her friends clinging to the granite at her feet. "We're not fooling anyone."

The others stood up and brushed the moss and rock chips off their clothes.

"I don't think we're going to catch them," BillFi said. "I don't think we're going to get close enough. I don't think we're going to catch them."

"Yes, we will," Logan said. "Now that we know we can stand up, it's, like, that much easier! Get your clubs ready. See that big dark one over there? Seals can't move very fast on land. When I say 'Go,' we'll all run over to it and totally hit it on the head. It'll be quick, and we'll get our seal."

The seal Logan pointed to was large, fat, and chocolate brown, with white whiskers that stuck out like porcupine quills. It wasn't looking at them. It was resting in the sun, eyes closed, about ten yards from the water's edge.

"Get ready," Logan said.

The hunters turned slowly to face their target.

"Get set."

The hunters gripped their belaying pins.

"GO!"

The hunters bolted. They dashed across the rock, leaping nimbly over cracks and ridges. In an instant, they were almost upon their prey. They raised their belaying pins, drew in close—and the seal rolled over twice toward the ocean. Logan dove through the air toward it, his belaying pin raised high. He landed with a curse on the rocks, his belaying pin jammed painfully beneath his shoulder. Joy tumbled after the seal, but the seal shifted subtly, and Joy scrambled into waist-deep, chilly water. BillFi tried to anticipate its movements, darting this way and that. The seal anticipated his movements, darted that way and this, and left him standing alone on a rock. Then, apparently bored with the antics, the stout seal yawned, let fly with an audible belch, and flipped into the ocean.

It bobbed to the surface about twenty yards out and watched the three hunters standing still, sunburned and bleeding and hot, their belaying pins drooping downward.

Logan shook his head, wincing as he moved his skinned knees and scraped elbows. "Ham," he said, flicking his hair away from his face. "I totally like ham. Don't you like ham? I love ham. Some of my favorite food is ham. Fuck these seals. Let's get back to the ship."

The others nodded. The *Dreadnought* seemed far away, but it also felt like home.

"*Muy bueno.* We love ham," Joy said quietly. "Especially that canned kind with that yellow jelly all around the outside. I love that stuff."

"Shit," Logan said. He could feel his chance to impress Crystal slipping swiftly away.

Back on the *Dreadnought* that evening, the other sailors were supportive—at least, as supportive as they could be without laughing. They sat around the dining table, beneath Joy's latest Bible sign, which read, "With God all things are possible—Matthew 19:26," eating a delicious ham and potato-au-gratin casserole Dawn had prepared.

"I had a hunch we'd need it," she said. Logan sighed. No one had any faith in him at all, he thought, and he wasn't sure they were wrong.

Jesse raised his rum and Tang. As he grinned, the fresh green-and-black tattoos on his jaws stretched outward. "Noble hunters," he said. "Loyal to the end."

"To the hunters!" everyone cheered as they toasted their friends. Everyone except for Marietta. She brushed her hair and scowled. "It was a stupid idea," she said. "You people looked like idiots out there."

Arthur stood and held up his wine with a flourish. "My friends," he said, bending his deep voice into something like a British accent, "there comes a time in the history of all great ships when some members of the crew must sacrifice everything—dignity, composure, even grace—in the interest of educating and enlightening the others on board. Our fearless hunters, of course, could have captured a dozen seals easily, but that wouldn't have served their higher purpose. No, my friends, they were intent on reminding us all that food is not to be taken for granted. They were intent on teaching us of the difficulties and challenges that face those who rely on the earth and sea for sustenance. They were intent on demonstrating for us the staggering odds that hunters must overcome every day. They did not set out to replace our ham, my friends. No! They set out to replace our tired and cynical attitudes. They set out to replace our contempt for ham with appreciation, with admiration, with affection. They accomplished their goal in fine fashion, and we shall be eternally in their debt."

He drank a swallow of wine and raised his glass again. "And they looked damn silly doing it!" he said.

"Damn silly!" cheered the others.

Logan grinned and shook his head. "Shit," he said. He raised his glass and drank.

☠   ☠   ☠

Marietta was at the helm the next day, and Arthur instructed her to keep the ship far away from the seal-covered shoals. "Rocks like that could smash a hole in our hull," he explained. The wind was strong and stiffening, turning slowly counterclockwise. The *Dreadnought* heeled sharply and cut through the waves with impressive power, tossing salt spray high into the air.

After lunch, most of the crew lounged on deck, enjoying the breeze and reading paperbacks they had bought in Freeport. Jesse busied himself with the task of tattooing his right calf, weaving increasingly intricate patterns like spiderwebs and hedgerows across his skin, while BillFi added swirls

and elaborate knots to Jesse's back. Crystal ripped off an endless string of sit-ups on a vinyl mat on the bow, and Dawn sat
with her legs crossed, facing the sun and chanting some mys-
tical mantra over and over again.

But Logan seemed restless. He poked around one hold
after another, digging through mildewed life jackets and fray-
ing ropes, fishing out an empty nylon sail bag or a fading
windbreaker. Whenever he found something that seemed to
satisfy him, he disappeared below and deposited it somewhere. Then he re-emerged and continued his hunt.

"What *are* you doing?" Marietta asked.

"Just, like, looking for some stuff," Logan said, arching his
eyebrows. "Shhhhhh! It's for a totally top-secret project I'm
working on."

Marietta scowled. "Well, tell me what you're doing, or I'll
get Arthur to order you to tell me."

Logan paused, looked over at her, and then resumed his
poking about.

"Did you hear me?" Marietta screeched. "I said, I *order* you
to tell me! Arthur will do what I ask him to. You have to do
what I say."

Logan paused again. Then, with uncharacteristic swiftness, he marched over to Marietta and stood in front of her,
his pale face just inches from hers. "Arthur might think he's
the captain here, but he's not—and I don't think either one of
you should push it," he said in a barely controlled tone. "In the
meantime, just steer the fucking ship."

Around four o'clock, Logan entered the captain's quarters
and closed the door behind him. The room was cozy and
quiet and thick with the power of the imagination.

Logan chuckled to himself. His mother hated to hear him talk like that. "Thick with the power of imagination?" she would say. "Thick with something, anyway." Then she would snort and give him some task to do, to keep his mind in the real world "where it belonged."

But his father understood. His father was an actor, a playwright, a dreamer, and a fool. He would leave his briefcase on top of the car when he pulled out of the driveway, scattering papers and turkey sandwiches all over the street as he drove away. He would put his pen in the cup in the bathroom, and then wonder later in the day why he had a toothbrush in his shirt pocket. He would call people on the phone and then forget who he had dialed, engaging the other person in charming conversation until he at last remembered whom he had called and why.

People called him "Loopy." His real name was Lawrence, but he had long ago acquired that nickname, and it stuck with him wherever he went. Loopy McPhee. People made good-natured fun of him, and he seemed to enjoy the embarrassing attention. But Logan never made fun of him. He loved his father deeply, and he was proud of Loopy's creativity and passion. Loopy could bang out some words on his old manual typewriter, and a year later audiences would cry at the little boy, or the old woman, or the brave mother who walked across the stage. Or they would laugh at the characters that Loopy invented in his mind and brought to life before their eyes. He created clowns of all kinds. Clowns in business suits. Clowns in prison stripes. Clowns in military uniforms, French-maid costumes, or nothing but their underwear. If Loopy wanted people to laugh, they laughed. If he wanted them to cry, they cried.

Loopy had hated the idea of sending his only child off on a "Leadership Cruise." Sounded too harsh. Too tough. Too boring. He would have been happier letting Logan spend the summer hitching rides on freight trains or camping on his own in the woods. But Logan's mother had insisted. "It'll do him some good," she said. "Bring him back down to earth, where he belongs." Loopy was a creative wizard and an absent-minded magician, but he was not the most assertive of men. When his wife insisted, he agreed.

Logan shuffled through the pile of fabric and canvas that sprawled across the Captain's bed in front of him. He smiled. He was doing this for Loopy, and he could feel his father's soul and inspiration and genius fill his mind and his fingers. He was ready to make a little magic of his own.

He worked in the captain's quarters all afternoon. He emerged for dinner, but he refused to tell anyone what he was doing. Once the meal was over, he went back into the captain's quarters and locked the door.

He stayed in there all night. He came out from time to time, fetching a tall glass of rum or visiting the bathroom, but then he disappeared again behind the wooden door. Arthur, curious and a little put-out, slept in Logan's bunk that night.

Breakfast was nearly over when Logan came out the next morning. His red hair was straggly, his clothes were rumpled, and he carried a dark green tarp under one arm. He placed his bundle on his bunk and took his place at the head of the table.

He smiled. "I'm totally starving," he said. "What's cooking?"

"We were going to ask you that same question," Arthur said, stretching his lanky frame and stifling a yawn. "Are you going to tell us what this is all about?"

Logan took a bite of the scrambled-egg-and-ham dish BillFi had made. He nodded. "Right after breakfast," he said. "I'd like the crew to assemble on deck."

It didn't take them long. Fired with curiosity, the crew gathered on deck just as soon as the dishes had been gathered and left to soak in the galley. The only straggler was Marietta, who always took her time getting ready to start the day.

When everyone was present, Logan carried his green package to the base of the mainmast. "Sorry for all the secrecy," he wheezed, "but I didn't know if this would turn out well or not. If it didn't, I, like, wasn't going to say anything to anybody."

"If *what* didn't?" Dawn asked.

"Well," Logan answered, "I figured that since we were pirates—the Pirates of the *Dreadnought*, you know, the Plunder Dogs, and stuff—we totally ought to have a flag. A pirate's flag. 'Avast, ye maties,' and all that stuff. Something that would make it clear to other boats that we, like, shouldn't be messed with. You know, Dread nought, 'Fear Nothing.' I wanted a flag that would let the world know we weren't afraid of anything it could dish out."

"So you made us a flag?" Arthur asked.

Logan nodded. "A big one," he said. "It'll be our symbol, if you like it. Something we can use to show we're a team."

"Let's see it!" Joy said.

Logan carefully unwrapped the bundle. As the green tarp fell away, the crew could see a black background with flashes of color. Logan held the flag by the corners and lifted it high; Dawn grabbed two corners and helped. It was square and big, and across the blackness curved four ragged slashes—gold, green, blue, red.

The crew was silent.

At last, Joy spoke. "*Me gusta*! I like it!" she said with awe. "Those marks look like dog teeth."

"Or shark gills," Dawn added.

"Or bear claws," Jesse said.

"Or gashes made by bear claws," Crystal said.

Logan grinned. "Right!" he said. "All of you!" He grinned most at Crystal.

"Dread *nought*," Arthur said with a dramatic flourish. "Logan, you did it! With this flag, we fear nothing. Let the Maritimes beware! The Pirates of the *Dreadnought* dare to show their colors! Watch out for the Plunder Dogs!"

Everyone cheered—except for Marietta. "It looks like a rainbow at night," she muttered as she crept back down below.

No one paid any attention to her. They were busy congratulating Logan for his contribution to the ship and the team.

"But how will we get it up the mast?" Joy asked.

"No fucking problem," Crystal said with disdain. She took the flag from Logan and tied it around her neck like a cape. Then she kicked off her shoes, jumped up, and grabbed the rigging. With spiderlike swiftness, she scuttled up through the lines and sails to the top of the mast, forty feet in the air. She attached the flag to the highest lines and shinnied back down. Logan vowed to remember forever that image: his flag fluttering in Crystal's hand.

The flag was magnificent up there. It flapped slowly in the wind, its bright and rich colors commanding attention. It seemed to give the whole ship a center, a focal point under which day-to-day life could be conducted with a constant reminder of the power and responsibility of the ship and its crew.

That night, the pirates talked around the dining table long past sundown. The flag gave them a sense of excitement and identity that they hadn't realized they lacked, and as the oil lamp flickered and sputtered overhead, they shared fantasies and dreams and confidences that they had, until now, been holding back.

Joy talked about Leo, her boyfriend back in Austin. She showed the others her ring, a thin gold band that glittered with diamond dust. It was a sign, she said, of deep affection, God's glory, and everlasting love.

"Everlasting love? Give me a fucking break!" Crystal laughed. "No such thing. All there is is shared agendas. Guys aren't husbands. They're allies—and alliances end when people change their minds."

"Maybe for you, but not for me and Leo," Joy retorted, her chestnut face frowning gently. "We're in love, and we're going to stay in love forever. He's not exactly the latest Hollywood hunk, but he's sweet, and he's loyal, and he's kind, and he's strong, and he's—"

"And he's enough to make me barf," Crystal said. "Get real. The best you can hope for from a guy is a great body and a slow mind. Like Jesse, here. Knockout bod. Not the swiftest brain on the planet."

Jesse looked up at her. He shrugged. "Loyalty is what counts," he said. "You'll know that once you find it."

"Hey, babe, I've experienced everything. You name it. Been there. Done it. Moved on," Crystal said. "Not like Joy here. She's more like, 'scared of it, won't do it, wouldn't be prudent.'"

Dawn turned toward Crystal, her green eyes blazing with anger. "You don't know—"

But Joy interrupted. "You don't know love, Crystal," she said with astonishing gentleness. She patted Crystal's arm. "You'll feel better about yourself when you do."

And to everyone's amazement, it was Crystal who stomped out of the room in tears. She spent the rest of the night high in the rigging, alone with her thoughts and the stars.

☠   ☠   ☠

The evening ritual was beginning to shift. For the first weeks of the trip, the crew would anchor the ship safely before sundown and gather in the mess hall for dinner. Then they would drift apart in small groups, find quiet places on the deck or in the cockpit or somewhere, and talk. Eventually, they all would return to the mess hall for a final lamplight conversation around the table, beneath Joy's Bible Saying of the Day.

One evening they ended up talking about the worst jobs they had ever had. Logan started that theme when he commented that he'd rather be a pirate than a professional clown.

"You were a fucking *clown*?" Crystal asked.

"For one summer," Logan said. "It was hell. All I did was, like, entertain at kids' birthday parties. A bunch of screaming, rowdy eight-year-olds who think Wiffle bats were invented so you could hit clowns in the nuts with them. And my job is to keep these monsters busy by showing them how to, like, make dachshunds out of balloons. 'Look, kid—a doggie!' Kids are ripping apart the furniture, punching out the windows, setting fire to my wig—and all the parents are hiding in the rec room downstairs, saying, 'Just call us if you need us.' No wonder I ended up being a pirate."

"Why didn't you just quit?" Joy asked.

"I couldn't," Logan answered. "My mother had gotten me the job, and she had totally made it clear that if I wanted to buy a motorcycle, I'd have to earn the money doing *that* job."

"You must have really wanted a motorcycle," Arthur said.

"Badly," Logan said. "Still do. By the end of that summer, I had managed to save all of, like, two hundred and fifty dollars. Cha-*ching*! I couldn't afford *gas*."

"I know what you mean," Joy said. "I once worked the night shift as a short-order cook. It was a little diner that was the only place open all night. When the bars would close, everyone who hadn't managed to pick up a date wandered in there. The order was always the same: cheeseburger with everything, apple pie, coffee. And the conversation was always the same: 'When do you get off work, baby?' 'I'll have a cheeseburger and a great big helping of you.' 'That grill ain't the only thing that's hot around here!' I finally went to a flea market and bought a picture of some big ugly boxer. I put it on my counter next to the grill, and whenever anyone gave me a hard time, I'd just point to it and say, 'Don't let my boyfriend José hear you talk like that!' And after an entire summer of putting up with that stuff, I saved four hundred dollars."

Dawn nodded. "That kind of hassle can be a real pain, but it's easier to take from a lot of lonely strangers. I once spent a summer working as an intern for an anthropology professor at the university near where I live. It started out with me doing typing and filing and stuff like that, helping him with things while he worked on some big research project he was doing. I loved the work—the thinking, the theories, the realization that we're all basically human no matter how different we look and act. But then we started working later and later into the evenings, and he started telling me how boring his wife was. It got pretty spooky. Then he asked me to go with him to some anthro conference in San Diego. It was a week long, and he explained, with this stupid little smirk, that he could only afford one hotel room. 'Two beds, of course,' he said."

"What did you do?" Joy asked.

"I told him that I would be happy to go with him to that conference. It would be a great experience for me," Dawn said. "But I also told him flat out that I would need a room of my own, a return airplane ticket, and the right to bring along a friend to keep me company."

"I'll bet the pervert *loved* that idea," Crystal said.

"He did—until I explained that my friend was Hank Henry," Dawn said. "Hank was a right tackle for the school's football team. He was about six-and-a-half feet tall, about three hundred pounds, and he shaved his head. I met Hank through my church group—we weren't dating or anything— but I figured it would scare this professor off."

"Did it?" Logan asked.

"It's hard to say," Dawn said. "His conference plans suddenly fell through—surprise, surprise—but a little while later, he told me he was going to the Australian Outback to do some fieldwork. He asked me to go with him, and he said he could only take one tent! By then, though, the summer was over, and I got out of there."

The pirates continued to share their stories. Arthur had worked on a highway crew, hired by a manager who wanted him to show the union workers how to apply themselves. "Three months of anger and hatred from my coworkers," he said.

Jesse had worked for a roofer in southern Florida, where the afternoon sun would melt the shingles and the soles of his boots. "I fell off a roof once," he said. "Everybody laughed. 'You damn near killed yourself, boy!' they said. I was lying on my back on the ground. Those people had no loyalty."

Joy had worked for a daycare center. "It was me and twenty kids for most of the day," she said. "I had to hire the older kids to help me with the little ones."

Crystal had worked for a private investigator, shooting videotape from the passenger seat of his Volkswagen. Marietta had worked for a modeling agency, showing off preteen dresses on creaky catwalks in the middle of aging malls.

When most evenings drew to a close, the pirates would stand one at a time, say goodnight, and wander off to the bathroom. When they returned, dressed in some assemblage of T-shirts and shorts or cotton pajamas, they would climb into their bunks, roll over to face the wall, and go to sleep. The last two or three to end the evening would clean up the glasses and blow out the lamp.

But things had begun to change. Signs of affection were becoming more open. On this night, for instance, Crystal stood up, stretched, and announced that she was going to take a walk on the deck before turning in—and Logan stood also. Crystal sat back down, and Logan sat back down. Crystal stood again, said goodnight quickly, and glowered at Logan. Logan stayed in his seat.

When Arthur was ready to call it a night, he announced that he was going to check the anchor before going to bed. Marietta offered to help him. Arthur climbed the steep gangway and disappeared into the night, and Marietta was close behind him.

It was a hot night with little breeze. The humidity made clothes sticky with moisture. Arthur stood in the bow and studied the anchor chain. It seemed to hold its original position, so the ship clearly wasn't adrift. He turned—and Marietta was close to his face.

They kissed for a long time. Then Marietta made her move. "I'll join you tonight in the captain's quarters," she said. "Just you and me. We'll be together, alone, and private. It'll be romantic."

Arthur shook his head. "I don't think we—"

Marietta kissed him again. It was a deep, involved, physical kiss, and it made her intentions clear. "Let's go," she said. "No one's going to care."

CHAPTER SEVEN

THIRTY-FIVE KNOTS OF FREEDOM LEFT

Breakfast the next morning was unusually quiet. Tension was sharp in the air, and it was Logan who broke the silence. "So," he asked Marietta, "did you, like, totally sleep well?"

"Just fine," she said.

"Oh, good," Logan said. "Yea! Whee! We've all been totally wondering how comfortable that captain's bed is—"

"It's absolutely luxurious," Marietta said, brushing her blond-streaked hair. "I haven't felt that good in a long time."

"—but of course," Logan continued, "since we're all, like, stuck out here in these little bunks, we thought we'd never know. I think you two ought to totally give us updates every morning. That way we'd know if, you know, the mattress was beginning to sag, or if the pillows were losing their plumpness. In fact, I think you should start a newsletter. You could give us the undercover scoop every morning."

"Or you can damn well sleep in the bunks like the rest of us," Crystal said to Arthur. "Who the hell gave you permission to move in there in the first place?"

"Who said I *needed* permission?" Arthur shot back. "If it weren't for me, you'd all be sleeping with mommy and daddy this summer. If any of you are so petty that you're upset over something this stupid, then that's your problem. I mean, we're out here in a boat that isn't ours, we dumped a body overboard without telling anyone he was dead, we're stealing the stuff we need, we all might end up in jail—and you're all bent out of shape because I sleep in the big bed. Well, maybe you all should just grow up. I really don't—"

"Apology accepted," Dawn said. She faced the rest of the crew. "Listen, everybody. After McKinley died, Arthur moved into the captain's quarters. I agree with Crystal"—she fixed her green eyes on Arthur—"it would have been nice if Arthur had talked about it without just moving in like that. But we're all okay. We just have some talking to do right now. We don't—"

"Oh, please!" Crystal snapped. "Look, gang, here's the deal. From now on, I say we rotate who gets to sleep in the captain's quarters. In fact, I say we rotate who gets to be the captain! Arthur got this trip started, but that doesn't make him Emperor for Life."

Oh, shit, Arthur thought. Mutiny. Crystal's trying to strip me of my position. What should I do? What would Dad do? "Never show weakness," he would say. That's it. Never show weakness.

"Forget about it," Arthur declared. "I'm the captain, and that's my room."

Good. Strong and forceful. Back her down. The minute you open the door, she'll come charging right through.

"And another thing," Arthur continued. "I'm tired of having you always whining and complaining about my being the captain. I'm the captain, and the job isn't open. If you don't like it, leave the ship."

"If I don't like it?" Crystal charged. "I've got news for you, pal. If anyone's leaving this boat, it's you."

Call her bluff. Force her to play her hand. When she loses in front of everyone, she'll stop being such a pain.

"Let's put it to a vote," Arthur demanded. "If you win, I'll move out of the cabin and we'll all share the captain job. But if you lose, you have to leave the ship."

Good one, Arthur thought. There's no way she'll—

"You're on!" Crystal said.

Dawn shook her head. "This is a bad idea, folks," she said softly. "We're not going to vote on who we'll listen to or where people get to sleep. Crystal, we respect your thinking just as much as anyone's, and we all know that our days on board the *Dreadnought* would be a lot harder if you weren't here. And Arthur, we know you got us started on this wonderful adventure, and we appreciate your willingness to make tough decisions. Let's chalk this up to a minor storm at sea and forget it ever happened. Okay?"

The chilly silence that followed, Dawn knew, was the best response she could have hoped for.

☠   ☠   ☠

Several days later, the crew staged another raid on lavish yachts. It went flawlessly. Crystal and BillFi were the raiders again, and Jesse worked the oars. The first target was a white cabin cruiser with a flying bridge and a mass of radio and navigational gear blinking expensively all over it. Crystal had been the scout, and she noted that the owners never bothered to lock the door. She and BillFi slipped inside and found a surprisingly stark interior—little furniture beyond a simple table and a sleeper sofa. The fridge, though, was crammed full of food—mostly sausages and cheese—and the raiders filled a duffel quickly.

The second target was a white sailboat with the words *Never Better* scripted across its stern. The key was hidden under a hibachi grill, and the interior was similar to many others they'd seen: the beds, the galley, the tiny bathroom. There wasn't much food on board, but there was a significant amount of cash stashed underneath one mattress. "Looks like a thousand dollars!" BillFi whispered as he slipped the money into the duffel. "Must be a thousand dollars!"

They went on to hit a third yacht to fill out their bags. It was a powerboat, white and impressive on the outside, with a flying bridge and teak deck. Inside, though, the galley and cabins were cluttered with dirty clothes, empty beer cans, and stuffed ashtrays. The blue smell of cigarette smoke clung to the air, and streaks of ash littered the unmade bed. Food and dishes filled the tiny sink.

"Owners left more than an hour ago. Walked. Said something about a bar with a big-screen TV," Crystal said.

"This is disgusting," BillFi said, pushing his glasses and looking around the disheveled room. "It's a mess. It's disgusting. We should steal a lot of stuff, just to clean up in here."

"Better yet," said Crystal, "we should take what we want and torch the fucking place. We should—"

Rustle. Something in the bottom of the small forward closet moved. It rustled again.

"Oh, great," BillFi said. "Just great. This place has rats. I hate rats. The rats in the shelter where I lived were huge. They were huge. I hate rats."

From beneath the heap of clothing on the floor of the closet came a sound. Half scream, half whisper. Hoarse and tired and scared. Not the sound of a rat. More like a mew.

"It's a cat!" Crystal said. "These people keep a cat in their closet."

She grabbed the clothes and tossed them aside. There, in a small cage, was a tiny kitten. It was gray with darker gray stripes. Its ribs corrugated its sides, and its face was gaunt and tight. It mewed again.

The cage, not much bigger than a shoebox, had an empty water bowl and a small paper plate for food. The food left in the plate was dry and dark brown, and it wiggled.

"Fucking maggots," Crystal muttered. "This is sick. Let's get out of here."

"Sounds good to me," BillFi said. He picked up the cage, holding the wires from above to keep his hands away from the damp sticky newspaper on the bottom of the cage. He followed Crystal up and out of the boat and into the clear night air. They carried their haul down the dock to the dinghy, where Jesse waited for them.

"Brought you a present," BillFi said. "A present. It's for you."

Jesse took the cage gently and looked inside. The kitten stared back, afraid and hopeful, mewing quietly. Jesse opened the cage door and pulled the tiny animal to freedom. He cradled her in his giant multicolored hands and petted her softly. He held her to his face, nose-to-nose, and stared into her eyes.

"We found it on one of the ships," BillFi explained. "It was badly treated. Badly. So we took it. We took it, and you can have it."

Jesse shifted his weight and moved forward in the dinghy. "You row," he said. Shrugging, Crystal took the oars and rowed back toward the *Dreadnought*. As the dinghy cut through the black water, Jesse grabbed the empty filthy cage with one hand and hurled it angrily overboard. It hit the waves with a splash and sank quickly. Jesse's eyes never left the tiny kitten that trembled in his oversized hands.

☠   ☠   ☠

The sky was clear, and the moon was three-quarters full. Dawn stood at the rail of the *Dreadnought* and watched the sparks of moonlight dance on the ripples in the sea as the dinghy approached. It was a magical sight, and the air was cool, the stars bright; she lost herself in the weaving, waving light.

She thought about home. Along about now, in late July, her father would be in Zurich scheduling press conferences to alert the media to the latest robotic inventions cranked out by the company he worked for. Then he'd be off to Israel to alert the media there, and then he'd be back home for a few weeks, then off to some other place. To alert the media.

Dawn smiled. It seemed a bit ironic—her father off hawking the virtues of cutting-edge technology, while she lived on a wooden boat and ate her meals by the flickering warmth of an oil lamp. But maybe the irony wasn't all that surprising. After all, ever since her mother died and she left for boarding school, she and her father had hiked down different paths.

He had wanted her to be a lawyer. That plan, and his constant travels around the globe, prompted him to consider boarding school for Dawn. A few years ago, they spent several weekends visiting schools, reading brochures, talking to teachers and students, and evaluating matriculation lists. Dawn was dead-set against the idea of going away to school. Not only was she tempted by the freedom of living at home while her father was away, but she also hated the idea of immersing herself in the stuffy world of the super-rich and super-bored. She had met enough of the upper-crust to know that she didn't want to join it.

Then they learned of Mount Greylock School. In Dawn's eyes, at first, it was barely a contender. It was founded by an evangelical Christian minister, but Dawn considered herself a firm believer in a more Hindu/Islamic/pagan/Baha'i sort of religion. Okay, she'd admit, it varied. And it wasn't very tightly nailed down. But it meant something other than sterile churches and expensive "show off" outfits and empty rituals and hollow words. There was no way she'd be happy in an evangelical school.

Plus, Mount Greylock was huge. The school had an enormous campus, and it was in western Massachusetts—not exactly the most glorious place Dawn could think of.

Her opinion changed swiftly when she visited the school. There was no dress code. No "I'm richer than you are" feeling. And no forced religion; the students studied the religions of the world and learned what they could about all of them. They talked a lot, and they shared their ideas, and they seemed genuinely happy.

And they sang. The whole school sang. Once a week, the students would gather in the chapel, share announcements and stories, and sing. The school song was "Jerusalem," the lyrics by William Blake; it was a song of hope and freedom, of building a beautiful, all-embracing world "amidst these dark, satanic mills." For someone who held Socialistic/Libertarian/anarchistic views—okay, it varied—Mount Greylock seemed like home.

It was while Dawn was at Greylock that she was inspired by her teachers to figure out what she really wanted to do with her life. One English teacher encouraged her to imagine her retirement party. What would she be proud of? What would she shrug off? "And," the teacher had said, poking her bony finger at Dawn's heart, "what would you regret?"

It was then that Dawn knew she didn't want to be a lawyer. She wanted to be a musician. A singer. And play the dulcimer with small wooden hammers that dance like lovers' fingers. She got a job in the school's library—without telling her father—and she saved enough money to buy a beautiful maple dulcimer and a cordless microphone headset that allowed her to play and sing at the same time without the intrusion of a standard mike. She practiced hard, often late into the night, and she performed at a few small parties. Finally, she demonstrated her art for the students at the all-campus meeting.

"Won't your father kill you?" her roommate asked over pizza late one night. "I mean, you're supposed to be going into law."

"My father has plans and goals," Dawn answered. "His plan is for me to be a lawyer. But his goal is for me to be happy. I think I can convince him that his *goal* is more important than his plan."

☠   ☠   ☠

The moonlight. Something was wrong with the moonlight. Dawn stared down into the water, trying to figure out what her eyes were telling her.

The light seemed to linger too long. As the dinghy approached, Crystal would pull on an oar, and the moonlight would reflect off the ripples. But then the light somehow persisted for just an instant after she lifted the oar and swung it, dripping, back for another stroke. Dawn watched intently, then she got it.

"It's glowing!" she called out. "The water is glowing!"

The others peered over the dinghy's rails. Sure enough, somehow the water glowed every time an oar swept along it, then faded back to black a moment later. As the dinghy bumped against the side of the *Dreadnought* with a barnacle crunch, Dawn grabbed a life ring and tossed it with a splash over the side. She held onto its line and gave it a vigorous shake, causing the ring to swish and wiggle in the water. All around the ring, the ripples glowed a rich yellow-green.

"Amazing!" Arthur said, joining Dawn at the rail. "What is it?"

"Plankton," Dawn offered. "There are certain kinds of plankton that glow when they're stimulated. We must be in some kind of plankton field."

"It's . . . kinda beautiful," Arthur said.

"Yeah," Dawn said. "It's beautiful—and alive." Jesse clambered up the side of the ship and disappeared down to the galley, hunched over something in his hands. Crystal and BillFi handed the duffels up the ladder, and Dawn hauled them over the rail. When the dinghy was empty and everyone was on board the ship, Dawn turned to Joy. "How deep is the water here?"

"About twenty-five feet," Joy said.

"Any rocks?"

"*Aqui?* No. Not here," Joy answered. "At least I don't think so. We wouldn't have anchored here if there were."

Dawn smiled in the moonlight. "That's what I wanted to hear." She walked over to Arthur, who still stood at the rail of the ship and stared at the black water. "Hey, Arthur. Have you ever done anything really impulsive, really crazy? Have you ever done anything just because it seemed wild and fun at the time, without worrying about what people might think?"

Arthur looked away from her. "Sometimes," he said. "You might even say recently. I'm still trying to figure out what to do about—"

"Lighten up," Dawn said, poking her long fingers into his ribs. "A little controversy is good for the soul." She stepped back, smiled again, and faced the crew. "I'm *glowing* swimming," she said. "Anyone up for a skinny dip?"

She kicked off her shoes, shook off her clothes, bounded to the port rail, and disappeared over the side.

A short, baffled, breathless moment later, Arthur and the others ran to the port side. They looked down, and there was Dawn, swimming the backstroke, whooping and laughing and splashing.

"This is great!" she said. "Come on in!"

Around her the sea glowed with living light. The moon still sparkled on the waves, and the plankton beamed with every move Dawn made. She was swimming naked in liquid starlight.

A moment later, an intensely glowing splash marked the spot where Crystal had jackknifed into the sea. Then Logan held up the gin and lemonade he had poured for himself. "You only glow around once in life!" he declared. He downed the drink, dropped his clothes to reveal his pale and pudgy body, and jumped awkwardly over the side.

BillFi grinned. "To boldly glow where no one has—has *glawn* before?" He shrugged, took off his clothes, and hurled his tense, overwrought frame into the sea.

It didn't take the others long to "glow overboard," as Joy put it. She jumped over the edge wearing her shorts and T-shirt. Jesse remained below, and the only other people who stayed on board were Arthur, who volunteered to mind the ship, and Marietta, who announced that she didn't do such stupid stuff.

"Besides," she said to Arthur, "it'll be nice to be alone again."

Arthur looked out at his friends, swimming, splashing, and spinning glowing webs in the water. Then he looked back at Marietta. He wondered why he ever found her attractive in the first place. She never seemed to have fun, unless she was putting down someone else. She never took crazy risks or did something goofy just for fun. Everything was calculated. Her whole look—the tight skimpy outfits, the tan, the streaked hair, the makeup, the carefully arranged poses—had been sexy at first, but now they just seemed desperate and needy. Dawn, on the other hand, was confident and intricate and *deep*. She didn't need to cozy up to some guy to get attention.

Arthur shook his head. He could see now that Marietta was attracted to him because he was the captain, not because she liked him. She craved power and superficial success, just like—

Arthur took a sharp breath. Just like my father, he thought.

"Actually," he said, "I think I'll go swimming after all." He took off his clothes and climbed up on the rail. The wind felt magical and powered against his bare skin.

"Hey, Arthur!" Dawn called out. "Glowing our way?"

"Glowing down!" Arthur shouted. He pushed off the side and arched gracefully in a gentle, dying-swan dive. He knifed through the chilly water and shot down fifteen feet below the others. At the low point of his dive, he spun around and looked up.

The saltwater stung his eyes, and the murky water blurred the images. But the sight above him nearly knocked the breath from his lungs. Overhead the water radiated with shimmering plankton, and the bodies of his friends danced in dark silhouette, treading in energized air. As they swam together and apart in kaleidoscopic patterns, Arthur imagined that they were all part of one body. He could see legs and arms release from one person, attach onto another, then move away again like contra dancers changing partners. New people were formed, then dissolved, then reborn again as the black shapes teased and wrestled and embraced. He tried to figure out which one was Dawn, but these bodies had no names. They were the absence of light in human form, solid shadows in ethereal plasma. He pushed against the buoyancy of the water and watched for as long as he could, then he kicked to the surface to join in.

☠　☠　☠

Arthur surfaced next to BillFi, who was treading water next to Dawn. Arthur shook the water from his hair and wiped his eyes, then he looked around. BillFi followed his eyes in the darkness, noted their gaze, and swam out of the way.

"This is great!" Arthur said to Dawn. "It's like swimming in a cloud. It's like Saint Elmo's fire underwater."

"Like what?"

"Saint Elmo's fire," Arthur said. "It's kind of like the northern lights all around the rigging of a ship. If it happens to the *Dreadnought*, I'll show it to you."

"Well, you might think this is Saint Erwin's fire—"

"Saint Elmo," Arthur said. "Saint Elmo's fire."

"Well, you might think this is Saint Elmo's fire," Dawn said, "and you might think it's plankton, but I think it's the sea goddess." She whirled in the water, hitting Arthur with the spray from her ponytail. "The sea goddess is giving us her light as a way of showing us her blessing."

Arthur smiled.

"Don't laugh," Dawn said. "When you live on a ship, the blessing of the sea goddess can save your life." She spun around and swam toward the others. "Logan," she called out, "let's play freeze tag. You're it!"

Logan wasted no time. He thrashed out and tagged Crystal in an instant, then he swam off after Dawn. Crystal cursed and tread water and watched as Logan closed the gap.

"Gotcha!" Logan wheezed as he tagged Dawn in a splashing flurry of glowing seawater. With flailing strokes from his soft legs and loose arms, he hunted down the others in a hurry. He caught Joy easily, but BillFi put up a surprising struggle, thrashing a storm of spray that kept Logan sputtering and squinting, until he kicked in one final swift lunge and caught him, too. That left Arthur. Catching his breath, Logan turned and swam toward him like a hungry shark.

"You're good at this," Arthur said with a grin, "but not good enough!" Arthur dove, intending to surface near BillFi and set him free so he could release the others. But Logan was crafty. He held his position, treading water gently, and watched the glow that betrayed Arthur's position underwater. When Arthur came up for air, Logan was waiting for him.

"Gotcha!" Logan shouted as he tagged Arthur. "You're it!"

"Oh, shit," Arthur said.

Logan grabbed him by the shoulders. He spoke softly but urgently. "Don't be totally stupid. I made sure to tag everyone else first. Now you're it. Bing! Freeze us all and, you know, save Dawn for last. Don't blow it."

Arthur smiled. "Thanks," he whispered. Then much louder he shouted, "Gotcha!" and tapped Logan on the head.

The others swam off in all directions. It didn't take

Arthur long to freeze BillFi and Joy, and Crystal acted bored and "let" Arthur tag her. All that remained was Dawn. Arthur swam toward her slowly, and she backed off at the same pace.

"Never in a million years," Dawn taunted, grinning broadly, the glowing water hugging her naked body. "You'll never catch me."

"I can catch you any time, any place," Arthur said. "Like now!" He faked a lunge toward Dawn. She screamed and thrashed away. When the glowing water settled, Arthur was exactly where he had been. Smiling. "Anytime, anyplace," he said. He began pressing forward once again.

A few minutes later, Dawn had slowed, and Arthur was close. Then Dawn looked past his shoulder. "Where did everybody go?" she asked.

"Like I'm going to fall for that," Arthur said, not turning around.

"No, really," Dawn insisted. "They're all gone."

Arthur glanced quickly behind him. The gentle waves were unbroken, and Crystal and Logan were the last to climb the ladder up the side of the *Dreadnought*. "Aha!" Arthur said, turning quickly back to face Dawn. "They fled! They couldn't stand the sight of your impending capture."

"Impending capture? Don't you mean *depending* capture? As in, depending on whether I let you catch me?"

"*Let* me catch you?" Arthur said. "I could tag you with one arm tied behind my back."

"You couldn't catch me with one arm tied behind *my* back," Dawn said with a grin. "I'd bet my queendom on it."

Arthur kicked forward and tagged Dawn's shoulder. She didn't try to flee.

"I retire as the reigning champion," he said. He hadn't lifted his hand from her skin. He let it slide down her back, and he encircled her waist with his arm. "However, I'd be happy to discuss that queendom offer."

Dawn leaned against him for a moment, then she shook her head and pushed him away.

"Discuss it with Marietta," she said. She swam back to the ship, leaving Arthur alone in the chilly water.

☠ ☠ ☠

In the dining room, Jesse stroked the tiny kitten on the table. He pushed a plate of milk toward her, making soft sounds of comfort and welcome. The kitten sniffed the milk and backed away. Jesse petted the kitten some more, slowly and without tension, and then offered the milk again. The kitten took a quick lap with her little pink tongue and backed away again.

The other sailors watched from around the table, dripping and drying from their skinny-dip. They were mesmerized by the impossibly small kitten and her powerful multicolored protector. For a long time, no one said a word.

As Jesse coaxed the kitten toward a long-overdue meal, BillFi told the story of the animal's rescue from the depths of a stench-filled closet. Joy offered a prayer for the tiny bundle of life, and Dawn's eyes filled with tears and anger over her mistreatment.

"It's not living on *this* ship, is it?" Marietta said.

Jesse bolted to his feet. He glared down at Marietta. "Yes, she is," he declared. He added nothing. He asked nothing of the others. He simply sat back down and focused his attention on the kitten.

Dawn was delighted at the new addition to the crew. "What will you call her?" she asked.

Jesse looked up.

"Ishmael," he said.

The next day, as Arthur was trying to decide where the *Dreadnought* should go, he called BillFi over to the chart table in the captain's quarters. The two of them studied a chart of the Gulf of Maine carefully, looking over the islands and the bays and the rivers, and then BillFi closed his eyes. He jabbed a finger at the chart, held it steady, and peeked.

"Haddock Island," he said to Arthur. "On the west side of Muscongus Bay. I don't know why, but that's where we should go. We'll meet someone there who can help us. That's where we should go. I just know it. Don't ask me how."

Arthur gave the helm to BillFi and ordered the crew to weigh anchor, and then he took over the bow watch. "We're heading west," he boomed. "To Haddock Island."

The day was cold, damp, and blustery. The crew, chilly and stiff in their oiled slickers and miscellaneous sweaters taken from a deep hold in the ship's bow—except for Marietta, of course, in her elegant cashmere—hoisted every sail, and the *Dreadnought* made good time. The swells were twelve feet high, and cold spray blew vigorously across the decks. Except for BillFi and Arthur, everyone scurried below to Joy's hot chocolate.

On the bow, Arthur straddled the bowsprit and held tightly to the rigging. He didn't mind being out in the cold wet air while most of the others were warm and sleepy down below. It was all part of leadership. He smiled to himself. Leadership, he was discovering, had its ups and downs—kind of like the bowsprit on a swelling sea. He would have loved to go below, pour himself a hot chocolate, and swap big stories and thin lies with the laughing crewmates around the table.

But someone had to be on bow watch, and Arthur knew that when the going got tough, the real leaders assigned the tough jobs to themselves. Builds confidence and trust among your subordinates, his father would say. They can't complain about the jobs you assign them if you give the tough tasks to yourself. It's a kind of investment. A few hard hours at a tough task, and you reap weeks' worth of willing obedience. Leadership is about being smart. Don't ever forget that.

Arthur sighed and stared across the windswept waves. Sometimes he would rather just be one of the gang, but something inside him forced him to push, always push for the top, the front, the pinnacle. It's not enough to try out for the school play—you have to audition for the lead role. It's not enough to play football for your school—you have to be the starting quarterback. It's not enough to date nice girls—you have to date the prettiest, the most popular, the most *sought-after* girl in school. There's no point in winning the consolation prize, his father would say.

"Just once," Arthur said out loud, shivering and holding tight to the rigging, "I'd like to forget about being first. I'd rather just be happy."

There was no one around to hear him. The wind was stiff and loud, and his solitary words were whisked out across the waves and scattered among the droplets of foam. Arthur didn't really want anyone to hear him, but he did want some nice company. If Dad were here, he thought, he'd tell me to go downstairs and invite Marietta to join me at bow watch. He'd say that she is the prize, and that I should go collect her. But just once, it would be nice if something I wanted came to me, on its own. I'm tired of chasing the things I'm supposed to want.

The bow, especially on a day like today, would make a perfect place for an important, intimate talk. He stared out at the sea, watching for lobster floats and hoping he didn't look like he was eager for her to join him. He tried to look like he was settled in, comfortable, ready for a long haul under rough conditions, capable and independent, mysterious and strong. That way, when she came up and approached him, he could pretend that he wasn't starving for her company. He could pretend that he was an island, a rock against the sea, gracious to those around him but needing no one else to complete his own self-definition.

He could pretend.

But Dawn never came.

CHAPTER EIGHT

THIRTY-THREE KNOTS OF FREEDOM LEFT

By early evening, the *Dreadnought* had dropped anchor on the southeast side of Haddock Island. The water was only six feet deep there, and the ocean bottom tapered up to a small pleasant beach. The island rose steeply toward a single hill at its center. There were no buildings or boats in sight.

The winds were still strong, so the crew dropped a second anchor before scurrying below to change into warm sleeping clothes and enjoy hot tea and conversation around the dining table. Arthur and Dawn exchanged comments from time to time, and Dawn responded warmly. Like she'd treat a friend. Arthur could hardly stand it. Marietta, on the other hand, sat next to Arthur and laughed loudly at all of his jokes.

Sipping tea at the table, beneath a sign that read, "Count it all joy, my brethren, when you meet various trials, for you know that the testing of your faith produces steadfastness—James 1:2–3," Joy turned to BillFi and looked puzzled. "Didn't I hear you say that we would meet somebody here?" she asked. "Somebody who could help us? There's nobody here at all."

BillFi nodded, pushing his glasses. "When I get a feeling, I get a feeling," he said. "They're never wrong. When I get a feeling, I just follow it. I don't know why I get them. I don't know where they come from. Sometimes I can even make myself get a feeling. Most of the time, though, they just happen. But they're never wrong. We'll meet someone here. Count on it."

"BillFi," Arthur said. "When you said this person could help us, what did you mean? We don't need any help right now. Do you think something's going to happen—something that will make us need his help?"

BillFi shrugged. "Don't know," he said. "I don't know how he'll help us. But he will. He will. He'll help us get through something. I don't know what. Just something. Maybe everything. I don't know."

"Bill's my friend," Jesse said. "He's always right about these things."

Arthur nodded. "I'm beginning to get that," he said.

Marietta laughed loudly, then stopped when she realized that Arthur meant what he said. "I'm beginning to understand it, too," she said with a serious expression.

Arthur stood up. "I think it's time I went to bed," he said.

"Goodnight, Arthur," Marietta said. "Sleep well."

"Goodnight, everyone," Arthur said to Dawn. He entered the captain's quarters by himself and closed the door behind him.

Jesse was the last to head for bed. He sat at the table in his underwear, drawing permanent-marker tattoos across his chest. His body was mostly covered now—both feet, both legs up to his upper thighs, his left and right arms from the biceps down—and he found a strange delight in the power that the body art gave him. He had always been strong, but the tattoos, he thought, gave him a presence that he had never felt before. He had worked so hard his whole life to be invisible, to be alone, to be enduring, that he had never noticed how exhausting that effort could be. With the tattoos, though, invisibility was impossible. He had no choice but to let people know that he thought for himself.

When the intricate lines and corners and curves across his chest had advanced to his satisfaction, Jesse tucked the markers under his mattress and returned with his bent and ragged copy of *Moby Dick*. A piece of torn cardboard marked his place more than halfway through the thick book. It was his third lap; each time through, as soon as he reached that last sentence, he turned to the front and began again. He was captivated by the descriptions of the South Pacific and the powerful intensity of the Maori warriors. He escaped into the descriptions of the whales and the ship and the sea, even with a real ship and sea all around him. He could feel the pull of adventure grip his heart as he read. The shelter in the Bronx seemed especially far away when he was reading the book.

Jesse put the book on the table and walked, naked except for his underwear and the swirling colors that covered his body, to the kitchen. He dug a can of tuna out of the deep shelves and opened it.

The sound brought Ishmael skittering out from underneath a bunk. The kitten, plumper now and overflowing with energy, scrambled across the galley floor and hurled headlong between Jesse's ankles. Jesse poured the juice from the tuna can into a paper bowl, pried out a few chunks of meat with his finger, and bound the can in plastic wrap. He carried the bowl back to the dining table, taking careful steps as Ishmael darted under and between his feet, mewing hoarsely.

Ishmael jumped onto the table with a burst of awkward kitten grace, and she lapped at the beige liquid in the bowl.

Jesse ran his hand down Ishmael's thin but sturdy spine. "You're welcome," he said softly, petting the kitten with a gentleness that contradicted his size and the tight tendons in his forearms and legs. "Feel like reading?" The kitten responded with a little kitten sneeze.

Jesse opened *Moby Dick* and began reading out loud, in a quiet whisper, to the kitten. Ishmael finished off the tuna and sat between Jesse's arms, licking her paws and cleaning her face. She dug her sharp little claws affectionately into Jesse's muscular arm. Jesse smiled and kept on reading.

In her bunk across from Jesse, Joy looked up from her Bible. In her heart, she knew that God was on this ship, bringing love and small reassuring islands of peace from time to time. She vowed to remember this moment, this feeling, and never forget that she couldn't have experienced it—couldn't have helped bring it about—if she had quit. Dawn lay in the bunk above Joy, chanting quietly and thanking the Goddess of the Sea for the gentle rocking and cool fresh air that made sleep so pleasant.

And alone in the captain's quarters, Arthur took off his shoes and reached toward the wall. He untied another knot from his calendar ropes, and he noticed that even though the summer was still young, it was clipping along at a good pace. Eventually he would be down to his last rope, that final knot growing closer and closer. He wasn't at all sure what he would do once it arrived.

He blew out the oil lamp and slid into the broad chilly bed.

☠   ☠   ☠

Crystal woke everyone early the next morning. She had just come back from her sunrise swim; her short blond hair was wet, and she had a towel wrapped around her shoulders for warmth. Her thin muscled legs bristled with goosebumps in the chilly morning air. "Hey, everybody," she said. "We're not alone. Get the fuck up! There's another boat here. It might be the guy BillFi was talking about."

It took the crew little time to leap out of their sleeping bags and scramble up the gangway. The morning was thick with silvery fog, and everyone blinked and strained their eyes to cut through the murky air. Tucked up close to the beach was a small dark-green sloop with rust-colored sails. The boat had a tiny cabin—not much longer than a bed—and the rails were cut low to the water.

On the beach was a woman dressed in ragged khaki shorts and a faded blue chambray shirt. She was thin and fit, her skin the color of mahogany and her gray-and-black hair loose and coarse. She was tending to a small smoky fire. She looked up at the *Dreadnought*, nodded a stiff greeting to the eight onlookers standing on deck, and turned her attention to a black frying pan resting on the sand. She squatted next to the pan, sitting on her bare heels, and scraped something out of a tin can. She put the pan on the fire and began breaking driftwood into more kindling.

"Is that the 'guy' you were thinking about, BillFi?" Crystal asked, putting her hands on her hips.

"It must be," BillFi said. "It has to be her. There's no one else around. It has to be her."

"It's a bit foggy—BOOOO-oooo—" Logan said, giving his best impression of a foghorn, "but can I, like, interest you all in breakfast on the beach?"

Two quick dinghy-trips later, the crew was on the beach. As Logan built a fire and cracked eggs against the edge of a battered frying pan, Arthur stepped forward and introduced himself to the woman in the ragged shorts.

"Bonnie," the woman said, shaking Arthur's hand briefly and turning back to her cooking. She was frying some pancakes in the pan, and she had pushed another tin can into the near edge of the fire. She had ashes in her hair and black streaks of soot on her hands. Around the second toe on her right foot was a diamond ring, and around the same toe on her left foot was a golden band; both rings were wrapped with string to make them fit. "I only have enough food for me."

"That's okay," Arthur said. "We have plenty. In fact, we were wondering if you'd like to join us."

Bonnie looked straight into Arthur's hazel eyes, unimpressed. "I don't mind eating with you," she said, "but I'll eat my own food. I don't take anything from anybody unless I can replace it." She turned back to her cooking without a word.

Dawn shrugged and helped Logan with the sausage. They worked quickly, and by the time Bonnie's pancakes were dark brown and littered with bits of sand and ash, Logan had served the *Dreadnought* crew sausage and eggs, cereal with powdered milk, biscuits he had made by winding thick dough around a stick and heating it over the fire, and grapefruit juice. Bonnie peeled her pancakes from the pan, and she pulled the tin can, bubbling with a thick seafood stew, out of the fire with her fingers.

"So what brings you out here?" Arthur asked.

"Wind, mostly," Bonnie answered. She shoved half a pancake into her mouth and stared out at the ocean while she chewed.

"No, I mean, are you sailing around here for fun, or are you doing something?" Arthur asked again.

"I'm always doing something."

Arthur smiled. He straightened his back, leaned forward, and looked Bonnie right in the eye.

"Hey, Bonnie," he said in a deep but gentle voice, "we've been out here for weeks. A little conversation won't kill you."

"There's nothing to tell," she said. "Nothing that would matter, anyway. Not everybody has a story that—" She cut herself off. Then she shrugged and shook her head. "Oh, what the hell. Maybe you kids can learn something from it." A trio of black flies buzzed around her face, but she paid them no attention. Eventually they swooped over to bother Logan.

The *Dreadnought* crew ate silently as Bonnie talked.

"Hell, it's probably been three years or so, but I used to be a marketing executive. For a big appliance company in New York," she said, scratching the back of her neck. "I didn't live in New York—never could stand the city. No, I lived with my husband and twin sons in a real nice house near the beach in southern Connecticut. The job paid well, you see. And I was good at it. We made dishwashers, toaster ovens, dehumidifiers—all sorts of things. And I could direct the marketing so well that our sales force barely had to work at all. The orders just came pouring in."

She drank a deep swig of the steaming stew, swallowed quickly without chewing, and continued. "I took the train into the city every morning at six forty-five, and I rode it back home again at six-thirty in the evening. I'd go home, take my shoes off, pour myself a vodka tonic, and spend the evening sitting in a chair, reading the *Times*, and trying to breathe normally.

"Our nanny was doing a good job of raising our kids, we had a housecleaner and cook who kept the place neat and made all our meals, so I would just sit back and relax. Let my pupils dilate. Loosen the muscles in my jaw. My forehead. My ribs. And I'd do nothing. I guess that's what the problem was. If I wasn't in the office, I wasn't doing anything. I wasn't being anything. Just drinking myself to sleep and trying to recover for another big day of pushing microwaves.

"I started to get scared. I began to think that maybe life was just gliding by, and that someday I'd wake up—and I'd be old. I'd be retired from work, my kids would be grown and gone, and I'd be sitting at home with my husband and nothing to do, nothing to remember but a long series of signed purchase contracts. My life would have passed me by, and I wouldn't remember any of it. I'd pray and dream and hope, I'd exercise and travel and cry—but nothing would work. My life would be over, and it wouldn't have mattered at all. I wouldn't have mattered at all. I guess that thought just got a little intense for me."

She accepted the mug of grapefruit juice that Joy offered her "in exchange for the story."

"So one day, I just did it. Just changed tack, you might say. I was waiting in line for the train one morning—it was a Wednesday, I think, early in the spring. Kind of chilly. Anyway, all of a sudden, I just stepped out of line. It seems like a small thing, I know, but you have to understand what it meant. *I stepped out of line.* I wasn't going to play the game anymore. Suddenly nothing was the same. I walked back to my car, drove home, and freed myself from my pantyhose and my push-up bra and my killer business suit. I changed into jeans and an old flannel shirt I found deep in the back of my closet. Then I took a big black marker, I picked up my beige briefcase, and I wrote 'I QUIT' in block letters on the side. Mailed it to my office. Then I drove to the bank and took out all our money. We had saved some, but not a lot. It was enough, though, for a down payment on a 52-foot sailboat that was strong enough to take me and my family all the way around the world."

Arthur grinned. The freedom of this summer's adventure was thrilling, and he could appreciate others wanting that experience.

"It was going to be great," Bonnie continued. "We would sail east to Ireland, all around Great Britain, then down along the European coast toward the Mediterranean. We'd stop a lot, see things, do things together, learn some languages, maybe get jobs here and there to bring in some money. I figured we could survive just fine. We'd go all the way around the world like that. Just me and Malcolm and the boys. It was going to be great."

She cackled awkwardly.

"The divorce happened in a hurry," she continued, her eyes glittering coal. "My husband told the judge about my sudden 'behavior change' and was able to get most of our assets and custody of the twins. They sold the sailboat to get the down payment back, or some of it, anyway. I was left with a little bit of money and a BMW. Still, it wasn't so bad. I was able to sell the car and buy this little sloop, and that's really all I need in this world. Just myself and my little sloop. She's a good boat. So anyway, now I just sail around. In the summers, I work my way up the coast to this area, and when fall comes, I head south toward the Georgia islands. I can always find stuff to eat, and I give people sailing lessons whenever I need a little money. I figure some day I'll get real sick, or I'll have a bad accident, or a killer storm will come along and catch me off guard—and that's when I'll die. But I'll *never* wake up and find myself old and bitter, with nothing to show for my life but a billion sold appliances. No, I figure the end will probably come quickly out here, and I'll smile on my way out."

Bonnie gulped down the last of her stew and put the can in the sand. The fog swirled, lightening at times and then growing thick again. No one said a word. Bonnie chuckled again.

"And you know what's really funny?" she said. "I could be rich again in three days. Anytime I choose. Hell, I could probably get rich enough to lure my husband back, get another chance to be a mother to my kids. Unless he's married again. I don't know. But money is evil. It's really the devil. People say the devil is some guy with horns and a pointy tail. But he's not. He's green. He's fashionable. He's expensive. Selling your soul to the devil is *literal*—and almost everyone has a price. So I don't even look for it. I don't want it, and if I found it again, I'd just leave it right where it is." She shot a glance at the teenagers around her. Marietta returned her stare with eager interest.

Arthur looked around at the others. They seemed as puzzled as he was, so he decided to ask. "If you found *what* again?"

"The treasure. Blackgoat's loot. You've heard of him. Some pirate two hundred years ago. Sailed all around here. Vicious bastard. Raided a lot of boats and killed a lot of people. All for the love of money. The love of the devil. He got a lot, too. A whole lot of loot. Hid it in a cave on a little island east of here. I came across it looking for mussels for my stew. You'd never know it was there—you'd never know the cave was there—unless you were right on top of it. But I wasn't about to poison my life with that stuff again. I decided then and there to leave it be and to head off in my little sloop. Money will kill you, and I didn't want it back in my life. So I left it there. Vicious stuff."

Then Bonnie stopped talking, and she wouldn't say anything more about her life. Whenever Arthur asked her a question, she answered with a one-sentence, vague reply. Eventually she stood, brushed the sand off her shorts, and walked away. "It's time for my nap," she said. "No point in sailing in the middle of the day. Too hot, if you ask me."

She waded into the ocean, swam out to her sloop, and flopped over the side. Without a wave or a look back, she ducked down into her cabin.

The *Dreadnought* crew was silent, thinking about all Bonnie had said. Then Marietta spoke. "Did she say *treasure?*" she asked.

☠   ☠   ☠

The crew spent the rest of the morning and much of the afternoon swimming, reading, and gathering fuel for the lunch fire. Crystal practiced windsprints up and down the beach, tightening her already tight abs and quads and glutes. Jesse sat on a rock near the water's edge and drew colorful swirls on his shoulders and touched up lines that were fading elsewhere. He had covered almost every part of his body that he could reach, and the abstract patterns gave him a frightening and primitive air. Not that Bonnie had given him a second glance, though. She didn't seem to think he looked odd at all.

Dawn recognized the gift offered to her by the Goddess of Quiet Mornings, and she took the opportunity to stand on her head. It was a form of meditation she had always wanted to try, so she found a secluded bit of beach some distance away from the others—and she planted the top of her head on the sand. Bracing herself with her hands, she kicked her feet into the air.

"Mantra," she said to herself as sand trickled from her feet to her face. "I need a mantra. Can't chant without one."

She thought through words that felt in tune with the foggy sun below her feet and the waves that curled upside-down before her eyes. *Pineapple*, she thought. No, that's stupid. How about *flip*? No. Too silly. *Three*, like three-dimensional. Seems like the right idea, with me upside-down and all. But not quite right. Oooff! She struggled to keep her inverted balance. The strange movement of the waves before her didn't help. "Goddess, help me," she said out loud. And then she waited.

"*Alignment*," she said firmly. It was just the right word. "Alignment," she chanted, grateful for the blessing she had received from the Goddess of Insights. She began to repeat the word in a loud whisper.

"Alignment.

Alignment.

Alig-nment.

Ali-gnment.

A-line-ment.

A line meant."

The word began to sound strange, alien, wrong. She continued the chant, and she watched as the odd world laid out before her—a ground made of blue air, a world made of churning seawater, a sky made of straw-colored sand—shifted and melded and merged in her mind. It was at this level, where all that matters is earth and water and fire and fog and life and gravity, that Dawn felt her spirit soar in breaching leaps around her. This is what she was after. This is why she did this. This is why she chose to stand on her head on a beach and chant while others were tossing Frisbees and building fires and talking about hidden treasure. There are other worlds in this world, other universes in this universe, other realities in this reality, and Dawn felt them pull her in deep and passionate ways.

When Dawn had finished her journey into alternate dimensions and was lying on the sand, trying to get the spots in front of her eyes to disappear, Joy and Logan roasted several long skewers packed tightly with chicken, peppers, and onions. The *Dreadnought* crew gathered around the fire, and as they ate, they talked about the lure of the treasure Bonnie had mentioned.

"It's a lie," Crystal said as she helped herself to a chicken shish kebob. "It's some fucking line she's come up with to find out whether she's talking to brainless tourists or not. If we fall for it—if we ask her where the treasure is—she'll know we're just stupid kids, and she'll laugh about us for months. Besides, think about it. Do you really think she knows where a fortune's worth of treasure is, and she doesn't want to get her hands on it? Her story is cute, but it doesn't make sense. And whoever heard of a pirate named Blackgoat?"

"I have," Dawn said. "I read about him in one of the books in the captain's quarters. Bonnie is right. He sailed all around here, he gathered a lot of gold and things from the ships and towns he raided, and he was nasty. We're lucky he's not around today."

Crystal shook her head. "Okay, so he was real," she said. "That doesn't mean anything—and it sure as hell doesn't mean that Bonnie stumbled on his treasure and then just left it there. I'm telling you, it's a test. I think we should try to pass it like adults."

"And I think we should grab the treasure while we can," Marietta said, pulling a piece of chicken off her skewer with her teeth. "This is the chance of a lifetime. We meet up with some crazy lady who's decided that money is evil. Then she tells us that she left behind a treasure worth a fortune. And you're telling us that we should just ignore it? Not me. I want to know where the treasure is, and I want to go get it."

The crew nibbled food off of sticks and debated the issue well after lunch. Then Bonnie emerged from the cabin of her sloop and began to rig her sails. It was time for a decision. It was time for leadership. Joy dug the Saint Christopher/Saint Francis coin from her pocket, but Arthur cut her off.

"It seems to me," he said, standing up and watching the little sloop, "that we're missing the point. It doesn't matter whether the treasure is real or not—if we don't pursue it, we'll never know. And it really doesn't matter what Bonnie thinks of us—we'll probably never see her again. So the question really boils down to whether we're willing to go over to Bonnie's sloop and ask her about it. That doesn't seem too tough. She's the one who told us so much this morning. It seems only natural to want to know more. Some of you might disagree, but I'm *going* to go over there and talk to her about it. And besides, we're forgetting one important thing. BillFi said we'd meet someone today who would help us. I'm beginning to trust his crazy little hunches, and I figure Bonnie can't help us if we don't follow her lead. Who knows—we might find enough treasure to let us stop stealing stuff from boats."

Arthur rowed the dinghy alongside Bonnie's sloop. Through the light fog, he could see Bonnie moving around down in the tiny cabin.

"Ahoy," he said. "Permission to come aboard?"

Bonnie was packing some odd pieces of scrap fabric into a box. She didn't look up. "I can't exactly stop you, can I?" she said. "I don't carry a gun."

Arthur wasn't sure whether that constituted an invitation or not, but he tied up the dinghy and scrambled over the side. He sat down in the boat's shallow cockpit.

"Got a glass of water down here for you," Bonnie said, still without looking up. "Don't mind sharing water. It's free in most places around here."

Arthur glanced over at the towering *Dreadnought*, shrugged, and climbed down into the cabin.

The space was almost entirely filled by a table that had a wooden bench on each side. There were no other rooms. A counter along one wall held a small green camping stove that was surrounded by a clutter of spice bags and stained mugs. The air was musty with odors of mildew, sweat, and cooking fuel. Tucked under the bow was a roll of soft crumbling foam; Arthur guessed that Bonnie rolled it out each night across the table and slept right there. He sat down on the port bench as Bonnie filled two smudged glasses with water from a plastic jug. She put the glasses on the table and sat down opposite Arthur.

"So," she said, "you're here about Blackgoat."

Arthur accepted the glass and took a drink. "Well, you got us kind of curious," he said. "What exactly did this guy do?"

"Who are you kids?" Bonnie asked, her gaze solid. "What are you doing out here?"

"We're part of a camp," Arthur said. "A summer sailing camp. Our instructor sent us out for a while on our own to improve our sailing skills."

Bonnie looked out the tiny porthole at the looming mass of the *Dreadnought*. "Bullshit," she said. "Try again."

"It's true," Arthur insisted. "We all signed up for a sailing—"

"Yes, yes, a sailing camp," Bonnie interrupted. "That much I believe. But your instructor didn't trust you with that ship just so you could learn a jib from a jenny. What happened? He dead?"

Arthur gasped. "What? Um, no. Not—"

"Okay, so he's dead," Bonnie said without a smile. There was no hint of accusation or fear in her eyes. "You kids kill him, or what?"

Arthur took a deep breath and told Bonnie the whole story—McKinley's oppression, his suicide, the burial at sea.

When he was done, Bonnie chuckled. "Slid him off a plank, did you?" she asked. "Right into the ocean? Hell, probably serves him right." She chuckled again. "Okay, you've done your bit. I'll tell you about Blackgoat and his treasure."

Arthur returned to the beach about an hour later. He said he'd tell everyone about Bonnie once they were back on the *Dreadnought*.

A short while later, sitting at the head of the dining table, Arthur smiled at the others.

"What did she say?" Marietta asked. "Did she tell you where the treasure is?"

Arthur nodded. "She told me where it is, and she told me how to find it," he said. "It was weird, though. I got over there, and she acted like she was expecting me. She poured us glasses of water, and we sat in the cabin and then she asked about McKinley. I told her the truth. She didn't seem to care. Then she told me all about Blackgoat and the things he did around here. He was a serious pirate for about twenty years before he finally disappeared. People say his ship went down in a battle with an English warship, but no one knows for sure. All they know is that he suddenly stopped raiding boats."

"Fine," Marietta said, "but what about the *treasure*?"

"When she was done telling me about Blackgoat," Arthur continued, "I asked her about the treasure. She just sighed, took out an old chart, and pointed to an island. Then she said, 'You'd better hurry—sail all night, if you have to. Tomorrow morning, the tide will hit a half-year low. That's when you have to be there. You can't see the cave normally. It's underwater.' Then she rolled up the chart, put it away, and pointed toward the door. 'You got what you came for,' she said. 'Goodbye.' The next thing I knew, I was back in the dinghy."

"What do you think all that meant?" Joy asked.

"I don't know," Arthur answered. "I think we disappointed her—" he tried to look tough, "but I got what I wanted."

Dawn opened a chart, and Arthur explained that the treasure was hidden just southeast of Vinalhaven Island, right in the middle of Penobscot Bay, on the southwest side of a small piece of rock called Brimstone Island.

"*Brimstone* Island?" Crystal asked. "Give me a break."

"That's what she said," Arthur replied. "It's right here on the chart. She said we should approach from the south, just west of the Buffalo Ledges. We'll come to a steep cliff with rocks at the base. The cliff is maybe a hundred feet high. At the base, way below the high-tide line, is a small opening that leads back into the rock. It's only visible when the tide is really low, like it will be tomorrow morning around eight o'clock. The cave goes back and up, and then it opens into a large room that Bonnie says has a big old box in it. She said that's the treasure—and she said she hoped, for our sake, that we don't ever find it."

"She might get her wish," Dawn said. "We'll never make it to Brimstone Island by eight tomorrow. The wind has died down a lot, and even if we sailed for another five hours today and three hours tomorrow, I don't think we'd reach it. The only way to get there in time is to sail all night."

Logan grinned. "We could totally sail all night," he wheezed. The others nodded.

Dawn fixed them all with a serious stare. "Do any of you know the first thing about sailing at night?" she asked. "Can you tell a chime from a gong, just by the sound? You'd better, because that's how you know which buoy you're passing. Do you know what an occulting light is? You'd better, because otherwise you'll never know which marker you're looking at. If you mess up, we could all go down with the ship."

"Now wait a minute—" BillFi argued.

"BillFi," Arthur said, "Dawn is right. If we want to sail all night, we'll have to learn about night navigation. I'm sure Dawn can teach us—she's been reading McKinley's books. And whoever is at the helm should have someone else up there with them—it would be too easy to fall asleep by your-self. Besides, the night will be long, cold, and lonely. Some company will make it a little easier."

Logan shook his head. "Well, then maybe we shouldn't, you know, do this at all," he said. "Why don't you go back and, like, ask Bonnie when another really low tide will be. We'll just make sure we're at the island then."

"That'll be tough," Arthur said. "She's heading out to sea."

He pointed to a porthole. The rust-colored sails of Bonnie's sloop were far off in the distance, fading in the foggy air.

"Great," Logan said. "Then I totally change my mind. I think we should forget all about this stupid treasure myth and just keep on sailing, you know, the way we have been. It's probably all just a whoop-de-doo fairy tale anyway."

"No," Arthur said. "I say we find out what's going on. This is too great an opportunity for all of us. Just think—we spend the summer by ourselves at sea, and we end up rich in the process. We could each own an island with a mansion on it. We're going to find that treasure if we have to sail all night, and as—"

"Yeah, yeah," Crystal interrupted. "As your captain."

Arthur nodded seriously, trying to look authoritative. "Yes," he said in his strongest low voice. "As your captain, I say we go for it. Who is willing to take the helm for the night sail?"

No one said a word. The possibility of treasure was tempting, but not if it meant standing on a cold deck all night, staring at charts and buoys and markers and lights, and trying to keep the ship from hitting an invisible rock. Arthur looked around the group, one face at a time. Never be afraid to let them see you mad, his father's voice flashed across his mind.

"This is great," Arthur said to his crew, scowling in the best anger he could muster. "You spend all our money in Freeport, so now we're raiding yachts to stay alive. Now we have a chance at some treasure. Some of you want the treasure, but no one's willing to do the work. Fine. That's just fine. If you won't do it, I will. I'll sail all night. I'm not afraid to do what has to be done."

An instant before Marietta could say a word, Dawn spoke up. "I'll do it with you," she said.

CHAPTER NINE

With Crystal at the helm, the *Dreadnought* turned to catch the gentle fog-laden wind and head toward Brimstone Island. Marietta was supposed to be on bow watch, but as usual, she talked someone else into doing it for her. Logan took the job, happy for the chance to serve on duty with Crystal. He clung to the bowsprit rigging and watched for lobster pots with a self-conscious air of importance and gravity. He pointed out every lobster float he saw, even some that were harmlessly off to one side or the other. Anything to keep in contact with the vigorous and daunting Crystal Black.

Logan even took to calling out the color, position, and distance of each lobster float: "Pink and green, eleven o'clock, like, fifty yards!" "Solid orange, three o'clock, twenty yards!" "Black and white, one o'clock, like, thirty yards!"

Then he paused for a long time. His voice sounded different when he called back again. "White with orange and blue stripes, ten o'clock—and coming right at us!"

Puzzled, Crystal glanced off to port. Through the fog she could see the gray outlines of a Coast Guard cutter heading toward them.

Logan scrambled back to the cockpit. "What do you think?" he asked Crystal, standing just a bit too close. "Are they, like, after us? Do you think they know about McKinley? Should we, you know, say anything to them? Hold our course? Turn and head back to port? Totally raise a white flag and surrender? What do you think we should do?"

With an exasperated sigh, Crystal said, "Look, Logan, they probably don't even—" But then she stopped. Logan's only courage, she thought, comes from a pathetic booze bottle. He wouldn't understand the value of a showdown. "We're holding our course," Crystal declared.

Logan dashed downstairs. Arthur was in the captain's quarters, getting some sleep before the night sail, and Dawn was in her bunk, reading sailing books. Joy was in the galley, extracting life from the ancient kerosene stove with a level of violence that seemed to clash with her peaceful attitudes. The other Plunder Dogs were sitting around the dining table, playing poker.

Logan threw open the door to the captain's quarters and shouted, "Get up top, everyone! The Coast Guard is, like, bearing down on us! We're in a lot of trouble!"

Arthur leapt out of bed and dashed up the ladder. The others followed right behind him. They gathered on deck and watched the cutter grow steadily nearer.

"Crystal," Arthur said, "what's up?"

"Coast Guard cutter," Crystal said flatly. "I hear the U.S. owns one or two of them. Tend to cruise around the offshore waters. Big deal."

The nervous energy on deck sank a bit in the fog. "Is it trying to intercept us?" Arthur asked.

"It's been on a collision course ever since we first saw it," Crystal answered. "Doesn't mean a thing. The worst thing we could do now is turn around and run away. I'm holding my course."

"Maybe we could just steer a little bit away from them," Logan wheezed. "You know, like, slowly and innocently. Like nothing was wrong."

Arthur shook his head. "Bad call. If we turn away, they end up crossing our wake just a short way behind us. Too close. I think we should turn a bit toward them, so we cut in behind them and let them sail on their way. That way, if they do want to talk to us, they'll have to change course—and we'll have some time to plan what we're going to say."

"Forget it," Crystal commanded. "I'm at the helm, and I've already told you what we're doing. We're holding our course."

"But didn't you say it was a collision course?" Joy asked.

Crystal nodded with a tight grin. "You bet your ass," she said. "Sailboats have the right-of-way over powerboats—right Dawn?"

Dawn nodded.

"So let's make *them* turn away," Crystal said.

The nervous energy on deck returned. All eyes watched the foggy cutter growing ever larger. Five minutes passed, and no one on the *Dreadnought* said a word.

"Crystal," Logan broke the silence. "I think this is a totally bad idea."

"So?" Crystal shot back.

The cutter came closer, holding its course. Crystal held course as well, staring defiantly at the giant mass of metal moving toward them. She could see a few of the Coast Guard sailors on the cutter's deck, leaning against a rail and watching the *Dreadnought*. They seemed calm.

The distance between the two ships dwindled. Arthur thought he could see the Coast Guard sailors grinning as the cutter maintained its collision course. The *Dreadnought* stayed true to course as well.

Closer . . . .

Closer still . . . .

BOOOOOOOOPP! The cutter sounded an air-shredding blast on its horn—and then slowly began to turn to starboard. Crystal held the *Dreadnought's* wheel steady, letting the cutter pass close to the schooner's stern. As the *Dreadnought* slipped in front of the cutter's wave-slicing bow, Crystal saluted to the sailors on deck. They waved back, and one of them, laughing, blew her a kiss.

☠   ☠   ☠

As the afternoon faded toward evening and the fog dwindled into mist, Arthur noticed BillFi on bow watch by himself. With nothing else to do and feeling too awake to get another nap before the all-night sail, Arthur climbed out onto the bowsprit and joined his little friend.

BillFi was not cut out for bow-watch duty. The incessant swelling up and plummeting down, crashing and soaring and crashing again made his stomach uneasy, and the powerful curve of his glasses magnified the effect. He held tightly onto the rigging with a tension that was both reassuring and draining. He tried not to throw up, and he kept reminding himself that he felt no immediate danger coming.

One day a few weeks ago, when BillFi had been on bow watch, Logan had decided to be irritating. He called up to

BillFi and asked whether he could see the lobster float at eleven o'clock. BillFi, clinging to the rigging and paying attention only to his digestive processes, shouted back, "Yes! We're clear of it!"

But there was no lobster float. Logan got a shallow chuckle out of the joke, and when BillFi realized the trick, he felt even more out of his element on this narrow shaft of wood that jutted perilously over the jaws of the icy waves.

Arthur lay back across the bowsprit rigging across from BillFi, laced his fingers behind his head, and stared up at the swaying and bobbing clouds. He let the minutes go by lightly, with the crashing of the ocean and the breathing of the wind, hoping to put BillFi at ease through the sheer force of relaxation. After a long moment of calm, Arthur asked BillFi the question that had been bothering him since they voted to stay on board the *Dreadnought* after McKinley died.

"So, BillFi," Arthur said. "I've been thinking about how all this should end. Eventually we'll wake up one morning, and it will be the day our families are supposed to pick us up in Rockland. They'll all be there at the dock waiting for us, and they think they're going to thank McKinley for taking such good care of us all summer. The way they imagine it, we'll pour across the gangplank, all sunburned and skinny and happy, with stories to tell about how much we learned on board. We'll talk about discipline and leadership and strategy, the tools young people need to get ahead in this world. And they'll give things to McKinley—nautical clocks and model square-riggers and checks—to show their appreciation for a wonderful and educational summer.

"But you know, that's not how it's going to happen. At some point, they'll all show up at the docks, and we'll sail toward them in the *Dreadnought,* and we'll tie up and march out and greet them. No McKinley. No stories about the Leadership Cruise. No—what will we talk about? Raiding yachts and stealing food? Bobbing for other people's lobsters? Drinking rum and listening to music and having a great time? How do we explain that to our parents? What do we say when they ask about McKinley? What's the *first thing we do* when we sail up to the dock?"

The conversation was having the desired effect. BillFi was more relaxed now, leaning against the rigging and listening to Arthur's thoughts. He was silent for a long time, staring out at the friendlier sea. Then at last, he spoke.

"I don't know what we'll do, Arthur," he said. "I don't know what. I just don't know. But I'm sure that something will come to us. Something will come. We'll know what to do. Then."

☠   ☠   ☠

The night grew chilly, and the *Dreadnought* crew drifted below. The last to leave Dawn and Arthur alone was Marietta, but at about ten o'clock, she abruptly stomped down the gangway and disappeared. The air was damp but clear, and the sound of conversations bubbling up from the dining hall blended with the rhythmic churning of the bow through the low even swells of the sea. The horizon had long since transformed, slowly, from a vista of pine-green land and slag-green water to a shimmering slice of tiny lights, blinking in cacophony, confusing and tranquil and mesmerizing. The air was crisp with the smell of salt and seaweed. Dawn took the first turn at the ship's wheel, her baseball cap pulled low with her ponytail flopping out behind, and Arthur sat on the railing next to her. At her commands, he jumped down to adjust the sails.

"We need to sail on a bearing of 150 degrees until we see a red flashing light straight off to the east," Dawn said. "It should flash every four seconds, according to the chart. It has a whistle on it, too, but we're still too far away to hear it. Once that light is directly east, we should turn and head straight for it."

"Okay," Arthur said, "but I see a million lights. Which one is right?"

They searched the broad band of lights off the port beam, trying to spot a small red flash that repeated every four seconds. Arthur counted "one thousand one, one thousand two, one thousand three, one thousand four" out loud as Dawn fixed her gaze on one red light after another. She checked and dismissed radio-tower lights far in the distance, running lights of other ships, even occasional taillights on cars that flickered as they passed behind houses and trees on shore.

"Wait a minute," she said. "I might have it. Keep counting."

"One thousand one, one thousand two, one thousand three, one thousand four. One thousand one—"

"Are you sure your count is right?" Dawn asked. "The light I'm looking at is blinking too slowly."

Arthur turned on a small flashlight, checked his watch, and counted again.

"That's it!" Dawn said. "It's right over there." She pointed off the port bow and counted with Arthur. "One thousand one, one thousand two, one thousand three, one thousand four—we found it! It looks like it'll be due east in about half an hour or so."

"Thank goodness," Arthur said. "That counting was really getting on my nerves."

Arthur sat back down, and the two settled into comfortable silence. The night began to take on a magical air, the way it does when friends huddle close outdoors. The sky overhead, undimmed by streetlights and unsoftened by clouds, was a sea of blackness sparkled with a billion tiny suns. Looking up past the main mast, Arthur tried to imagine just how far away those stars were. He knew that the light that reached his eyes had left the stars long ago—they had all moved by now, and some had exploded or sputtered out altogether before he was born. There was life out there—he could feel it—but suddenly, he and Dawn were the only living souls in the universe.

"Do you ever wonder where we're going?" he asked.

"Sure I did," Dawn answered. "But then we found that blinking red light."

Arthur laughed. "That's not what I—"

"I know what you meant," Dawn said with a sweet smile. "I was kidding. Sure, I wonder where we're going. And think about what that means. Where will we be tomorrow? Will we find this cave, climb in, and discover huge amounts of treasure? Or will we miss the island entirely and wind up sailing into a crowded harbor on Vinalhaven? And what about the day after that—where will we be then? And next month? And next year? And a hundred thousand years from now? Where will Arthur Robinson and Dawn FitzWilliam be a hundred thousand years from this exact moment? Will we be here on Earth as other people? Or will we have disappeared for good? Or will our sun have exploded or sputtered out altogether?"

Arthur looked at Dawn. He was sure he hadn't said that out loud. He studied her pretty freckled face as she watched the lights and minded the wheel. He hadn't felt this content in a very long time.

☠ ☠ ☠

"Oh, hey," Arthur said as he hunched against the chill of the night, "I found the *Dreadnought*'s log when I was poking around McKinley's cabin earlier. I was trying to find more books about night sailing, and I found this old logbook."

Dawn grinned. "Well, go get it!" she said. "Let's find out what this old boat has been up to."

Arthur scrambled below and returned with a large leather-bound book. He clicked on his small flashlight and skimmed the pages quickly.

"Wow!" he said. "This ship has done a lot of things before we found her."

"We have time to kill," Dawn said. "Tell me where she's been."

Arthur settled himself down on the rail. "Let's see," he said. "Looks like she was built in 1892—way more than a century ago! She was launched on June 12, and they really did smash a bottle of champagne on her bow when she slid into the water."

"I love it!" Dawn said. "I think a great boat like this deserves a fancy beginning. What was her maiden voyage? Exploring the South Pacific?"

"Not exactly," Arthur said. "She hauled boxes of stuff from Maine to Newfoundland."

"Oh," Dawn said, disappointed.

"The boxes were filled with ordinary stuff—fabric, paint, candles, rope, bullets. One box even had a bunch of shoes in it. And she sailed back from Newfoundland filled with tons of salted cod."

"Gross," Dawn said, wrinkling her nose. "I hope they didn't put any in *my* bunk."

Arthur laughed. "It looks like the *Dreadnought* hauled boring cargo for a long time," he said, flipping through several pages of the logbook. "In the 1950s, she was sold to a guy named Dr. Hector. I don't see his first name in here at all. He sailed the ship to Annapolis, Maryland, and it looks like he hired a bunch of people to fix her up for a sailing trip around the world."

"Cool!" Dawn said. "Maybe we should do that sometime."

Arthur glanced at her. He wasn't sure how to interpret that, so he turned back to the book. "Looks like Dr. Hector died in 1974, and a bunch of people in Gloucester, Massachusetts, turned the *Dreadnought* into a tour boat." He chuckled. "They offered dinner cruises in Boston Harbor— lobsters and all. Just like we've been doing, sort of."

Dawn smiled. "Sort of."

"Then the ship was a kind of floating classroom in Mystic, Connecticut," Arthur said, turning the pages. "It looks like that's when they built our bunks down below, for the students to sleep in. Then she was a bed-and-breakfast off Long Island, and then she was a museum in Provincetown, Massachusetts."

Dawn patted the steering wheel. "You've gotten around, haven't you, girl?" she said to the ship.

"And then she was sold to Howard McKinley," Arthur said.

"And then McKinley killed himself, and a bunch of teenagers took over the ship, and now we're sailing off in search of pirate treasure," Dawn said. "Maybe we should write our own entry into the log."

Arthur smiled. "Let's wait to see how it all turns out," he said. "Maybe we won't want to admit to anything in writing." Arthur riffled back through the pages of the logbook, and a piece of paper fell out. He pounced on it before the wind could blow it overboard.

"What's that?" Dawn asked.

Arthur studied the paper. "It's a letter from McKinley, and it's addressed to his mother in Greencastle, Indiana."

"What does it say?" Dawn asked.

Arthur read the note in the dim beam of the flashlight.

May 18

Dear Mother,

I know it has been a long time since I wrote last. Sorry about the delay. I've been working very hard—lots of irons in the fire, you know. The business world is tough, but I'm making it work for me. I think Dad would have been proud.

"Was his father dead?" Dawn asked.

"I guess so," Arthur said.

"I didn't know that."

I took the money I made from the Tex/Mex restaurant and used it to launch the Norfolk Notebook, sort of a touristy, family-oriented, general-interest regional magazine. You would like Norfolk, Mother. It's a nice city.

Anyway, the magazine was so successful that I was able to sell it after just a couple of years. And now I've parlayed that money into the biggest venture of my life. I'm buying a fleet of tall ships, and I'm going to use them to help young people learn the value of discipline and respect. The ships will operate like

> summer camps on the ocean, and students will be
> able to test themselves against the elements and learn
> a lot about their ability to overcome obstacles.

"Well, that *is* what he said in the brochure, anyway," Dawn said. "It didn't work out that way, but I guess that is what he was trying to do."

> I've already bought the first ship. It's called the
> Dreadnought, and it's a beauty. It's a 156-foot
> schooner, and it was—

"A hundred fifty-six feet!" Dawn exclaimed. "Not even close!" Arthur nodded and continued:

> It was once used as the personal yacht of the Duke
> and Dutchess of Wales. It's in perfect condition, and
> I think the students who live on board will be able to
> feel how they ought to behave. This ship commands
> respect, Mother, and I'm sure the others in my fleet
> will do the same.

> I am taking a bit of a gamble, though. I have used all
> of my liquid assets to purchase the ship, so I'm count-
> ing on everything going well. If I don't get enough
> students, or if something goes wrong during the first
> summer, things could get a little tight. I wouldn't
> have to sell the ship or anything—I've planned too
> well for that to happen—but if the first summer
> doesn't go well, I might have to take your advice.

Working for Pete at the lumberyard would be hard,
of course—being the older brother, I have always felt
that I could do a better job at getting ahead—but if
I have to do that for a few months to keep my cash
flow in the black, then I guess I'm ready for that.

Arthur and Dawn were silent for a long moment. Then Dawn took a deep breath.

"Good Goddess," she said softly. "When the counselors walked out, he decided to die rather than admit failure and work for his little brother."

Arthur shook his head. "It was worse than that," he said, his breath gently fogging in the chill air. "He would have had to admit that he had been a failure at everything—the restaurant, the magazine, the *Dreadnought*—and he would have had to admit that his brother—his *younger* brother—had done better by working his way up through the ranks at a lumberyard. And he would have had to admit that he had been lying to his mother about his success at business. It obviously was more than he could face."

"Does he say more?" Dawn asked.

Sorry—I had to put this letter aside for a few days
so I could hire the crew for the Dreadnought. They
are a fine bunch of young men and women. They're
skilled sailors, compassionate counselors for young
people, and they're absolutely loyal to me. When
you're sailing around the North Atlantic trying to
whip a bunch of teenagers into shape, it's good to
know that your crew is behind you 100 percent.

*After I get a few more ships in my fleet, I'm going to
set up an around-the-world cruise. I'll take the
Dreadnought, and I'll sell berths on it for a hand-
some price. The teens who go with me on that trip
will have the experience of a lifetime. And I'll make
sure to save one cabin for you, Mother. Maybe the
nice one in the bow, with the extra-large porthole
and the private bathroom.*

"What's he talking about?" Dawn asked. "No one has a
private bathroom, and the portholes are all the same."

"McKinley had a strange relationship with the truth,"
Arthur said.

*Well, I have to go now. I'm expecting a call from
some financial backers who might want to buy into
my latest venture. I get a lot of these calls, but most
of them aren't worth bothering with. People always
wait until something is a success, you know, before
they're willing to invest in it.*

*Give my best to Peter. And please don't tell him about
my cash-flow problems. If things go as planned, I'll be
able to buy his lumberyard in a year or so.*

Howard

"Why do you suppose he never mailed it?" Dawn asked.
"Sheet in the main, please."

Arthur tugged on the main sheet and sat back down.
"Maybe it was too full of lies, even for him," he said. "I don't

think I could send something like this to my mother. It would feel so . . . pathetic, I guess."

"I have an idea," Dawn said. "When this summer is over, we should write to McKinley's mother and tell her what a wonderful commodore he was. It might make her feel better."

Arthur shook his head. "I don't think so," he said. "From the sounds of things, she's been lied to enough."

Around one o'clock, Arthur took the wheel, and Dawn walked briskly around the deck to warm up and keep herself awake. She jogged in place for a bit, taking tiny little nowhere steps while her ponytail flopped behind her, and she beat her fists against her shoulders. Her feet thumped on the deck with a hollow bass note. She went below to get an extra sweater, and when she returned, she had a strained look on her face.

"What's the matter?" Arthur asked. The ship had passed the first red marker, and Arthur was keeping an eye on another one, dead ahead, that was flashing a regular twice-then-once pattern. He was supposed to keep that marker to port as well, but not by much; the ship was nudging through Two Bush Channel, a narrow passage with ledges and small islands littering the water on both sides.

Dawn sat down on the stool. "Maybe I shouldn't say anything, but you're bound to find out sooner or later," she said.

"What?"

"It's Marietta. Everything is dark and quiet down below, but Marietta isn't in her bunk," Dawn said.

Arthur groaned. "She's probably in the captain's quarters."

"She *is* in the captain's quarters," Dawn answered. "Logan was in there, too. They left the door open, but I think she was trying to talk him into spending the night with her in there. Kinda in your face, isn't it?"

Arthur was silent for a long time. He watched the red light flash twice-then-once, twice-then-once, and he felt the gentle rocking of the deck as the *Dreadnought* rose and fell with the swells.

"It didn't work, though," Dawn said. "Logan left in a hurry, all red-faced and glancing over at Crystal on his way out."

Arthur chuckled. "Hey, it's not like I'm in charge or anything," he said. "She can go after anyone she wants. Marietta and I were close in certain ways, but it never felt like much of a relationship. I was probably an idiot for even spending time with her."

They sailed on for almost ten minutes without saying a word. The only sounds were the whisper of the wind and the creaking of the ship.

Then Dawn kissed him lightly on the cheek. "It *is* a magical night, isn't it?" she said.

☠   ☠   ☠

At three o'clock, Dawn had the helm, and the night seemed endless. She and Arthur had talked about many things during their long sail alone, and the conversation turned to the hazards of ending relationships.

"So what's the worst you've ever been dumped?" Dawn asked Arthur.

"The worst?" he said. "Hmm, I'd have to think about that. Wait—I've got it. Her name was Christie. We'd been dating for about two months. This was maybe a year and a half ago. But she was seriously into drugs and heavy partying, and I wasn't, so it got to be tough after a while. I was about to break up with her, but she beat me to it. At least, I think she beat me to it. I'm still not totally sure."

"What happened?"

"Well, we went to a restaurant for lunch one Saturday, and we met up with one of her friends there. This friend had a magazine with her—*Cosmo,* or something—and the next thing I knew, the two of them were pointing at pictures in the magazine and giggling. They were clearly enjoying some kind of joke that I wasn't allowed to see, but I tried to pretend it was cool. Apparently, this wasn't the response Christie was hoping for. So she began to point to pictures—still without letting me see them—and whispering to her friend that the people in the picture looked like me. She whispered it loud enough for me to hear, and the two of them kept on giggling. They even got into a pretend argument about which of the pictures looked more like me. Then they giggled some more.

"Finally, I figured I'd been polite long enough. I told her to stop, because this wasn't very fun. She kept on doing it. So finally, I grabbed the magazine and took a look for myself. There were two pictures on the page. One was a little baby, and the other was a painting of a pine tree. That's when it struck me that the whole thing had been set up—Christie had asked her friend to meet us at the restaurant and go through this little drama just to make me angry."

"What did you do?" Dawn asked.

"I took my cue and left the restaurant, and the next night, I asked someone else to go to the movies with me. I saw Christie a little while later with some other guy, too. It was all pretty stupid. I don't know why we couldn't just talk about the fact that we weren't working out. Anyway, about a year later she got pregnant and dropped out of school, and I figure I'm better off without her," Arthur said. "How about you? What's the worst dumping you've ever gone through?"

"Okay," Dawn said, "let's see. Yes. Robert Amadeus Thompson. Notice how his initials spell 'rat'? Anyway, he and I had been seeing each other for more than half a year. Then one day, we're at his house, and no one else is home. Which was cool—we had been there alone before. Well, he told me there was something in his room that he wanted to show me, and he asked me to wait in the living room for a few minutes first. He went to his room, and a couple of minutes later, he called for me. I went in, and he was lying on top of his bed, absolutely naked. I said, 'What is this?' And he said, 'Come here, baby—it's time.' Well, I had never slept with anyone before, but I wasn't all uptight about sex. But I was *furious* that he thought he could simply declare that 'it's time' and expect me to rip my clothes off on his command. I told him to forget it, and he told me that if I didn't go through with it, he would go out that night and sleep with one of my friends. I told him to remember a condom and think about baseball. Then I left his house."

"What happened next?"

"Well, I found out later that he had tried to hook up with three different friends of mine, and they had all turned him down," Dawn said.

Arthur shook his head. "Doesn't count," he said. "I'm not sure whether you dumped him or he dumped you. So you owe me another story—what's the worst job you've ever done of dumping someone else?"

Dawn nodded and told Arthur about the time she wrote a "Dear John" letter to her boyfriend but accidentally stuck it on the wrong person's locker at school. Arthur told the story about how he called his girlfriend, broke up with her, then was so upset by her crying that he changed his mind. A week later, things still weren't working out, so he had to do it all over again—and he changed his mind again. The third time worked, though. "I broke up with her just before my family and I took a four-week vacation to the Rockies," he said. "By the time I came back, she was dating someone else and had told everyone that she had to break up with me three times to get me to go away."

He also told Dawn about the couple he had seen on the dock when he arrived to board the *Dreadnought* in Rockland. "I keep flashing back to them, when I let my mind wander," he said. "They weren't kissing or anything. Just holding each other—and staring more deeply into each other's eyes than I thought was possible. I don't know why they got to me like that, but they did. It's like they were seeing a part of the universe that I didn't know existed."

Dawn smiled. "Maybe that's what love does," she said. "Makes your universe a little bit bigger."

☠   ☠   ☠

Arthur and Dawn were still awake and on duty at five o'clock, but their perceptions of the world were suffering from the long chilly night. The *Dreadnought* was cruising through open water between Matinicus and Vinalhaven, crossing an open stretch of the Gulf of Maine. The swells were higher, and navigation was simple. Still, it seemed like the night would never end, that there was no one else alive on earth, and that the ocean was all that was left of the world.

"I have an idea," Dawn said, stepping aside as Arthur took his turn at the helm. "I played this game at a party once. It's a lot of fun."

"At this point," Arthur said, "I'm ready for anything. Especially sunrise. But a game sounds good, too."

"Okay, here are the rules. We can talk about anything we want to, but we can only talk in questions. Get it?"

"No," Arthur said.

"Don't you understand the rules? How could they be simpler? Can't you see how easy it is to talk only in questions? Do you want to give it a try?" Dawn said.

"What if I don't?" Arthur said with a grin.

"Do you think that'll bother me?" Dawn said.

Arthur glanced at her. "Am I correct in believing that you aren't bothered by much?" he said.

"Should I be?" Dawn said, grinning.

"Maybe. Oh, shit," Arthur said.

"Can you say that as a question?"

Arthur smiled. "Oh, shit?"

Dawn shook her head. "Can't you do better than that?"

"Why should I?"

"Shouldn't you always try to do better?" Dawn said.

"Hmmm . . . aren't goals overrated?" Arthur said. "Whatever happened to just doing what you wanted to do?"

"Can't you do that now?"

"Are *you* free to do anything you want to do?" Arthur said.

"To be free, do you have to be *totally* free?" Dawn said.

"Isn't 'partial freedom' a contradiction in terms?"

"Why isn't it enough to be free in spirit?"

"Is that all you want to be?" Arthur asked.

"What else is there?" Dawn said.

"Can't you be free in body, too?" Arthur asked.

Dawn smiled. "Why are we talking about my body?" she said.

"Isn't it arrogant to think that freedom of body is the same thing as freedom of *your* body?" Arthur said.

"Do you object to arrogance?"

"Isn't arrogance just a defense against vulnerability?" Arthur said.

"Are you now objecting to vulnerability?"

"How do you feel about 'vulnerability' and 'your body' being talked about in the same discussion?" Arthur asked.

"Why do my feelings matter to you?" Dawn said.

"Damn, you're good at this," Arthur said. "Okay, wait. Um . . . shouldn't your feelings matter to me?"

"Doesn't concern over someone's feelings imply a certain intimacy?" Dawn asked.

"Are you afraid of intimacy?" Arthur said.

"Are you?"

"No fair."

"Okay," Dawn said. "Would you be worried if I were afraid of intimacy?"

"Would it bother you if I were concerned about your feelings?"

"Weren't we talking about intimacy?" Dawn asked.

"Okay, would it bother you if we were intimate?" Arthur asked.

Dawn was silent for a moment. A long moment.

"No," she said. "It wouldn't."

They kissed for a long time, warm and safe inside their thick sweaters and oiled slickers. The air was cold, and the stars were fading to advancing light. From below came the sounds of people getting out of bed and Crystal clanking pots in the galley. The aroma of coffee and hot cocoa drifted upward.

Dawn smiled. "Does this mean what I think it means?" she said.

Arthur returned the smile. "Does it mean as much to you as it does to me?" he asked.

"Why do you suppose we took so long?"

"Shouldn't something like this take a long time?" Arthur asked.

Dawn nodded. "The best things always do," she said.

CHAPTER TEN

THIRTY-ONE KNOTS OF FREEDOM LEFT

Brimstone Island suffered from overstatement. It was an ordinary little island, a small green teardrop bobbing close to the southeast side of Vinalhaven. Its most impressive feature was a façade of steep cliffs that surged up from rocky ocean to pine woods above. The *Dreadnought* approached from the southwest side of the island, where the cliffs were especially steep and the water was deep close in to shore. Marietta was at the helm, and with sarcastic complaints and backhanded orders, she guided the ship into anchor position. The other sailors, stretching and yawning in the early morning chill, dropped and stowed the sails with automatic efficiency.

The cliffs were full of holes. Dozens of them. White-and-black terns swirled and darted through the air in a rapid-fire ballet, screaming at the unjust swiftness of insects.

Marietta scanned the coast for some kind of sign, but she found nothing. "It's a lie," she said with a scowl. "That crazy bitch told us a lie. She just wanted to see whether we'd spend the rest of our lives crawling in and out of those stupid caves. Even if there is treasure in there, we'd spend the rest of the summer just trying to figure out which cave is the right one."

"Not necessarily," Dawn said, pulling her ponytail through her red cap. "Bonnie said we had to get here by eight o'clock, because that's when the extreme low tide would happen. It's six thirty now. I think we should wait a little while and keep our eyes on those cliffs."

Logan glanced at Crystal. "We don't need, like, everyone for that," he said, hoping to sound adventurous. "Let's leave a lookout or two and go ashore. I'm totally curious about this Brimstone Island."

"So am I," Arthur said, "but I'm going to bed. I need a nap before we explore the cave."

"I need some time to meditate," Dawn said, flashing a smile at Arthur. "It's much more refreshing than a nap."

"I'll go to the island with you, Logan," Joy said. Several others—Crystal, BillFi, and Jesse—pulled on their sneakers and agreed to join the shore party. With a dismissive wave of her hand, Marietta stretched out on deck and oiled her skin with a perfumed tanning lotion despite the sun's faint gleam from low across the water.

The dinghy shoved off, and the oarlocks screeched as Jesse pulled against the oars.

"Be back by 7:45," Dawn called after them. "We'll need everyone here to watch for our mysterious cave."

Logan smiled. "Wouldn't, like, miss it for the world."

When the dinghy bumped against the base of the cliffs, the reality of this side trip set in. The cliffs rose almost straight up a good ninety feet, and while cracks and ledges made climbing seem possible, one mistake would cause a body to plummet to a swift death on the rocks below. Dark-green moss clung to the rocks at the base. A stiff breeze rustled the pine branches far overhead.

"Oh, well," Logan said. "Maybe there's, like, an easier way on the other side of the island."

"Not likely," Crystal said. "This whole island is steep. Besides, this doesn't look all that bad." She grabbed two large coils of rope from the bottom of the dinghy and looped them over her head and one shoulder. Then she kicked off her shoes and vaulted nimbly out onto a rock. Without another word, she began to climb the cliff.

"You're crazy!" Logan shouted. "You'll totally get yourself killed."

Crystal said nothing. She climbed slowly, scanning the coarse face for handholds and ledges. Her long legs were an asset; at times, to get into the best position, she would reach one foot nearly up to her shoulders, bending with a supple grace that complimented her physical strength. The dusty ledges left white marks on her callused feet. When she was thirty feet up, she paused for a moment on a wide ledge, her breathing hard but controlled. Then she climbed on, disappearing from time to time behind outcroppings, then emerging again as the rock face jutted into the air.

"She made it!" Logan shouted when he saw Crystal wave from the top. "I wonder what it's like up there."

"Only one way to find out," BillFi said with a grin. From above, Crystal's rope tumbled down in a coil, unfurling as it fell. The last few feet of the rope splashed into the water just a short distance from the dinghy.

"It's tied off!" Crystal shouted down. "Use it to climb! The view is incredible!"

Logan studied the cliff, the crumbling ledges, the gull droppings, the lichen and weeds. He watched as a small pebble bounced and popped down the cliff, spinning wildly and crashing into one rock after another, then landing with a dull clack against the granite that barely rose out of the ocean nearby. His stomach churned sourly from nerves and last night's gin. But at the top of that cliff was Crystal, and this morning might represent his only chance to be alone with her.

The climb would be long, and he knew it wouldn't stop at the cliff's rim. Logan had found Crystal attractive from the start, with her tight muscles and her short blond hair. Even while McKinley was screaming orders and the "campers" were enduring soggy sleeping bags and incessant "demotions," Logan had admired Crystal's coolness, her confidence, and her willingness to keep herself just a bit distant from the rest of the crew. Early in the second week of McKinley's cruise, a squall had swept through, catching McKinley and the crew off guard, and everyone had to scramble to keep the ship from heeling too far or taking on too much water. The crew was doing reasonably well for a young and inexperienced team, but everyone on board was getting tired. Then without warning, a gust hit that caused the ship to lean sharply. BillFi lost his balance and slipped on the wet deck—and his thick, plastic-rimmed glasses skittered across the floorboards, through a scupper, and over the side of the ship.

Crystal didn't miss a beat. She leapt up from her position tending one of the sheets—Logan swore she had started moving before the glasses left BillFi's head—and she grabbed a tied-off halyard and bounded over the side. No one was quite sure whether she actually hit the water or not, but an instant later she was standing near the bow with the halyard in one hand and the eyeglasses in the other.

When she handed the glasses back to BillFi, he nearly cried. Without them, he was blind, and their loss would mean an end to his summer at sea. Crystal didn't say a word—she acted like she did this sort of thing every now and then just to pass the time. She just coiled the halyard, returned it to its cleat, and once again took her position at the main sheet. Logan had pulled the sheet as tight as he could, but Crystal braced her feet against a support and pulled it even tighter.

McKinley glowered toward the crew.

"What are you all staring at?" he had bellowed. "Don't you have work to do?"

Standing at the bottom of the cliff, Logan knew he'd have a lot of work to do trying to keep up with Crystal. But he thought he saw Crystal wave at him, encouraging him to climb. It was the only encouragement she had ever given him, so he clambered over the side of the dinghy, wobbled gracelessly across the short expanse of rock, and grabbed the cliff.

At first the rope was unnecessary and in the way. Cracks and shelves in the rocks made climbing easy, and Logan— despite jeans too tight for his soft and rounded frame, despite high-top sneakers that were never laced up, despite the skein of red hair that harassed his eyes, and despite the geyser in his belly that boiled in protest against a long stretch of over-drinking and a short burst of adrenaline-fueled acid—groped clumsily for large handholds and luxuriously solid footholds. He ignored the rope and pulled himself upward, grunting higher and higher off the ground until his body wavered and quivered fully five feet above the rocks. He looked up at the spinning cliff above him. He looked down at the surging waves below. He looked straight ahead at the tiny spider that moved with inefficient flailing across the knuckles of his right hand.

It was all too much. He let go of the cliff and shook off the spider. Then, reeling for balance, he twirled around and grabbed the rope. At that moment—with his feet wedged in a notch in the rock and his sweaty hands clinging to the coarse and solid rope—his stomach, sick from days of abuse with sugar and nights of abuse with alcohol, emptied itself into the air. He vomited from five feet up, waited until the heaves were finished, and then lowered himself awkwardly down. He staggered back to the dinghy and flopped into its cool bottom, his face twisted into an embarrassed grimace. "I hate this shit!" he wheezed out loud.

From the top of the cliff, Crystal waited to see whether her friends would join her. She peered over the edge of the cliff and saw the others still sitting in the dinghy, Logan lying on his side. She watched for a moment, then knew she was alone.

She looked around. The view from the top was indeed incredible. To the northwest, the island of Vinalhaven, with houses and roads and radio towers. To the east, Isle au Haut, a dark-green mass silhouetted against the sun. To the southwest, the low shapes of Matinicus and Wooden Ball. And to the south, nothing but open ocean and misty sky. Some gulls flew by, off in the distance, unfazed by altitude and gravity and travel in three dimensions.

Crystal looked around. The top of the island was a large bluff covered with low pines and shrubs, interrupted here and there by grassy meadows filled with short briars and small bright-yellow flowers. She followed a narrow break in the trees. No people moved among the bushes, but a shallow, mossy cellar hole showed that someone, a long time ago, had tried to make a life here. Crystal jumped down into the depression.

The ground was cool and damp, the earth a rich and pungent black.

Probably the rotten old boards of the house, Crystal thought. Why would some idiot build a house clear out here? And how did they get up here?

She imagined a small cottage, tidy but unpainted, with a porch that faced the morning light. A living room, a kitchen with a wood stove for cooking and heating, a low sleeping loft overhead with a narrow ladder and a kerosene lamp. Outside, a root cellar and a small garden with carrots, potatoes, snow peas, and onions. Long dark winters, bitter and desolate, followed by the salvation of spring and the warm caress of the summer sun. Then brief, brilliant autumn, and yet another winter. An endless cycle of seasons in a dollop of acreage bound in by the sea. And the mainland so far away.

She sifted through the loose loam of the cellar hole and found pieces of ancient glass, broken and rounded soft, and some small bones. A modest earring. A ceramic bowl. Part of a shoe. In one corner was the rusted skeleton of a shopping cart.

"How the hell did *that* get here?" she wondered aloud.

She climbed out of the pit and continued her walk. The path snaked through the scrub pines, and as Crystal rounded one corner, she stopped abruptly. Just a few feet in front of her, facing her with a menacing stare, was a large ram. Its horns curled back over its head, its wool was shaggy and brown, and it seemed wholly unafraid of this odd human who had arrived out of nowhere.

"Hello," Crystal said, once she had regained her composure. "This island must belong to you."

The ram didn't move. It didn't blink. In the distance, Crystal could see dark shapes moving through the brush.

More sheep. Easily forty of them. Probably the bastards of the herd kept by the people in the shack, she thought.

Crystal smiled at the ram. "Hungry?" she said. "You don't look hungry, but let's see if we can be friends." She dug into the pocket of her denim shorts and pulled out a small bag of raisins. She poured some into her hand and held it out slowly.

The ram remained motionless.

"Oh, come on," Crystal said. "They're fucking raisins. Here, watch." She took a raisin from her hand and popped it into her mouth. "They're good. Give them a try."

She sprinkled the raisins on the path and took a few steps back. The ram held its position for a moment, then stepped forward quickly. It sniffed at the raisins and snorted.

"Well, if you don't like—" Crystal began.

The ram turned quickly and trotted off through the brush, leaving Crystal alone again.

"Maybe raisins were a bad idea," she admitted out loud. "They look a lot like sheep turds."

She shrugged and continued down the path. The sheep kept their distance, watching her through the bushes. The path looped around the flat top of the island, cool with breeze and prickly with mosquitoes, and twenty minutes later it brought her back to the cliff she had climbed. She looked over the edge and saw the others stretched out in the dinghy, talking and laughing and enjoying the warmth of the early morning sun. Crystal sat down on a rock and dangled her legs over the cliff edge.

It didn't surprise her that none of them had joined her. People never seemed to join her. They always wanted to just hang out together and make small talk, something Crystal hated with a passion. She pulled her journal out of her back pocket and popped the cap off a pen. She wrote quickly, describing the island and explaining about Blackgoat and the treasure. Then, as she sat alone, out of reach on the top of the cliff, she turned her comments inward.

Just once, she wrote, it would be nice if someone came along who liked to do things with me. A guy— tall, strong, quiet. Someone who can't stand to waste time sitting around. Someone who isn't afraid of heights or risk or exercise. Someone who wants to know what it's like on top of the next mountain or inside the next cave. Someone who wants to know what I'm like. Someone who will take the time to find out.

"Oh, well," she sighed. "Whoever he is, it's fucking sure he's not going to suddenly appear up here."

She put the journal back into her pocket. She pulled up the rope, tied it with the second one into a long loop, and tossed one end of the loop over a large boulder. She then snaked the rope around her waist and between her legs, put one hand on each side, and backed off the cliff. Pushing off the rocks with her feet and letting the rope slip slowly through her hands, she rappelled with bounding arcs down to the rocks below. At the base, she untied one knot and pulled both ropes down.

"That was totally cool!" Logan shouted with a grin. He was enjoying the relief that throwing up had brought, and he was trying to recover his dignity as well. "Like, where did you learn to do that?"

Crystal shrugged. She wasn't in the mood for conversation.

☠   ☠   ☠

Dawn sat on the bowsprit, staring at the cliffs. The waves inched lower down the stone face as the minutes slipped by. Dawn whispered a meditative chant asking the Sea Goddess to bring them good fortune.

"Sea Goddess!" a voice shrieked behind her. It was Joy, standing just aft of the bowsprit. "Look, I don't mean to diss your beliefs or anything, but where do you get this stuff?"

Dawn resisted the urge to flip back a sarcastic answer in irritation over the shattering of her meditation. Instead she shrugged. "People have been worshipping the sea for millennia," she said. "A lot of people in this world understand that everything is alive—animals, birds, plants, and fish, but also rocks and continents and oceans and the Earth itself. We're surrounded by spiritual beings, but most people don't bother to notice."

Joy clambered onto the bowsprit and sat down next to Dawn. "Some of those things might be living, yes," she said in the tones of a patient teacher, "but that doesn't mean they are spiritual. We are spiritual beings crafted in God's image—but dogs aren't, and birds aren't, and seals aren't, and the ocean certainly isn't. God made all these things so that humans would have the food, medicine, stability, and inspiration to live and grow. All these beautiful things are gifts from God Himself, and they aren't just strange-looking people in other forms."

Dawn shook her head. "Haven't you ever *felt* it? Like at night, when we're in our bunks and someone just blew the lamp out. The *Dreadnought* is alive—I'm sure of that. I've felt her wrap herself around us at night, holding back the waves and the wind and keeping us safe. *Dreadnought* responds to our moods and our actions just as clearly as animals and people do. Doesn't that make her alive?"

"No, *mi amiga*. That makes your *imagination* alive," Joy said, patting Dawn on the arm. "But this ship is just a bunch of wooden timbers and canvas sails. It responds to us because we make it respond, by pulling on ropes and turning the wheel. But the *Dreadnought* is no more alive than the lobster pots are. They're things made by people to help us in our lives. They're tools. God made only one creature in His own image. Us. We're it. And we're all there is. Everything else is just things, put here by God to help us."

Dawn looked out at the waves curling over the face of an ocean she knew was alive. "But God couldn't have made us in His image," she said. "Just look at you and me. Your hair is black. Mine's brown. Your skin is light brown. Mine is almost pure white, except for the freckles. And look at Arthur and Logan. If God made us in His image, is God male or female? He can't be both, can he? I don't think the logic holds."

"The logic holds just fine," Joy shot back. "It isn't your body that's in God's image. It's your soul. Your soul is a little part of God. *Me entiende?* Do you understand?"

"But then why do you think that seals and whales don't have souls?" Dawn said, pulling the brim of her baseball cap low over her eyes. "If the shape of the body doesn't matter—if we can be built in God's image whether we're male or female— then why can't we be built in God's image whether we're homo sapiens or cetaceans? Humans or whales? And for that matter, why not birds? Fish? Trees? Mosses? Water? Stone? Air? The ocean? The planet? If shape is less important than spirit, then why don't you think all these things have souls?"

"I gave you a Bible," Joy said firmly. "Read it. God made all those things so that we would have the food, the shelter, the medicine, and the glory that we need to thrive in this world.

And he gave us those things so that we could turn our attention to the most important thing in the universe—getting to know God better. We're all here to serve Him."

"The Bible is a great book," Dawn said, "but so is the *Bhagavad-Gita*. The Koran. The Talmud. *Illusions*. *Jonathan Livingston Seagull*. Don't you understand? The world is full of spirit. Not just one spirit. Not just one book. *Everything*. All around us. Haven't you ever felt it? Haven't you ever felt the joy of knowing—of *feeling*—that you're surrounded by an infinite web of spirits, all connected to each other, to the life force itself, to *you*? It's such an intense and magical feeling that I can hardly breathe when it comes over me."

Joy smiled. "*Si*. I have felt that," she said. "I have felt the joy that comes from the knowledge that God—the greatest and the only force in the entire universe—the force that *made* the entire universe—cares so much about me, about my tiny little hopeful life, that He reaches down from time to time, from Heaven, just to touch my soul. And when that happens, I don't breathe for a long time."

Dawn stared off at the sea, the living spirit-filled sea that spoke to her and shared this existence with her. Joy stared off at a different sea, a sea filled with water for human life and fish for human nourishment, all courtesy of the loving God.

At last, Dawn spoke. "In a world too often damaged by cruelty, hatred, bitterness, and violence," she said, "I am glad that there are people like you around."

Joy smiled. "Amen, sister," she said.

☠   ☠   ☠

A short while later, with the island crew back on board, Dawn pointed toward the dripping cliffs as the crew gathered around her. "Three caves have surfaced since we arrived," she said to Arthur, who had just come up from below. "Blackgoat's treasure could be in any one of them."

Arthur took command. "We should send over three groups of two people each. The other two will stay on board the ship and watch things from here. Each group will go to a cave and explore it for half an hour. Then we'll all meet back here and talk things over."

"Sounds complicated," Marietta said, adjusting the straps on her blouse.

"It's important," Arthur said. "We don't have much time before the tide turns and starts covering up those caves again, so we need to explore them all at once. I've thought it over, and that's the best plan."

Marietta shrugged. "Fine," she said. "Who wants to be in what group?"

Arthur and Dawn formed one group, and BillFi and Jesse formed another. Crystal and Marietta reluctantly formed the third—and Logan joined it quickly, hoping to impress Crystal and overcome the humiliation of the disastrous cliff climb. Joy agreed to wait on the ship to serve as anchor watch—"I want to put a new Bible sign up in the dining room anyway," she said. The dinghy shoved off, and with Jesse's strength at the oars, the groups were dropped off at the chilly mouths of the caves.

"Good luck, everyone!" Joy called out.

Crystal scrambled lightly over the rocks and ducked into a small dark fissure just above the water's edge. Logan followed gingerly, and Marietta was not far behind. They clicked on their flashlights and dropped down to their hands and knees.

"Jeez, this is small," Logan said. The passage was barely large enough for a person to wriggle through. The rocks dripped with seawater and kelp as the three inched their way forward on hands, knees, and bellies. Logan felt cold water drip onto his back and sharp rocks break the skin of his knees. His stomach had regained its fury.

"It gets bigger up ahead," Crystal called back. She shimmied up through a tight break and found herself in a tiny room with dry walls. There were no signs that other humans had ever been there before. The rocks were dark and sparkling and dirty. The air was musty, and it clouded with dust whenever Crystal moved. Outside the beam of her flashlight was absolute darkness.

Logan and Marietta puffed and coughed their way up through the hole and sat down.

"This treasure had better be worth it," Marietta said. She looked around. "Now what?"

They scanned the walls with their lights.

"There," Crystal said. She pointed to a narrow, vertical gap that twisted up into the far wall.

"I was, like, afraid you were going to say that," Logan groaned.

Crystal slipped nimbly into the crack and wriggled slowly upward. The crack was too small for her arms to move much, so she had to inch forward on one side.

"I'm not sure I'll fit in there," Marietta said. "Some of us have big chests, you know."

Crystal's chuckle echoed down from above. "Some of us are flexible enough to go where we need to," she called back. "Lying around in the sun isn't exactly good exercise."

Logan wisely chose to keep quiet. He squirmed upward through the crack after Crystal, trying not to worry about the close pressure of the solid rock. He jiggled and panted his way forward, his back arching as he followed the corkscrew turn of the cramped shaft. He wished that he had entered on his other side, so he could bend more naturally as the crack spiraled upward. It was too narrow for him to change positions, and the arch was getting uncomfortable.

He wriggled forward a bit with his arms outstretched, his belly squished tight on all sides. A small spur of rock was pulling his shorts down, making him feel even more awkward. He could barely move his chest enough to get air into his lungs. Sweat slithered down his face, and he began to breathe more rapidly.

"I can't make it," he called out, but he couldn't get enough air to make himself heard. "I'm coming back down." He hoped that Marietta wasn't too close behind him.

He pushed with his hands, but his body didn't budge. The rock squeezed against him; he could see in his mind hundreds of feet of cold granite above him, below him, around him, thick and solid and unmoving. He tried to find a better angle with his hands, but he flailed against nothing but soft dust and uncaring air. He pushed again. Nothing.

"Marietta," he wheezed, "pull my feet." His sneakers dangled in open air behind him. He kicked. He couldn't gain an inch downward. He thrashed with his hands, unable to breathe. His flashlight smashed against the rock and went black. He pushed his shoulders against the granite, but it would not let him go. Suffocating. Hot. He could feel blood dripping down his hands.

From below, Marietta's voice drifted up. "Hurry up, lardbutt," she said. "You're slowing us all down."

"Pull!" Logan tried to call out. Barely a whisper. "Feet!"

The rock seemed to tighten. Logan couldn't get enough air. Crying, he pounded the dust with his hands, his head squished against his upper arm. He kicked his feet against the uncaring air. He peed, the warm liquid adding to his panic.

And then from below, he felt Marietta's hands grab his ankles and pull. Granite gouged the doughy skin of his stomach. She pulled some more. Logan got his shoulders free and pushed himself downward. He landed with a dull thud on the floor of the little dry room. He gulped air and curled up into a pudgy ball against the wall, turning so Marietta wouldn't see him cry.

"Jeez, you didn't have to piss yourself," Marietta said. "There's no way I'm climbing up that tunnel now that you peed in it."

Crystal climbed on alone, unaware of the two she had left behind.

"There's another big room up ahead," she called out, "and I think I hear something."

A few minutes later, all three teams—minus Logan and Marietta—had arrived in the same chamber. Beams from five flashlights arced around the cave, crossed their faces, and settled in the center of the chamber. In the middle, under yellow stalactites, were two large wooden chests.

CHAPTER ELEVEN

"Well, here we are," BillFi said, catching his breath. "Here we are. Could be a fortune. Could be nothing. Could be either one. Here we are."

"Who goes first?" Dawn asked.

"I think BillFi should," Arthur said. His low voice echoed in the small chamber. "He's the one who led us to Bonnie. We owe this discovery to him."

BillFi pushed his glasses up and nodded. "I accept," he said with a grin. "I'll do it. I accept." One box looked quite a bit older than the other, stained dark and soft with time. He bent down and peered at the older box, his face just inches from its cracked surface. "Here goes."

He fumbled with the latches on the front of the chest and lifted them slowly. They moved with complaint, and flakes of rust spattered his hands. He opened the lid and aimed his light inside. He held up something small that glinted with a dull shine. It was a dagger, short and menacing, its steel handle forming a skull that seemed to be screaming in agony. The skull's eyes were rubies that flickered dark red in the glare of the flashlights.

"Shit!" Crystal said, taking the knife from BillFi. "This is one serious blade."

Arthur whistled low. "Wow!" he said.

"Think of the history behind that," Dawn said. "Think of the stories it could tell."

"Screw that," Crystal said. "Think of the money it could bring!"

BillFi reached into the trunk and pulled out another item.

"Here's a silver baby's rattle," he said. "A baby rattle. It's engraved. 'Elizabeth.' That's what it says. 'Elizabeth.'" He passed it to Arthur.

"He *stole* a little girl's rattle?" Dawn asked. "That's awful!"

BillFi opened a small wooden box, peeked inside, and passed it to Dawn. "And here's a bunch of teeth," he said. "A bunch of teeth, all with gold fillings."

BillFi held up the remainder of the items in the chest: a gold wedding band, a locket with a mildewed photograph inside it, a child's pewter drinking cup.

"We can't take these things!" Dawn said. "This is horrible! Blackgoat forced people to give him things that . . . that *mattered!*"

BillFi dug through the moldy shreds of wood that cushioned the contents, and he pulled out an urn, heavy and about two feet tall. It glinted deep yellow in the flashlight beams.

"Gold?" Crystal asked.

"Brass," Arthur said. "BillFi, what is that on the front?"

BillFi examined the urn. It was empty. On the front was an engraved coat of arms, intricate and finely wrought. BillFi brushed off two centuries' worth of dirt and grime.

"It's Blackgoat's, all right," he said. "It's his. It has his family name carved across the bottom. And on this coat-of-arms thing are a lantern, a pineapple, a tree, and a fish. At least I think it's a fish."

"Do you think Blackgoat was royalty?" Crystal asked. "He had a fucking coat of arms?"

"Maybe," Arthur said. "But it's odd. Most coats of arms have swords, or armor, or some other war image on them. Part of the point was to let others know that you were strong and willing to fight. But this has nothing like that. These are symbols of food, growing things, showing the way. Not exactly ferocious images."

"The pineapple is an almost universal symbol of hospitality," Dawn said. "It's a very welcoming, generous sort of thing—exactly the opposite of a sword, which tells people to stay away from you."

Arthur shook his head. "So somehow Blackgoat started out in a prosperous and decent family, but ended up a bloodthirsty pirate. I wonder what happened."

BillFi sat up tall next to the chest. "Look," he said. He lifted a book, dark and mildewed. "Look at this. It looks like a Bible. Wish Joy were here. She'd like this. She'd like this a lot."

"I wonder what a guy like Blackgoat was doing with a Bible," Crystal said.

BillFi opened the book. "*The Holy Bible*," he read. He turned the page. "Someone wrote on it. 'Presented to Billy Blackgoat on this the Eve of his Christening, September 1782. May God watch over your soul.'"

A small piece of hemp rope, thin and crumbling, jutted from between the pages. BillFi opened the book to the pages it marked.

"Some parts are underlined," he said. He read slowly and carefully.

I called to the Lord, out of my distress, and he answered me; out of the belly of She'ol I cried, and thou didst hear my voice. For thou didst cast me into the deep, into the heart of the seas, and the flood was round about me; all thy waves and thy billows passed over me. Then I said, "I am cast out from thy presence; how shall I again look upon thy holy temple?" The waters closed in over me, the deep was round about me; weeds were wrapped about my head at the roots of the mountains. I went down to the land whose bars closed upon me for ever; yet thou didst bring up my life from the Pit, O Lord my God. When my soul fainted within me, I remembered the Lord; and my prayer came to thee, into thy holy temple. Those who pay regard to vain idols forsake their true loyalty. But I with the voice of thanksgiving will sacrifice to thee; what I have vowed I will pay. Deliverance belongs to the Lord!

The cave was silent for a long moment.

"Noah," Crystal said. "The Great Flood."

Dawn shook her head. "It isn't Noah. It's the story of Jonah. That's the prayer he offered when he was inside the belly of the fish that swallowed him. After Jonah prayed, God had the fish put Jonah on dry land, and he was able to warn the people of Nineveh to change their ways and avoid the destruction God planned for them. They did, and their lives were spared. But Jonah was rejected as a liar, because the destruction he predicted never happened. He was a hero, but everyone thought he was a liar."

BillFi nodded. "It seems to have been Blackgoat's favorite passage."

Crystal frowned. "I wonder why he—"

"This might tell us," BillFi interrupted. "I think I found his diary." He lifted a thick leather-bound book from the chest. The crew was silent as he opened the cover. Powdery mold filtered up through the flashlight beams. BillFi squinted his eyes close to the elaborate handwriting on the pages.

"What's it say?" Crystal asked.

"The name seems to be Reginald Branigan," BillFi said. "It isn't Blackgoat's. It belongs to Reginald Branigan. It was written—or at least started—in 1799. The first page gives information about the ship Branigan was on. It was called the *Wormwood*."

"What the hell is *wormwood*?" Crystal asked, her blue eyes bright in the flashlight beams.

"It's a plant that gives off this really strong, bitter, dark green oil," Dawn explained. "The oil was used to make absinthe, a liquor that people drank even though it was toxic. It's now illegal almost everywhere in the world. *Wormwood* can also refer to a terrible, unpleasant, or mortifying experience."

"So the guy's a monster," BillFi said. "Who else would name his boat *Wormwood*? The guy's a monster."

"Or a lover of beauty," Dawn answered. "*Wormwood* has very pretty yellow or white flowers."

BillFi turned some pages. "It's mostly just information about where the *Wormwood* sailed and what cargo it carried. It seems to be an actual cargo ship—not a pirate ship at all. It does mention Blackgoat, but he doesn't seem to be the captain. This Branigan guy talks a lot about a Captain Carr. Seems to have been a decent sort of guy. Captain Carr."

"What does it say about Blackgoat?" Arthur asked.

BillFi flipped through the book and stopped at a page near the end. "Here's something. It says at the top, 'The Tragic Story of William Blackgoat.' That's what it says at the top. 'The Tragic Story of William Blackgoat.'"

"Well, read it," Crystal said.

BillFi began:

> *Aug. 17th, 1809. It has been full fourteen months since I wrote in this booke, but yea I never forgot about it. It just seemed there was more to do than I could get done. Had no time to make the usual notations. But as this is my last entry, I've a mind to record my recollections of Captain William Blackgoat before I depart this weary worlde.*
>
> *Never have I seen a more tortured soul. The man seemed obsessed with getting riche, any way he could, and it tore him apart that he never made it.*
>
> *It started when he was a mere first mate on the Wormwood. He had this idea that he had to be the captain else nobody would respect him. And then, if he became captain, that he had to be the best captain in the North Atlantic. It was all or nothing, for him. He had to be the greatest, or his whole life would be for nought.*
>
> *Well, after a few years of shipping work—a few years of doing mighty well, too—we all was taking good shares of the cargo we was hauling for merchants in London and New York—and the merchants were right glad for our services, too—well,*

after a few years, Mister Blackgoat started getting right anxious. Said he should have been captain by now, and that once he was captain, he'd make sure those bloody merchants paid us right. Didn't know what he was talking about. All us on board thought our pay was right fair. Still, you could see that Mister Blackgoat was getting eager to take charge of the ship and negotiate a bigger cut.

Sounds familiar, Arthur thought.

He got his chance when Captain Carr was out with two men searching out a small island for a good place to anchor. They took one of the dinghies, and they had been gone about half an hour when Mister Blackgoat came up on deck with a flintlock in his hand. He called the men together, told us all a bunch of lies about how Captain Carr was selling us out to the merchants, and he declared that he was now captain of the vessel. I don't know whether the men believed what he said or were simply afraid of his firearm—we always knew Mister Blackgoat was a bit daft—but we all went along with him. Shouldn't have, but we did. We pulled sail and left the three of them on that island. They had some rations, and we all figured they'd manage well enough. But we never heard from them again.

"That's horrible!" Dawn said.
Crystal grinned. "Talk about bad karma," she said.

So now we was sailing a stolen boat. We took down the ship's flag and sanded her name off the hull. And the first merchant cargo vessel we saw, we boarded. Set the crew adrift in the lifeboats, took all the victuals and valuables on board, and sank that ship straight down to the bottom of the ocean.

Now it might be sounding like Captain Blackgoat was nothing but a miserable fellow, but that wouldn't be an accurate understanding. In fact, I wouldn't be alive today if it weren't for Capt. B. I was climbing rigging a few years back, lost my footing, and went over. We were in right shallow water, just a fathome or so, and I must have spooked a shark that was sleeping on the bottom. The next thing I knew, the beast had a hold of my leg and was dragging me under. I couldn't move, and I knew that I was going to die. As I looked up at the ship through the silver surface of the water, I saw Capt. Blackgoat climb the rail. He jumped into the water and landed right on top of that shark. The shark let go of my leg in a trice, and some mates pulled me into a lifeboat. I looked back to see Capt. B wrestling that shark, sticking it in the eyes, twisting its flippers, and I could see it was hurt. I figure that Capt. B broke its back when he landed on it, and so he was able to get the upper hand in the fight. Well, it took about twenty minutes, but Capt. B killed that fish, and he didn't suffer a scratch! We hauled that black-eyed shark on deck and carved it up in a hurry. There's nothing in this world I like better than a good shark steake, and Capt. B gave me first choice of the fillets. That dinner was the best I ever ate!

"Sometimes a man has to fight the sea," Jesse observed. "The good ones win."

I ended up losing the leg a few weeks later—the blood went bad, and there was nothing else for it. But I'd be long dead if it weren't for Capt. B, and my only regret is that I didn't have the dedication to return the favor and stay by his side until the end.

And then there was that gale that bloody near killed us all. It happened a few years back. We could see that some weather was coming. The wind was backing around toward the northeast, and we could see dark lines of storm clouds far off on the horizon. So we dropped anchor in a safe harbor, used the lifeboats to set some extra anchors, and made sure the hatches were tight and the sails were furled.

Through his glass, Capt. B could see a small cargoe ship sailing south right along the storm line. He couldn't figure out what the devil they were doing out there—couldn't they see that a gale was brewing? Well, he watched until he saw the ship disappear in the squall line. He knew it couldn't survive out there in that storm, so he gathered us all together. He told us that he wanted to go out and rescue the crew of that ship, fools that they were. He also said that we might not survive it, either. He said that we were safe, here in the harbor, and that anyone who wanted to go ashore and wait there could do so. Three people left. They took a lifeboat in while we raised our anchors. Then we went out to see if anything was left of the foolish little ship.

It was a bigger storm than we had thought.

Waves took out our foremast and half our rigging. A few of the cannon got loose and crashed about the deck, doing a great deal of damage. The ship pitched so hard that no one could keep their footing. We had to tie ourselves to our stations and do our work as best we could without moving.

We got to that ship just as it was going down, and we used a lifeboat to get the twelve crewmen out of the sea. Capt. B was in the lifeboat, of course, with a line tied around his waiste, lunging out over the gunwales and grabbing at any waving arms he could see. We saved them all, the fools, and we brought them back to the harbor. They said their captain had died of dysentery just a few weeks before, and no one on board had much experience. They had thought they could outrun the storm.

Well, rather than rob these people blind, as we had done with that first ship, Captain Blackgoat up and decides to help them out! Said it wouldn't be sporting to plunder an inexperienced crew that we came across in distress. Wouldn't help his image as a pirate. He wanted to take on the biggest and the strongest, not some sodden crew we had to pluck out of the sea. So we put them down on the mainland and gave them some food and told them to be on their way. Odd fellow, Capt. B.

"No shit," Crystal said.

We lived off the booty from our first plunder for about a month, then we ran down another ship and

did to it what we'd done to the first one. This crew
put up a bit of a fight. Fired pistols at us and even
tried to wheel a cannon into place. But we was too
fast. The Wormwood's a fine ship. We came alongside and took that vessel in a few minutes' time. Got
a little bit of money and some food. But not enough
to satisfy Captain Blackgoat.

 Nothing ever seemed to satisfy Capt Blackgoat.
That eventually was the end of him. We gathered
more money and more supplies with each attack, but
it was never enough. He once told me that he
planned to attack an Armada vessel or a ship from
the British Naval fleet. I told him he was mad, that
we'd all be killed and deserve the dying. But he wanted the world to know that he was the most fearsome
pirate in the sea. He wanted to attack a British
Naval vessel, strip it clean, and leave the crew naked
on board to sail her back to England and tell the tale.

 Well, he did it. We came across a British ship,
the HMS Queensborough, and Captain gave the
orders to attack. Now I'm no coward, but I know
when I'm outmatched. I grabbed a chest on deck, put
in some provisions and a fair bit of our treasure, and
snuck off in one of the dinghys.

 I watched the battle as I rowed away. The
Wormwood didn't last an hour. The Navy ship put
its first cannonball right through the deck. The next
cannonball was heated red hot—I could see it glowing as it shot through the skye. When it hit the
Wormwood, right in the main cabin, the whole ship
seemed to burst into flames.

> *The Wormwood went down in a trice, and I believe all hands went with her. Captain Blackgoat, gunner Mitchell, Roberts the sailmaker—they all went down, God rest their souls. And everything on board went down with her.*
>
> *I made it to this island in short order, and I hid out among the caves to avoid capture. I was hoping that some of my mates would make it to the beach, but none of them showed up.*
>
> *It's been nineteen days now. I've used up the food I brought with me. So I've made up my mind to turn myself in, and I'll be heading off soon. I'll stash this book and the sea chest deep inside one of these caves. It isn't much, but it's all that's left of the Wormwood, the ship I called home for more than 10 long years.*

The crew was silent for a long moment, thinking about history and ships, loyalty and death.

"What about this other trunk?" Crystal asked.

BillFi looked at her, sighed, and lifted the lid of the other chest. The objects inside this trunk were much newer. BillFi pulled out a pair of black high-heeled shoes, a woman's navy blue blazer, a leather-bound book. He handed the book to Arthur, who unzipped the cover and opened it.

"It's a daily planner," Arthur said. "A calendar book. From four years ago. And it's filled with appointments and lists of things to do. 'Contact Alberts in Chicago.' 'Check on timetable for focus group.' 'Notify Bradley about Singapore opp.'" Arthur looked up. "I think it's Bonnie's. This is how she planned her work marketing washing machines."

"What the hell is it doing here?" Crystal asked.

Dawn smiled. "Don't you get it? Bonnie carried this stuff around with her on the boat for a while. Maybe she thought she could go back to this life someday. Then she found the cave, read Branigan's diary—just like we did—and she turned her back on her old life forever. She put these things next to Branigan's because they go together. The last remnants of a mindless quest for wealth."

"So where's the loot?" Crystal asked. "This stuff doesn't look like a fortune to me."

It was Arthur who answered. "Listen to this. On the last page of the planner, in really big letters, it says: 'Whoever finds this should know. I tossed most of Blackgoat's riches into the Atlantic Ocean. Trust me, you should thank me for saving your life. Now go home and be good to your children.' It was Bonnie's last message."

"That bitch!" Crystal exploded. "She had all this great stuff, and she chucked it into the damn sea? We could've sold it and gotten really rich. What the hell was she thinking?"

Dawn nodded. "She was following her heart. That's why she told us about this place. So we would understand the lesson she was trying to teach us. So she told us about the caves, and the low tide, and—"

"Low tide!" Arthur said. "Oh, shit. What time is it?"

Crystal held her watch in her flashlight beam. "Twenty minutes after nine."

"The tide!" Arthur said. He grabbed Dawn's arm. "Dawn—when would this cave—"

"Now," Dawn said with horror. "The mouth is probably underwater already."

They scrambled down the passage that Crystal had climbed, gathering Marietta and the still-shaken Logan with them. Below the small room at the bottom, they found nothing but murky saltwater.

CHAPTER TWELVE

"We're trapped!" Marietta screamed. "We can't get out!"

The crew sat down quietly and didn't say a word. The only sound was Marietta's panicked breathing and the soft plopping of water dripping off some stalactites.

"Dawn," Arthur said at last. "We know that the tide doesn't go as high as that upper room, the one with the chest in it. How long could we last up there?"

"We wouldn't run out of air," she said. "These chambers are pretty big. But an extreme low tide comes along only a few times a year. Without water and food, we'd never hold out long enough."

"Okay, then we'll have to get ourselves out of here," Arthur said. "Everyone listen to me. We need to know how high the water is and how far it is between here and the outside." He turned to Jesse. "Listen, you're the strongest person in this crew—and you might be our only hope. We need you to dive down there and find out how deep it is and how long the passage is from here to the outside. Take a deep breath, keep track of where you are, and don't go so far you can't get back. Are you willing to help?"

Jesse nodded, and Arthur smiled with pride at the respect the others were giving his command. As the rest of the crew sat in silence, Jesse untied his boots and took off his pants and shirt, revealing the elaborate mosaic of swirls and colors that covered every inch of his body. He took a gulp of air. Without saying a word, he disappeared into the dark water.

"Crystal, check your watch," Arthur said. "I want to know how long he stays down there."

"And, like, what if he doesn't come back?" Logan whimpered.

Arthur sat down on a damp stone. "Then I'll go in after him," he said. Dawn glanced at him, her expression a mixture of admiration and fear.

Time passed with agony. The six trapped crewmembers sat in the cramped passage, their flashlights aimed at the water in the hopes that Jesse could follow the beams back to them. Echoing drops of water splashed down from the walls. Jesse was gone for two minutes. Then three. Then four. Arthur took off his shoes and began to unbutton his shirt.

"How long can he hold his breath?" Logan asked.

"Not this long," Dawn said.

Suddenly it all became real to Arthur. He stopped with his shirt half-unbuttoned, and he stared at the inky black water. He had commanded attention. He had given orders. He had been a leader. And his friend Jesse might well be dead as a result. Arthur sat down, pale and sick. He had just sent a friend to his death, and suddenly leadership and authority didn't seem to matter much anymore.

"Never show weakness," his father's voice echoed through his head. "Raise for discussion only those points you're willing to lose. It doesn't hurt to let them see you mad. If you pull that stunt again, I'll resign as captain. Don't talk to me in that tone of voice. I'll give you something to cry about."

Arthur shook his head. His father wasn't making any sense. In fact, he—Arthur shook his head again. He thought about his father, trim and tidy in his crisp business suits, armored with his smug smile and glinting eyes. In fact, Arthur thought, he doesn't make sense in my world at all. But if I can't get help from him, who can I get help from?

"Trust yourself and no one else," his father's voice said.

"Shut up," Arthur answered silently.

They waited. Six minutes. Seven. Arthur knew that Jesse was either free on the outside or trapped beneath the tide in the narrow passage. Arthur took off his shirt and stepped to the edge of the black seawater. If Jesse couldn't make it, Arthur knew that he would also—

SPLASH! Jesse burst through the surface, showering the others and gasping for air. Arthur grabbed his shoulders and hauled him out of the sea. A rope was tied around his waist, and it trailed down into the murky water.

It took several minutes for Jesse to slow his breathing.

"It's long," Jesse said. "The water is deep, and it's a long way to the outside. We should hurry. Follow the rope."

"How did you get this rope?" Dawn asked.

"Joy," Jesse answered between gasps. "Loyal friend. She saw the tide getting high. She swam over to the dinghy with this rope. She tied it to the dinghy. She gave it to me when I got out."

Arthur shook his head slowly. "Remind me to kiss her when we get out of here," he said.

Dawn smiled. "I'll be sure to do that."

Crystal led the way, with Marietta right behind her. They

each grabbed the rope, lowered themselves into the chilling water, and took a deep breath.

"Remember," Arthur said, taking command once again, "keep your hands on the rope. Pull yourselves along quickly. And don't bunch up—you don't want to get kicked in the head by the person in front of you."

They nodded, and one at a time, they vanished.

Arthur counted slowly to sixty. "If they run into trouble, I don't want all of us down there trying to hold our breath," he explained. "We need to give them time to get out."

"Jesse," Arthur continued. "You and Dawn go next. BillFi, Logan, and I will take the last shift."

Jesse nodded. He lowered himself into the water, with Dawn behind him. "Don't take too long," Arthur said. "As the tide comes up, this passage just keeps getting longer."

Then they were gone.

Arthur counted to one hundred, then he turned to the other two. "You ready?" he asked. They nodded. Logan looked green and queasy in the glare of the flashlight, his stomach still unsettled from his heavy bouts with alcohol. He was panting in rapid, shallow bursts. "Let's go," Arthur said.

Sixty seconds later, the three of them were in the water. BillFi was in the lead, and Arthur took the rear, placing the flashlight on a rock and aiming its beam into the water. They filled their lungs with the clammy cave air and dropped below the inky surface.

The cold was shocking. Arthur held the rope in his left hand and slid his right hand forward. No flashlight beams guided them, and the blackness was complete. He tried to develop a rhythm—reach, pull, glide, reach, pull, glide—and he hoped that he was going fast enough to get out before his lungs forced his mouth to open. Reach, pull, glide. It felt good. He thought he could make it.

Then his foot bumped something soft. Definitely not a rock. He thought at first that it was a shark, but it didn't come after him. Besides, he thought, sharks wouldn't swim where they couldn't see.

Logan. The word flashed through his mind. *It's Logan.* He stopped, held the rope, felt around in the darkness. He couldn't take any chances. Whatever it was, he would try to drag it out of the cave.

His hand hit a rock, then another. Then, holding the rope with his right hand and straining into the midnight water as far as he could reach, he felt the soft object again. It was a shoulder. Logan's shoulder. Arthur grabbed onto Logan's shirt and pulled hard with his right hand.

He was running out of air. With only one hand on the rope, he had to be careful not to let it slip away. He knew if that happened, neither he nor his friend would ever reach the surface.

He tried another rhythm. Pull, slide. Pull the rope, slide along it. His left hand ached from clenching Logan's shirt so tightly, but he wasn't about to loosen his grip. Pull, slide. He had to breathe. He let some air out of his lungs, hoping to stall the need to inhale.

Pull, slide. A faint glimmer up ahead. More bubbles out. Some seawater spasmed into his throat, and he coughed out valuable air. Pull! Slide! The light grew brighter. Arthur gave a final tug on the rope, and he felt Logan slip from his grasp. His mouth opened and he felt cold water rush down his throat. He didn't feel arms grab him from above and lift him into the chilly breeze.

☠ ☠ ☠

When he woke up, Arthur looked around the captain's quarters of the *Dreadnought*. Dawn was next to his bunk. Arthur tried to sit up, but the bunk—and the cabin, and the world—twirled out of control, and he sank back down to the cool security of the mattress.

"Are you all right?" Dawn asked.

Arthur took a deep breath of clear air. "Dunno," he slurred. "Howslogan?"

Dawn smiled. "He's okay. He's asleep in his bunk. Another few seconds though, and he wouldn't be okay at all. You saved his life."

"I can't—" Arthur spoke, but he cut himself off. In a single quick move, he rolled over, thrust his head off the bunk, and threw up into a large bucket Dawn had placed there for just such an occasion. When he was finished, he sputtered, "I don't—" and he threw up again. "Oh, shit," he said, and he lay back down to sleep.

That night, the entire crew enjoyed a dinner of shish kebobs on deck. The sunset was a deep red, and the boat rocked gently in the harbor. BillFi invented a new drink for the occasion—he called it "Inky Blackness," and it seemed to be mainly rum and grape juice—and he offered a toast to Arthur's heroism.

"To Arthur, who pulled Logan out with one hand and himself with the other," he said. "He's one handy guy." BillFi laughed out loud at his joke.

The crew raised their glasses to Arthur, who waved dismissively. He looked pale and tired, but he grinned at his onboard friends. He felt a deep warmth in his heart, grateful that everyone was okay.

"And to Jesse," Joy said, "who went back into that water with a rope, just to save his friends."

They raised their glasses to Jesse, who sat without moving.

"And to Joy," Dawn said. "She's the one who swam over with the rope in the first place. That showed a lot of courage and foresight."

They raised their glasses to Joy, who grinned and blushed.

"And I'll offer a toast," BillFi added, "to Reginald Branigan. We'll probably never know what became of him after he left the island, but I hope he received the ending he deserved. I hope he ended well."

All eight members of the *Dreadnought* crew lifted their glasses high and held them aloft for a long silent moment. Then Dawn stood, walked to the rail, and emptied her glass overboard. "And that's for Captain Carr," she said to the sea. "All good sailors like rum, and I'm sorry about the grape juice."

Then Logan stood and walked over to BillFi. "Pour me another drink," he said. "And make it a strong one."

Crystal rolled her eyes, and Arthur shook his head. Another night, another round of Logan's binge drinking. Logan took the overfilled glass to the side of the ship. He drank one long swallow of the rum and grape juice, and then with surprising anger, he hurled the glass and its contents far overboard.

"I've had enough of that shit," he said, facing his friends. "I damn near died today. I can't run. I can't climb cliffs. I can't swim. I can't do a fucking thing. I've been letting that shit mess me up for a long time, but it stops now." He turned to face Arthur. "I owe you big time."

Arthur shook his head. "You owe yourself a great life," he said. He pointed to the pitcher of purple booze. "And I think you're right—you won't find it in there."

Logan nodded, brushed the hair out of his eyes, and sat down.

Then Arthur sat next to Dawn, wrapping a blanket around their shoulders. He said nothing, and he still stared straight ahead. Logan inched as close to Crystal as he dared, and BillFi and Jesse watched from the top of the hold. Joy sat alone, and Marietta fumed. Seagulls cried from time to time, waves murmured below, and the *Dreadnought* crew chatted quietly, their faces growing indistinct in the darkening evening.

"What should we do about the treasure?" Marietta asked. "We didn't get the things out of Branigan's chest. When is the next really low tide?"

Logan shook his head. "I'm totally not going back in there," he said.

"I agree," Dawn said. "I can see why Bonnie calls that stuff evil. It is evil. Blackgoat ripped apart people's lives, and I don't want to risk *my* life going back."

"That's ridiculous," Marietta said. "Some of that stuff is worth good money. We could sell it to a museum or something. And we won't risk our lives—we just have to watch the time, that's all."

"*Perdone*. Sorry. I'm for leaving it there," Joy said. "I don't want any part of it, and besides, I think Bonnie might be right. Look at us—some of you nearly died trying to find that stuff."

"Well, I'm going back for the treasure," Marietta said in a firm voice. "Who's going with me?"

The only sound was the creaking of the ship and the gentle lapping of the waves.

"Fine," Marietta said with a scowl. "I'll go by myself then. Some other time. Without any of you. And I'll be rich all by myself." She stomped down the gangway to the cabin below.

The sky was nearly dark now, and the rest of the crew remained on deck, pressed close together for warmth and companionship, talking and laughing and dreaming together. Gradually, everyone but Arthur and Dawn drifted below and slid into their sleeping bags. The silence held them close for a long time.

"I don't get it," Arthur said at last. "I don't know what I'm doing wrong."

"What makes you think you're doing anything wrong?" Dawn asked.

"Are you kidding? Logan nearly died. I nearly died. Crystal seems ready to mutiny. Marietta seems ready to explode. I thought all we'd need was strong leadership, and everything would be fine."

"Oh, I see," Dawn said with a gentle nod. "And you thought that Arthur Robinson, age seventeen, with no experience in stuff like this at all, could simply *decide* to be a leader, and never make a mistake? I see clearly. You're full of yourself, and now you want pity for screwing up."

Arthur shook his head, knowing that Dawn couldn't see the anguish on his face. "No," he said with surprising calm. "I don't want pity. I want to understand. I'm giving clear orders. I'm thinking things through as clearly as I can. I'm taking the needs of the crew into consideration. I'm trying to anticipate—"

"No, you're not," Dawn interrupted.

"Not what?"

"You're not taking the needs of the crew into consideration."

"Sure I am," Arthur answered. "I think about what they'll need. I try not to yell at them too much. I give them time to do their jobs and time to have fun. I let them take the helm a lot—"

"Big deal," Dawn said. "So *you* give us time to have fun. So *you* give us a chance to take the helm. So *you* give us at least some of the respect we deserve. You aren't giving us what we want most."

"What the hell's that?" Arthur snapped.

"Freedom," Dawn said. "Maybe we don't want you to *give* us time to have fun—shouldn't that be our own choice? Maybe we don't want you to *give* us a chance at the helm—isn't this our ship, too? Maybe we don't want you to *give* us the things you think we need—can't we make those decisions for ourselves? The people on this ship respect you, and they trust your leadership, even when you screw up. But if you want things to work better, you need to lead *less*, not more. You don't have to make every decision. Let us talk things over and come to a group decision. You don't have to think things through all the time. You have some pretty smart people on this ship. And you don't have to make mistakes all by yourself. We all deserve the chance to try and to fail and to learn—and not to beat ourselves up over it. You deserve that same chance, too."

Arthur let some silence go by. He wasn't sure he liked what he was hearing. "So what are you saying?" he asked at last. "You want me to step down as captain?"

"There is no 'Commodore,' Arthur," Dawn replied. "We're all in this together. I just think you should realize that and stop acting like you're in charge. No one here has to listen to you, and I don't think Crystal is going to go along with this arrangement much longer. Marietta either. But I don't want you to step down as captain. I want you to share the job. What do you think would happen if we took turns being captain? Would the boat sink? Would we get lost somewhere at sea? Maybe. We might just do that to ourselves. But then it would be *our* fault, not yours, and *we* would figure out how to handle it. Together. As a team."

Arthur pulled the blanket tighter across their shoulders. "But my father—"

"Your father," Dawn said, "is wrong."

CHAPTER THIRTEEN

TWENTY-EIGHT KNOTS OF FREEDOM LEFT

Early one morning, the *Dreadnought* set sail for Rockland Harbor, just north of Owl's Head. Rockland Harbor was the site of the *Dreadnought's* launch, and the crew had longed to revisit its quaint shops and cozy restaurants ever since the ship had set sail. They had been afraid to go there, though, after McKinley's death, but time was realigning their thoughts.

Joy was enjoying her first shift as the official Captain of the Ship. After the attempt to find Blackgoat's treasure, and after several long talks with Dawn, Arthur had announced that they would rotate the captain's position from now on. He packed his gear, and it took little time for him to move out of the captain's quarters and into one of the bunks in the main room. He expected people to treat him with contempt. He was weak, he thought. A loser. But they didn't. They seemed to appreciate the gesture. Even Crystal looked at him with new respect. He still wasn't sure he understood, but he was beginning to learn that Dawn held wisdom he hadn't seen at first.

Joy stood at the helm and grinned. "*Muy bueno,*" she said. "I'm going to like this." She planned for the crew an afternoon of shopping, laundry, and maybe dinner of corn chowder on the deck at sunset. She steered the ship steadily across West Penobscot Bay. Shortly after lunch—Dawn served seafood salad and cornbread, sharing tidbits as she cooked with Ishmael, who rubbed against her legs—a cheerful "Ahoy!" from across the bay changed the day's plans. It was the *Elkhart*, and Richard Turner was at the helm.

"The *Dreadnought*, isn't it?" Turner called out through a bullhorn. "A reasonable opponent in a race, but a bit slow to windward, as I recall."

Logan jumped up from a vinyl mat and did his best "Queen of England" wave. "The *Elkhart*, isn't it?" he yelled across in a foppish British accent. "A reasonable opponent, a bit clumsy on the tacks, but quite graceful in victory, as I recall."

Turner nodded with a flourish. The wind was strong and straight out of the east. He gestured to windward.

"A couple of inviting markers out there," he said, as the ships sailed side by side. The crew of the *Elkhart* lounged along the rails, nibbling on bagels and sipping cappuccino out of tiny cups. The crew of the *Dreadnought* sat along her rails, biting chunks out of an angel-food cake they passed around for dessert.

"Indeed," Logan called back, wiping the hair from his eyes. "Lovely red nuns, one with a gong. Care for a closer look?"

Turner smiled. "Wouldn't miss it. Shall we say counter-clockwise around, the first one back to the breakwater wins?"

Logan smiled. "Winner buys dinner for everyone?"

Turner put on a mock frown. "Again!" he pouted. "If I didn't know better, I'd think you were just mooching."

Logan put on a mock frown of his own. He turned to Joy. "What do you say, Captain?" he asked. "Up for a race?"

"If you are," Joy said uncertainly. She didn't feel entirely confident as the decision-maker, but she didn't want to squash the crew's fun.

"Awesome!" Logan said. "Hey, everybody—battle stations!"

The crew of the *Dreadnought* was in place in seconds. They had weathered fierce storms, internal bickering, bad food, weird drinks, and unsettling romances. There was nothing they couldn't do together.

Dawn scrambled to stand next to Joy. "We need to jibe," she whispered.

"Okay," Joy said. "Please prepare to jibe, everyone!"

"Ready!" Arthur yelled.

"Jibe ho," Joy said. She turned the wheel cautiously.

The *Dreadnought* turned its stern across the wind. The crew hauled on the sheets and let them out again, positioning the sails with a smart "Pop!" Before the *Elkhart* crew had finished rinsing their cappuccino cups, the *Dreadnought* was tacking through the waves toward the first marker.

The large wooden *Dreadnought*—even with all her heritage, her years at sea, her spirit, and her crew—was no match for the sleek fiberglass *Elkhart*. Turner was an able skipper, and he timed his tacks with experienced precision. The *Elkhart* slowly gained on the *Dreadnought*.

"Are we going to let them win again?" Arthur shouted as he pulled in the mainsheet.

"Hell, no!" Jesse shouted. He joined Arthur and pulled the sheet even tighter, his multicolored biceps rippling as he strained against the rope. The *Dreadnought* picked up a bit of speed. It rose and rocked through the waves, heeling sharply in the wind.

Joy held onto the wheel tightly. The ship cut through the waves as it sped toward the buoy.

"Joy," Dawn said. "I think we should come about now and get farther to the right. That sound good to you?"

Joy shrugged. "If you say so," she said. "Ready about!" she called.

"Ready!" the crew shouted back in unison.

"Hard alee!" she shouted, turning the wheel to move the ship's bow across the wind.

The *Dreadnought*'s bow cut a graceful arc across the wind. The boom crashed across the decks—and everyone ducked without looking up. The sails puffed out crisply, and Arthur and Jesse hauled on the mainsheet. Crystal and Marietta tightened the foresheet.

"Turner's still gaining!" Dawn shouted. "Joy, try to cut him off at the buoy!"

Arthur glanced up from his mainsheet position and shook his head. "We don't have enough room," he said.

Joy checked the positions of the buoy and the gaining *Elkhart*. "Arthur's right," she said. "We won't make it. We need to know where the wind is strongest. It's our only hope."

Crystal kicked off her shoes. "I'm going up," she said. "I'll tell you where the wind is." She grabbed the ratlines and swung out over the water, her feet landing lightly on the rigging. She scrambled to the top of the mast as though gravity were powerless to pull her down. She shouted directions down to Joy, and the *Dreadnought* picked up speed.

"We're almost at the marker," Arthur called back.

"Ready about!" Joy shouted.

"Ready!" the crew responded.

"Crystal, hold on tight," Dawn called.

"Hard alee!" Joy yelled. She spun the wheel sharply counterclockwise. The *Dreadnought* pivoted around the buoy, and the sheet crew let the sails swing wide. The ship passed within a few feet of the *Elkhart*, which was still traveling in the original direction and just beginning its turn.

"Impressive," Turner called over, saluting. "Very impressive. You've been practicing to become sailors."

Dawn grinned. "We *are* sailors, Captain," she shouted back. "And we're winning." She turned to Joy. "We need some kind of magic," she said quietly, "or he'll pass us on the next jibe. We can't stay ahead of him at this pace."

Joy nodded. "I know," she whispered urgently. "I hope Crystal can help us, but I don't want to ask her about the wind until the *Elkhart* makes its turn. The flapping of its sails might keep them from hearing what she tells us."

Dawn nodded, impressed. "I'll let you know when," she said, watching the other boat. "Wait . . . wait . . . ready . . . .now!"

"Crystal!" Joy called.

Standing on the rigging near the top of the mainmast, Crystal scanned the water ahead. To port, the waves were rolling and smooth. To starboard, they chopped into angry foam. She pointed to the right. "The wind is over there!" she shouted. "To starboard!"

"Okay," Joy said. She turned the wheel clockwise.

A moment later, BillFi climbed up from below, holding tightly to the rails as the *Dreadnought* crashed through the waves.

"Wrong," he said.

Joy looked at him. "*No comprendo*. I don't understand. What do you mean, 'wrong'?" she said.

"The wind," BillFi answered. "We should go to the port side. Definitely the port. To the left."

"Crystal is up in the rigging looking at the waves," Joy said. "She said the wind is to the starboard. You were sitting in the cabin. How could you know what to do?"

"You're right," BillFi said softly. "I was below. You're right. But I *know* that the waves to port are calm, and the waves to starboard are choppy. Calm to port, choppy to starboard. I know. I also know that in a few minutes, those calm waves to port will be hit by a blast of air. Warm. Out of the southeast. Warm air. I don't know why I know this. But I do. I really do. The gust won't reach the starboard waters for several minutes—enough time for us to leave the *Elkhart* behind for good. Behind for good."

"But I can't steer us toward calm water!" Joy said.

BillFi nodded. "Then we will lose the race," he said.

"Look, I'm . . . I don't . . ." Joy said. "Please just go back below."

BillFi didn't leave. Dawn stared at Joy. For the next sixty seconds, the only sounds that could be heard were the wind in the rigging and the gurgle of the *Dreadnought*'s wake. Astern, the *Elkhart* was twenty yards away and closing.

"Turn harder to starboard!" Crystal shouted from above. "Now!"

"See?" Joy said.

"She's telling you what she *sees*," BillFi said. "I'm telling you what I *know*. Turn to port. I'm telling you what I know." Fifteen yards astern, the *Elkhart* began to creep to starboard, chasing the higher wind.

Joy shook her head. "I need some help here. *God* will tell me what to do." Holding the wheel with her left hand, she dug the coin out of her pocket and spun it smartly on the deck. Dawn and BillFi watched with her as the coin twirled—Saint

Francis, Saint Christopher, Francis, Christopher, Francis—
and then with a tiny wobble, the coin lurched through a
drainage hole in the deck and plummeted into the sea. Joy
screamed. Time froze for a petrified moment.

"I need that!" Joy cried. "I need it to help me decide what
to do!"

Dawn put her hand on Joy's shoulder. "I think," she said,
"God wants you to decide this one on your own."

Joy, her face pale at the thought of her precious coin—her
decision-making connection to her Lord—fluttering slowly
toward the sandy muck at the bottom of the ocean, looked
straight into BillFi's eyes. "You better be right," she said. Then
she turned to Dawn.

"Tell your sea goddess to kick up a storm," she said. "We're
heading toward calm water."

She spun the wheel hard counterclockwise.

"No!" Crystal yelled. "*Starboard!*" Joy didn't answer.

For a long moment, the *Dreadnought* stalled in a faint
breeze. The *Elkhart*, still pressing to starboard, drew even and
began to pull away. The *Dreadnought* slowed to a near stop.

"Oh, no!" Joy cried. "We could have won, but instead we're
sitting here like a rock. We had the lead, and we might've kept
it if we had stayed in front of the *Elkhart*. But no. I dropped
my coin overboard, and then I—"

"Here it comes," BillFi said.

"*Que?* Here *what* comes?" Joy asked.

"The wind," BillFi said softly. "Tell Crystal to hold on tight."

"I don't feel anything," Joy said.

Dawn smiled. "Hey, Crystal," she called up, "BillFi says you
better hold on tight!"

"Aye!" Crystal called back.

The wind slammed the sails. The *Dreadnought* heeled sharply and nosed down into the water. Her bow seemed to snag on a running wave. Then the ship stiffened, gathered the new gale into its system of power, and shot forward like a world-class sprinter. The next waves were mere murmurs beneath her hull; she cut through them with ease. The deck hummed with vibrations from the rigging, and unseen beams creaked and limbered in adjustment to the strain. The surge toppled three members of the crew, sending them sprawling backward and sitting abruptly on the deck. BillFi didn't move—he was quite ready for the wind's arrival—and in the rigging, Crystal tightened her usually casual contact with the lines.

On board the *Elkhart*, Turner looked over at the *Dreadnought* just in time to see her leap ahead in water that had been calm just an instant before. "What the hell!" he shouted. He snapped out a few orders—tighten that halyard, let out that sheet, ready the spinnaker—but nothing mattered. His ship, lolling along in a pleasant breeze, was powerless to catch the gargantuan *Dreadnought* with a full head of steam.

The finish wasn't close. The *Dreadnought* thundered into Rockland Harbor, and Joy turned her smartly into the wind. The crew, leaping to the task with the get-it-done speed of experienced sailors, lowered the sails and stowed them below. The anchor dropped with a confident splash. By the time the *Elkhart* tied up alongside, Joy was leaning casually against the wheel.

Turner looked impressed. He nodded solemnly and raised his martini glass in salute to the victors.

Dawn smiled at Joy. Then she turned. "Hey, Arthur—let's make one heck of a banquet!"

☠   ☠   ☠

Dinner that night on the decks of the *Dreadnought* was the most elegant meal the crew had ever put on. The storage chests were covered with sheets, sails—anything that would pass for tablecloths—and each one gleamed beneath small flickering candles. Candlewick Imports, Freeport. Eight dollars apiece. Arthur was actually glad the crew had bought them.

For the first course, the two crews enjoyed crackers and artistically sliced vegetables, offered with both a hummus and a bleu cheese dip by waiters BillFi and Jesse, although the *Elkhart* crew was somewhat unnerved by Jesse's homemade tattooing. The colorful lines now covered every inch of skin that could be seen, including his face and even his eyelids, and he drew strange and unsettled stares as he wandered among the crowd with his tray of hors d'oeuvres.

Everyone was scattered throughout the main, fore, and aft decks, standing in small circles, leaning against the rigging, staring out to the moonlit sea, or clustered around the candlelit tables. Ishmael even ventured out on deck, staying close to Jesse and keeping an intent watch for dropped bits of seafood. Once the glasses had been filled, Turner called everyone together on the main deck and offered a toast.

"I offer these friendly challenges because they put a bit of spice into life," he said. "And I believe that spice is important. But it should be noted that until today, only one ship had ever beaten us, and it was a Navy vessel full of hot-headed cadets. I raise my glass to the fine crew of the *Dreadnought*. The sea is a talented teacher, and you have learned her lessons well."

All on board raised their glasses in salute, and BillFi, after a quick drink, busied himself with the capture and demise of a fly. Despite the ruse, however, he could feel Arthur's stare. When he looked up, he saw Arthur raising a glass to him in salute. BillFi nodded, raised his own glass again, and finished his wine.

The clanging of a ladle on a pot signaled the start of dinner. Marietta and Logan ate with the *Elkhart's* first mate, a middle-aged cousin of Turner's who owned a large chain of movie theaters across upstate New York. Named Elwood Richardson at birth and called "Woody" since his college days in the late 1970s, he was a meticulously flat-stomached man who wore a meticulously tailored outfit consisting of a blue blazer and a light-blue shirt over khaki chinos and leather Top-Siders. He meticulously combed his hair over his bald spot and meticulously hoped no one would notice. Marietta found him attractive in a moneyed sort of way—wealthy, stiff, flattered by a young woman's attention. Also at the table were the *Elkhart's* cook, a somber man with tense features and nervous habits; the meteorologist, a loud and bawdy woman who delighted in shocking the people around her with off-color words and foul puns; and the "rigging mate," a nine-year-old boy whose title and position were manufactured to give him a place on the boat. The group chatted and laughed at the meteorologist's tales of the strange and irreverent characters she had met at sea.

Joy, Crystal, Arthur, and Dawn ate with Turner and other members of the *Elkhart's* inner circle. To Turner's left was his navigator, Jim Greenfeather, a young, ruggedly attractive Shawnee man who was attending the University of Maine. He had recently borrowed money from his father to launch a new enterprise in the Oklahoma oilfields, and he talked with excitement about the prospects. After Greenfeather came the Hennessey sisters, twenty-six-year-old twins who were slightly old-fashioned in appearance but who carried an air of mystery and depth, as though they had just stepped out of an old novel and were withholding a profound and magical secret; Garrison Chevalier, the *Elkhart's* tremblingly sensitive "poet laureate"; and Heather Heath, an actress who had landed a few supporting roles in major movies and who had received some positive murmurs of critical and public attention.

The rest of the *Dreadnought's* crew was scattered among the remainder of the *Elkhart* riche. At the head table, Turner smiled formally to Arthur. "So," he said, "you've come a long way since we last met."

Arthur nodded. "We've been sailing every day, so we were bound to get better at it."

"But your captain," Turner continued, raising his glass to Joy, "is not the same one I raced against last time."

"We take turns being captain," Joy said. "It seems important that we each get to see what it's like." Arthur smiled a halfway smile and took deep delight in the sparkle of pride in Joy's eyes.

"Smart," Turner said. "You don't know what power and responsibility feel like until you try them on."

Arthur nodded, and he raised his glass to Dawn.

As they ate, Turner told a long and lively story about his adventures in Borneo. "I took an extended visit there," he said between mouthfuls of ham and scalloped potatoes. "Looking for new sources of timber. The jungle was dense, and the insects and leeches were all over us. I got a leech stuck inside my ear once, and we had a devil of a time getting it out." He told them about hacking through the jungle with machetes, climbing slippery rocks as they worked their way up waterfalls, and encountering wild boar and enormous snakes. He told them about the people he met, the young native woman he had fallen in love with, the tearful departure at the end when she decided to stay with her family. Arthur listened attentively. He couldn't tell how much of the story Turner was making up, and how much—if any—was true.

While Turner was talking about Borneo, Crystal and Jim Greenfeather, the young oil entrepreneur, slipped away from the table. They stood in the bow of the ship, talking in low whispers.

"I've been working on this oil project for two years now," he told her, "and I think it's finally beginning to go someplace." He paused and stared out at the moonlight. "So, what kinds of stuff do you like to work on?"

Crystal felt a solid wall spiral up around her. Nice try, but no dice. "Nothing," she said. No one was going to catch her opening up. She was too tough for that. Too hardened. Too cool. She wasn't about to—

She looked over at Jim. He seemed like a nice guy, and he was certainly good looking. Athletic. Energetic. Great smile. She shook her head. "I'm going to get some dessert," she said, turning toward the tables and lights and conversations.

"Wait," Jim said. "Don't run off like that. What are you afraid of?"

Afraid! Crystal glared at him with blazing blue eyes. I'm afraid of nothing, she thought. Nothing at all. Who the hell does he think is? All I'm trying to do is keep out of some stupid, sticky relationship with some guy who—

Relationship. Isn't that what I've been wanting? Crystal asked herself. Well, here's a chance. So what's my problem? Why don't I just see what happens?

She took a deep breath. "I like to swim," she said. She glanced at Jim's face. He smiled gently. She took another deep breath and told him more about herself, her dreams, and the challenges she felt she faced.

After dinner, as the *Dreadnought* and *Elkhart* crews stood around on deck sipping champagne or ginger ale, Turner faced Arthur. "Tell me," he said. "The last time we met, you explained that the fellow in charge of your sailing camp was down below and not to be disturbed. Surely he's available this evening for some conversation with your guests?"

Arthur took a slow breath. "No," he said carefully, "he's still unavailable. He's been rather reclusive for the past several weeks."

"Reclusive?" Turner said. "Nonsense. Surely he'll tolerate a quick hello. Please take me to him."

"I don't think that would be a good idea," Arthur answered.

"Why not?"

"It just wouldn't, that's all," Arthur said.

"Ridiculous," Turner replied. "I gave you a tour of my ship, and I expect you to give me a tour of yours. And when I reach the room where this odd hermit is holed up, I'm going to pop in and introduce myself."

He stood up.

Arthur stood up to his full towering height.

"You can't do that," Arthur said in a dark voice. Shit, he thought. I'm doing it again. Taking charge. Not asking the others for advice or help. Still, there are times when decisive action is—

"Why the hell not?" Turner asked. "He is on board, isn't he? He is capable of communicating, isn't he? He is *alive*, isn't he?"

Dawn stared intently at Arthur. Joy fidgeted with her spoon nervously, rubbing it back and forth across a small span of tablecloth with rapid movements. Arthur put his hand firmly on Turner's arm.

"Captain Turner," he said, looking him straight in the eye. "I'm going to have to ask that you drop the subject. If you are unable to do so, I will ask you and your crew to leave our ship."

Turner returned his gaze. "Like hell. Nobody is going to—" Turner began, but the sentence was cut short by a shriek from high overhead.

Everyone on deck looked up. High in the rigging, faintly visible against the evening sky, were two human shapes—tan, slender, and totally naked. One of the figures leaned off to starboard, crouched, and leapt out into space. She was followed by the other. They knifed headfirst through the cool air, arms outstretched and feet together, and cut through the surface of the water with a pair of crisp splashes.

"It's Crystal!" Dawn said.

"It's Jim!" Turner said.

Both crews rushed to the starboard rail. The water was smooth, barely showing a ripple where the two had entered.

A moment passed in silence. Then a splash and some whooping laughs sounded from the port side, and Crystal and Jim Greenfeather clambered up the ladder and scrambled high into the rigging once again.

"They swam under the keel!" Arthur said.

"Good God, he's lost his mind!" Turner said.

Crystal and Jim flung themselves back out into the sky, two naked cannonballs laughing for forty feet straight down and crashing into the sea with enormous splashes.

"My navigator," Turner said with a tight smile. "Ordinarily, quite a respectable young man."

Jim and Crystal swam through the waves in an endless game of tag, tussled with each other amidst splashes and laughter, disappeared beneath the dark waves for long counts, surfacing far away but always near each other. When at last they tired, they climbed the rail, scrambled up the rigging, and dried off in the chilly air before getting dressed. Eventually, they returned to deck.

"Have fun?" Turner asked coolly.

"Yes, sir," Jim answered. He was tall and wiry, and he gave Turner a playful grin. Crystal did the same for Arthur.

"Nice dive," Arthur said with a small smile.

"Thanks," Crystal said, still catching her breath.

"Nice dive?" Logan shouted, his cheeks a crimson red. "That's all you can say? 'Nice dive'? It was crazy! It totally was suicide! Crystal, you could've gotten yourself—"

Crystal held up a hand. "But I didn't, did I?" she said. "And taking chances is what it's all about. But you wouldn't know about that, would you?"

Logan's face went ashen. I've just taken a huge step toward making you like me, he thought. Didn't you notice? Doesn't that count for anything? He opened his mouth to speak, but then he turned and stormed down the gangway to the dining room below. Ishmael followed hopefully behind, her gray tail held high as she darted down the steps.

Turner shook his head. "Jim, I must say I'm a bit surprised. I thought you had a more level head on your shoulders."

Jim flashed him an icy glare. "It's as level as it needs to be."

"Hey, gang," Crystal called out to the whole group. "Jim says there's a band playing in town. At the Crustacean Lounge or something."

"The Compass Lodge," Jim said. "I saw flyers in town. Starts in about an hour."

"The Compass Lodge?" Turner asked. "You've got to be kidding. You aren't thinking of going, are you?"

"Yes, sir," Jim answered. "Want to come along?"

"I don't think so," Turner answered frostily.

"I'll go," Dawn said.

"I'm there," Arthur said.

"Then I am, too," Marietta said smoothly. "Wouldn't miss it for the world."

Half an hour later, the *Dreadnought* crew was ready for a night on the town. Turner, for his part, decided not to press his desire to meet "the fellow in charge." Arthur thought that showed an uncommon flash of leadership.

☠   ☠   ☠

The Lodge of the Fraternal Order of the Compass in Rockland was a large boxy brown building on the edge of town. A hand-painted sign out front read, "Tonight: The Susan Coffin Band." Sounds of guitar, banjo, steel guitar, bass, fiddle, and drums escaped through the walls in three-four time.

The air inside was warm and blue with smoke. The building was hollowed out to form one expansive hall. At one end was a bar, outlined in strings of small green lights. The sole bartender looked like he had been hired more for his ability to break up fights than for his skill at mixing beverages. Stretching from the bar to the dance floor was a maze of picnic tables filled with country-and-western-looking patrons: yoked shirts, snug jeans, ruffled dresses with low-cut necklines. The *Dreadnought* crew and Jim Greenfeather, dressed in their nicest outfits, took a large table along one wall and ordered drinks. The waitress didn't look at them, and she didn't ask them to prove their age. Logan had agreed to come along, but he ordered a root beer and refused to look at Crystal. Jim Greenfeather ordered grapefruit juice, and Crystal did the same. The cowboys and cowgirls at the picnic tables stared and pointed at Jesse and his technicolor face.

Susan Coffin was dressed in a tight calico dress and played a plugged-in acoustic guitar. Behind her were five men, each in black T-shirts and indigo denim blazers, playing the other instruments. Susan was belting out the words to a foot-stomping country tune, and a block of dancers was moving in straight lines to identical steps, marching forward, spinning sharply, and stepping backward at right angles again. The song ended in a steel-guitar flourish, and the dancers applauded enthusiastically.

"Thank you," Susan said into the microphone. "I appreciate it." She flashed a sweet smile to the people sitting and dancing in the haze.

Marietta, sitting across the table from Arthur and Dawn, turned to Arthur and managed a brittle smile. "May I have the next dance?" she asked, fussing with her streaked hair.

Arthur looked at Dawn.

Dawn shrugged.

"Okay," Arthur said. He stood up.

On stage, the lights shifted to a cool blue. Susan moved closer to the microphone.

"This next song I'd like to sing," she said, "has been one of my favorites for a very long time. It's called 'There's Got to Be a Morning After.'"

Dawn chuckled as Arthur slid by to join Marietta on the dance floor. She leaned toward the others. "It's the theme to *The Poseidon Adventure*," she said to the others as she stared at Marietta, "an old disaster movie about a ship."

Once on the dance floor, Arthur and Marietta swayed without saying a word. They had their arms around each other, but Arthur kept their bodies from touching. Whenever Marietta moved closer, Arthur backed away. It looked like she was leading.

"Speaking of disasters . . . ." Crystal said, watching them.

"Yeah," Dawn said.

As soon as the song ended, Arthur turned and walked back to the table. Once he was seated again next to Dawn, he thanked Marietta for the dance.

"My pleasure," Marietta said dryly.

The *Dreadnought* crew sat around the table during the next few songs, chatting and laughing and enjoying an evening on land. Jim Greenfeather sat close to Crystal. Then Susan Coffin ended a song and spoke into the microphone once again.

"We're going to take a short break," she said. "Give us a chance to wet our own whistles a little bit. We'll be back in about ten minutes to bring you more music here at the Rockland Compass Lodge. In the meantime, feel free to come on up and entertain us for a while. Anyone who wants is welcome to play up here and sing a little bit 'til we get back. Just do us a favor—please don't sound any better than we do."

She smiled, and the band left the stage. The house lights came up, the noise from conversations rose, and Dawn nudged Arthur in the ribs.

"Go on," she said with a mischievous grin. "You heard her. Get up there and sing for us."

"Right," Arthur said. "Why don't you go?"

"I never sing without my dulcimer," Dawn said. "But I've heard you sing when you're on bow watch. You sound great. Go on."

"No way."

Dawn faced the rest of the crew at the table. She picked up her glass and began to bang it on the table. "Arthur! Arthur! Arthur!" she chanted.

The others joined in. "Arthur! Arthur! Arthur!" Only Marietta was silent.

Finally Arthur gave in with a shrug. He stood up and worked his way toward the stage. He took his time—he strapped on Susan Coffin's guitar, adjusted a microphone, cleared his throat. Then he looked up.

"First, let me say thanks to Susan Coffin and her great band," he said. The audience applauded. People milled about, lines formed in front of the bathrooms, but Arthur pressed ahead. "I'd like to sing a song that's kind of slow and maybe not the right thing for a Wednesday night dance at the Compass Lodge, but what the hell—it's pretty much all I know."

He strummed the guitar, listened, and began:

> *The lights of the harbor*
> *Are getting close now.*
> *We've had a great journey*
> *And we made it, somehow.*
> *But the pull of adventure*
> *Tugs hard at our bow.*
> *I don't want to go home just now.*

We weathered the storms
And we sat through the calms.
We sailed past the beaches
Of coconut palms.
We slathered our bodies
With oils and balms.
I don't want to go home just now.

He continued with the song, a slow portrait of good times, good friends, and the inevitable farewell.

These last days of sailing
The ocean with you
Are filled up with laughter
And some sorrow, too.
But tonight we've got music
And mugs full of brew.
I don't want to go home just now.

The audience chuckled at the "mugs full of brew" line, and Arthur realized for the first time that some of them were actually listening to him. He glanced over at the *Dreadnought* table and was surprised to see his friends facing the stage, smiling and enjoying the show. He smiled back at Dawn.

Then, out of the corner of his eye, Arthur noticed a denim-clad figure climb onstage and sit down at the steel guitar. Without missing a beat, this new performer slid into a solo that had all the right sounds: soft, slow, sad, but somehow comfortable and comforting. Arthur filled in the sound with a series of gentle chords. Then the fiddle player—

Arthur hadn't even seen him get on stage—started in with a sweet solo of his own. When he was finished, he nodded, and Arthur stepped up to the microphone once again.

> *These last days of sailing*
> *The ocean with you*
> *Are filled up with laughter*
> *And some sorrow, too.*
> *But tonight we've got music*
> *And mugs full of brew.*
> *I don't want to go home just now.*

> *I don't want to go home just now.*

He finished with his guitar echoing the melody, and then he strummed the final chord. The audience was silent for a long, respectful moment. Then they applauded, slowly at first, then louder and more exuberantly. Arthur smiled, bowed his head, and put the guitar down.

"Nice job," the fiddle player said. He was tall and thin, and he had a big smile. "But you missed that seventh back in the second stanza."

Arthur grinned back. "Thanks for joining in," he said. He shook the man's hand, then he turned to step down off the stage. As he did, Marietta downed her drink quickly and wobbled unevenly through the jumble of tables.

"Now it's my turn," she said too loudly.

CHAPTER FOURTEEN

Marietta and Arthur passed each other in the aisle; she didn't give him much room to get by. Then she took the stage, smoothed her hair, and strapped on the guitar.

"That was *nice*," she slurred into the microphone, "but now it's time to get this place rocking! What do you say?"

No one said anything. The fiddle player and the steel guitarist waited to see what she had in mind. Marietta paused for an awkward moment, as if trying to talk herself out of this, then she hit a G chord and turned up the volume on the guitar.

"One, two, one two three four!" she chanted, and she launched into the song. It was "The Whole Cone" from the 1990s movie, *Hot Fudge*. In the movie, the song was a funny, campy, oversexed bundle of double meanings. But Marietta tried to sing it in a sultry tone as she gyrated around the stage.

> *I like ice cream.*
> *I love ice cream.*
> *It refreshes me on a summer day.*
> *It cools me down in an exciting way.*

And gives me all the energy I need to play.
So take me out to go and get some ice cream today.

I like French swirl.
I love French swirl. . . .

Marietta had downed too many glasses of gin to perform anything well. Her left hand had trouble finding the chords, and her right hand had trouble keeping a rhythm. She was far too loud. She shouted the lyrics tonelessly, and she writhed and bounced around the stage in an embarrassing attempt at steamy sexuality. She wiggled her shoulders, she thrust her chest forward, she spun around and shook her hips. She pointed to someone in the audience and motioned for him to come forward while she sang. No one moved. The cigarette smoke seemed to settle slowly toward the floor.

So take me out
To go and get some

She hit a final thundering chord.

Ice cream today! she shouted.

The audience was silent. Then some people applauded good-naturedly, and someone said something off in one corner. Several people laughed. The applause ended quickly, and Marietta was left to climb down from the stage, no eyes on her, no smiles directed her way, no requests to dance. She tottered down the aisle, sat heavily in her chair, and sucked down another drink. She looked at Arthur and started to say something—but then she turned to Logan.

"What did *you* think?" she said. "Didn't know I could do that, did you?"

Logan shook his head slowly. "No," he said, "I can totally say I didn't."

Susan Coffin and her band reclaimed the stage, and Susan stepped up to the microphone. "I want to thank those brave performers," she said. "Let's give them a hand!"

The applause was kind.

"Now," she said, "I know that every now and then a waltz just feels like a good idea, so I think we ought to play one. Let's dim the lights, soften the mood—and fellas, this is the kind of song that you ought to dance to with someone you really, really care about. Now's your chance for romance."

Marietta leaned across the table toward Arthur, her dress falling loose at the neckline. "So," she said, "what do you say? We both can sing. Let's show them we can dance, too."

Arthur stood up. "Marietta," he said gently, "you've got to understand. I'm sorry if I hurt your feelings. Let's just forget about it, okay? Let's just forget about everything." He offered his hand to Dawn. "Will you dance with me?"

Marietta recoiled like she'd been slapped. "You—!"

"I'd be honored," Dawn answered quietly. She took his hand, and the two of them worked their way onto the dance floor. Most of the couples were older, and some had clearly been waltzing together for a very long time. They were synchronous. They were smooth. They were having fun. Arthur slipped his right arm around Dawn's waist, and he held her right hand at shoulder height. A few missteps, a few false starts, and a few warm laughs. Then they began to move together, turning gently, their bodies following the rhythms of the music and each other. One-two-three, two-two-three. It was old-fashioned, silly, almost antiquated. But it also brought them close.

When the song ended, the dancers applauded the musicians and the onlookers applauded the dancers. Dawn and Arthur kissed warmly and took their seats.

Marietta glowered like an angry child. She locked her eyes onto Arthur's, and she scowled, smoldering, dark, and bitter. Arthur smiled as pleasantly as he could.

"You shit!" she yelled. She stood up, knocking the table so sharply that drinks nearly toppled. "You'll regret this!" She turned to Logan. "Let's go back to the ship."

Logan shook his head. "I'm staying here," he said. "But like, thanks anyway."

Marietta held herself erect as best she could. She put on an icy smile and looked at no one. "Fine," she said. She straightened her dress. "That's fine."

She walked quickly out of the lodge and let the screen door slam behind her.

☠   ☠   ☠

The crew meandered back toward the shore at about one o'clock. They were talking and laughing, singing from time to time, arm in arm, side by side, friends and friends and lovers.

When they reached the end of the dock, BillFi stopped.

"It's gone," he said. "The dinghy. It's gone."

The black ocean rippled in the moonlight. The odor of mud was thick. And BillFi was right again—the dinghy was nowhere to be seen.

"Oh, great," Crystal said, her arm around Jim's waist and his around hers. "Marietta took it back to the ship. That little bitch. How are we supposed to get back on board?"

BillFi shook his head. "Give me a minute," he said. He pushed up his glasses and looked out to sea toward the *Dreadnought*. "No. It's not at the ship. It's not at the ship—and neither is she."

"How do you know? You can't see—" Crystal asked, but she stopped herself abruptly. This was BillFi she was talking to. "Okay, so what the hell do we do?"

"We fan out," Arthur said. "If she's not on the *Dreadnought*, then she must have come back on the dinghy. She probably just parked it somewhere else to give us a hard time."

They found it a few minutes later drifting sullenly in the middle of a small mossy inlet. Jesse took off his clothes, swam out to it, and brought it back. Crystal kissed Jim goodnight and, with several of the others, climbed into the dinghy. A couple of trips later, everyone was back on board. Everyone except for Marietta.

The sight in the dining room was shocking. An inch-deep layer of muddy rum and smashed glass covered the floor. The lamp was broken, most of the food had been dumped out of the kitchen shelves, and all the sleeping bags had been pulled down into the muck. Ishmael trembled underneath the table, staring with wild eyes and twitching her tail. The *Dreadnought* sailors stood, stunned, then they got to work. Crystal checked Marietta's bunk.

"All her stuff is gone," she said.

"So is our spare cash," Arthur called out from the captain's quarters.

Logan took the broom and dustpan from the bathroom,

and Joy produced a large supply of trash bags. The crew dug into the mess, cleaning with an energy fueled by anger. Broken glass and booze-soggy papers were scooped into trash bags and stowed in the stern. Sleeping bags were put up on deck to dry. Dawn salvaged as much of the food as she could. Ishmael sneezed and cowered out of the way, sodden with rum and seawater.

When they had cleaned the room and repaired the oil lamp, they all gathered around the table in the main cabin. Logan poured everyone—except for Crystal, Joy, and himself—tall glasses of rye and apple juice. It was all they had left.

"Where do you think she went?" Joy asked.

Crystal shrugged. "Could be anywhere," she said, sipping plain apple juice. "Where do her parents live?"

There was silence as each of the crew looked at the others. No one knew.

"Does she have any brothers or sisters?" Crystal asked.

No one knew.

"Friends in Maine?"

No one knew.

Arthur shook his head. "I'm beginning to see why she felt she didn't belong here," he said. "And most of it is my fault."

"Quit being so damn egotistical," Crystal responded. "She drove us all crazy, and none of us is too upset that she's gone. I'll even bet it's a relief to Logan."

Logan had nothing to say. The table grew quiet.

"So now what?" Crystal asked. "If we call the police or the Coast Guard, it's 'goodbye, summer' and 'hello, freaking Mom and Dad.'"

"We can't call anyone," Arthur said, "and we have to hope that Marietta doesn't, either."

That night, Arthur untied another knot from his calendar ropes. Twenty-seven knots left. The summer was running out.

☠ ☠ ☠

The *Dreadnought* spent the next thirty-six hours floating in Rockland Harbor, each crewmember hoping, for somewhat different reasons, that Marietta would return. The crew on watch kept an eye on the marina, looking for Marietta's familiar scowl, but only the yachtspeople wandered about. Jesse was captain, and the ship went nowhere. The sailors dozed on deck, took short swims, played idle games of cards. Ishmael stayed close to Jesse, and he petted her with reassuring hands. She sneezed some more, trembled, and seemed unable to calm down.

Crystal spent the time writing an entry in her journal.

I'm worried that it's going to end soon. Marietta took off in a huff, after smashing up the dining room, and knowing her I think she'll turn us in. It would take just one phone call from her to bring an end to this crazy and wonderful summer.

It has been great. The people on board are a lot of fun, except for Marietta, and I've had a great time getting to know them all. We've had some incredible adventures, and we've seen a lot of the Maine coast. And Jim is fantastic—I really think he's great. Ever since we dove off the mast together, I've really connected with him. It would be a shame to see it all end.

Especially since once it ends, I'm on my own again. It's obvious that some of these people are going to keep in touch with each other. Arthur and Dawn will, I'm sure. BillFi and Jesse will always be friends. Joy has a boyfriend back home to return to. But I'm worried that, once again, no one will bother to keep in touch with me. I might keep in touch with Jim for a while, but I'll bet he doesn't even come to meet me at the docks when we go back to Rockland. I'll write letters to Arthur and Dawn and the gang, send them cards at Christmas. But then, after a while, it will be just like all the other people I've met. They'll stop writing, they won't think about me, and if any of them get together and talk about this summer, they'll say, "And oh yeah, there was this tough tomboy. What was her name? Christine or something. Yeah, she was kinda difficult." And that will be that.

I hate feeling this way, but I don't know how to change things. Marietta's approach is to throw herself at guys—not exactly my style. Dawn and Arthur seem to make close friends easily, but I can't somehow. I don't know what to do myself. How to make a long-term friendship.

I don't know. Maybe I've been on my own for so long that I send out these "STAY BACK—DANGEROUS" vibes. Jim was the first guy I've ever really talked to, in a deep sort of way. That felt great—really great—but I doubt I'll ever see him again.

Well, maybe we'll get lucky and Marietta won't turn us in. Maybe she'll think she got back at us by smashing up the place. Maybe we can spend the next few weeks together, and maybe I'll make a good, close friend. Someone to keep in touch with forever. Maybe.

☠   ☠   ☠

Three days later, Crystal was captain. The *Dreadnought* remained at anchor until midafternoon, and then Crystal put her hands on her hips and gave the order to hoist the sails.

No one offered any arguments.

Crystal met with a few of the others and charted a course for Large Green Island, which lay farther out to sea almost due south. The wind was steady, the sails filled easily, and the crew trimmed and sheeted with automatic competence. The *Dreadnought* made good time downwind, cutting a rolling wake through the waves. There was little talking on board.

While the ship was underway, Joy scraped together a few more of the things that Marietta hadn't trashed and served dinner, but few of the crewmates noticed the herbs in the cheese spread or the wheatberries in the bread.

It was at that moment that Logan took charge. His energy—and his courage—had rebounded noticeably since he stopped drinking every night. "All right, gang," he told the crew on deck. "We can mope around all day, worried that Marietta is going to bring our summer's fun to an end. But if we do, then she's totally succeeded no matter what she does. I say we forget about her. We can always make other plans if we need to. We'll figure out something. In the meantime, as the official *Dreadnought* Morale Officer, I say we have some fun."

"Like what?" Dawn asked half-heartedly.

"I saw some people on television doing this really cool thing, and I've always wanted to try it," Logan said. "Well, now's my chance." He scurried below and returned a moment later with a large bundle of canvas in his arms. He clipped one corner to a forward halyard and the other corners to side sheets. When he pulled on the halyard and tightened the sheets, a huge red-and-white striped triangular sail opened in the breeze. "It's called a spindler," Logan said.

"Spinnaker," Dawn corrected with a smile.

"It's called a spinnaker," Logan said. He was smiling more, too. "You use it when you're going downwind. A lot of people think it doesn't help very much and isn't worth the trouble. They might be right—it's totally a pain to keep it filled. But these people on TV did something with it that I've always wanted to do. So here goes."

He let the port sheet out a long way, almost to the point of letting the spinnaker collapse. Then he cleated it off and ran over to the starboard side. He uncleated the sheet over there, tied a loop in it, put his foot in the loop, and with a goofy grin on his face, he stepped calmly overboard.

"What the hell!" Crystal shouted. Everyone jumped to their feet. They started to rush over to the side, but then they stopped. And they stared. Logan wasn't dragging through the ocean at all. In fact, he was rising—and he continued to rise higher than the ship's deck. He was holding onto the spinnaker sheet with both hands, his foot firmly in the loop, and the wind was blowing him high in front of the ship.

"Whhooooo—EEEE!" Logan shouted as he dangled and twisted and swung through the air forty feet over the ocean. "YEEEEE—haaaaaa!"

The rest of the crew burst out laughing. They shouted encouragement, admiration, and Tarzan jokes. After a while, they reeled Logan in and he collapsed, panting and grinning, on the deck. They rigged up a rope seat and attached it to the free corner of the spinnaker so they wouldn't have to hold on so tight, and they each took turns. Joy floated up a short distance and came down, insisting after she was back on deck that it was fun. Arthur took a long ride, controlling the sail carefully and rising high into the air, and Jesse and BillFi each took turns. Dawn took a running start and pushed sideways as she left the deck, causing her body to spin wildly through the air. And Crystal put her foot on the seat and flew high— then dove off and rocketed in a tight graceful arc down to the sea. The crew flashed into the "sailor overboard" drill and fished her out of the ocean.

"Thanks," she said once she was back on deck, dripping seawater from her blond hair but clearly pleased. She grinned at Logan. "I needed that."

☠   ☠   ☠

Crystal steered the ship to the southeast side of Large Green Island, where the water was just sixteen feet deep and somewhat sheltered by small ragged islands called the Seal Ledges. The *Dreadnought* clipped sharply between the island and the ledges, and Crystal gave the order to come about. "Get ready," she said, feeling better after Logan's spinnaker craziness. "Hard alee!"

The next sound—heard by everyone on the ship—wasn't quite a crash, and it wasn't quite a scrape. It was more like a pressing, and a popping, and a sickening crunch. The sound of rock on wood. The sound of rock *through* wood. A jolt shuddered through the frame of the ship, and everyone on board lurched forward and fell to the decks.

"Oh, shit!" Crystal shouted, regaining her footing quickly. "What the hell was that?"

"We hit the ledges!" Dawn called back from the port beam. "I can't tell if it did any damage."

The answer to that question came an instant later. Joy dashed up the stairs from the galley.

"Water's coming in—fast!" she shouted. "It's getting deep!"

Crystal wasted no time in organizing the crew.

"Arthur! You and Jesse get below and stop the leak. Use whatever you need. Joy! Figure out exactly where we are and tell us where the closest deep water is. Dawn! Get over the side and see how bad it looks from out there. Logan! You and BillFi salvage as much stuff out of the cabin as you can. I want all of you to report back to me in ten minutes or less. Go!"

The teams rushed to carry out their orders. Arthur was impressed at the authority with which Crystal gave her commands. He and Jesse scrambled down the gangway and waded through thigh-deep water toward the galley. The water poured against their legs; there was a current inside the ship. They fought their way to the galley—and saw no damage at all to the hull. The room was strangely calm. Floating on the murky water were half-empty jars of jam, knotted plastic bags of bread, a cookbook not yet waterlogged, some plastic forks. Ishmael, looking small and wet and terrified, dug her claws into a cutting board that bobbed on the surface. Faint ripples betrayed a bulge of water surging up from below.

"The break must be way below the water line!" Arthur said. "We'll never fix it until we get off this rock."

A few minutes later, Crystal had come up with a plan. She gave instructions to Arthur and Jesse below. She ordered Dawn to take the wheel, and Crystal herself moved to the port rail with a small sail in her hands and a line around her waist. "NOW!" she shouted.

Several crewmates rushed to the starboard side of the boat, causing the *Dreadnought* to tilt slightly away from the rock. An instant later, Joy and Logan hauled in the mainsheet, and the sail overhead popped into shape. The wind pushed the ship over even more, and down below, Arthur and Jesse braced their backs against the pantry and pushed against the splintered wood and submerged granite with their feet. Ishmael tumbled into the water, then scrambled, soaked and panting, onto a countertop. The ship drifted free from the rock.

Crystal, of course, had volunteered for the hard job. The rope tied around her waist had been snaked around a cleat on deck, and Logan had wrapped the other end behind his waist and was holding on tight. Crystal climbed over the rail and leaned backward. Keeping her feet in front of her and her legs parallel to the ocean's surface, she backed slowly down the side of the ship. It was like the rappelling she had done down the cliff on Brimstone Island, except that this was the wet and broken hull of a ship—in a brisk wind. She had a scrap of sail in her hands and a hammer and nails in her pocket.

As she slowly worked her way down, Logan paid out the line in gradual controlled movements, never letting both hands lose contact with the rope at once. If Crystal slipped or got in trouble, his job was to cross the rope all the way around his waist and hold on tight—the others would have to do the actual rescue. For the first time in maybe his life, he felt up to the challenge. Crystal moved down steadily, and within two minutes she had reached the damaged part of the hull.

With the sails tight and most of the crew on the starboard side of the ship, the bottom of the hole was just above the water line. Crystal could see that the wooden slats were bent and somewhat splintered, but they hadn't fully broken. Keeping her feet far apart to maintain her balance, and trusting Logan to hold the rope tight, she laid the sail scrap flat against the dripping mossy bruise on the *Dreadnought's* side. She held the canvas in place with one hand and pulled the hammer from her belt with the other. It was awkward, but she managed to drive in the first nail, pinning the sail against the wood. Now able to use both hands, she wasted little time hammering in another three dozen nails, creating a taut bandage over the wound. It wouldn't last forever, but it would do for now. She grabbed the rope and scrambled back over the rail.

"Let's go!" Crystal barked. The crew formed a bucket brigade, passing pots and pitchers of water up from the galley and emptying them over the rail. The crew worked quickly and quietly, passing full containers up the gangway and empty containers down. It took nearly three hours, but finally, the galley was only ankle deep, and the sail patch seemed to be holding. Using just the forward sail, the crew moved the ship into deeper water and repositioned the anchor.

Crystal wiped the sweat from her forehead. "We're going to have to keep an eye on this all night," she said. "And we're going to have to bail from time to time. Let's set up a watch rotation—we'll split into pairs, and each team will take a two-hour shift. Tomorrow we'll go into port and get some supplies for fixing that hole better. I'll take the first shift. Who wants to join me?"

Half an hour later, most of the crew was sitting quietly on deck. The evening was chilly for late July, and Logan passed around mugs of hot cider. To the west, a cluster of energetic lights blinked and moved with a tranquil appeal. Arthur pressed close to Dawn and wrapped a blanket around both their shoulders.

"So, *que pasa?* What happens now?" Joy asked to no one in particular. "How long can we sail with a leaky boat?"

"Depends," Crystal answered. "If we can fix the leak tight tomorrow, we should be fine. If it keeps on leaking, we can still sail, but we'll have to bail out all the time, and everything below will be damn wet, and cold, and clammy. Including our bunks. Not exactly the *Love Boat*."

"And the leak isn't our only problem," Joy added. "What do you think Marietta is going to do? I think she'll turn us into the Coast Guard."

"I agree," Arthur said. "She's angry, and she's not the sort of person who handles anger real well."

"So what will happen?" Joy asked. "I wish I could spin my coin."

"Your God will talk to you in other ways," Dawn assured her.

"What happens depends on what Marietta tells people," Arthur said. "That we stole a boat? That we've been raiding yachts all up and down the Maine coast? That we threw a dead body overboard? That we killed McKinley? Hell, there's no reason to think she'll stick to the truth."

"I don't care," Logan said, pushing his hair back. "I'm totally not worried about Marietta, and I'm not worried about the Coast Guard, and I'm not worried about the leak in our boat. We'll fix the leak, Marietta is just an annoyance, and as for the Coast Guard—well, it wouldn't take us long to sail into international waters."

There was a moment of stunned silence.

"WHAT?" Arthur shouted. "Sail into international waters? Are you crazy? What the hell are we supposed to do out there?"

"It's simple," Logan said. "Think about it. We're pirates, remember? You think Bluebeard or Jean Laffite ever cared whose waters they were in? They just moved around from country to country, from coast to coast, you know, like, raiding when they had to and living however they wanted. There's no reason why we can't do that. Go on up to, like, the Canadian Maritimes for a while. Sail up the New Brunswick coast, cross over to Nova Scotia, maybe even go all the way out to Newfoundland. Then sail back after people have forgotten all about us, and just totally keep on going. The Chesapeake. Florida. The Caribbean. Mexico. Hell, we could get enough money to sail through the Panama Canal if we wanted to—go on up to the Baja, California, or Alaska. Don't you see? We're all free. We can totally do anything we want to."

There was another long silence as everyone on deck sipped their cider and thought about Logan's idea. Finally Joy spoke. "You're saying that we should leave our parents for good," she said. "*Es todo*. That's all. Just disappear. Forever."

"That's not the end of the fucking world," Crystal said.

"But you're also saying that we should leave our friends, our schools, our families—everything," Joy said. "That's not what I thought would happen when I joined this crew."

Dawn nodded. "I don't think most of us are in a position to just—" She stopped in midsentence, interrupted by a loud, low wail from below. A moment later, Jesse staggered up the gangway, cradling Ishmael's tiny, gray, lifeless body in his hands.

☠   ☠   ☠

"What happened?" Arthur asked.

Jesse couldn't talk, his eyes dark with pain and his throat squeezed tight in anguish. BillFi came up the gangway behind him.

"It was all just too much for her," BillFi said gently. "Just too much. Marietta's tantrum, crashing into the rock, she fell into the water again and again, the tilting ship and the noise and the fear and everything. It was all just too much for her. I think she was sick when we got her, but she was getting better. But she couldn't take all this."

Jesse shoved past the others and sat alone at the bow, still holding Ishmael tenderly.

"She was alive when we found her under the stove in the galley," BillFi continued. "She was alive, but she was acting strangely and sneezing a lot. She wouldn't come out. Then Jesse pulled her out and picked her up. She mewed once, licked his face, and then died."

The crew was silent. Joy prayed softly. Tears trickled down Dawn's face. But there was nothing to say. The kitten—liberated from abusive owners, freed on board the Dreadnought, full of life and cuteness and spirit—was gone, replaced with stiff fur, glazed eyes, and a drooping tail. Joy whispered a prayer, in part for Ishmael but mainly for Jesse, asking God to ease his distress and calm his soul. Dawn let the powers of the earth and the sea wash through her and the ship, taking Ishmael's life force and returning it to the spirit energy that makes the world turn and the heavens shine. Crystal just stared out to sea; she never knew what to say or do when things like this happened. Arthur glanced forward, worried about his friend but wise enough not to intrude on the dark solitude he maintained on the bow.

Abruptly Jesse stood and stomped back below, carrying Ishmael with him. He returned a few minutes later with some scraps of wood and a small tin can. The crew watched as Jesse, his face grim and his eyes red, tinkered with the wood near the bow. Then he came back to the main deck, carrying the product of his work. It was a small raft, just large enough for Ishmael's damp body. Jesse had built a tent of sticks on top of her. Looking at no one, he carried the tiny boat and the can down the ladder to the dinghy. He pushed away from the *Dreadnought* and let the dinghy drift through the waves. Then he poured kerosene from the can over the little raft, set it on the water's surface, and struck a match. The blazing raft bobbed slowly downwind, turning friendship into fiery light. Jesse sat by himself in the dinghy and didn't move. From time to time, a deep wail would rise from the sea, and Jesse would grip his own shoulders and rock against the tilting of the waves.

The others were quiet on deck, watching the ritual taking place below. The small flame grew distant, sputtered, and went out. They sat in silence for a long time.

Their thoughts were shattered when Dawn leapt to her feet. "Oh, Goddess," Dawn blurted. "Look at that!"

Off the starboard beam drifted a huge wooden ship, double-masted and old-fashioned—dark, silent, and deserted.

CHAPTER FIFTEEN

TWENTY-FOUR KNOTS OF FREEDOM LEFT

The ship seemed oddly out of place. It was tall with a squat hull, and it seemed to absorb all flickers of light—flashlights, lighthouses, stars—turning them back in a bleak, desolate reflection, like the ashes of a long-dead fire. Its stern was tall and nearly vertical, and its bow came to a blunt and chubby point. The detail work, including an ornately carved wooden railing and an elaborate bowsprit that resembled a large and desperate bird, offered evidence that this was once both the product and the symbol of wealth. Now, though, it seemed tired and over-worn, a refugee that had drifted into another time.

Jesse was still in the dinghy, staring at the dark waves, but the rest of the *Dreadnought* crew crowded the starboard rail and stared at the derelict. "Ahoy!" Arthur boomed his low voice across the shortening gap of water between the two ships. "Anyone on board?"

There was no reply. The ship slid quietly closer to the *Dreadnought*. In the faint light of the stars and the glow from the distant mainland, the crewmates could begin to make out some details. The mainmast was broken. The mizzen-mast was angled sickeningly to one side. The ropes dangled limply, some in knots and tangles, some just rotting away. The bowsprit was mangled. The glass of the portholes was broken and dull. And the wheel turned aimlessly, with no hand to guide it.

"A ghost ship!" Logan said.

"Maybe," Arthur said. "Or maybe there are people on board who are sick or hurt. I think we should board it. As your captain, I—" He caught himself short. "Uh, I mean— what do you all think we should do?" Out the corner of his eye, he could see Dawn beaming a big freckled grin at him. He liked the way that felt.

"I'll go with you," Logan said.

"So will I," Dawn said. Crystal also volunteered, eager for some action to lift the oppressive sorrow of Ishmael's death. BillFi remained on the *Dreadnought*, waiting for Jesse's grief to ebb.

"Let's go," Arthur said. Let's go, he thought. That's what leaders say, isn't it? Not "Get going." At least, that's what he thought Dawn would say. This new approach still felt like he was wearing someone else's clothes. He called to Jesse gently and asked him to bring the dinghy over.

Jesse climbed over the ship's side and walked quickly below, speaking to no one. "Let's leave him alone," Arthur said softly. "He needs to work this out on his own for a while. We can talk with him when we're back from that ship." The others nodded.

Arthur, Dawn, Crystal, and Logan climbed down into the dinghy, and Arthur rowed them over to the strange ship. As they worked their way across the black undulating water, they could make out the name carved on the bow.

"The *Icarus*," Dawn read. "I see a ladder built in over there." She pointed toward the stern. Arthur pulled the dinghy in close.

"Halllooo!" Arthur called out. No reply. Only the sound of dripping water and creaking wood.

"Ahoy!" Dawn shouted. "Anyone home?"

Nothing.

"We're coming aboard!" Arthur called. "We're here to help you!"

"Yeah," Logan said softly, "if there's, like, anyone here to help."

They tied the dinghy to the wooden ladder and climbed up; the rungs were cool and soft with moss. Indistinct in the darkness, the deck of the *Icarus* looked like it had been abandoned a century ago. Planks were spongy in places, rotting underfoot and threatening to give way. The air was musty and mildewed. As the ship rocked in the waves, a door down below banged open and closed, open and closed.

"Look at this," Dawn said. Carved into the ship's wheel were crudely shaped initials and a number: I.R.C. 92. "What do you suppose this means?"

Arthur shrugged. "Irving Rutherford Cronkheit, 1892?"

"In Royal Company?" Crystal guessed. "Maybe the 'R' is for 'Royal.'"

"Maybe it's 'I'd Rather be Camping,'" Logan suggested with a grin.

"Cute," Dawn replied, smiling. "I wonder if it is 1892, and whether that's the year the ship was made, or the year it was abandoned."

A moment later, Logan called from the bow. "Over here! Look." When the others arrived, he pointed to the deck. The anchor chain had been carefully placed to form a large black X.

"Creepy," Arthur said. "I wonder why they did that?"

"Could be a warning," Dawn said, "or a message to anyone who finds the ship."

"A message like what?" Logan asked. "'Abandon Hope All Ye Who Enter Here'?"

"Maybe," Dawn said with a shrug.

In silence the crew took in the mood of the ship: the grayness of the wood, the uneasy slope of the deck, the rich odor of rotten planks.

"I totally hate this place," Logan said. "Let's get back to the Dreadnought."

"In a minute," Arthur said. "A ship like this must have had a crew of at least eight or nine and maybe a lot more. I wonder where they all went."

"I don't know," Crystal said, "but it doesn't look like a happy ending."

As they surveyed the dank and crumbling deck, wondering about the events that led to the abandonment of the Icarus, Arthur found himself thinking about the end of their own voyage. Only twenty-four knots remained in his ropeline calendar; just twenty-four days before families would gather in Rockland expecting to meet McKinley and eight happy campers. What story could they tell to make it all make sense? What could they say that would make the summer end well?

His thoughts were interrupted when Dawn suggested that they explore the rooms below before returning to the Dreadnought. At first, Logan chose to stay up on deck, but he changed his mind when he realized he would be completely alone. He climbed down the gangway right behind the others.

Below decks, the rooms were dark, clammy, and vacant. In the beams of their flashlights, the crew could see that the beds were damp and rumpled; no one had done any housekeeping before they all abandoned ship.

The captain's quarters was thick with the residue of ancient cigar smoke. The desk was collapsing in on itself, and the bed was greening with mold. Overhead, the low ceiling was streaked with cobwebs and darkened with spiders. Arthur poked through the damp rubble of the desk carefully, but he found little evidence that could answer any questions. No log, no diary, no coins with dates on them. The captain, it seemed, had time to gather his records. But only just barely. At the bottom of a shelf that had long since fallen down, Arthur found a small piece of ivory with part of a ship carved into its flat surface.

"Scrimshaw," Arthur said as he aimed his flashlight onto the off-white treasure. "Nautical scenes carved into ivory. It gave sailors something to do during their off hours. The captain grabbed his logbook and stuff, but he didn't have time to take the carving he had been working on." He looked around the small room. "This ship has been empty for decades," he said with wonder in his voice. "What made them all leave in such a hurry?"

"Pirate attack?" Logan guessed.

"Maybe," Arthur said, "or a sudden, hideous disease. Or starvation—they might have scrambled overboard at the first sign of land."

"Maybe they were all swept overboard by a storm," Dawn said.

"Or they, like, killed each other off," Logan offered. "A mutiny, and then a counter-mutiny, and then another and another."

"Whatever it was," Arthur said, "it was quick, and it was complete—no one stayed behind to take care of the ship."

The four *Dreadnought* crewmates continued their search of the ship. They found an old pair of leather shoes in one room, the moldering remains of a wool cap in another, but no indication that anyone had remained behind after the others had left. In the forward head, they saw a pair of black canvas trousers, soggy and shredded in small pieces scattered throughout the room.

"Rats did that," Arthur said. "But I don't even think they're on board any more."

"They ran out of food?" Dawn suggested.

Arthur nodded. "Or they knew she was about to sink," he said.

The crewmates stood in silence for a moment.

"I, like, totally think it's time to go," Logan said. The others agreed.

☠   ☠   ☠

Jesse sat on the bowsprit all night, staring off at the point where he had last seen Ishmael's light. When the sun rose, he climbed down to the main deck and rejoined the stretching and yawning crew, speaking not a word about the loss of his little friend. Joy gave him a hug. Arthur patted him on the shoulder. Dawn whispered a blessing that was designed to brighten spirits. And BillFi just sat next to him in silence.

And in the rational light of morning, there was no sign of the *Icarus*.

The *Dreadnought* sailed gently downwind to Matinicus Island, a large tourist destination a comfortable distance out to sea. The crew pooled the cash left in their pockets to buy whatever they would need to repair the damaged hull. Most of the crewmates toured the island, which was beautiful with trim cottages, wild blueberry bushes, and the rugged enchantment of rocky beaches and heavy tides—an odd contrast to the glooming hulk of the *Icarus* the night before. Jesse stayed on board, staring out to sea. While the others took in some sightseeing, Logan and BillFi hiked over to a marine hardware store.

"What do you need today?" asked the woman behind the counter. She was short and stocky, with silver hair and strong blue eyes, and she looked like she could weather the toughest storm ever suffered in the North Atlantic. Her stare was unnerving.

"Well," Logan said, "we have, like, a problem."

"It's a hole," BillFi said, pushing his glasses up his nose. "In our boat. In the side of our boat."

"Down low," Logan said.

"A big hole," BillFi said. "It's a big hole—well, pretty big, anyway—and it's in the side of our ship. Down low on the side, below where the water usually goes. Do you know the best way to patch something like that?"

The woman stared straight at them. She didn't smile. She just pierced them with her eyes, and then she shook her head in disbelief.

"Wood or fiberglass?" she asked.

"Wood," Logan said. He blinked behind a cascade of red hair.

"How big's the hole?"

BillFi pushed up his glasses and shrugged. "I'd say it's about a foot and a half in diameter. More or less. A foot and a half across. That's big, for a hole."

The woman stared at them. "A foot and a half?"

Logan nodded.

The woman stared at them. "You have a foot-and-a-half hole in your hull. Below the water line?"

BillFi nodded.

The woman stared at them. "You have a huge hole in your hull, below the water line, and you want me to give you something so you can fix it?"

Logan nodded.

The woman stared at them some more. It was becoming spooky. "I'll give you something, all right. I'll give you some advice. Admit to your father that you wrecked his boat and tell him to take it over to Minot's right away for repairs. They're pretty busy this time of year, but they could probably get it fixed in a few weeks. Until then, you'd best forget about your allowances and see what you can do about weeding the garden or something to pay him back."

BillFi shook his head. "You don't understand," he said. "It's our boat. Not our father's. The boat belongs to us. Well, you know— To us. It belongs to us. Pretty much."

The woman snorted. "Your father *gave* you a boat?" She obviously didn't approve. She shook her head and clucked. "Well, if it's patch material you need, I have that for you." Logan exhaled. She led them through the aisles of the cluttered store, past the folding ladders and the heavy-duty drills and the power sanders, and then she handed them a five-gallon can of marine pitch, some wide paintbrushes, some caulk, and a large copper patch. "Here. Pay me at the counter."

BillFi produced a small wad of bills and he paid for the supplies. The woman took the money without a smile. "Just be off with you now," she said. "Good luck with that patch of yours. And keep an eye out for those pirates we've been hearing about."

Logan and BillFi froze. "Pirates?" Logan asked.

"Sure," the woman said. "You've heard about them. Teenagers. Murderers. Filthy thieving bandits. Would sooner cut your throat than say hello. It's like one of them Los Angeles gangs, only on the water. Everybody's talking about them." She looked at Logan intently. "I'm surprised you haven't heard of them."

"Uh, we've been out on the water for a while," BillFi said. "Out of touch, you know. On the water."

They left the store quickly and almost sprinted down to the dinghy.

☠   ☠   ☠

Back on the *Dreadnought*, sitting with the others in a circle on the aft deck, BillFi described their encounter in the marine hardware store.

"She acted like everyone on the island knew about us," BillFi said. "Like they knew we were here."

Dawn shook her head seriously. "Marietta wouldn't come all the way out here," she said, "so people must be talking about us on the radio. It's safe to guess that every town all up and down the coast has heard about us."

"BillFi," Crystal said, "did the lady know what the ship looks like? Did she know our ship's name?"

"I don't think so," BillFi answered. "All she knew was that a nasty gang of teenagers was causing a lot of trouble. A whole lot of trouble. 'Murderous thieves.' She seemed to think that they were willing to kill people, even if they had no good reason. She looked at us strangely, but I don't think she figured us out. I don't think so."

Dawn, the captain for the day, stood up. "We had better get out of here, just in case. Let's head back to Large Green Island. It was pretty isolated—I don't think anyone'll find us there. Then we can fix the hull and talk over what we should do next. Agreed?"

The crew agreed.

"Okay," Dawn said. "Let's hoist the sails. Fast. And Joy—monitor the radio and tell us if you hear anything more about those nasty teenage pirates."

As the *Dreadnought* sailed west-northwest toward Large Green, Arthur sat on bow watch and thought about what had just happened. It seemed odd that rumors about the Plunder Dogs were circulating along the coast. If Marietta had talked to the police or the Coast Guard and turned them in, they would have been contacted by now. Officially. Permanently. It was strange that the only "evidence" that Marietta was talking was a wild rumor about cutthroat kids. Arthur knew it wouldn't last. Marietta was bound to turn them in.

The *Dreadnought* sailed for two more days, the crew watching the new stronger patch carefully but finding nothing more than a small trickle of seawater seeping in through the hull. Arthur spent an increasing amount of time sitting on the bow, trying to make sense of everything. His rope calendar was down to twenty-one knots—just three weeks of summer left—and he wanted to make sure it ended well. With Marietta out there, he thought, it might not.

After a while, Dawn joined him on the bow. "A penny for your thoughts," she said.

"A penny? I'm not that cheap," Arthur said with a smile.

"Okay," Dawn said. "Fifty thousand dollars and a new car."

"Sold," Arthur said. "But I want a down payment before I talk."

She kissed him.

"Close enough," Arthur said. "Actually, I was thinking about this rumor that BillFi and Logan heard. Why is Marietta spreading rumors about us instead of just turning us in?"

Dawn shrugged. "Just to make us suffer for a while?"

"Possible," Arthur said. "But I think there's more to it than that. She doesn't just want us to fold, to give up. She wants to win. She wants to win big. So I think she's trying to make us panic. If we get worried and then start doing stupid things, we could make this all really bad for us—and then she could be smug in the knowledge that she didn't go along with this whole idea."

"So she's hoping that we'll bolt for international waters," Dawn said.

"Something like that," Arthur said. "Or kill ourselves. Or raid the Maine Maritime Academy. Who knows what she's thinking. But it seems like she wants us to do something crazy."

They sailed on in silence for a while, the bow splashing through the shallow waves.

"You know what I hope?" Dawn asked.

"What?" Arthur asked.

"I hope that we—I mean you and I—"

"The hope will have to wait," BillFi said. He was suddenly behind them. "That hope will have to wait. There's a storm coming. A big storm coming." He pointed to the northeast horizon where some dark towering clouds had formed. The wind was blowing from that direction. "You ought to hope we don't sink."

   ☠ ☠ ☠

As soon as the *Dreadnought* returned to Large Green, the crew scrambled to get ready for the gale. Dawn issued commands, and the crew worked smartly through the drill. Portholes were clamped shut. Hatches were secured. Anything loose was tied down or stowed securely. The sails were struck and stored below.

  Arthur and Jesse worked on the anchors. They let out extra line on the main anchor to improve the angle and increase the anchor's grip on the sea floor. Then they climbed into the dinghy with two additional smaller anchors that were also tied to the *Dreadnought*'s bow. They rowed out as far as they could, angling off the starboard corner of the ship, and dropped the first anchor. Then they maneuvered over to the same position off the port corner and dropped the second.

  "That should hold her," Arthur said. They returned to the *Dreadnought* quickly.

  Down below, the crew braced the weakened timbers of the shattered hull with everything they could find.

  Once all the preparations were complete, the crew gathered on the aft deck and waited. They could see stars overhead in the evening darkness, but the sky to the northeast was black.

  "It'll be here in about half an hour," BillFi said.

  "What does the radio say about how bad it is?" Dawn asked.

  "*Feo.* It's bad," Joy said. "Gale-force winds, high seas, a lot of rain. There's an advisory out for the next eight hours. Everyone is supposed to seek a safe harbor."

"Well, we've done everything we can," Dawn said. "I think we'll be all right—if that patch holds. It should. Crystal nailed it down pretty—"

She was interrupted by an eerie glow, greenish yellow and electric, that danced around the rigging high overhead. The crew fell silent and watched as the crackling energy shimmered and sparked overhead.

"Wow!" Dawn whispered. "Arthur—it's that fire! Saint Erwin's Fire!"

"Elmo's," Arthur whispered back. "Isn't it beautiful?"

☠   ☠   ☠

The storm hit with malevolent fury. Within seconds after the winds started to rise, the *Dreadnought* was engulfed in a rage of wind, waves, and rain. The rigging screamed overhead, struggling against the masts in a windswept panic. Slashes of lightning crackled across the sky. Snarling curls of water and foam crashed over the decks, forcing everyone to scuttle below. The *Dreadnought* lurched and heeled, but its anchors seemed to hold.

The crew huddled around the table beneath Joy's latest Bible sign: "You shall love your neighbor as yourself— Matthew 22:39." Joy was in the captain's quarters monitoring the radio. She stuck her head into the main cabin and gave the crew an update.

"It's going to be five hours more, at least," she said. "The Coast Guard says it's one of the worst storms in the last ten years. It's all people are talking about on the radio—nothing about us right now."

"Well, that's a relief, anyway," Arthur said. But he knew that the silence would be temporary. If people on Matinicus had heard about these "pirates," then it was just a matter of time before the Coast Guard did, too. The source of the information was obviously Marietta, and Arthur knew she would turn them in before long.

He thought about Marietta, what she was doing right now. She's probably sitting in some hotel room, he thought, eating ice cream and watching TV. Her parents are probably on their way to get her, but she's enjoying her final night of freedom. He smirked. Hell, she might even go down to the hotel bar and sing a few catchy tunes.

The image of Marietta in a comfortable hotel, courtesy of the money she took from the *Dreadnought*, offered an interesting contrast to the dimly lit cabin of the stoic ship. As the waves outside pounded and thrashed, the ship rocked with a kind of strong grace. The lantern hanging from a hook overhead angled from side to side—or seemed to—as the ship was lifted and dropped by the swells.

Arthur looked around the table.

All in all, he thought, not a bad crew. Jesse gives us strength. BillFi gives us vision. Crystal brings toughness, Joy brings faith, and Logan brings a few laughs. And Dawn— Dawn brings passion, and beauty, and warmth, and depth, and love. He smiled, and he wondered why he hadn't recognized her extraordinary grace from the start. And I bring—

He stopped.

What do I bring to this crew? he wondered. A while ago, I would have said I brought leadership, and direction, and authority. But no one wanted any of that, and things have gone more smoothly since we started sharing the captain's job. So what do I give to the crew? If I'm not the leader, then what am I?

He didn't know. He couldn't answer his own questions. All he could sense were the gifts that the others had given to him. He felt stronger, more relaxed, more sure of himself—and ironically, less desperate to be in charge. But he couldn't sense his own place in the crew.

Dawn squeezed his hand. "Pretty cool summer, wouldn't you say?" she asked.

Arthur smiled. "Why shouldn't it be?" he asked back.

"Are all summers this wonderful?"

"Aren't all summers as good as they can be?"

"Was last summer this great for you?"

Arthur shook his head. "No," he said, "it wasn't."

Crystal stood up. "Well, I don't know about you all," she said, "but I'm beat. It's almost midnight. Let's work out a watch rotation and go to bed."

"I'll stay up," Arthur said.

"So will I," Dawn volunteered.

"Okay," Crystal said. "Then the rest of us—"

BillFi jumped to his feet. "She's going down!" he blurted out.

After a tense silence, Crystal spoke. "The *Dreadnought*? How?"

BillFi shook his head. "Not the *Dreadnought*," he said. "The *Icarus*."

The crew rushed to the starboard portholes. In the lightning flashes, they could see the decrepit ashen shell of the *Icarus* looming nearby once again, but this time listing sickeningly to port. A huge wave lifted her high into the air and sent her reeling down the other side. Another wave tossed her sideways onto a ledge; the *Dreadnought* crewmates could hear her ribs snap against the rock. Then she scraped off the granite, rose dizzyingly skyward on another wave, and settled slowly into the water. She was low and angled awkwardly, fat and clumsy in the water. Each new wave sent her into a lurching tumble; it seemed like she would roll completely over soon. Then she thrust her bow high into the air, proud and tall and arrogant against the storm.

A moment later, she careened over, hit the waves hard— and was gone.

The crew was silent, staring at the spot where the *Icarus* had gone down.

"Godspeed, *Icarus*," Joy said out loud. "May you finally rejoin your crew."

The cabin was silent as everyone returned to their chairs around the table. The dim light of the galley seemed strangely peaceful in the midst of the howling storm outside. Logan passed around a bottle of rum, and a splash was poured into every glass but Crystal's and Joy's. They took straight apple juice—and so did Logan.

"To the captain and crew of the *Icarus*," Logan said. "It takes, like, a really good ship to carry on, even after the loss of her crew. May Neptune keep them all safe from storms forevermore."

"May God keep them safe forevermore," Joy said.

"May the Goddesses keep them safe forevermore," Dawn said with a grin.

"Forevermore," chanted the crew. They lifted their glasses and drank.

☠   ☠   ☠

The storm raged on, but the *Dreadnought*'s anchors held fast to the ocean floor. Most of the crew settled in for some sleep, leaving Arthur and Dawn to monitor the radio and check the makeshift patch from time to time.

The two sat in the captain's quarters in comfortable silence, snug on the smartly made bed. The calendar rope that Arthur had fashioned at the start of the summer had dwindled down.

"It's all ending, isn't it?" Dawn asked. "I mean, we can't go on much longer. That copper patch is good, but it won't hold forever. Marietta's bound to tell the Coast Guard about us, if she hasn't already. And sooner or later, we'll get caught raiding somebody's yacht."

Arthur nodded. "And I don't think we're going to head for international waters," he said. "At least, I don't intend to."

"But if we don't go away somewhere, how will we end all this?" Dawn asked. "How can we just stop all this and go home? We sank a dead body in the Gulf of Maine, and we're sailing a ship that doesn't belong to us. We can't just buzz into Portland harbor, tie up to a dock, and wander off. Sooner or later, someone's going to want to know what happened to McKinley."

"I know," Arthur said quietly. "I've been thinking about that. He left enough notes and journal entries that I think we can convince people that we didn't kill him. But they won't believe us at first. And even if we do convince them, we're probably going to have to explain the yacht raiding. That's bound to come out. Even if Marietta doesn't tell anyone about it, someone from the crew will surely let it slip somehow. And I don't know what we'll have to say about that."

They sat on the bed for a while in silence, their arms around each other. The wind shrieked outside, but the noise only added to their sense of secrecy and promise—and sadness.

"Still," Dawn said, "it's been such a great trip. We've seen some amazing things. We've crawled through caves looking for treasure. We've gone skinny-dipping in a phosphorescent sea. We've sailed through the night, had cookouts on the beach, and weathered a lot of storms—this one included, I hope. I don't regret anything we've done. I just hope it all works out okay."

"It will," Arthur said. "We haven't come this far just to make it all end badly. Sooner or later, a path will become visible. BillFi said so. And we'll choose, maybe, to take it. And whatever path we choose will lead us out of this part of our lives and on to the next one. We'll be just fine."

"I hope so," Dawn said. "I don't want to look back on all this and feel sad, or guilty, or embarrassed."

"What I'm wondering," Arthur said, "is what will happen to us. You and me. One way or another, this summer is going to end, and we'll have to go home. I'd like to see you some more, even after all this is over. But how can we keep on seeing each other? We live almost four hours apart."

"Yeah," Dawn said, "but high school doesn't last forever. I'm thinking of going to the College of the Atlantic. It's a cool school in Bar Harbor, Maine—specializes in human ecology. How about you?"

Arthur sighed. "Dartmouth, if I'm lucky," he said. "That would get us closer, but it's not like we'd see each other very often."

"Maybe we could settle on a college we both like," Dawn said.

"How about the University of Tasmania?" Arthur said with a grin.

"I love it," Dawn said, a sparkle in her green eyes. "If we start sailing now, we might get there by the end of our senior year."

"Or how about Fairbanks?" Arthur said. "You know, in Alaska? I hear they have a great—" He was interrupted by the squawking of the radio.

"Mayday! Mayday! Mayday! This is an emergency! We are caught in the storm, and we're taking on water. We're going down. Please help. Please help NOW. Mayday! Mayday! Mayday! We're sinking, and we need immediate assistance. Repeat: We are sinking. If anyone can hear me, please help us."

"I know that voice!" Arthur said. "That's Richard Turner!"

CHAPTER SIXTEEN

Twenty-one Knots of Freedom Left

Dawn and Arthur awakened the crew and gathered everyone around the table. They had to speak loudly to be heard over the increasing howl of the storm outside.

"The *Elkhart's* in a lot of trouble," Dawn explained. "It sounds like they were trying to get to Matinicus Island, but the storm pushed them onto the Foster Ledges. They've rolled completely over at least once, their mast is broken, and their diesel engine is dead. They're taking on water around the propeller shaft, and it's coming in pretty fast. I figure they have maybe twenty minutes before she sinks completely."

"I think their radio was damaged when they rolled," Arthur said. "Their signal faded a lot. We relayed the distress call to the Coast Guard station in Rockland, but I don't think their cutters can get here in time. I think we're the closest ship for miles around."

"I think we should go get them," Dawn said. "We can sail in close and send some people over in the dinghy. The *Elkhart* is going to sink, but we can at least rescue Turner and his crew."

"What do you say?" Arthur said. Asking for input from the others was becoming more natural. "It's risky, and we could get in a lot of trouble out there. Our patch is holding, but it won't stay tight forever. But we can't just sit here and let those people drown. We're good enough at sailing to handle almost anything. Should we go?"

There was a long silence.

"We could totally get killed out there," Logan said, wiping his hair back.

Dawn nodded. "Yes, we could. But remember why we all came to the *Dreadnought* in the first place. We wanted to be stronger. More mature. More independent. We wanted to face challenges and overcome them. Well, right now we're facing the biggest challenge of our lives. Are we up for it?"

Joy reached for her Saints coin, then bowed her head when she remembered that it was no longer in her possession. She knew that Dawn was right; God wanted her to make her own decisions. She listened carefully for God's still voice, and then she nodded. "I'm here to help people," she said. "So I'm going. Who else wants to join me?"

Six hands rose high.

"Okay," Arthur said, "let's make it happen. Joy, how high are the winds out there?"

Joy looked at him solemnly. "They gust up to hurricane strength at times," she said. "Sixty-eight knots."

☠　　☠　　☠

It was just after midnight on August 1st, and Dawn was the captain. She assigned each crewmate to a position: Arthur at navigation, Jesse and Logan on the sheets and sails, Joy and Crystal on bow watch, BillFi down below to monitor the patch, and she took the helm. Within a few minutes, the *Dreadnought* slid out of its protected harbor and into the chaos of the storm.

The waves were ferocious, crashing again and again over the forward deck. The crew was dressed in full rain gear, with hoods pulled forward and low on their faces. Joy and Crystal tied themselves to the rigging and held on as hard as they could as they watched for rocks and debris. Whenever they saw something in the water, they would shout back to Dawn and point toward the hazard.

It was all Dawn could do to keep the *Dreadnought* on course. With each wave, the ship lurched to port, and Dawn pulled hard on the wheel to counter the blow. After each wave, she threw the wheel in the opposite direction to stay on course. Arthur held tight to binoculars and tried to catch glimpses of markers while the ship was high on a wave, and he shouted compass directions to Dawn as they pressed ahead.

Bolts of lightning illuminated the crew's gestures in blazing strobe flashes as the wind ripped their words out to sea.

It took more than forty-five minutes for them to reach the Foster Ledges. Arthur searched the sea with the binoculars, but he saw no sign of the *Elkhart*.

"Get BillFi up here!" Dawn shouted. Arthur dashed below to the galley.

"It's still holding," BillFi said, standing almost knee-deep in seawater. "The patch. It's leaking a little. But it's holding. The patch is holding."

"Good," Arthur replied. "BillFi, we need you on deck."

BillFi scrambled up the gangway and stood next to Dawn at the wheel. He hunched in his yellow slicker and closed his eyes. He listened to the wind. He listened to the rain. He listened to the waves. "They're over there," he shouted. He pointed off the starboard beam. "Half a mile or so."

"Ready about!" Dawn shouted. "Hard alee!" She turned

the wheel hard to the right. The *Dreadnought* came across the wind and headed off on its new tack. It was just a few minutes later that Joy called back from the bow.

"I see something!" she shouted. "Over there!" She pointed just off the port bow. Ahead in the water was an oily cluster of debris—scraps of fiberglass, splintered pieces of polished wood, a clutch of cognac bottles bobbing on the waves. In the midst of the wreckage, clinging tightly to a swamped lifeboat, were Turner and his crew.

How does BillFi do that? Dawn asked herself. She barked out some orders. "Heave to! Jesse, Arthur, Crystal—grab life jackets and get into the dinghy. Let's get these people on board!"

As usual, Jesse took the oars, and the three crewmates ventured out into the waves. The *Dreadnought* was close to the wreckage, but it still took Jesse, pulling with all his strength, nearly ten minutes to cross the violent swirl of ocean between the ship and the wild-eyed crew of the *Elkhart*. They were clustered around the swamped dinghy, holding on and kicking with their feet to stay afloat. The dinghy had enough buoyancy to help, but cold and fatigue strained the victim's faces.

Jesse pulled the dinghy alongside, and Richard Turner helped his crew grab onto the sides.

"There are too many of us!" Turner shouted over the shrieks of wind. "You'll have to make two trips. We'll wait with—damn! It's the *Dreadnought* crew!"

"Yes, sir," Crystal shouted back. "We'll get you out of this."

Arthur looked at the ashen faces peering over the gunwales. "Turner!" he shouted. "We'll take five in this dinghy—the weakest, any injured, the coldest. Let's get them in here."

"We can't hold five!" Crystal shouted back.

"Yes, we can," Arthur answered. "You and I are getting out. We've trained for this, and we know what to do." This is no time for democratic discussion, he thought.

Crystal spun around and locked her blue eyes on Arthur. Then she nodded. "We sure do!" she said.

Arthur grabbed one of the *Elkhart* crew under the arms. It was the cook, who looked just as somber and nervous as he had at dinner on the deck. Arthur planted a foot against the dinghy's hull and hauled the man painfully over the gunwale. The cook flopped into the bottom of the dinghy, lay stunned for a moment, then curled up on the bow seat.

Arthur next reached for the meteorologist, but she grinned and laughed out loud. "Hell, no," she said. "Take him first." She nodded her head toward the nine-year-old. Arthur wasn't going to waste time arguing; he grabbed the boy and dragged him into the dinghy. By this time, Crystal had helped the first mate, Woody Richardson, climb over the gunwales, and she was busy dragging the young actress on board. The dinghy lay dangerously low in the water, and waves spilled in over the side.

"Crystal!" Arthur shouted. "Let's go!" The two of them tightened their life jackets and vaulted into the sea, and Arthur helped Garrison Chevalier boost himself into the dinghy. Without wasting a second, Jesse heaved on the oars. The dinghy moved slowly back toward the solid safety of the *Dreadnought*.

The water was colder than Arthur had expected. He felt the icy water suck his strength out to sea. He grabbed the side of the *Elkhart*'s swamped lifeboat and hollered over the wind. "Everybody in! Now!"

Counting Crystal and Arthur, there were seven people left in the water. Arthur did not bother with discussion and consensus. "Everybody sit down!" he shouted. "Sit down in the boat!"

Crystal nodded. The swamped-dinghy drills. They had been fun, many weeks ago, but now the skills they had developed in those drills were going to matter. She modeled the proper position and signaled for everyone else to do the same. Jim Greenfeather and Richard Turner caught on and helped the meteorologist and the Hennessey sisters hunker down in the boat. The group worked well together, and they squirmed down into the chilly water inside the dinghy, held onto the sides, and waited for the next command.

The drill went perfectly. At Arthur's shout, the crew raised to a crouching position, and Arthur, Jim, Turner, and Crystal slapped and splashed water furiously over the sides. It took a long suspenseful moment, but gradually, the dinghy's gunwales inched above the surface. Once the others saw the progress, they all began bailing water out of the boat. Ten minutes later, the boat was high enough to make steady bailing possible. An occasional wave and the driving rain refilled the boat, but the crew was able to keep up with it. The dinghy was too overloaded to row, but the waterlogged people inside could at least keep themselves out of the ocean.

Half an hour later, Jesse returned with the dinghy. He had come alone to leave as many seats as possible for the *Elkhart* crew. Half the people in the *Elkhart* dinghy climbed over to Jesse's boat, and the two small vessels worked their way through the storm to the safety of the *Dreadnought*.

Even on board the ship, there was a lot of work to be done. Except for Jim Greenfeather and Richard Turner, who insisted on helping with the sails, the *Elkhart* crew was taken below and treated with bandages, hot soup, and warm blankets. On deck, the crew set some sails, and Dawn took navigational directions from Crystal, who had plotted a course to the nearest safe waters. Once the ship was tucked away between Matinicus and Ragged Island, with three anchors out and everything stowed and secured, the two crews squeezed into the dining room below. Some steady bailing had reduced the water underfoot to an insignificant layer of dampness.

Sipping hot cocoa and wrapped in a damp woolen blanket, Turner explained what had happened. "There are some people expecting us on Matinicus," he said. "Some old business partners of mine have a cottage there, and they invited us over for a few days. We knew the storm was coming, but we thought we could get there in time." He took a deep drink of the cocoa. "I guess we were wrong. The storm hit us quickly and drove us up on those ledges. The propeller shaft broke, and we started to go down. After we sent out our Mayday, we evacuated to the lifeboat, but we couldn't even keep it from swamping. That water is cold—we wouldn't have lasted out there much longer."

"It is a wild one," Dawn said, listening to the howl of the wind outside. "I'm just glad everyone is all right."

Turner shook his head, his face pale and his expression serious. "If I can ever repay you for saving us, you let me know," he said.

"On behalf of the crew of the *Dreadnought*," Dawn said, raising her mug, "you're welcome."

Crystal and Jim huddled under a blanket along one wall. Dawn and Arthur did the same. Everyone chatted about boats, storms, Maine, and life at sea. The storm outside raged for a while and then gradually diminished into spent silence.

Early the next morning, the *Dreadnought* dropped the pas-
sengers off at Matinicus Island and sailed on her way. No
mention was made of the "fellow in charge" of the *Dreadnought*.

☠   ☠   ☠

For the next several days, the *Dreadnought* sailed the Gulf of
Maine, Penobscot Bay, and a bit into Muscongus Bay. They
staged some raids on large fancy yachts, snagging summer
sausage, fruit, and other food along with some cash and the
occasional bonus trinket. On one boat, they picked up three
roasted chickens and a soccer ball. On another, they found a
dozen paperback books and a three-gallon tub of Greek
olives. Joy protested from time to time, but she drew strength
from the knowledge that she was bringing the grace of Jesus
among them, even if they sinned. She saw it as good prepara-
tion for her work on the streets of Austin. The House of Joy
had given way in her mind, replaced by a vision of serving
God among the unfortunate people on Earth.

One day, while anchored in a small and pretty cove, Dawn
took a swim through the waves. The saltwater stung her lips.
The sun, strong enough to raise small pink blisters on her shoulders, warmed the top two feet of the ocean waters, leaving chilly
regions of darkness below that licked at her feet. She smiled as
she paused to look around. Logan was on board the schooner
that they all called home, walking barefoot along the ship's edge
and clutching a bright green umbrella. He was making the
sounds of circus music: "BUM pa dittle ittle um pa dum pa,
BUM pa bittle ittle um pa dum pa . . ." as his flag fluttered in
the rigging overhead. Laughing at his antics, Joy and Arthur sat
in the stern and played checkers. Crystal lay on deck, pumping

situps on a mat, and BillFi and Jesse sat on a rock near the shore, debating intently with low tones and sweeping gestures.

"Ah, Goddess," Dawn whispered to the sky, "this is how life was meant to be."

They spent the next afternoon gathering mussels, which Joy used to make a stunning pasta dish with thick noodles and a hearty red sauce. The activity had been fun, with five of the crew wading along a beach at low tide, poking among the rocks and scraping the small meat-filled shells into tin cans. Logan got a nasty sunburn from the experience, but it was a pleasant way to spend a day.

A few days later, Logan declared that he would serve as the chef for the day. His breakfast was basic but tolerable: toast with peanut butter on it, a quivering mass of yellow scrambled eggs with bits of sausage and cheese mixed throughout, glasses of "Logan's Patented Breakfast Juice," which turned out to be a blend of cranberry and grapefruit. Lunch was hot dogs on the leeward beach of a tiny island; deli-made potato salad, pinched in one of the raids, completed the menu. But dinner, Logan said, would be something special. He issued tin cans to the entire crew—everyone was required to participate to get enough food for a meal—and he told his friends to put a little bit of seaweed and saltwater in the bottom of each can.

"I read about this in a Euell Gibbons book in the captain's quarters," he explained. He led them to the beach and demonstrated the procedure he wanted them to follow. "Watch this."

He grabbed a large patch of chocolate-brown seaweed, held his hand still for a slow count to five, then flung the seaweed aside and thrust his hand into the now-open space. Skittering in the sudden sunlight were four tiny crabs, each no bigger than a quarter, and with deft movements Logan grabbed at them and plunked them, one at a time, into his can. He got three, but the fourth escaped below a large rock.

"Greenback crabs," he said, showing the can's contents to the crew. "They're small, but they're totally tasty. We'll need, like, a whole bunch of them."

Joy's dark face looked skeptical. She gazed into the can, then looked up at Logan. "And once we catch a bunch of these," she said, "you're going to cook them, crack open their shells, and pry out the little tiny pieces of meat in there?"

Logan grinned and pushed his hair back. "Won't be necessary," he said. "Watch." He grabbed another mound of seaweed, paused for a moment, and then flung it aside. He plucked up a greenback crab and deftly popped it into his mouth. He chewed it quickly.

"Gross!" Joy squealed. "That thing was alive!"

Logan nodded. "When you eat them this way," he said, "you totally have to bite them before they bite you. But they're really not bad—crunchy, salty, pretty good. For dinner tonight, I'll cook them. You won't have to eat them raw. But we'll eat them whole like this. They're really good."

Crystal shrugged her taut shoulders, flung aside some seaweed, and tossed a crab into her mouth. "They're okay," she said.

The rest of the crew quickly lost interest in the enterprise and set about building small stone villages near the waterline. Undaunted, Logan and Crystal gathered a few dozen of the tiny crabs and dropped them into the cans.

"How exactly are you going to cook these?" Crystal asked.

"That's the really cool part," Logan answered. "First I'll boil them, but along with the crabs I'll boil up some Irish moss—that's the brown stuff growing on those rocks over there. It's, like, a special kind of seaweed I read about in the book. If you boil it and then let the water cool, it gels like a warm Jell-o. So I'm going to make the world's first Logan McPhee Greenback Crab Irish Moss Seafood Aspic. It's going to be fantastic."

Crystal seemed unimpressed. "It could be," she said.

Logan built a small fire in the shelter of a few rocks, transferred all the crabs into one large tin can with handfuls of Irish moss and some fresh water, and got the concoction boiling. Then he covered the can with a thick board he found along the high-tide line and left it on a rock to cool.

"Seafood aspic in two hours," he declared. To round out the meal, he hiked inland a bit and filled a large can with wild red currants. When he returned, he peeked under the board to see how his soon-to-be-world-famous seafood aspic was doing.

It was moving. There was some scum across the top of the water, but he was certain he could see things moving underneath. He put down the currants and looked more closely.

Worms. Or maggots. Or parasites of some sort. There were thousands of them, writhing in the warm thick water, undeterred by the boiling. The spectacular potential of exotic seafood aspic had metamorphosed into a vile, revolting sight. "Damn it!" Logan said. He leapt to his feet and kicked the can far into the ocean. "I hope you all drown!" he shouted after the creatures that had ruined his meal. Crystal hiked along the beach toward him.

"Dinnertime?" she asked.

"Yeah," Logan answered with a frown. "We're having wild red currants and Spam." For a fleeting moment, his thoughts took him home to his mother's homemade meatloaf and mashed potatoes. He sighed. The summer was beginning to drag on too long.

☠   ☠   ☠

It was a few days later, on August 15th, that they crossed paths with the *Chamber Pot* again. The *Dreadnought* was drifting slowly across the mouth of a bay when Logan spotted the odd little boat heading southward.

"Ahoy, Captain Smudge!" Logan called out. Smudge, wearing the same shorts and still dangling a sausage between his lips, responded with a wave and turned the wheel. A few minutes later, the two ships were lashed together and Smudge was on the *Dreadnought's* deck.

"Not much time just now," he told the teenagers. "Heading for warmer waters, you know. Won't be long before the seas turn cloudy and cold up here, but by then, I hope to be down around Key West, selling conch shells to the tourists and trading lies with the ladies. But I might have a few idle moments to share a story with you, if you've got perhaps some rum or a drop or two of whiskey."

Logan was already climbing the gangway with a mug in his hands. Smudge took an enormous swallow of the tepid rum, belched loudly, and began.

"Now this is just a short one, you see. Got to be heading south, you know. But I'll tell you about the race between the *Flotsam* and the *Jetsam*. They were sailboats, you see, and the captains were twin brothers. Now the *Jetsam* was an all-white boat, with sleek lines and tight sails. Her captain was named Archibald, and he was a prim-and-proper sort of guy.

"But the *Flotsam*, it was broad in the beam and high in the stern. It was built for adventure and fun but not for speed. And that captain, Alexander, he was a happy-go-lucky sort of guy with a smile on his face and a dream in his heart.

"One day, the two brothers decided to race their boats across the English Channel. So they got up early, made some sandwiches, and set off to see who could reach his destination the fastest.

"The *Jetsam* took off through the water like a rabbit, bearing down on the finish line with the intensity of a hawk. Archibald was a determined sailor, and he wasn't about to lose to his brother.

"But the *Flotsam* left the harbor and sailed along slowly. Alexander had some friends on board, and they watched whales and sang with the gulls and flew kites and swam alongside the boat when hove to.

"Well, Archibald had been waiting at the finish line for three days by the time the *Flotsam* pulled up. He was furious! 'Where were you?' he demanded.

"'Oh, here and there,' Alexander said with a smile. 'Wasn't it a beautiful sail?'

"'Beautiful? Hardly,' Archibald scowled. 'It was tough and demanding—at least, for those of us who know how to race. But never mind, never mind. What matters is that I won the race!'

"'Won the race?' Alexander grinned. 'Nonsense! I won a long time ago.'

"'*You* won! Not even close. I've been waiting here for three days,' Archibald sputtered.

"'Ah,' said Alexander. 'Quite true. But the race wasn't to this point, my brother. If you recall, the race was to see who could *reach his destination first*. Your destination was this spot. But my destination was a great trip on the water with good friends. I achieved that the moment I left the dock. So you see, Brother, you lost by three days.'

"And with that, Alexander rounded up his friends and set sail for faraway places, smiling every minute of the voyage, secure in the knowledge that as long as he was doing something he loved, he would always be a winner."

Smudge finished his rum. "And with that, I've got to be shoving off. Long way down to Key West, you know. And while the *Pot's* the best ship on the high seas, she's not necessarily the speediest. Goodbye, mates. See you next summer."

He climbed down to his little boat and cast off. With a wave, he tightened his mainsail and dug a shallow trough toward the South.

☠   ☠   ☠

The days continued in an easy vein, pleasant hours clouded by periods of worry or sadness. On the whole, a nice stretch of summer, but something was missing. The raids were becoming routine—no thrill, no variety. The sailing was glorious but mundane—the sailors chose courses, sighted markers, sailed with precision, and reached their destinations with little difficulty. The coastline of Maine, stunning in greens and grays, became monotonous, the same stark beauty again and again, dulled not by any intrinsic loss but muted by the crew's own sense of change. They chatted less frequently. There were fewer jokes. And each crewmate, privately and silently, began to think more often about families, school, and life at home, with its delicious imprecision and glorious irresponsibility.

On August 18th, a warm and slightly hazy day with a light breeze and few cares, Logan was at the helm. He was feeling better than ever since he decided to lay off the rum, but he was thinking more and more about home. He steered a steady course, trying not to let on that he missed his family.

That evening was quiet. Arthur made a light dinner, just sandwiches and soup, and the crew ate silently around the table. Their bodies were on board the ship, but their minds were far away. At home.

The stillness of that evening was shattered by the squawking of the ship-to-shore radio in the captain's quarters: "Schooner *Dreadnought*. Schooner *Dreadnought*. This is Captain Robert Fernandez of the United States Coast Guard Station at Rockland, Maine. Schooner *Dreadnought*, come in, please. This is the Coast Guard."

"Oh, shit," Arthur said, tossing his napkin onto the table. "Marietta has finally turned us in."

CHAPTER SEVENTEEN

FOUR KNOTS OF FREEDOM LEFT

Logan steered the ship into a narrow bay tucked deep inside a small island that was little more than a dot on the map and dropped anchor. Then he gathered the crew in the dining room.

"What are we going to do?" BillFi asked, pushing his glasses. "Marietta called the Coast Guard. She told the Coast Guard about us. She told them. What are we going to do now?"

Dawn's freckled face was calm beneath the brim of her battered red baseball hat. "I think we need a negotiator," she said. "One of us who will be the designated person to talk to this Coast Guard guy. Someone who's good with words. Someone who can debate and make our case clear and with conviction. Someone who—oh, I don't know—someone who got us into this in the first place?"

All eyes turned to Arthur.

Arthur paused for a moment. "Oh, hell, I can't argue with that," he said. "But listen. I made a big mistake early in the summer. I didn't try to take charge—I tried to take over. I know the difference now, and I have all of you—" he looked at Dawn, "—to thank for that. But if you want me to lead these negotiations, I will. And I'll do my best to get us out of this. I can't promise anything. We're in a lot of trouble—the ship, the raids, McKinley. If I'm going to talk our way out of this, I'll need a lot of support from all of you. I'll tell you everything that's going on, but I can't be second-guessing everyone. I'll talk with you about everything I do. But you'll have to agree to stand behind whatever deal I can make."

The response from his crewmates—warm, loyal, grim—made it clear that he would get all the support he needed.

"Okay," Arthur said. "I guess I have a lot of talking to do."

"What should we do in the meantime?" Logan asked. "Like, pack our bags?"

Arthur looked him straight in the eye. "That might not be a bad idea," he said.

Everyone stayed in the dining room while Arthur poured himself a glass of water, dug out a notebook and a pen from underneath his mattress, and entered the captain's quarters, leaving the door open so the others could hear. Once he was ready, he picked up the radio's microphone.

"Captain Fernandez of the United States Coast Guard," he said in a low steady voice. "Captain Fernandez of the U.S. Coast Guard in Rockland, Maine. This is Arthur Robinson of the schooner *Dreadnought*, responding to your hail. Come in, please."

In the main cabin, the crew whispered. "He said his name!" BillFi said. "He shouldn't have said his real name."

Crystal scowled. "Marietta fucking talked to them, Billy Boy," she said. "The Coast Guard knows our underwear sizes by now."

They listened some more. There was a long pause of silence in the captain's quarters, and then Arthur repeated his reply. Logan began to hope that maybe they would be ignored and forgotten, but then the radio crackled with static. "Arthur Robinson of the schooner *Dreadnought*, this is the Coast Guard," a woman's voice said. "Please switch to channel four and stand by for Captain Fernandez. That's channel four. Do you read?"

"I understand," Arthur said. "Switching to channel four." He turned the dial on the radio until the number four appeared in a backlit square at the top. He waited. The crew waited.

An eternity later, Captain Fernandez's voice boomed out of the radio. "This is Captain Fernandez," came the voice. "I understand I am talking to Arthur Robinson. Is that correct?"

"Yes, sir, it is," Arthur said. His voice was clear and strong, revealing nothing of the concern, worry, and fear that gripped his friends. "How can we help you?"

"Well, son, it seems you and your friends are on a boat that doesn't belong to you," Fernandez said. "And the owner is missing. And a whole lot of yachts are missing valuables and food. Son, we even have reports of public nudity and under-age drinking. We have reason to believe that you and your friends are somehow involved in all of this, and I'd like to ask you to visit me here at the station to talk it over."

"I appreciate the invitation, Captain," Arthur said, "but we would be more comfortable doing our talking over the radio. We have a lot of things to get straight before we leave this ship."

Static.

"Son, I can understand your concerns," Fernandez replied, "but you need to look at the big picture. I have reason to believe that your boat is damaged and leaking. The Maine State Police, with whom I am in direct contact, have a warrant out for your arrest. And I understand that there are even some people on board who are being held there against their will. Now why don't you sail on over to Rockland and get this all taken care of?"

Arthur let a long lapse of silence fill the air. Then suddenly Dawn appeared behind Arthur and rested her hands on his shoulders. "We all want you to know," she said, "that every-one on board this ship is behind you. Don't let him bluff you." She kissed him lightly on top of his head and returned to the dining room.

"We won't sail in until you and I have reached some agree-ments," Arthur said into the microphone. "I don't think you've been given an accurate picture of what's been going on here."

"I understand, son," Fernandez said gently. "Listen, it could have happened to anybody. McKinley was hard to deal with, he was threatening, so you panicked. You were stuck out at sea. You didn't know what to do. So you overreacted. I'm sure the judge will take into account—"

"That wasn't it at all," Arthur interrupted. "McKinley killed himself. We have notes he wrote that will show that. We did not murder him. We never panicked. We never over-reacted. We talked things over every step of the way. We knew what we were doing at all times. We will not give up all we have gained just to beg for mercy. Panicked? Overreacted? Captain, the people on board this ship have never been so thoughtful, so mature, and so responsible in their entire lives. You will *not* take that away from us."

Fernandez's voice took a harder edge. "How can you say you're being mature when you've been doing the things you've done?" he said. "That does not look like mature behavior to me."

Arthur thought for a moment. Then he squeezed the radio microphone. "Captain?" he said. "With your permission, I'd like to tell you a story."

He leaned back in his chair, took a deep breath, and began to tell Captain Fernandez about the crew's long vivid summer on board the *Dreadnought*. He talked about the wrath—and the tragedy—of Howard McKinley, even reading from

McKinley's letter to his mother and his suicide note. He talked about the summer dream that everyone on board had agreed to share. He talked openly about their mistakes and passionately about their joys. He wove a tale of love and adventure and ultimate betrayal, and he placed blame on his own shoulders without apology.

When he was done, he waited for Fernandez's reply.

"It's getting late, son," the captain said. "Let's pick this up again in the morning. Oh-seven-hundred hours sharp. Channel four."

Then there was silence.

The crew gathered on deck to enjoy the evening air and talk over their situation. "Sounded nice," Dawn said.

"Thanks," Arthur said. "Fernandez needed to hear our side of the story. It was pretty clear that Marietta had told him a lot of lies."

"Who's captain tomorrow?" Crystal asked.

"I am," Dawn answered.

"Well, Captain," Crystal continued, "there are a few things we need to think about. First, we should move the ship every night, and during the day, we should stay hidden away in little bays and things. If the Coast Guard comes looking for us, we sure as hell don't want to make it easy. We have to give Arthur all the time he needs."

Dawn nodded. "Sounds good," she said. "We'll wait until it gets a bit darker and then hoist the anchor."

"We should also choose locations that move us farther and farther away from the fucking coast," Crystal continued. "We have to stay in radio range—if Fernandez loses contact with us, he might send out a whole bunch of helicopters to find us and force us in—but I think we should put some distance between us and Rockland."

"*Por que?* Why?" Joy asked.

Arthur answered. "To keep our options open," he said. "We got lucky—Fernandez seems like an okay guy to deal with. But we don't want to make things too easy for the Coast Guard. We have to make it hard for them to find us, and hard for them to figure out what we'll do next. We need as many cards in our hands as we can get."

Once the color of the sky had changed from blue to black, the crew of the *Dreadnought* got into position. They raised the anchor quickly, filled the sails, and eased out of the bay. Dawn was at the helm, and Arthur stayed with her. The others tended the sails. The night was beautiful: an explosion of stars dancing across the sky, a warm and soothing breeze, a ship full of friends and uncertainty and lovers. Arthur studied the charts and called out the markers—gongs, beacons, lighthouses—and between sightings, he and Dawn talked about themselves and their futures.

"College of the Atlantic?" Arthur mused. "Hmmm. Could be perfect. I've been thinking lately about studying environmental law."

"That would be perfect," Dawn answered with a smile. "Maybe I'll see you there."

By two o'clock, the *Dreadnought* was tucked into a small bay on an unremarkable island, and the crew was below. They talked for more than an hour—about each other, about the ship, about how it all might turn out—and then the conversation wound down into comfortable silence. Just before everyone drifted off to bed, Logan lifted a glass of apple juice.

"Well, gang—it's been an awesome cruise," he said.

☠   ☠   ☠

The radio came to life at seven o'clock the next morning. Fernandez seemed to be in good spirits.

"Good morning, son," he said after the initial hail and response.

"Good morning, Captain," Arthur said calmly. It was clear that he was prepared to talk for as long as was necessary.

"Son, I've been thinking about the things you said yesterday," Fernandez pressed ahead matter-of-factly. "I checked up on some of the things you said—I talked to McKinley's mother and his brother in the hardware store—and I spent some time this morning talking to the District Attorney here. Everyone is prepared to accept that McKinley killed himself. You won't be charged with that."

Arthur leaned back and took a deep breath. One important step was behind them. But many more steps lay ahead.

Fernandez continued, "There's the problem of your dumping his body overboard, but I think the judge will overlook that. What else are you going to do with a dead body at sea? We've also dismissed the charges of underage drinking, public nudity, and hunting seals out of season and without a license—I forgot to mention that one yesterday, didn't I? And the bit about holding people on board against their will— well, we talked again with our ... with our source, and we now know that everyone is there willingly. There's no issue there."

More steps forward. Things were beginning to look good.

"That only leaves us, basically, with the problem of the money, the valuables, and the food that you stole," Fernandez said. "Starting with McKinley's money and the other things on board, and going all the way through the stolen lobsters and the items taken from boats along the coast. We have twelve complaints on file, and I'm guessing there are a lot more we still don't know about yet. Now I'd like to resolve this peacefully, and I think you ought to come on over here and tell us what happened. Give us your side of the story. Then we'll all make sure that the outcome is fair for everybody. Sounds good, doesn't it? No more running, no more hiding, no more worrying about getting caught. We'll just move ahead to the next step and take it from there."

Arthur shook his head and picked up the microphone. "Captain, I appreciate all you've done for us. We've come a long way already. I need time to talk to my crewmates and decide how to proceed. Let's talk again this afternoon. Fifteen hundred hours. Same channel."

"Fair enough," Fernandez said.

☠   ☠   ☠

"There's no fucking way I'm going to jail or juvey or whatever," Crystal said, shaking her head. The crew was sitting on a small beach, eating charcoal-grilled hot dogs and bowls of baked beans. "I'll *never* agree to that. Never."

Dawn took a drink of iced tea. "So far," she said, "Fernandez has been pretty vague about what would happen if we sailed into Rockland. He talks about 'the next step' and things like that, but he hasn't spelled anything out. I think he's trying to keep his options open, but it also means we have some room to wiggle. Going to jail might not be the only possible outcome."

"Well, we'd better get things spelled out pretty clearly," Crystal said. "Because if turning ourselves in means going to fucking jail for theft, then I won't do it."

"Listen," Logan said, "I'm telling you, the only way out is for us to, like, sail into international waters. The Coast Guard doesn't know where we are right now. Boom! We can totally get out of here free and clear. If we don't, we're all going to be arrested, taken to court, charged with a whole bunch of thefts, convicted, and sent to jail or some kind of juvenile detention home. I don't know about you, but I'd totally rather take my chances on the open seas."

Dawn shook her head. "Forget it," she said. "I'd rather turn myself in. I'm tired of worrying about getting caught, and I'm tired of not dealing with anyone else except for ourselves. There are a lot of people out there who care about us. I don't want to leave them forever."

"But Logan has a good idea," Arthur said. "I don't want to leave the country either, but the Coast Guard doesn't know that. We might use that option—the *threat* of that option—to get some of those other charges dismissed."

"I don't know," Dawn said. "It sounds risky. We don't even know where international waters really are, or what the Coast Guard is allowed to do out there."

"It won't matter," Arthur said. "The Coast Guard is presenting us with their plan for the near future: We turn ourselves in, go through the courts, and take whatever comes. And Fernandez has hinted that he is willing to back that up with force—that line about resolving this peacefully was intended to be a threat. Well, what we need to do is present Fernandez with a plan of our own: We sail into Rockland, hand over the boat to Fernandez, and if we have to, go through the courts with the promise that even if convicted, we won't serve any jail time. And then we back that up with our own threat. If they don't promise to forget about jail, we'll sail into international waters and vanish. Fernandez will just have to choose between the two plans—and the two threats."

☠   ☠   ☠

In the captain's quarters, the negotiations continued over the radio. Arthur stated clearly that whatever outcome was discussed, going to jail could not be one of the possibilities.

"Let me get this straight," Fernandez said. "You want to be able to break into yachts and haul up lobster traps, take all sorts of things that don't belong to you, and you shouldn't be punished for it? What kind of society would this be if we allowed such things to happen?"

"First of all," Arthur said, "let's address the issue of the lobster traps. In court, all you would have, I suspect, is your one witness's opinion against all of ours. I'm willing to talk with you, in private and off the record, about things that might or might not have happened. But in a courtroom, you'd have a hard time proving much."

Fernandez was silent for a moment. "I like the way you see things," he said. "Clear. No clutter. And you're right—we would have a hard time proving the lobster theft. But the yacht thefts are a different story. We have all kinds of witnesses—people who were out on the docks at those times and will testify that you were there as well—and we have fingerprints and other pieces of evidence. So that one won't just go away."

"I understand that," Arthur said. "But jail can't be in the equation. What would it take to get a guarantee—a *guarantee*—that the worst would be fines or community service or something?"

"You want a guarantee!" Fernandez said. "Look here. One word from me, and a fleet of helicopters will be in the air within an hour, and they'd waste little time finding you. Then the cutters would go out, seize your ship, arrest the whole bunch of you, and drag you here whether you like it or not.

Don't talk to me about guarantees, son. You're using up my patience."

"Captain Fernandez," Arthur said, his voice still calm and pleasant, "I am quite aware of the position we're in. We are willing to admit to our mistakes and do something to make up for them, but we won't go to jail. There are several people on board who want us to sail off to the east, out of U.S. waters, and just disappear. Take our chances on the ocean. Go to Europe or something. Most of us have families that we don't want to leave, but without a promise that we'll avoid going to jail, the people who want to escape might just take the helm and get us out of here. So please, if you can find a way to end this without sending us to jail, it would make everything a whole lot better."

Fernandez sighed. "Let me talk to the judge and the D.A.," he said. "I'll get back to you."

☠   ☠   ☠

The crew spent the afternoon swimming in the deep waters of the bay. A cluster of jellyfish drifted by, large and clear with purple centers, and Logan scraped up the nerve to touch one.

"Wow!" he said. "They're more solid than I thought. And it didn't sting me!"

BillFi scooped one out of the water in an easy motion. He studied it closely. "I wonder if you can eat these things," he said. "I wonder if they're edible."

"Doubt it," Dawn answered. "I don't know why, but I really doubt it."

No further word from Fernandez had come by evening, so the sailors made a delicious dinner and talked quietly for several hours. A few of them idly cleaned up their bunks, getting their personal belongings in order. It seemed like the thing to do.

That night, the *Dreadnought* moved silently to a new bay, on a new island farther out to sea. Dawn pointed to a chart. "We're running out of land," she said. "If we keep this up, we'll have to drop anchor in Iceland."

The night passed with subdued conversation, the swapping of addresses, some comments about plans and keeping in touch. Dawn and Joy filled much of the time with a lively debate about God and the Goddess. Crystal wrote in her journal. Jesse touched up the fading lines of his tattoos.

The next morning, Arthur was on the radio once again. When he was finished talking, he sat down with the others on deck. "Fernandez is helping us a lot," he said. "He could easily haul us out of here if he wanted to." Arthur smiled. "And he pointed out this morning that U.S. waters extend two hundred miles off the coast—if we bolted for international waters, we'd never make it. The Coast Guard ships would catch us before we got halfway there. Still, Fernandez talked to the D.A., and he came back with an offer. If we turn ourselves in and plead guilty to the theft charges, we won't have to go to jail. We will have to pay for everything we stole, though, and we'll have to pay a fine. We'll also have to do a *lot* of community service— two hundred hours apiece, working in homeless shelters and after-school programs. But we wouldn't go to jail. I think that's the best deal we're going to get."

"Thank goodness," Dawn said. "Now we're getting somewhere."

For several minutes, the only sound was the breeze in the rigging. Then Joy spoke: "*Cuanto?* How big are the fines?"

Arthur took a deep breath. "They're big—twenty thousand apiece, for a total of one hundred forty thousand dollars. And to pay for the things we stole will take a total of thirty thousand more. So somehow, we'll have to hand over one hundred seventy thousand dollars."

Logan whistled low. "I'm a bit short this week," he said. "Try me again on Monday."

"Shit," Crystal said, "my parents wouldn't pay that kind of money, even if they had it."

"Mine either," Dawn said. "That's impossible."

A mood of gloom settled over the crew, but just for a moment. "Treasure!" Logan said. "We know where there's some treasure. Let's tell them about that treasure stuff we found in that cave—the spoons and things—and see if that settles things up. It might be worth a lot to a museum or something. Maybe that will take care of everything."

Arthur shrugged. "Only one way to find out," he said. "I'll talk to Fernandez."

He was gone for just a few minutes before he returned on deck. It was clear from his expression that the discussion had not gone well. "He laughed," Arthur said. "I mentioned Blackgoat and Branigan, and he laughed and said, 'You've been talking to Bonnie, haven't you?' He was impressed that we had actually crawled through the caves and found the stuff, but he said it wouldn't do the trick. He told us that giving its location to the judge might help—it might make it look like we're trying hard to do the right thing—but he said the fines and restitution have to be in cash. Real, modern, American cash."

"So much for that," Logan moaned. "I hear Iceland is lovely this time of year."

"We'll have to talk about that," Arthur said. "I still don't think most of us are willing to—" He was interrupted by Jesse.

"Why not ask Turner?" Jesse said slowly, his tattoos making his voice seem deeper. "He has a lot of money. And he owes us a *big* favor."

Arthur looked at him with surprise.

CHAPTER EIGHTEEN

ONE KNOT OF FREEDOM LEFT

The next morning, Arthur radioed the idea to Fernandez, and the captain agreed to check it out. The radio reverted to unsympathetic static.

Arthur sat in silence in the captain's quarters. He looked around. There was the bed where McKinley had left this earth, and where, it turned out, power was not free for the taking. Next to it was the desk, which held the radio that served as both lifeline and finale. Along the wall, next to the rope calendar that was now nearly free of knots, were the *Dreadnought* log, several books that held the secrets of sailing, and the letter that McKinley had written to his mother. Arthur knew that the summer's adventures were coming to an end, and he was surprised at how sad he felt about it. The summer had been difficult at times—even dangerous—and Arthur had never held illusions about continuing the cruise into autumn. September was not far away, and with it would come school and textbooks and tryouts for the soccer team. The end of the summer was not a surprise, and Arthur couldn't figure out why he felt so close to tears.

Maybe some things aren't supposed to end easily, he thought.

The radio crackled with Fernandez's voice. Arthur sat up quickly.

"I'll be damned," Fernandez said over the air. "Turner has agreed to pay for everything you people have done. He must owe you a lot."

Arthur smiled and lifted the microphone. "I think we just broke even," he said. "Let's work out the details."

Half an hour later, Arthur gathered the crew on deck and explained the situation.

"We are to surrender the ship tomorrow at noon," he said, "so we'll have to get an early start. Our parents will be in Rockland Harbor to pick us up, and we'll be ordered to appear at the State Police office sometime later for the filing of formal charges. But the D.A. has agreed to the deal, so Turner will pay the fines and restitution, and we'll all have to do the community-service work. That's not small—we each have two hundred hours of working with kids who are in trouble with the law. Think about it. During the school year, we could maybe do five hours every Saturday afternoon. That means that our Saturday afternoons will be booked for the next forty weeks. That will be a lot of hard work, but it's worth it. When we're done, we'll be off the hook."

"Will homicide charges be filed against our parents?" Logan groaned. "I think my mom is totally going to kill me."

Arthur smiled. "You're on your own for that," he said. "But we're going to make it, and now it's important that we end this trip in style."

The crewmates spent the evening getting the ship ready for surrender. They finished packing their belongings, they scrubbed the decks, they cleaned up the galley and the cabins, and they put all of McKinley's things in order. It took several hours, but everyone in the crew wanted to impress the people who would be waiting for them.

In the captain's quarters, Arthur received a radio hail from a newspaper reporter who had been following the conversation with Fernandez. She asked Arthur a long string of questions, and Arthur patiently put together the entire story for her. He was tired and had a lot to do, but he thought the publicity would help in case something went wrong.

That night, as the sailors sat around the table in the main cabin for the last time, Logan poured cranberry juice and raised his glass. "Well, gang—it's been a wild ride."

The crew drank to that. Then they talked with each other, openly and freely, about their lives, their dreams, their fears, and the summer they just spent together. The sky to the east was growing light when the last of them went to bed.

And Arthur untied the last knot in his rope calendar.

☠   ☠   ☠

August 22nd dawned crisp, cool, and windy. After breakfast, Arthur gathered everyone on deck.

"When we get to the dock," he said, his low voice calm and certain, "there will be a lot of people waiting for us. The Coast Guard, reporters, our parents. We need to make this look good. We have to show them that we know what we're doing—that we're not just a bunch of crazy teenagers." He paused and looked at Dawn. "We also need to say our goodbyes now. We won't have much chance when we reach Rockland."

Logan turned to Crystal. "This has been really great," he said quietly. "Do you think I could call you sometime?"

Crystal smiled—a surprisingly soft and gentle smile beneath her cap of blond hair. "You need to find someone closer to home," she said. "But it's been good getting to know you, too."

Joy went around the circle, hugging each of her friends and whispering blessings and solemn wishes into their ears. "It's been a pleasure ministering to you all," she said. "If you ever need help, give me a call."

Jesse clapped a huge hand on BillFi's shoulders. "Does this mean we're going back to the shelter?" he asked. "Back to the Bronx?"

BillFi smiled. "What do you think?"

Jesse returned the grin, distorting the tattoos on his face. "After all this?" he said. "Hell, no. I never again want to take orders from people who don't know what they're doing. I like the way things have been this summer—free to do whatever we want. So let's go wherever we want." They shook on it.

Arthur put his arms around Dawn and gave her a strong hug. "If I can . . . um, College of the Atlantic . . ." he said, "would that make any sense . . . if I—"

"Yes," Dawn said softly. "It would make all the sense in the world."

After a long moment of heartfelt and sad farewells, Crystal announced that she had one more thing to do. She ran below and returned with something held behind her back.

"This is for you," she said to Arthur. "You've been a pain in the ass at times, but we wouldn't have had this summer without you." She held out her hand. In it was Blackgoat's dagger, with ruby eyes in the handle's skull.

Arthur stared at it and then looked up with amazement at Crystal's smiling face. "You kept it!" he said. "I didn't think we had saved anything from that cave." He took the dagger and held it respectfully in his hand. "Thank you," he said. "This really means a lot to me. A lot." He gave Crystal a quick hug and stowed the dagger in his duffel bag.

As the goodbyes dwindled down, the crew got ready for their return to their families and their futures. They wanted the ship to be perfect.

Space had been cleared at the main dock in Rockland Harbor, and Fernandez waited there with his Coast Guard officers and two dozen members of the Maine State Police. Waiting on land was a cluster of adults—the parents of the *Dreadnought* crew, some reporters, curious townspeople. Noon was just minutes away.

"There they are, sir," said one of the Coast Guard uniforms. He pointed to the east, where the sails and masts of the *Dreadnought* were coming into view. The ship was in full regalia: every sail had been hoisted, colorful banners fluttered from the rigging, and the four gashes of the *Dreadnought* flag—the one Logan had made so many weeks before—flew from the top of the mainmast.

"That's one beautiful ship," Fernandez said out loud.

The *Dreadnought* approached the dock smoothly, with Arthur at the helm. Flash bulbs and murmurs popped through the crowd. The crew, dressed in dark T-shirts and light pants, lined the rails, standing not at attention but with a steady air of confidence. Arthur called out his orders with a clear sharp voice. "Prepare to jibe!" he boomed. "Jibe ho!"

The crew leapt into action, sheeting in the sails and preparing to let them out on the other side. Arthur twirled the wheel, and the *Dreadnought* spun around smartly. The starboard side of the ship slid gracefully against the side of the dock, Jesse and Logan threw lines over the dock cleats, and

Dawn and Crystal secured the gangplank. The sails were lowered and stowed in an instant. Then once again, the *Dreadnought* crewmates stood along the starboard rail. Their faces were serious, respectful, and proud.

Fernandez and two of his officers approached the gangplank.

"Nice docking. Permission to come aboard?" Fernandez asked in a strong military tone. He saluted, and his officers did the same.

Arthur stepped forward and returned the salute. "Permission denied, sir."

Fernandez looked startled. "What?"

"Just a moment, sir," Arthur said. "Crystal? Now, please."

Crystal turned from the line of crewmates, kicked off her shoes, and scrambled up the rigging. At the top of the mainmast, she unclipped the *Dreadnought* flag and carried it down to Arthur. Dawn and Arthur folded the flag into a triangle with great care, and then Arthur climbed onto the gangplank and crossed over to the dock.

"Sir!" he said firmly. "Presenting the crew of the *Dreadnought*—the finest sailors ever to cross the Gulf of Maine."

One at a time, the crewmates walked solemnly across the gangplank as Arthur called out their names:

"Joy Orejuela." She held her hands before her and paused for a moment in prayer. Then she stepped onto the dock.

"Crystal Black." Crystal marched across the gangplank and gave Captain Fernandez a playful punch on his shoulder.

"Jesse Kowaleweski." The crowd gasped at his multicolored skin. He walked across without looking at anyone.

"William Fiona." BillFi pushed his glasses up his nose and trotted off behind his friend.

"Logan McPhee." Logan crossed the gangplank and stood smartly in front of Fernandez. He locked eyes with the captain—something he would have been afraid to do a few months ago—and then he nodded and continued down the dock.

"And Dawn FitzWilliam." Dawn smiled at the crowd and at Arthur, and she walked across the gangplank with the casual grace of someone who knows where she's going.

"I'm Arthur Robinson," Arthur said, stepping onto the dock. "One crewmate unaccounted for, sir."

Fernandez smiled gently. "We know, son," he said. "She's on her way home."

"And it is my duty to report a suicide and burial at sea," Arthur continued.

"Very well," Fernandez responded.

"Presenting the *Dreadnought* colors, sir," he said. He held the flag out toward Fernandez. "Permission to come aboard now granted."

Fernandez shook his head. "We don't need to take your ship just now, son. And you keep the flag. I think you all earned it."

Then the *Dreadnought* crewmates, escorted by the Coast Guard and Maine State Police officers, walked down the dock toward land, toward their parents, and toward some tough questions and painful answers.

Logan trotted over to his parents, gave them an awkward hug, and turned with them toward their car. His mother, prim and severe, glared at him sharply, but his father wore a tie-dyed hat and maintained an odd grin. He couldn't help noticing that Logan seemed to stand a little straighter and carry himself with more pride than he had before. He winked at his son. "Cut out the booze, didn't you?" he whispered. "I was hoping you would."

"You knew?" Logan asked, wide-eyed.

"Why do you think I sent you on this cruise?" Loopy answered with a grin. The two of them walked side by side toward the car.

Crystal's parents, classic middle-aged overweight Americans, greeted her with joy and concern and then ushered her off toward a waiting station wagon. Crystal scanned the parking lot—and saw Jim Greenfeather standing at the edge of the crowd. She tore herself away from her parents and bounded over to him. "You came!" she said.

"Had to," he replied with a smile. "I don't have your phone number." The two of them talked for a moment, exchanged addresses, and kissed goodbye. Then Crystal climbed into the station wagon and waved to Jim until she vanished in the distance.

Jesse and BillFi walked across the parking lot toward a waiting taxi. The driver, a bored-looking heavyweight woman, held a hand-scrawled sign bearing their names. The shelter in the Bronx had obviously hired a taxi to take them to the bus station—things were probably too hectic to spare anyone. Jesse and BillFi approached the taxi, side by side, and then looked at each other for a moment. Without a word, they walked past the taxi and vanished down the road. Arthur watched them dwindle, not sure if they'd be all right but confident that somehow, together, they would survive. He wondered if he would see them later at the police station. Or ever.

Joy burst through the crowd and wrapped her arms around Leo. Her parents waited quietly, not staring directly at the young couple, and then hugged her in turn. "You've lost so much weight!" her mother shrieked with a giggle.

With her arm still around Leo's waist, Joy said, "Mother, I've been ministering to my shipmates, and I want to work at a street mission. I know it's not the House of Joy, but it truly is God's work. I'm on the right path now, and it's time for me to start getting the job done." Her mother grinned and kissed her on the head.

Dawn gave Arthur a final hug and a deep kiss, and she whispered in his ear, "College of the Atlantic. One year from now. I'll see you then—if not before."

Arthur hugged her back. "Count on 'before,'" he said. "We're only four hours apart. Won't we be able to see each other pretty often?"

"Would you like that?" Dawn answered.

"Do seagulls poop on the foredeck?" Arthur said with a grin.

Dawn laughed. "'Do seagulls poop on the foredeck?'" she said. "Couldn't you ask something a little more romantic—like 'Do the stars shine beautifully on your radiant face'?"

"How about 'Do you think hurricanes could keep me away'?"

Dawn nodded. "Don't you agree that it's a nicer way of phrasing things?"

"Do you realize how much you've taught me this summer?" Arthur asked.

"Isn't that what special summers—and special friends—are for?"

"Do you think we'll ever spend a summer as wonderful as this?"

"No," Dawn said. "Not unless we're together."

They hugged again, parted, and walked toward the crowd. Dawn's father gathered her up and hurried her away from the reporters. She glanced back at Arthur, and then she was gone.

Arthur walked up to his father and stepmother. He held his hand out to his father, man to man, handshake and nod and understanding.

It didn't happen.

"What the hell were you thinking?" his father screamed at him, ignoring the offered handshake. "When we get home, young man, you've got one hell of a lot of explaining to do."

Arthur stopped walking and stood tall. "No, Dad, I don't," he said in the same solid voice he had used with Fernandez.

"What?" his father asked. The new wife drifted off into the crowd. "Don't tell me you think—"

"Dad," Arthur said in a firm and gentle voice. "This is important. There have to be some changes between us. You sent me here to gain some maturity, some authority, some sense of command. Good call, Dad—it worked. And it's working now. If you want to talk with me—*with* me—I'd be happy to chat with you all night. But if you want to lay down one of your lectures, if you want to talk *at* me all night, if you want to play the Authoritative Dad role and have me play the Subordinate Son role—then forget it. If that's your plan, tell me now and I'll just keep on walking. You've done a lot for me, Dad, but you don't own me. Whatever happens between us from now on, Dad, it happens between men. Between adults. I made some mistakes—some big mistakes—and I'm prepared to do community service for them. But stop treating me like a child. If you want to talk things over, hear about how my summer went, maybe tell me a little about your life—then I think we should find someplace comfortable and start talking. But I don't want your lectures anymore." His gaze never left his father's eyes. At last, it was the elder Robinson who blinked.

"This is going to take some getting used to," the elder Robinson said. He tried to suppress a reluctant half-smile as he appraised his son, tall and tan and strong. Then his expression sharpened. "You still have a lot of explaining to do." He turned and walked down the dock with his son—toward the car, toward the mainland, toward the rest of their lives. He didn't put his arm around Arthur's shoulders. He didn't walk especially close to him. But he was working to understand all the things he had learned about his son in the past forty-eight hours.

And Arthur walked slowly, with confidence, with the kind of centered calm that experience and courage and self-reliance can bring. He let the silence blossom, unconcerned about filling the time with idle chatter. The time would come soon, he hoped, for long bouts of serious talking.

Suddenly Arthur felt someone grab his shoulder and pull him around. It was Dawn, with a beautiful smile and a tear on her freckled cheek. "One last goodbye," she said. She threw her arms around Arthur—and stared deeply into his eyes. Arthur stared back. They didn't kiss. They didn't move. Arthur felt the universe peel away. He said nothing at all. They just gazed deeply into each other's minds, letting their souls intertwine in an intimate and spiritual embrace. Arthur wasn't aware of the passage of time or the position of the sun or even his own breath. He just let himself open to her eyes and felt her open to his. The world stopped turning, and nothing on Earth mattered to him at all.

At last, he became aware of the people around him once again, and he noticed off in the distance a young man watching them. He seemed oddly envious, and after a moment he broke away to follow his own path. Arthur smiled at Dawn.

"True feelings never end," he said. "I'll be with you soon."

Then Dawn's father returned and took her arm. She disappeared into the crowd once again.

And so they were gone. The Plunder Dogs had become, in an instant, part of the scattered world of teenagers and their dreams. They would cross paths in the courthouse, perhaps, and then try to stay in touch, but most of them would let it drop after a while. Only a few would keep the bonds strong forever. Arthur had no doubt that he would keep the promises he had made—to the others and to himself. He walked with his father toward the black Lexus SUV.

And bobbing gently at dockside, trim and clean and old and proud, the *Dreadnought* waited quietly for her next assignment. The Maine breeze rustled through her rigging, and the late-summer sun warmed her decks. The ice would come soon. But after it would follow longer days and open waters, beckoning with promises of new adventures and a few more chances to sail.

ABOUT THE AUTHOR

MICHAEL ROBERT EVANS is an award-winning, associate professor of journalism at Indiana University, teaching courses in magazine writing and editing, among others. He focuses his research efforts on indigenous media movements, having spent a year in the Arctic on a Fulbright Fellowship, working with Inuit videographers, and three months in the Australian Outback working with Aboriginal radio and video producers. He is currently working on media issues involving North American native groups.

Evans was a magazine editor in Massachusetts for thirteen years, and his freelance work has appeared in numerous magazines and newspapers. Author of a book on magazine editing published by Columbia Press in 2004, he has two other books on journalism under contract. *68 Knots* is his first novel.

Michael, his wife, and his two sons split their time between homes in Bloomington, Indiana, and New Hampshire.

For study guide questions on this book
and activities developed for all of our titles,
please visit Tanglewood's website at
www.tanglewoodbooks.com